Tim,

Come back to Las Vegas! There are so many casinos that need your email address. Thanks for the support. Hope you're doing well.

Much love,

Bill

Honey and Hand Grenades

Honey and Hand Grenades

LOGAN SHEFFIELD

Copyright © 2013 by Logan Sheffield.

Library of Congress Control Number: 2013906361
ISBN: Hardcover   978-1-4836-2226-2
               Softcover   978-1-4836-2225-5
               Ebook   978-1-4836-2227-9

All rights reserved. No part of this book may be reproduced or transmitted in any form or by any means, electronic or mechanical, including photocopying, recording, or by any information storage and retrieval system, without permission in writing from the copyright owner.

This is a work of fiction. Names, characters, places and incidents either are the product of the author's imagination or are used fictitiously, and any resemblance to any actual persons, living or dead, events, or locales is entirely coincidental.

This book was printed in the United States of America.

Rev. date: 05/24/2013

To order additional copies of this book, contact:
Xlibris Corporation
1-888-795-4274
www.Xlibris.com
Orders@Xlibris.com

For Catherine,

Your help has been invaluable.

"I know not if't be true,
But I, for mere suspicion in that kind,
Will do as if for surety."

—Iago, *Othello* Act I, Scene III

"Demand me nothing. What you know, you know.
From this time forth I never will speak word."

—Iago, *Othello* Act V, Scene II

ACKNOWLEDGMENTS

The biggest thanks goes to my mom, who for whatever reason still has a copy of the very first 'novel' I ever wrote. Titled *Trouble Worldwide*, it's basically a 4th grader's retelling of *Miami Vice*. Written in pencil and everything. Also, a thank you to Lauren Conrad. One day we'll laugh when telling our grandkids about this.

HONEY AND HAND GRENADES

Do you ever watch a movie desperately hoping the ending will change? Not even hoping. More like expecting. Do you ever do that?

Think of a film. One you know every detail of. Doesn't have to be your favorite. Just one you know really well. One you can quote in your sleep. One you've seen fifty times or more.

Things develop the way they always do. Exposition, conflict, character development—all the same. No surprises or tricks. But for some reason, against your better judgment, you think this time will be different.

Quite the suitable analogy for the eternal optimist.

Those who, despite evidence to the contrary, give people the benefit of the doubt, think they'll learn from their mistakes. Despite the fact that things play out the same way every time.

This optimism, a problem I no longer face. A burden removed long ago. No longer expecting anyone to surprise me. They never let me down in that they always let me down.

I'm not a monster. I'm doing this for your own good. To make the world a better place. Not as if I'm some comic-book asshole flipping a coin to determine the fates of those he encounters.

I make my decisions based on character. On intellectual capacity. On whether or not they can explain why you should never defrost a windshield in the middle of a Chicago winter by throwing hot water on it.

Believe it or not, it happens.

As the saying goes, everything happens for a reason.

Most of the time, that reason is "You're a fucking idiot."

Alas, here I go again, jumping to conclusions. Or not. Fairly certain my assumptions about the guy in the Arizona State alumni sweatshirt are correct. Never gave much credibility to an academic institution that rejects fewer people than a Thai hooker. Even if they aren't, rectification isn't really my thing.

Get Kendall's attention. Give her the signal. Send a couple drinks to the guy in the maroon-and-yellow sweatshirt. Tell her to drop a blue pill in each glass. Sucks to be his friends. Guilty by association. The casualties of war.

Enlisting her help, fantastic move on my part. Instrumental in assisting my cause. Don't be fooled by her demeanor. Or the throat tattoo. She's sweet as honey and smart as they come. You know the saying. Never judge a book by its cover. Easier said than done. Is everyone capable of such impartiality?

Are you already fed up with the clichés? Plenty more where that came from.

The things I contemplate. Drinking alone in a stench-cloaked bar. Accounting for 10 percent of the clientele, 50 percent of the revenue.

Whoever put these songs on, they're inside my head. Each tune, one immediately followed by another. All products of artists cut short in their prime.

Sublime, "What I Got"

Nirvana, "Smells Like Teen Spirit"

Sex Pistols, "Anarchy in the UK"

As if the entire jukebox is a shrine. An ancient relic, possibly one of a mere hundred remaining in the country, posthumously worshipping those troubled by demons the likes of which most will never know.

Demons.

Everyone has them. Some refuse to acknowledge them. Some fight them off for decades. Others welcome them with open arms. Some win and some lose. Make no mistake, we've all got them—not in equal numbers, but everyone has a few. Bradley Nowell, Kurt Cobain, Sid Vicious—books whose covers didn't even begin to tell their stories. Merely a fraction of the whole. A poor representation of the majority. Buried beneath their covers tragic stories begging to be heard. Never were or too late when they were told.

What about everyone else? What if a cover is all you have to go on?

The mindless masses, roaming the streets, taking up space, wasting resources. Judge them by their covers. Not like they have anything else to offer.

Whether a famous artist or common folk, life goes on. As I sit here, pouring one-hundred-year-old whiskeys down my throat, their trials and tribulations seem irrelevant. No one cares that they're gone. Sure, they'll say how tragic it was. Then they're on to the next topic. As long as we have fun songs to sing and dance to, their legacy thrives.

You and I, profiting off the misery of others.

Welcome to the Entitled States of America.

The land of opportunities abandoned.

Opportunity.

Fortune laughs at those who recognize it, commends those who take advantage of it, and favors those who make their own.

Guess which category I fall into. If you're reading this, you were probably an accident. That's not to say that no one loved you. But truth be told, your presence on this planet was due to a long string of coincidences.

Maybe you think everything happens for a reason. All part of some master plan, devised by an omnipotent creator. Maybe you think that's complete garbage. Long story short, I don't care.

I don't care if you make a yearly trek to mecca. I don't care if you've never seen the inside of a church. I don't care if you hate abortions. Or if you wander the streets waving baling wire at every baby bump you see. Maybe you hate military intervention. Maybe you roam the streets dressed like Rambo. Saving yourself for marriage? Maybe you fornicate with any willing participant.

So long as the world travels around the sun, there will be disagreement. Simply inevitable. Apathy on the other hand, a different monster entirely.

If you learn nothing else from my legacy, remember this: the actions of one person with solid resolve, no matter how nefarious, cannot be stopped by a unanimous but apathetic majority.

Your life is a book. What does your cover say about you? How many pages? Are you Edwardian Script *or* Courier New*? Like it or not, everything you do goes into that book. Some things carry more weight than others. But nothing is left on the editor's desk.*

Thing is, no one has enough time. No one will read the whole thing. So make sure you have one amazing graphic designer. Because you will be judged by your cover. Therein lies the injustice. Decades of hard work and good deeds ignored because no one likes being inconvenienced.

Clichés get repeated because they're often true.

So once again, don't judge a book by its cover.

Don't assume the blonde girl with 44DDs isn't a calculus wizard.

Don't assume the black guy in the fancy car stole it.

Most importantly, because it works both ways . . . don't assume that the guy who once set out to save the world will feel any remorse over destroying it.

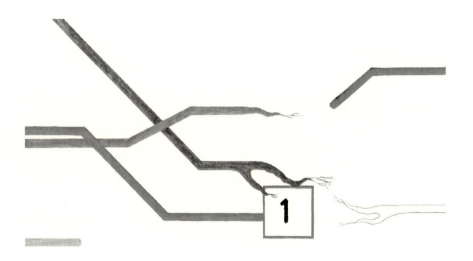

1

Every night beginning on my seventh birthday, I prayed for cancer. Not for a cure. Not for others. For me. I wanted it. I wanted the disastrous growth to ravage my body worse than any natural calamity the world has ever known. It never came. Rather, it never took hold of *my* organs. Slowly the prayers became wishes. Eventually, those dreams went by the wayside. Sure, calling a tumor a "dream" doesn't resonate with logic. You'll understand. Give it time.

Simply put, I was a prodigy. Had a gifted mind from day one. Proper nurturing has only increased its potential.

You might say I'm being egomaniacal.

I call it an understatement.

When I said the death sentence never took hold of me, I never said it didn't crash into my life at all. Mom got it when I was fifteen. Let's back up first before more cancer talk. When I say Mom, I mean the woman who took care of me. Raised me. Not the worthless bitch that abandoned me.

In a dumpster. In February. In Chicago.

That's right, I was a dumpster baby.

Paul Watts was the hardest-working man I ever knew. Loyal, honest, and proud, that was him. The calluses on his hands were so thick, you could shove a thumbtack into his palm and he'd be none the wiser. He could do it all. He *did* do it all. Working in manual labor from age twelve would wear most people down. Make them jaded. Not Paul. Saw the good in everyone. With all the shit happening in his life, he was never too busy to help someone in need. Every single hour of his days were usually packed with activity. All twenty-four of them. Dad was the guy who wasn't slowed down by that. He could force a twenty-fifth in there somewhere. For anyone who needed it.

I wasn't old enough to recognize his generosity when it impacted me most. How could I? I was less than a month old. No one knows my exact date of birth. The cunt that popped me out couldn't be found (I'm not very fond of the sperm donor either). There were no records I even existed. One night in February, Dad was headed for his bus home. He'd just finished the night shift doing repair on the expressway. He was running just a second late. The bus was not. Go figure. The one morning he's not standing on the corner at seven sharp for the #15 bus (typically rolled in around 7:07 a.m.), it was on time. Virtually unheard of in the Windy City.

Call it fate, if you believe in that type of thing.

I don't. I'm a man of science.

But Mom and Dad loved that stuff. The only reason I've never fully dismissed the possibility of an almighty creator.

He knew it would be at least twenty minutes before another one came. If he was lucky. Coffee—Dad hated the taste. But when it's four degrees, hard to justify being selective. The donut shop two blocks down had been open for a couple hours. That's where he heard me. Crying in a dumpster behind a donut shop.

So I'll take this opportunity to give you a moment to consider why cynicism is so deeply rooted in my brain.

I wasn't always like this. I used to believe in things like love and compassion. Optimism was once in my vernacular.

Things change.

After nearly a week spent in intensive care, Paul and Josephine adopted me. Gave me a home. A place to sleep that wasn't full of used tampons and rotting egg salad. I probably had a name during that first month or so after my birth. No clue what it was. It's of little concern to me. Dad wanted to name me after someone renowned for their intellect. He wanted to push me in the direction of excelling with my mind. Albert and Edison were quickly vetoed by Mom.

Theodore won.

It means "gift from God."

I'd hate to see what passes for a practical joke up in heaven. But that's what she always called me. I believed her too.

As I've said, a man of science such as myself doesn't really buy into talk of fate and things happening "for a reason." But Mom made a believer out of me. For most of my youth at least.

It wasn't until after she'd passed that Dad told me the truth. They could never conceive. They tried for years. Sex twice a day, fertility specialists, artificial insemination—nothing worked. Suddenly, things made more sense. They'd always raised me to believe I was capable of greatness. My peers disagreed. When you're young, the wisdom of your elders seldom prevails. Early formative years of education are a fragile time, especially for someone of my intellectual capacity. Mom and Dad convinced me the other kids were jealous. I wanted to believe them.

But through it all, they never gave up on me. Constant encouragement, unconditional support. I very quickly overcame any complex my classmates might have instilled in me, thanks to Mom and Dad. They were quite an ego boost.

Oddly enough, they were also why I wanted cancer. From an early age, I was convinced that I was going to change the world. My impact would be felt, remembered forever. I was certain of this. It would make more sense if I told you I wanted cancer because I hated my life. That I had feelings of inferiority due to my dumpster abandonment. Not at all. I wanted cancer because I wanted to eliminate cancer. Dad kept lead soldering wire in the basement. I used to chew on it after dinner. That's how badly I wanted it. I was certain that given the right resources, I could rid the world of one of its most devastating afflictions.

I was also wise enough to know that no one will trust a kid in underoos to treat their Hodgkin's lymphoma. People with myeloid leukemia tend to gravitate away from the medical advice of those who don't eat the crusts on their sandwiches. The only way I was going to have the specimens I needed was to get it directly from the source. That's why I prayed for cancer. Every time I blew out a birthday candle, I wanted mesothelioma. If I tossed a coin in a fountain, I imagined melanoma taking over.

Depressing to some, I saw it as a potential opportunity. I knew it was my destiny to change the world. There was no doubt in my mind.

Then Mom got it. Tore me apart. Overwhelming trepidation consumed me. I was afraid for her. But also saw this as my chance. I could save not only her but also hundreds, if not thousands, of people. I was going to be a hero.

I was wrong.

A healthy dose of reality: losing my mother tortured me incessantly. But what bothers me more is that I wept longer over my failure to change the world. I'd just lost half of the most important thing in my life. My driving force. Yet all I could think about was my shortcomings. Thankfully, Mom was never a quitter. Knew she wouldn't want me to give up. Whenever one of my projects as a young scientist went awry, she was always there with an anecdote to pick me up.

"Sweetie, no one believed Copernicus. They laughed at him when he suggested the sun was the center of the universe," she would say.

"But he was *right*, Mom! I'm just stupid."

"Oh, come on now. He might have been right, but the point is he didn't give up. He believed in himself. He knew he was right, and he kept trying. So what about you? Are you going to quit just because of one little failure?"

I hated when she was right. "No, Mom."

Then she'd make me cookies, oatmeal-raisin. And I was back in the lab

For Christmas when I was ten, she crocheted a blanket for me. Had a small embroidered message.

It read: A person who never made a mistake never tried anything new. You probably know him as the guy with the crazy hair. $E=MC^2$. That guy. I slept with it every night until I was exiled out of town.

After I composed myself once Mom was gone, I knew she'd want me to keep at it. Dad wouldn't let me quit either. Sadly, I never cured cancer.

I did cure AIDS though. I probably should have mentioned that earlier.

Yes, I'm the guy who put an end to a worldwide pandemic.

And it was the biggest mistake of my life.

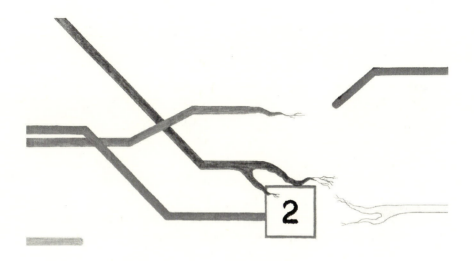

2

For every action, there is an equal and opposite reaction. Or so they say. I buy the "opposite" part. The "equal," not so much. One thing is certain: all actions have consequences far more profound than their immediate results. You've probably heard of the butterfly effect. It's bullshit. What I'm referring to is quantifiable. The results are palpable. They can be measured and calculated. The conclusion traced back to a very definitive origin.

In Boston Common, a sign warns against feeding the birds. Explains that feeding them prevents migration, leading to over population. More birds mean more physical damage. This links to poor quality of water. Finally, public health suffers as a result. Feed the birds, spend a week bent over a toilet. It's that simple.

A prominent university raises tuition. The price of lap dances drops. More female students struggle to make ends meet. The number of exotic dancers increases. The consumer reaps the benefit of competition in the market.

The government places a tax on ice to promote water conservation. In turn, a chemist develops an additive to keep beverages colder without it. Three years after its release, thousands of people develop tumors. Coincidence? Unlikely.

Surely though, curing AIDS could not possibly have negative repercussions? Really, it depends whom you ask. Roughly fifteen years after FDA approval, it wasn't even news. Maybe fifty people worldwide died each year from it. Tops. Carpal-tunnel syndrome was linked to more fatalities. People lifting things they had no business carrying. But all in all, everything was great. Arguably flawless.

Unless of course, you're in the business of profiting from the threats it imposed. Condom companies were not fans. Their sales steadily declined every year after my discovery. Coupled with improvements in birth control methods, prophylactics became effectively obsolete.

Nine billion people thought I was a hero. A handful wanted me dead. Although heavily skewed, the odds were not in my favor. I left town. Went into hiding. Escaped to a desolate area, virtually uninhabited. Maybe three people knew where I went—under my real identity that is. Had to leave the country to ensure my safety. Spent the last several years traveling and studying all over Europe and Asia.

Samuel Clemens.

That's me now.

Sound familiar? If you recognize the name, you're part of a small group. No one these days has even heard of *Huckleberry Finn*. Definitely haven't read it.

Figured Mark Twain wasn't too fond of it. Might as well put it to use.

Ted Watts is no more. He died in a chemical explosion. Or was it mercury poisoning? The details escape me. Don't believe everything the media tells you.

I left Singapore a few days ago. Welcome back to Chicago. Can't run forever.

Being back after this much time away is odd to take in. Not what you would call nostalgic. But it's still home. *Was* home anyway. Everything altered since I left. It's an entirely different world. Or might as well be. The upside is no one seems to recognize me. A feat I took countless steps to achieve once I decided to come back. My long scraggly hair has been neatly trimmed. Kept tidy with a dollop of pomade. I'm clean-shaven for the first time since puberty. Most importantly, the tattoos are gone. No expensive laser surgeries. When I first immersed myself in the world of permanent ink, I heard all the clichés.

"You know that's gonna be there forever, right?"

"What if you want a good job?"

You know the remarks.

Never thought they applied to me. Always knew if for some reason I didn't like them, I'd find a way around it. So I did. I invented a salve a while back. Rub it on the area twice a day, for three weeks, and you're back to normal.

Rather, *I'm* back to normal. No one else knows about this solution. I'm still debating whether or not to release it. After my last breakthrough, I realized I must consider potential outcomes more seriously. If monetary gain was my sole motive, there would be nothing to debate. But understand, I do these things because I like to.

Not to mention, my last cure ensured I'd never have to worry about money ever again. The only personal upside I've seen so far.

No, money's not an issue. How do you think I'm funding my latest venture? I'm paying for all of it. No way would a company associate itself with this. Too much bad press. Not worth it.

Fine by me. I hate answering to investors anyway.

I'm putting away the last of my coffee. Cream, two sugars. I hate it, but Ted Watts never drank coffee. Samuel Clemens does.

As resolved as I am to get this project underway, paranoia inevitably sets in. No one knows me. I'm a foreigner. Still, can't help thinking that everyone in the Bumpin' Grind Café knows who I am. Unlikely. I was a regular at Addison Grill three blocks down. But showing my face there . . . not ready to chance it yet. Still, I doubt that even the owner Steve would recognize me.

Just keep reminding myself I'm being irrational. The people here are too focused with their text messages and Sabretooth devices to notice a 9.0 earthquake. But that one lady, she keeps looking at me. I look back at her, and she retreats. Looks the other way. I don't exactly fit the mold of the normal clientele here. It's going to be like this everywhere I go for a while. Going to assume everyone is out to get me. To drag me down. I'll be fine soon enough. Just need to keep a focused mind.

Finish my coffee, wipe my mouth, take a bite of my bagel.

"Will there be anything else, sir?" the waitress asks me.

"Just the check, please."

She nods, pulls out a slip of paper. The service has been just fine, but I ask her, "Oh, one thing though?"

"Sure, what is it?"

I pause, presenting the illusion of pensiveness. "Well, I was wondering. What do you want to do with your life?"

Taken aback, confused, she clarifies, "Huh?"

"I mean, this place is nice and all. But I assume you don't want to bring cups of coffee to guys like me for the rest of your life, right?"

"Oh, gotcha. Well, it's OK for now. But I don't really know what I wanna do. I've got time, ya know? I'll figure it out, but for now just takin' it slow, havin' fun. That's about as good as anyone can do I guess, right?"

A slanted smile. "Certainly."

"Is that all?" I nod, she walks away.

Pulling out my wallet, I find the exact amount for the food, place it on the table, dig into my pocket and grab three nickels. Heard the U.S. Mint will discontinue them next year.

Hope she spends it wisely. Maybe invests it. Ultimately her decision. She earned every penny.

I look back through the window. She's counting her tip, cursing me.

In hindsight, she was probably worth a quarter.

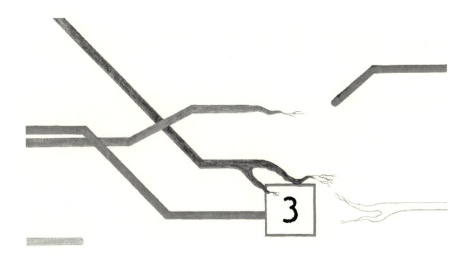

The last place a person with my net worth would live is a two-bedroom apartment fifty feet from the Blue Line. Noisy as fuck. Not much fun. I'll deal. Never set foot in it. Not this *exact* place at least. I've spent more than my fair share of time in shoeboxes like these over the years. You've seen one then you've seen them all. Glad I found a furnished place though. Just want to pass out. Any bed will do. Never been a fan of narrow stairwells, and I momentarily reconsider my living arrangements. I could easily afford a place by the Water Tower or near the Hancock… fuck, I should just buy the Hancock Tower itself.

But inconspicuous is key.

Keep a low profile, at least to start.

That's typically where people in positions of power begin to falter. They get an ego, a swollen head. Think they're unstoppable. For the most part, they're right. But then they underestimate those who try and bring about their demise.

Not me.

This will all work better if I draw as little attention as possible.

Unlocking the door to my new place for the first time, it's somewhat ominous. The shades are drawn, the air stale. All I can hear is the thrashing of metal as the *L* goes racing by. *Doors open on the right at North and Clybourne.* Never gets old. After a few seconds, the atrocious clamor subsides, yet I'm not left dwelling in silence.

A buzz is coming from somewhere. Looking left, it's not the fridge. It sounds like water splashing. The shower is on. Here's where most people wind up fucking themselves. They try and assess the situation, walk slowly. Maybe they call out hello or "Who's there?" Here's what I know: I'm supposed to be alone.

But I'm not.

I immediately run toward the noise, trying not to trip in the halls of the murky apartment.

A thin horizontal glow bounces off the hardwood floor. Probably maple, not that it matters. Even in the darkness, I can tell that whoever laid it did a subpar job. Dad would flip if he saw this. I'll tear it up and redo it later. But right now, more pressing matters await.

The door is closed, so I kick it in. Take it out of my security deposit.

Sure enough, the shower is occupied. Surprisingly, still going about their business. Apparently, breaking and entering (and showering) is routine for them. Lowering my shoulder, I lunge at the large person I can hardly make out through the opaque curtain. Instantly, he hits the ground, the floor slicker than greased owl shit. I begin throwing fists left and right, landing all over.

He just takes it. Doesn't fight back. But occasionally uses one of his mitts to deflect my punches. Then I look down.

Don't know how I didn't spot it immediately.

Staring back at me, the largest cock I've ever seen.

That bright orange tip. Like a number 5 billiard ball perched atop a Genoa salami.

A look of recognition finally comes across my face. Still not uttering a word, he begins to clap his hands.

"Damnit! What are you doing here?" is all I can spit out.

Now he's laughing. Silently, as no sound comes out.

I sit back, water still pouring down on us.

Finally, I catch my breath. My eyes are still drawn to that python of a penis, polished off with the most bizarre tattoo I've ever seen.

"You know, if you ever want to get rid of that, I've developed something that removes the ink."

Laughter subsiding, he just shrugs as if to say "maybe."

We stand up, hug one another.

"It's good to see you, man. It's been way too long."

Again, he nods in agreement, smiles. With one arm, he throws me over his shoulder. Then walks me over to the living area, throws me on the floor, and returns to finish his shower.

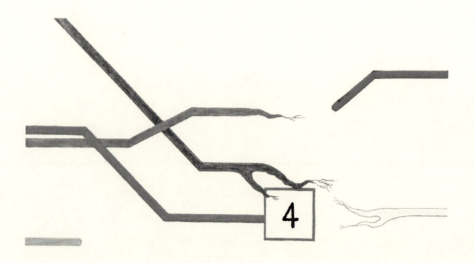

4

Dillon Pulaski has been my best friend since third grade. I was by no means antisocial. Merely felt I lacked a common ground with my classmates. They obsessed over cartoons and video games. I was reading George Orwell and Ayn Rand. You might think that would bother a young kid. I just accepted it early on. My ambitions and interests differed from theirs. Any condescension on their behalf was merely jealousy manifesting itself.

Water off a duck's back.

I was acclimated to my lack of a social circle. Then there was a new kid in class. So immersed in the *New York Times* crossword puzzle that I failed to notice something so blatant. On the other side of the room, an unfamiliar face towered above everyone. My only thought, *Surely he must be lost.* Looked like he belonged in high school. A growth hormone experiment gone far more successful than anticipated.

In need of a ten-letter word for *addictive*, my concentration was broken by Mrs. Clay's cheerful chirping.

"Class, we have a new student joining us. His name is Dillon, and his family has just moved here from Florida. Please do your best to make him feel welcome and help him if he needs anything." Then she made some joke about adjusting to Chicago's "amazing" weather. Most people laughed. Her humor was starting to grow old with me.

Typically, we would go right into either a math lesson to start the day or exercises in cursive writing. I received benefit from neither and was admonished any time I napped during the rudimentary assignments. Dillon's arrival was apparently a cause for a departure from the norm.

"OK, everyone, please take out your pencils and paper, we're going to continue with multiplication," Mrs. Clay announced. Her declaration met with a collective groan. Diffusing their angst, she added, "Settle down now. *First*, we're going to play a game." Cheers ensued. "I'm going to write down a number between one and one hundred on my notepad. I would like each of you to write down a number as well. Whoever is closest to mine, higher or lower, will win a homework pass." She was immediately exalted upon uttering this condition. I had little interest in the prize. I needed homework passes like Zeus needed an atomic bomb. Academics were my essence.

The new kid's hand was in the air.

"Yes, Dillon? What is your question?"

"Well, Mrs. Clay, not to be rude, but you're asking for something impossible."

A puzzled look, debating his sincerity. "I'm sorry, but I don't think I understand."

"With all due respect, there are far too many numbers between one and one hundred."

Again, looking confused, she elaborates, "No, Dillon, there are only one hundred options. So, everyone, please write down your number, and don't forget to put your names on your papers as well," she adds, assuming the topic is closed.

But the new kid persists, "Again, Mrs. Clay, I mean no trouble, but I respectfully disagree. There are actually infinite numbers between one and one hundred. Or even between one and two." She is bewildered. He goes on, "You see, Mrs. Clay, you didn't specify if the number you were thinking of was a whole number, a rational number, or even a real number for that matter. I believe you just made the assumption that we would in turn assume you would pick a whole number, but you never specified. For all we know, your number could be 12, but it could also be 12.3851. It could be pi. So I ask with the utmost courtesy . . . what kind of number are we dealing with here?"

I can't believe what I'm hearing. His sincerity is inconsequential. His mere awareness of rational numbers, impressive. Most kids look at him with disdain for showing off. I stare in awe.

She gradually recovers from the lecture the new kid has just delivered. Composes herself even more slowly, and responds, "It's a *whole* number, dear." Blatant mockery, and immediately the regret on her face from talking to a student in such a tone was evident. "No tricks, no fractions. So please class write your numbers down and pass them to the front."

All the numbers are passed forward. Everyone in the class starts asking who chose what. Explaining why Mrs. Clay would *never* pick an even number, she's just not that predictable. There was a meager attempt to start the next lesson after collecting the papers, but the class won't allow it. They want the results. Piercing pleas are heard from every corner. Mrs. Clay knows tranquility is a pipe dream until a winner has been announced.

"OK, OK, class, calm down. I'll write the number on the board." She picks up a marker, begins to draw on the board. A collective gasp ensued. All of the students hold their breaths. Except me. Depriving the body of oxygen is unhealthy, and rather juvenile if you ask me. She quickly marks a 9 on the board, and most of the class utters something indicating they are out of the running. She puts the pen on the board once again, and the few kids who chose in the 80s and 90s await the results. Mrs. Clay quickly draws a couple more lines. The number is revealed to be 94 while a select few cheer.

"OK, class, who thinks they have the closest number?" she asks pleasantly.

"Seventy-one," a boy says with a false confidence.

"Seventy-eight," one girl shouts.

"Eighty-two," another girl counters with great certainty.

The class is impressed, and Mrs. Clay asks if there is anyone who thinks they are closer than eighty-two. When no one responds, she goes to the stack to find Beth's paper to verify that she did in fact choose the closest number. But as she's flipping through the pile, she pauses. A bizarre look appears. Then she stares at Dillon. Back to the paper, back to the new kid.

"Dillon, is this your paper?" she asks, knowing it obviously belongs to him, unsure why he hasn't said anything prior to now.

"Yes, Mrs. Clay, it is."

"Why didn't you say that you had a closer number than Beth's?" she asks with concern.

"Oh well, I must have forgotten what I wrote down," he explained, poorly faking ignorance.

The class demands to know what he put. Mrs. Clay shows the class what his paper has scribbled on it. Intrigue turns into frustration as no one knows what is going on.

Danny yells, "Mrs. Clay! That's not a number, it's just some stupid letters! What the heck!"

She gives him a stern look to mildly admonish him for speaking out, and then explains. "Well class," she continues, drawing the letters XCIV on the board. "Does anyone know what roman numerals are?"

Images of grandeur immediately flood my brain. This new kid . . . he and I are going to run the world.

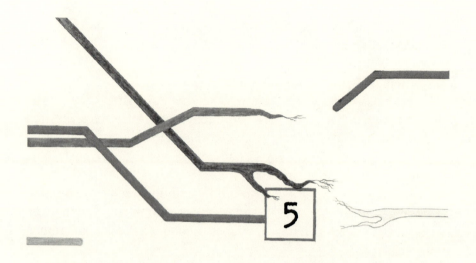

5

Nearly three minutes have passed. Dillon's expression remains unchanged. Effectively just stares down Medusa. Impulse was his trademark. He's shifted away from that over the years. Still, his thinking lasts longer than I anticipated. Finally, he looks up at me, begins a rapid series of facial contortions. Nostril flares, winks, eyebrow raises. It's his own language that he developed. I in turn became fluent. It's very complicated, but he prefers it to sign language. Long story short, Dillon lost his ability to speak several years ago. More to come.

Sorry, man, but what you're asking me to do is crazy. Are you aware of just how ridiculous this whole plan sounds?

Ridiculous, no. Complicated, absolutely. Still, I'm always up for a challenge. If he thinks this part is crazy, it's a good thing I didn't give him *all* the details. I can tell he's on the fence. Too much information, and he'll never get on board.

I don't need to remind you what ensued after the last cure you developed got out, he gestures to me.

If he's referring to the time I cured AIDS—later forced to flee the continent, change my identity, abandon everything, all the while my best friend was being assaulted on a weekly basis . . . then yes, I remember quite well.

"Dillon, believe me," I begin, "I know just how absurd this whole thing sounds. But trust me, I've given it a lot of thought. I've had *years* to think about it. Not only do I want to do this, I feel like it's my calling." As that last word leaves my mouth, I'm flooded with regret. Not one to dodge accountability for what I say, still want to take that back.

Dillon's eyes bulge with excitement. *Really?* The conversation hangs in suspense. He's thinking even more deeply. I already know where this is going. *I'll tell you what. I'm going to pray on this . . . and you're going to come with me.*

I knew it. "Dillon, you know that's not going to happen."

Fine. I would never force you to, but I just thought it might be good for you. But I must be on my way. He stands up, pushes in his chair, and heads for the door.

Can't believe what I'm about to do. At this point I feel my options are rather limited. A small sacrifice to make when viewed on the scale of my final objective. Still, going to mass with Dillon is not something I ever saw happening. A rigid atheist as long as I've known him, no longer the case. Apparently, when I cured AIDS, that was all the proof he needed. This threw me. People cure diseases all the time. People live, they die. That's the cycle of life. Science had been looking for a cure for decades; it was bound to happen. Why is this any different?

I'm easily among the smartest people in the world. Not being cocky. That's reality. Compared to Dillon, though, it appears I was raised in the Mesozoic Era. There isn't a word suitable to describe his level of genius.

His biggest downfall, however? His lack of drive. Ambition is not his strength. Given all the abilities in the world, he squandered most of it. He argues otherwise, will feed you some bullshit about it being part of his life's "journey." Don't buy it. People who ramble about "finding their way" in life are painfully aware of how much they screwed up. Dillon being a prime example.

We were virtually inseparable from the day we met. All the way through high school. Neither of us spent much time studying. Everything was elementary. Came naturally. So we spent a lot of time being asshole teenagers. Not getting into too much trouble, just enough to frustrate most adults. No drugs, maybe a little booze at home with some X-Box, but that's about it. We didn't vandalize or harass, with one notable exception. Dillon was in a perpetual state of sedation. Not induced by narcotics, just naturally calm. But one thing set him off like you wouldn't believe. A complete Jekyll-and-Hyde scenario.

Most businesses have those neon signs. They flash Open during operating hours. Unfortunately for them, they would occasionally neglect to shut them off. I saw nothing wrong with it. Dillon on the other hand . . . "irate" is an understatement. The mattress store on Belmont wasn't actually open at 11:00 p.m. Dillon put a rock through their storefront glass. Contrary to what the sign said, the shoe store on Dearborn wasn't selling hush puppies at 3:00 a.m. They did spend the next day ordering new windows though.

He never stole anything. Had no need for it. Each time he did this, he tied a note to the rock. Always worded differently, the message never changed: "Turn off your sign when you leave."

I didn't think much of it at the time. Just kids being kids. Or so I thought. But really, Dillon was just starting to let out his wild streak.

We graduated, went to different colleges. Me, I focused on biology and chemistry. For a few weeks anyway. Turns out, I really did know more than my mentors. Every single one of my professors freshman year had penned at least one book. I found flaws in all but one of them.

Resignations followed.

Wanted to feel bad. But I didn't. We were all scientists. In search of facts. Truth. If anything, they are in my debt. They didn't see it that way. Mildly put, their understanding of the world was off at best.

Needless to say, offers to the world's best medical schools were arriving before I could legally drink. Harvard. Maybe. Johns Hopkins. No, thanks.

Figured since I already knew more than just about everyone around me, I'd simply have fun. So I majored in industrial design and art history. For those of you considering this . . . don't. Art degrees are bullshit. If you can puff-paint a Japanese character on a park bench, you can be an artist.

If you can simulate a stuffed bear dry-humping a facsimile of the U.S. Constitution, you can probably run the department. Curious what it takes to make it to the Guggenheim?

It's simple really.

Garage sales.

Seriously. This isn't exaggeration. Rather, documented fact.

Junior year I landed an internship working with the curator for the Guggenheim in New York City. If you're ever near Eighty-seventh and Fifth, stop in and check out the building. Don't actually pay to see the exhibits. The architecture, by far the most fascinating aspect, is free. You can pay $25 to see sun-dried fruit glued to Swedish clogs. Just don't say you weren't warned.

My duties were mundane at best. But perseverance pays off. I showed promise. Totally unrelated, but some people were "let go." Have my suspicions why. Their loss was my gain. I pounced on the opportunity. When I found out I would have the coveted task of organizing a collection in the third-floor gallery, I smiled ear to ear. I should have been researching Caravaggio, Picasso, or at least Pollock. Looking for the best of the best. Pull in some big names.

Instead, I waited and waited. The day before the installation was to be put in place, I dropped $72 at a local thrift store. Old record players, swim fins, coffee-stained blankets. The pieces were put in place. I fabricated several phony descriptions. Long story short, overwhelming success. The *New York Times* said it was the best display they'd seen in *any* gallery within the last thirty years.

I knew then I could never again take the world of art seriously. Another reason in the ever-growing list of why talks of fate, destiny, and the like drive me insane. I can't even count how many artists over the years I've met who blab about their purpose in life. In my experience, destiny is simply a euphemism for "unemployed." People who are in a perpetual state of "finding themselves" are only doing so because they have so much free time. People with jobs can't do much soul-searching. They're too busy being productive members of society.

After we complete the mile walk, Dillon and I are staring up at the massive spire out front of Our Lady of Mercy. My knees shake slightly. Not because I mind organized religion. I don't love it, don't despise it. The last time I set foot in this, or any church, was for my mother's funeral. Dad passed while I was out of the country. Wanted to come back. I really did. Wasn't safe yet.

This day had to come sooner or later. Let's get it over with.

You catch more flies with honey than with hand grenades. If doing this will sway Dillon in my favor, it's a worthwhile sacrifice.

Still trembling mildly, we enter the cathedral. Everything is different, yet the exact same.

The congregation might be comprised of different people, but not really. The guy in the third pew, chronic masturbator. Lady just to my left, three abortions this year. Old dude in the back beat his wife for thirty years. These three, along with half those in attendance, are staring me down. Just like anywhere else I go. Some lady in the front, I can feel her eyeballs burning a hole in my soul. Paranoia strikes again. Everyone else here has their share of indiscretions. But in sixty minutes, all is forgotten. Forgiveness is only an hour away. It seems to me forgiveness is merely an excuse to be flawed. Validates weakness. Don't fuck up then there's no need for it. It's merely comfort for the substandard.

If I were flawed, I'd ask for forgiveness too

Don't have that problem.

The priest is giving his sermon, cluing us in on how to live forever. Telling us how the poorest among us will be first into heaven. Seems a blessing to have been born in the third world. Why bother help those starving globally? They'll be given eternal life. Instead, focus on massive errors in judgment then say you're sorry. Heaven awaits.

Then he goes into sex. If God denies access for this, then he's getting lonely up there. Or loves his personal space. But again, looking around, so many ugly people have no idea how blessed they are. How noble are you if you're never tempted? What sacrifice have you made if no one wants to sleep with you? Blonde bombshells have it much worse. Sure, they'll never pay for a single drink in the earthly realm. A lifetime of free mimosas, a poor tradeoff compared to eternal misery.

I'm exaggerating, but still have a point. I'm agnostic. Although I don't really think there's an omniscient creator, I'm not sold there isn't one. I hear people don't believe because there's no proof. Understandable. Can't prove the contrary either. The fact is, if God exists, God makes the rules. If God wanted to strike you down for jerking off to porn, he most certainly could. So what if you think drinking alcohol is no big deal. God can despise it if he wants. Not my belief. Not impossible either.

Being back here with Dillon brings back so many questions. So many unanswered conflicts from my youth. Not sure where I stand on fate and divine intervention. Not really my thing, but only a fool would rule it out completely.

The fact is, Mom and Dad ate it up. Whether right or out of their minds, I value their opinions. What can it hurt to pray on this decision? As Dillon kneels down to give thanks for his well-being, I decide to join him.

I think to myself, *Dear God, if you don't want me to bring about the outright annihilation of human existence, by all means . . . please stop me.*

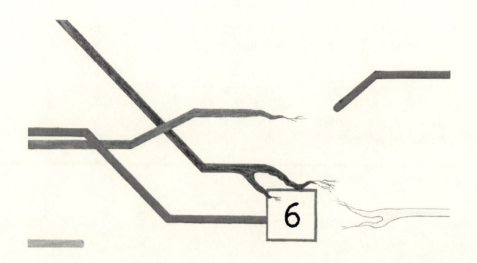

6

Dillon Pulaski wasn't always this precious. You see him now, you want your daughter or your sister to marry him. Few people know this was the same guy whose on-camera fuck list outnumbers the population of Alaska. I'm low-balling that figure. You get the point.

So it's really no surprise when I tell you that Dillon was a big reason as to why I cured AIDS. When you only have one parent and your best friend is terminal, you fight. That's what I did. His life choices were questionable at best. I had to help him. No-brainer at the time. Still not sure how it would play out in round two.

Remember when I said throwing rocks through storefront windows was the first indicator that Dillon had a wild side? When he got to college, he let it rip. Despite having the most gifted mind the world has seen in centuries, he chose to major in film. Wasn't very fond of film classes though. Diagesis, crane shot, swipe, Orson Welles, sound bridge, subtitles, boom mic, Rosebud . . . he hated it. Just like any smart kid, he was able to bullshit his way through classes. Grades weren't an issue. He saw his hours in film lab as a massive joke, a waste of time. Didn't mean he wasn't interested in making movies. Just wanted to make a different type.

He shot his first porn sophomore year. Walked in on his roommate banging his girlfriend. They stopped at first. But he encouraged them, picked up a camera. An addiction was born. He directed a handful of scenes that floated around on the Internet for the rest of that year. His libido quickly took over. Like I said, Dillon was so well endowed, you'd think he was running in the Belmont Stakes. Any bar he walked into should have had a dress code requiring enormous floppy hats. Put mint juleps on special. It's no surprise he decided having sex on camera was his undeniable vocation.

Handsome, funny, and ruthless. Dillon could sleep with any woman he wanted. So he did. Three hundred seventy-four were lucky enough to find this out firsthand over his last two years in college . . . that's what was documented at least. Certainly more participants off-camera.

With that much exposure, it's no surprise he was among the most highly sought male adult film stars ever. Sure, every man's dream. Sleep with gorgeous women, get paid for it.

It's never that simple.

Quickly, he became known as Jack Avalanche. The guy came with so much force, it could drown a rhinoceros. Sperm banks kept empty five-gallon buckets lying around just in case. Still not ringing a bell? How about *Dickabod Crane*? Yep, Dillon's fiftieth professional film became notorious not for the enormous jugs or fake orgasms. No, what catapulted this title immediately to porn immortality was much different. He shot the entire film with a pumpkin on his head. Is the orange tip of his penis making more sense? That's right, he had the head of his cock tattooed orange with black markings just for this film. Still hard to say which of the two jack-o-lanterns was heavier.

Not exactly surprising, Dillon eventually contracted every STD known, including HIV. We weren't as close as we had been growing up. But he was my best friend. I had to help him for that reason. But also because I knew I had been given another chance to do something amazing.

I isolated myself in the lab. Tried everything. Intense research and testing. Within five months of the news, I was ready. When I finally got in touch with Dillon, he was in bad shape. I don't think he remembered me. No doubt strung out on the flavor of the week. I found him in Van Nuys, California. He wanted to die. I couldn't blame him. He looked worse than death. After days of fierce arguing, he conceded. I gave him the shot, and we waited.

Gradually he felt better. Showed no signs of malady within three months. I knew the cure worked. The AMA was skeptical. It was as if Dillon was a new man. He had a renewed passion for life. Couldn't thank me enough. Swore he would make it his duty to not only help distribute the cure throughout the world, but to also make me famous. He said "hero" was trivializing my role. I said I wanted to fade into the distance. Secretly, I was thrilled. Saving lives was by far the most important aspect. The prospect of fame wasn't so bad either.

He kept his promise. I really wish he hadn't. Part of his plan to spread the word was let the world know just how healthy he was. Sounds nice, right? Dillon effectively considered himself invincible. Didn't see this as a second chance at life. Didn't think to maybe put aside his reckless ways. Instead, he became *more* immersed in his old lifestyle. Began making films far raunchier than anything he'd ever done. He slept with women, men, androgynous, animals. Anyone and anything willing, he put his dick inside. What did he care? He couldn't be stopped. The deadliest disease known to man: irrelevant. I want to believe his intentions were good. The plus-side: his actions turned skeptics into believers in virtually no time. The down-side: you don't sleep with that many people, publicize it, and not reap a serious backlash.

Since the cure, he's slept with countless people. Many of them married. They looked at porn as a way to spice up their life. Make someone jealous. Or terminate a dead-end marriage altogether. There were a lot of pissed-off husbands in the coming months. Dillon was attacked almost everywhere he went. Taunts and jeers followed him in a parasitic fashion. Couldn't go ten minutes without being insulted or threatened. Most of the abuse was verbal. Still, some of it was physical.

That's why he can't talk.

The blink of an eye is all it takes. Piss off the wrong person, you might get away with it. Piss off dozens of them, chances of escaping unscathed drop substantially. Sitting in a restaurant one night, near the front, a four-pound rock smashed through the main window. It hit Dillon square in the head. Talk about irony. At least the place was open for business.

Obviously, it didn't kill him, he's a giant. He walked around dazed for a few minutes. When he finally stood up and left under his own power and that was it: a baseball bat to his skull. Wooden, luckily. All caught on camera, too many witnesses to count. Turns out Dillon had fucked this guy's wife *and* both of his daughters on film. Drove the guy to drinking heavily. Some people can't hold their liquor. He's locked up, no idea where. Call it "justice" if you want but it didn't cure Dillon's inability to talk. Aside from a myriad of shattered bones, the nerve damage was unbelievable. Bones, they heal. Surgery will fix scars. But his brain was permanently tainted. Though it still functions in every conceivable way. When it comes to enunciation, nothing. You never realize how much you miss someone's nonstop yapping until it's gone. Condemned to a life as a mute.

Could be worse.

At least that's Dillon's take on it.

The cure for AIDS wasn't enough for him. He kept living fast and hard. It wasn't even the assault that hit home. Watching the video of his attacker—that broke his heart. Stockholm syndrome. Sympathize with your captor. Whatever. Dillon's heart went out to this guy. He blamed himself. Ultimately, realized he forced no one to do anything. They were governed by their own free will. Still, Dillon took this hard. Months went by that he couldn't forgive himself. Wouldn't forgive himself.

Certainly, losing the ability to speak took its toll on him. His outlook: losing that was nothing compared to losing those you love.

Throughout it all, I wanted to see it from the eyes of this other guy. I wanted to feel sorry for him. I don't know his story. Did his wife hate him? Was he a deadbeat dad? Maybe he was devoted in every way and never saw this coming. That's beside the point. His actions were beyond crazy.

But Dillon's resentment wasn't with his assailant.

He resented himself. Made a vow: never hurt another person. Ever again. Physically or emotionally. He was a man of peace.

To his credit, he has absolutely lived his life according to the promises he made himself. Sought counseling. Became very active in church. It's not for me, but it helped him. Who am I to argue?

Did I think about healing him? Naturally. But Dillon won't even let me broach the topic. Last time I cured something, shit hit the fan. That can't stop me though. Progress is inevitable. The friend in me saw his side though. He also saw his new lot in life as his fate. The work of God. There was a reason behind this.

I'm still trying to figure out what it might be.

No one exemplifies redemption and second chances like Dillon Pulaski. He had a rough youth, but he is one of the greatest, kindest men alive.

It's his benevolent nature that I love. It's also the reason I should encounter little resistance manipulating the shit out of him. Although there is one person who would make this go a lot faster.

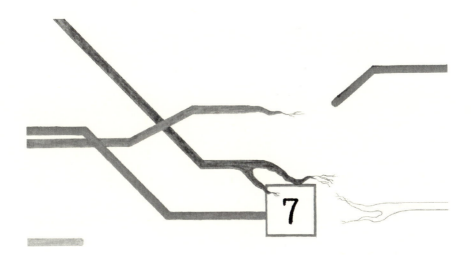

7

Mackenzie Desjardins. Where do I begin? She's something else, that's for sure. Like most people, you're thinking Dillon has no capacity to love. Because he fucked anything with a pulse, he wasn't like you. Didn't want to settle down.

Wrong. Let he without sin loosen up and live a little.

If anything, his burning desire to fall in love drove him to porn. He didn't handle rejection well. No one does, especially not him. His insecurities compounded. It eventually got the best of him.

Enter Mackenzie. First year of high school, freshmen English, under Mr. Burke. Cakewalk for all three of us. Homer's *Iliad*. Dillon and I taught her Latin just so she could read it in another language. The English translation was too rudimentary. Naturally, Dillon fell for her.

The feelings weren't mutual. That would make life too easy.

Mackenzie was adopted. Her circumstances not as bad as mine. Still, it gave us something to bond over. I guess she felt connected to me. Just to clarify, her adoptive parents are French-Canadian. She's Japanese. A jujitsu master. Call it racist, stereotypical, whatever. On many occasions, I witnessed her force an all-state linebacker into submission. The girl is five-foot-one, ninety-three pounds . . . dressed and assuming she just ate an entire cheesecake.

She taught me the basics. I honed my skills during my time as a refugee. One of many Eastern crafts I focused on. Acupuncture was another.

High school was awkward enough. Two guys and one girl parading as friends rarely make it better. We made it out alive.

College came. She ended up at the same school as me for the first two years. Then she transferred. To Dillon's school.

Let me lay out for you a complicated love triangle. More linear than anything, really. Dillon worshipped Mackenzie. She wasn't into him like that, so he did the next logical thing: sleep with every other woman. Apparently, it worked. When she eventually transferred, they made one of his famous films together. Her intention was to make me jealous. I know this. I know this because she was in love with me. I'm hoping she still is. Would cut my workload in half.

A woman sleeping with your best friend to make you jealous would infuriate most people. Here's where this situation shatters the mold.

I'm not attracted to her. Yes, I think she's stunning.

Now you're thinking I'm gay.

I'm not.

But I'm not straight either. Attraction is all biological impulses. We see something, it evokes a reaction. Very few women incite anything within me.

Now you're thinking I'm a virgin.

Wrong again.

I'll save you some time. The answer to your next question is three. Certainly not very many given my age. It was a conscious choice.

Fact of the matter is I lost my virginity long before I could drive a car. Not my proudest moment. It was shortly after Mom died. A dark and troubling time. Didn't mean I refused to accept reality.

I went to her grave regularly. I cried. A lot.

A fragile frame of mind is not conducive to great life choices. Enter Krystal Madigan. I first noticed her at the funeral in the church. Saw her at the burial too. Call it irony. Call it fate. Her mom died three months prior. Krystal was older than me by a couple years. Yet her mother was younger than Josephine. Never found out her connection to my family. Why she was there that day.

We vented. Screamed profanities. Helped the other one adjust to a new life.

It was after the third time we'd crossed paths. It wasn't getting easier, but the other's presence seemed to prevent it from getting worse.

We grabbed some burgers. Then a movie. Then a quick fuck.

Aside from being an emotional wreck, trepidation consumed me. Performance anxiety. I fumbled around with the condom for at least two minutes. Dropped it. Tried putting it on backwards. Eventually, we got going. Ended as quickly as it began. She told me to pull out when I was about to cum. Wanted me to shoot it on her. A foreign concept to me at the time. I had yet to see a pornographic film. The raincoat didn't seem like it would make this request any easier. I pulled out. She ripped the rubber right off. Caught me by surprise. Milliseconds before climax, my dick flung up, shot up my nose.

Long story short, it was a while before I tried it again.

What about the other two? If you're wondering if Mackenzie is one of them, she's not. Not opposed to it though. Sex is a powerful tool. If she still has feelings for me . . . well, I'll do who I have to do.

She wasn't hard to find. Always been very driven, prominent in the art community. Mention her name to anyone who's set foot in the Chicago MOMA, they'll know her. Three degrees of separation. Four at most. Our interest in art was another reason we got along so well. Notice I didn't say "love" of art. Her talents are off the chart. Watching her work go unrecognized while dumpster-divers sold pieces for seven figures got old. Couldn't handle it. One of myriad reasons I got out of the art world.

To her credit, she stuck with it. I'm glad she did.

I step inside Gumball Alley on Belmont. Nothing about the name says "restaurant." Immediately, I'm blown away. Most of the work is hers. The parquet tables? Her blood, sweat, and tears. The steel ornamental flower ceiling decoration. That is hers too. She did the Dia de Los Muertos mural on the far wall. Only took her a week. Every single chair in this place is unique. Sure, similar in height. The designs are all different. All made from scratch. Not a single prefabbed piece.

Did I mention she owns the joint? The entire operation. It's all her. The pizza is her own recipe too. Heard nothing but great things.

I grab a seat at a booth. Upholstered with blue-and-green checkered vinyl. It's middle of the day; busier than I expected. I look at the menu, wonder if she's here today.

I pan my head around the room, admire the artwork. Scope the strangers, make quick character judgments. Most people carry on; business as usual. Not her. Not the brunette in the corner. Hiding behind massive sunglasses. They're a dead giveaway. This isn't a Vegas nightclub. They're superfluous. Whatever . . . just another crazy Chicagoan gone mad from the cold.

I look at her, back at the menu, back at her. She ducks her head. Focuses on her pasta and salad. I dismiss it; look at the menu once again. This time with intent.

Too late, my server approaches.

"Hey, sugar, what can I grab you to drink?" I look up.

It's Mackenzie.

If I'm at all surprised, I hide it well. Without hesitation, I say root beer, no ice. Breaking protocol here. Ted Watts drank tepid soda. Will she notice? It's not a bizarre request. Not exactly standard either.

She seems unaffected, walks away for less than a minute.

"There you go, darlin'," she says, slaps the warm beverage in front of me. "What are you having?"

Time to test my new look. I gaze up at her. Each movement deliberately drawn out. I have my suspicions, but I ask anyway. "Um, yeah, what exactly is this Buddha Pizza?"

"Oh that. It changes every day. Basically, each day, we decide what five toppings will go on it. We don't tell you what they are. It's kind of adventurous, gets you to try something new. It's based on the philosophy that you should be thankful for what you get. Even if you hate green peppers, eat them anyway."

My assumption dead-on. I'm very familiar with such practices. Years in the Orient paying off.

Feigning disgust, "Oh wow, I don't think I'm that spontaneous. Could I just have a personal pepperoni please?" I'm staring her in the eyes the entire time. She's hiding her discomfort well. Either doesn't recognize me at all or is messing with me to see if I'll break first.

"Sure thing" is all she says as she walks off to the kitchen.

I wait, sipping my warm soda. People come in, others leave. The lady in the corner is stabbing at the same three romaine leaves. Has been since I sat down. At least now she's looking elsewhere.

Mackenzie grabs my cup, gives me a refill. Doesn't say a word. This is encouraging. If she of all people has no clue who I am, odds are no one else will either.

The pizza comes; she asks me if I need anything else. Looks at me with what I take to be recognition. Likely, I'm merely projecting that desire. Just because I want it to be doesn't make it so.

I eat the pie quickly. The first pizza I've had in years. Regardless, it's delectable. Mackenzie knows her stuff. Good for her.

The brunette eventually gets up and leaves. I don't think she paid. Mackenzie is back with my bill.

I give her a heads-up on the lady not paying. A worthless retroactive warning. Should have spoken up earlier, so I offer to pay her bill.

"Oh, don't worry about it. She's in here every day. I think she's been a regular for about a year now."

"How long have you guys been open?" I inquire with genuine intrigue.

"Wow, we're coming up on eight years here pretty soon."

"Congratulations. Well, with pizza like this, I can see why."

A small smile, the first I've seen on her all day. Since I left the country years ago in fact.

"Thank you," she says. "Will that be all?"

I nod, but then out comes, "I'm sorry I didn't get your name."

"Mackenzie." She wasn't always this terse.

"Great name. Let me ask you, Mackenzie, what do you want to do with your life?"

As if she gets asked this question by every customer, in stride she replies, "I'm doing it. I make art. I made almost everything in this place. The tables, chairs, sculptures. Most of it is mine. I own the joint."

She says it with so much conviction, anyone else would believe her. It's not a *false* answer. But it is an *incomplete* answer.

She wants a family.

She wants kids.

Congratulating her, "Wow, that's fantastic. Good for you." I hand her my credit card; she returns with the receipt and a pen.

"There you go, Mr. Clemens."

"Thank you."

"If you don't mind sir, I have a question for you."

"Sure thing. What is it?"

"When did you change your name from Ted to Samuel, and how long have you been back in America?"

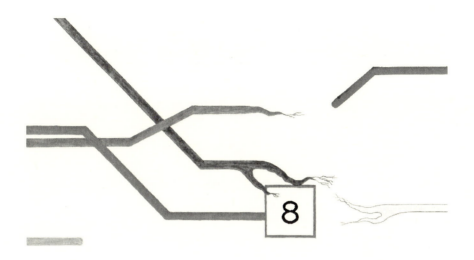

8

"I'm in," she tells me with that bravado I've been missing. I'd forgotten just how confident this woman is. A true asset to the operation.

Full disclosure. She knows what I'm up to. Unlike Dillon, I've hidden nothing from her. No secrets. We're in this together.

Her zeal will come in handy. But that's also the problem. Why is she so eager? No hesitation whatsoever. Had I suggested a plot to blow up the Louvre, would she have batted an eye? Her compliance I expected. Eventually. I didn't even have to ask twice. Something is off. I make a mental note. Bold, italics, and underlined. I'll get answers.

"So tell me, Ted, how exactly are you going to pull all this off?" she wonders with a mix of genuine curiosity and sarcasm.

"Easy." I hold up both hands, palms out. "Look at my fingers," I tell her. First she's confused, doesn't get it. I make her take a closer look. She notices something, not that it explains much.

"Are those warts? Calluses, what?" she asks.

Not quite. Embedded in each of my thumbs, index, and ring fingers are tiny ball bearings. No bigger than a mustard seed. I ask her what she knows about acupuncture. Not much, she tells me. Lucky for us, I know more than most of Asia. Studied it rigorously while in exile.

I step even closer to her. "May I?" I ask as I place my right hand on her left ear. She looks confused. "Trust me," I tell her. No irony, no mockery.

"OK," she confides in me.

I walk her over near the oven, open it. The heat pours out, several hundred degrees. Apprehension is on her face. Standing behind her, my left hand now grasps her left ear. I squeeze high up on the ear, center, just underneath the helix. Distracting her, I ask, "So how long have you owned this place?"

Puzzled I just asked her this question, she tells me, "Oh well, the building was a pizza place for probably over forty years, but I didn't take over until about eight years ago." She carries on wearily. I grab her left hand with mine and shove it in the oven.

She screams.

Silence quickly ensues.

Human nature dictates you scream. If someone threatens you by sticking your hand in a scalding oven, of course your first instinct is to expect pain.

But that didn't happen.

She felt nothing. She turns around, dumbfounded. "How the fuck are you doing that?" Her mind is blown, yet she still wants to hit me. I don't blame her.

I back her away from the oven. "Would you like another example?" I offer.

Her eyes bulge. She's seen enough for one day. She's sold. Confused, but convinced. That's good enough for now.

I tell her it's simple. There are hundreds of pressure points all over the human body. Dozens located in the ears alone. They all correspond to varying body parts and sensory organs.

I could make her cum just by pinching the skin at the bridge of her nose.

Could whack her shins with a pipe, and she'd be none the wiser if I applied proper pressure to the tip of her tongue.

"Here. Take this." I hand her a butcher's knife. There's trepidation. She's terrified at the thought of cutting me. I tell her I'll be fine. If she's going all-in on this mission with me, I need to be fully convinced that she feels likewise. There can be no doubt on her part that this will work.

"Kick me in the balls as hard as you can," I tell her.

"What?"

"Just do it, I'll be fine. I didn't burn your hand, did I?"

She wants to know what the knife is for. I tell her it's for later, need not worry about it right now. I grab my lower left ear, the lobule. She kicks. Hard. The temptation to let out a fake scream and scare her crosses my mind. I suppress the urge. Must remain professional.

"See? I'm fine."

She is in awe. I expected as much. I've seen men bathe in boiling tubs of water. Not a peep. My cynicism ran deep the first few times I was a witness. Must have been a trick. Eventually, I worked up the courage to do it. Rather soothing to be honest. Make no mistake. The skin will still be severely damaged. Some will never fully heal. Lucky I know the best surgeons the world has to offer.

I give her a better explanation of how this information will be practical. That I can force someone to pass out before they know my hand is on their ear. I can temporarily impede someone's short-term memory. I've utilized it more times than I can count.

Doesn't take long to make her an apparent believer. I'm still suspicious. Why? She hasn't seen me in years. Somehow she's fine with this. I know she had feelings for me. Probably still does. Nevertheless, it feels off.

But her agitation has already transformed into blatant fervor.

"What does this do?" she asks repeatedly as she pinches all over my ears. "How about this, huh?" Moving so fast, she's making me a little dizzy. Acting as if my face was a new toy she'd been given for her fifth birthday.

She picks up the knife. "So what are we gonna do with this?" She flails it around while my concern grows. I cautiously bring her arm to rest and take the knife away.

"Oh well, that pizza was great, but I'm still hungry. Can you make me a sandwich?"

She rolls her eyes, insults me for my poor attempt at humor. I tell her I was going to have her stab me but changed my mind. That's a little advanced.

Mackenzie runs back and forth for the next several minutes, helping customers, refilling drinks. I wash some dishes. Eventually, she gets some downtime. I'm on the cusp of asking her flat-out why she's so willing to help.

She beats me to it. "So, Ted"—I calmly shake my head—"sorry, *Samuel*. I'm more than willing to help you out. But you're gonna do something for me in return."

Seems fair. What might that be?

"I know you came to me because you want Dillon's help. You think I can sway him." My look of surprise gives me away. I don't deny it. "It was pretty obvious. Look, we're all adults. He wants me, he'll do what I ask. You knew I'd say yes to just about anything you asked of me." Her candor and relaxed nature throughout this entire discussion are incredible. Time will tell if that's advantageous or detrimental.

"Hey, I know Dillon's all 'born-again' and living a pretty respectable life. But he's still human. We'll get him to crack," she tells me with a nefarious grin. Oddly enough, it's the most comfortable I've felt all day.

"I like your attitude," I tell her.

"I thought you would. But like I said, I'm not in this entirely for you. I've got some business I want to take care of," she tells me like she's the one running the show. Her increasing assertiveness excites me. My decision to include her reinforced every second.

"Sure thing, Mackenzie. Whatever you want, it's yours."

Another sinister grin. "I hoped you would say that. Well, first, I want to test this system out on my ex-husband," she says very nonchalantly.

"Wait, you were married?"

"Wow, Ted"—I shake my head again—"sorry, Samuel. That's gonna take some getting used to." I nod in agreement. There are going to be a lot of changes. Most of them difficult, but necessary nonetheless. "You sure have missed a lot over the years. But yes, I was married. It ended badly. I'll give you the dirty details some other time. I'm not really in the mood right now."

"That's fine. He must have been some piece of work if you want to do *this* to him."

She chuckles, "You have no idea. But in addition to that, there's something else I want."

"Anything."

"You know how long I've dreamt of having children. I ain't getting any younger. I want a kid . . . and you're gonna fuck me senseless until I have one."

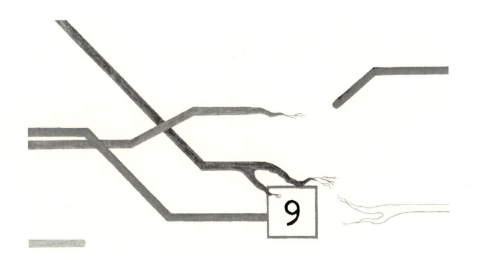

9

Beating a dead horse, but art is a joke. For lack of a better term. Debate it all you want, I have my reasons. However, there is one inspiring thing about it. A truly amazing artist comes along once or twice in a generation. At best. But they do exist. Sadly, their greatness is not recognized in their lifetime. It takes decades, maybe centuries, before their work is fully appreciated. In this age of instant gratification, that's comforting. A light at the end of a very small and twisted tunnel.

Most notably, Vincent Van Gogh. I'm not partial, but I recognize his enduring impact. He achieved little to no recognition while alive. That didn't stop him. Emily Dickinson, same thing. This is where I applaud art. Where it converges with science.

We study celestial bodies that possibly ceased to exist billions of years ago. Attempt to predict the workings of the solar system millions of years from now. Ever heard of scientific notation? 8.5×10^{28} light years. We do that standing on our heads.

So believe me when I say I'm well aware of the consequences of my undertakings. Results not measurable until long after I'm gone.

That doesn't mean my impact won't be felt. I'll live on in infamy.

Even if no one knows who I am.

Imagine though. My legacy: the man who single-handedly saved the human race.

Who subsequently wiped it off the map.

Feel free to call it delusions of grandeur. I believe my attitude is reasonable. I can back it up. I'm not on the same playing field as God, but I'm close. Only a step below.

For now.

Maybe a messenger carrying out his will. I'm no expert on religion, but find me the biblical passage where it says the world will last forever. This was bound to happen sooner or later. I happen to prefer sooner.

A five-year-old girl dies of leukemia. Unfair, no doubt. Fate? Perhaps. A heroin junkie contracts every form of hepatitis known to man. Calms his nerves by saying everything happens for a reason. He doesn't regret it; he'll learn a lesson from it. It was meant to be. Keep it up. Rationalize everything. Let's tell ourselves there was nothing more we could do. Be content with less than perfect.

I don't work that way. Not anymore. I tried playing "fair." Only one problem. Fair is simply an idea. Intangible. Always evolving. Once you get close to what you think it is, shifts once again. Perpetually on the run. You'd have better luck chasing rainbows. The fight to end slavery turns into the right to vote. Which becomes a fight for equal pay. Don't interpret this as me saying these aren't noble pursuits. They are. Merely that every hurdle cleared inevitably leaves an isolated few on the outside looking in. Gay marriage, a prime example.

Make no mistake; eventually, people will get it right. Sooner or later, everyone will pull their heads out of their asses. A few states have already set the pace. We're on our way. Still a long road ahead. Point being eventually, it will be fair. But there are no free lunches.

If you don't like opposite sex partners, why can't you marry someone of your own gender? Valid point. But what if you don't like humans? Why can't you pledge your love and devotion to your Doberman? Dogs are loyal pets. So what if a grown man wants to fuck his cat? But why stop there? Which is why I'm passing around a petition to let blind people drive cars. Not their fault they were born without sight.

After all, the Founding Fathers would want it that way. What part of *all men* did you not get? Clearly Thomas Jefferson would throw a fit. Good ol' TJ, founder of democracy. Owner of slaves.

That's right. The man whose writings and philosophies you hold so dear couldn't comprehend a dictionary. A whole new world of contradictions unfolds. Remember, he wrote we're all *created* equal. Nothing about staying that way.

He said *pursuit* of happiness. Nothing about actually getting there.

A 2,000-year-old collection of writings is worthless. A 250-year-old document however . . . a product of the divine.

Ironically, the very people who flip out about religious doctrine impacting their lives are the same people who desperately cling and feed off the beliefs of a crazy man.

Which is fine. We're all crazy. I'm certainly out of my mind. An eternal catch 22. Actions inconsistent. Hypocrisy flowing through my veins. My biggest credit: determination. Unlike most, I follow through. I won't make my intentions known. If I did, it would likely make no difference. No one cares. Sure, they'll make everyone *aware* of the problem. Start a group on a social networking website. Wear a T-shirt with a catchy slogan. Wash your hands, move on. Let someone else deal with it.

Fine by me. The more complacent, the better. This will come in handy, as Mackenzie's ex-husband is twice my size. More massive than she described him. Not that he could stop me. I've mastered the principals of leverage. Even with conventional fighting, I could take him. But with my mastery of acupuncture literally at my fingertips, it's a non-issue.

Mackenzie closed up Gumball Alley for the night, told me all about her past. I really was out of the loop. The major outline of her story, nothing you haven't heard. She met a guy a few years ago. A real charmer. Handsome, established, but lots of fun. Too good to be true. That cliché didn't materialize out of nowhere. Most people aren't what they appear. Jarrett was no exception. Did just about everything wrong minus domestic violence. Truly a piece of work.

She's my friend. I would have done this for Mackenzie regardless. Then she told me more. A common conflict in marriage. Some people work through it, some don't. Kids. She wanted them. He didn't.

Not with her, anyway.

He was sleeping around, for at least two years. Three different women that he confessed to. She suspects more. Proof of the three? Babies. He has at least three kids, all with different mothers. Maybe they know about one another. But doubtful.

For all I know, Jarrett is devoted and coaches all three of their soccer teams. Maybe he pays child support in full and on time without fail.

Ask me if I care.

Just to clear up any confusion, I don't. Never waste time debating. Make a decision, stick with it. Sure, you'll do things you regret. You'll fuck up. Give it some consideration. Deliberating for days or more is, however, fruitless. Weigh the pros and cons, but do it quickly. Go with your gut. If it all goes to shit, improvise.

Sure, maybe he's a great guy deserving of a second chance. Maybe I'd feel bad about this if I got to know "who he really is." Don't have time for that. I'll be the first to admit my choices in the coming months will be irrational. Calling them sporadic and inconsistent? Putting it mildly.

Simply put, that's how it goes.

Some make the cut, others don't.

Many deserving people go unrewarded. Meanwhile, the parasites of the world thrive.

I'm behind on my Bible studies. Sodom and Gomorrah—sound familiar? Places so corrupt and depraved, God was ready to wipe them clear off the map.

He didn't. Not right away that is.

Said that in a world filled with sinners and hedonists, he would spare the wicked for the sake of a righteous few. None could be found.

I'm not that nice. Don't have the time to scour the world for something that likely disappeared decades ago.

If I had 1 percent the grace of God, I wouldn't be sitting in this shitty bar, observing Jarrett and his friends.

Happy hour. Not sure what's so happy about it. Everyone looks miserable. Neutered dogs smile with more conviction.

I glance down at the crumpled photo Mackenzie gave me, the image blurry. That devious smirk, unmistakable. The second I see him in person, I know why Mackenzie was drawn to him. Everyone knows him here. She tells me he's been coming here every day after work since she's known him.

Sometimes you want to go where everybody knows your name.

But sometimes, you really should have stayed at home. Or gotten as far away from your past as possible.

Most people are sitting in groups, an occasional solo patron here and there. Despite the appearance of social activity, most of them are typing away. This is who we are. Make plans only to make new plans while making plans to make plans, killing time while they pretend they haven't wasted their lives. The moderately full bar not as loud as you'd expect. The chatter is low but far from silent.

Jarrett is chatting up the bartender. A woman in her late twenties, early thirties. He's lost a step. His jokes are awful. She laughs regardless. Desperate for tips. That or popsicle sticks provided the only literature she's ever read.

Listening to him talk hurts my brain. Yes, I'm biased. Still, nothing about him is endearing. Apparently he's wealthy. Like it or not, helps with women. That's not what Mackenzie was drawn to. Not the primary reason, at least. She's been great with money. Makes sound fiscal decisions.

She liked him because he's a carbon copy of me. The way I *used* to look that is. Scruffy beard. Shaggy mop of dark brown hair splaying out in every direction from the edges of his Cubs' hat. Covered in tattoos. Owns Belmont Inkworks, one of the city's best studios. Word is that he's the best in town. Maybe so. The same can't be said for the nine-year-old who must have tattooed him in a drunken daze. An epileptic at a disco is capable of better work.

I'm new to this scenario, but she was into Jarrett for all the wrong reasons: filling a void. Projecting her fascination with me on him. Whatever does it for you. The important thing: he's out of the picture. Fortunately for the bartender with no standards, I'm about to end his reproductive capabilities.

I approach the bar, ready to order. Her gaze fixed on him. I wait patiently. All the time in the world. I even eavesdrop to pass the time. Despite her vapid veneer, she appears quite driven. She pays her way through school. Botany-Government, double major. A worthless skill set. Admirable nonetheless.

My patience is rewarded. She eventually catches my eye. Excuses herself from my target, approaches me. I'll have a White Russian. As she grabs the bottles, I plot my attack: steal her attention long enough, Jarrett will leave.

She returns with my drink.

"Eight dollars, hon."

I slap a twenty on the bar, tell her to keep it. Not the biggest tip she's ever received, but impressive still. Her pleasant surprise registers with me, so the lies begin.

"I couldn't help overhearing that you're in school. I was a history major, about as worthless as they get, right? How much longer do you have?"

Just like that, I'm in control.

"Oh geez, way too long. I only go part-time because of work, so probably at least three more years. It'll be worth it though."

"How so? Is there a great demand for people who stay up late debating the democratic relevance of the Dracuunculus vulgaris?"

Her jaw drops. During my travels, I saw several of the world's rarest plants and animals. I don't tell her that. Just that I'm an avid fan of nature.

Jarrett's impatience is evident. He's growing fidgety. Hilarious. His nerves get the best of him, "Hey, Daivey, can I get another one? I'm runnin' on empty over here."

She politely excuses herself. I use this opportunity to break the ice.

"Hey, man, you mind if I check out your work?"

This puts him at ease, relatively speaking. He's hesitant but sees a potential client, so he obliges.

I lie, very convincingly. "Wow, these are great. Who did your work? I'm looking to get something done."

"Well, I've had several people do my work over the years, but you don't wanna go to them. They're good, but not as good as me."

I feign aloofness. "Oh, you're an artist."

Daivey butts in, says he's the best in town.

Just like that, this is too easy. Fish in a barrel.

We chat for a while. Mostly about tattoos, nothing too serious. I set up a time to come in. Tell him I'll bring some sketches. If I didn't know any better, I'd start to think he was a decent human being. He's a charmer, all right. Says he's gotta piss, he'll be right back.

Time to strike. I order two pints of stout. The darker the better. Palming a blue pill, I pick up the glasses by the rims. Pretend to look at the logo on the glass. A generic excuse.

"Wow, this looks delicious." Just like that, the pill slips out of my palm, into his glass. Dissolves quickly, not that anyone could ever see it swimming in that sea of darkness. I throw Daivey another twenty; Jarrett returns.

"It's about time. I was about to check and make sure you didn't pass out in a stall. I bought us another round. Drink up."

Jarrett puts the glass to his lips, and just like that, the game begins.

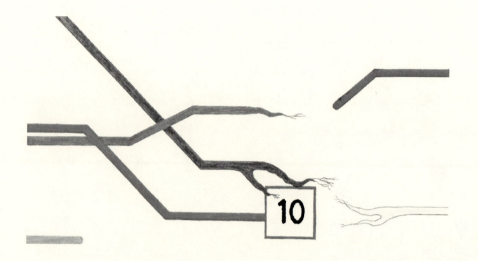

10

I'm not out to create a master race. Black, white, green—makes no difference. This isn't a quest for a planet populated entirely of blond-haired / blue-eyed musclemen. If you expect me to say, "Hitler was misunderstood," think again. Gay or straight, big deal. In fact, gays might get special treatment. They tend to not produce in large numbers.

Don't mistake my "open-minded" nature for altruism. I have my criteria.

Do I like you? Do you annoy the shit out of me? Are you stupid beyond repair?

I need people with ambition. Any society will have those of superior intellect juxtaposed with their cerebral inferiors. I'm out to raise the bar. By getting rid of the bottom-feeders in our current state, eventually the standards will change. Those of moderate intelligence today will be at the bottom of the pyramid.

Those currently occupying the bottom rungs will drop off entirely. With more intelligence running around, surely someone will undo what I've started. Seems counterintuitive. What can I say? I'm a real loose cannon. You never know what's coming next.

My plan was officially set in motion when I gave Jarrett a dose of the blue. This tattoo appointment serves multiple purposes. I want to learn more about his sexual habits. What's done is done. I still want to know if he really is the dirt-bag Mackenzie says he is. Next, he needs to be having unprotected sex. Lots of it. That's the fastest way for my plan to take effect.

It's sexually transmitted. Won't make anyone ill though. No vomiting. No making your skin pale. Undetectable.

But very easily contracted. No one wears condoms anymore. This will spread virtually overnight.

Is there a cure?

No.

Is there a vaccine to prevent it?

Certainly.

The recipients are handpicked by me of course. Quite simple really: do something I like, you get the white vaccine. Aggravate me: blue pill for you. Sterile for the rest of your days.

Belmont is exceptionally crowded for this time of night. The Inkworks is just around the corner. I stop to grab a bite. I've dined on cuisine from all over the world. Nothing like a Chicago hotdog. I throw down three in a matter of minutes. It's been years. Well worth the wait.

Keeping with my motive of breaking old habits, I put ketchup on them. Ketchup on a Chicago hotdog.

Like I'm a fucking tourist.

Ketchup. On the greatest culinary achievement the world has ever known.

#Sacrilegious

I step inside a studio sandwiched between a coffee shop and locksmith. The inside clean and well lit. The neon sign above the door has seen better days. I grabbed the last appointment of the evening. Should take a few hours.

Jarrett acknowledges me. Tells me to take a seat, he'll be ready shortly. I browse the art on the walls. None of it looks like Mackenzie's work. His portfolio average at best.

The stereo in the shop blasts a punk cover of a Lady Gaga classic.

A clipboard is slapped down in front of me. Shifts my attention.

"Hey, buddy, what's up? Could you fill out this consent form when you get a sec? I'll also need to copy your ID." This kid has tough exterior. He seems genuinely intimidated. Not sure why. I look like the typical corporate clone these guys love to talk shit about. First day on the job? Unlikely.

Fill out the form, give him one of my many fake IDs. To Jarrett and company, I'm Eric Blair.

See also "War is peace/Freedom is slavery/Ignorance is strength." Or *Animal Farm* if you're feeling rustic.

Jarrett won't remember the evening's events. Anyone else around tonight might. The less they know and remember about me, the better.

Back to glancing at the stock images people can put on their bodies. Nautical stars galore. Dragons? Oh my. What's the Chinese character for "narcissist"? Here we are, 2021, and somehow tramp stamps are still in style.

Despite the room tempting me with a barrage of cliché images, I stick to my original plan. Something bordering on original. But not so unique it could be used to identify me exclusively. Not that it matters. Jarrett will at best get the outline done before I make my move. Whatever he puts in my skin will only be there three weeks tops.

He cleans up his station, ready to begin. I hand him a sketch of a stein of beer. Seeing as how tonight I'm from Milwaukee, I reason that it reminds me of home. Mackenzie sketched up a twisted mug, foam splashing out of it. Jarrett glances at it, doesn't think twice. Couldn't recognize her style if it punched him in the dick.

The song has switched to Chicago's very own Alkaline Trio.

He scans the image onto transfer paper, shaves the hairs off my right shoulder, and applies the image. Time to begin.

I pretend the needle piercing the skin for the first time is uncomfortable. I've been through this literally dozens of times. What can I say? I'm a sucker for Stanislavski. Method is the only way.

He works fairly quickly, keeping great focus. For being quite the talker at the bar, he barely utters a word to me now. Perhaps if I grew labia, he'd show more interest.

Slowly the other artists begin cleaning up for the night. Sweep the floor. Windex the glass cases of body jewelry. Aside from Jarrett and myself, the kid who took my ID is the last one around. He does some quick math and shouts out the day's take to the owner. Jarrett shrugs. Not a great day, but they've done worse, he seems to imply. Just like that, he's out the door.

Only Jarrett and I remain. The kid at the front desk locked the door on the way out. We're there after hours. Don't want random passersby stumbling inside. Foot traffic outside has subsided noticeably. A few drunken people wander by every few minutes. Then a woman with an apron sticking out of her jacket flashes by, rushing to catch the bus. Can't help but wonder: if she misses it, what will she do while waiting for the next one? Stay away from dumpsters. The only thought cycling vigorously through my mind.

Jarrett finishes the line-work. Tells me to stand up, take a look at it so far. He needs a smoke break. Wants to relax his hand for a few minutes too. It's starting to cramp. Says we'll get to the color in a few. He offers me a smoke, I decline.

As I study his work in the mirror; he steps out the back door.

Places everyone. The show is about to begin. I check my pockets, make sure I have the pills I need.

All set.

To kill the time, I peruse the artwork in his personal booth. The walls are only four feet tall. Sort of a tiny cubicle. Covered mostly in paintings and drawings, there is a small section of photographs. Jarrett and some woman. Jarrett and a child. Him with two different children. Him with an older woman. One with him hugging a half-naked woman doused in more mascara than a lab rat. The banner in the background is for a porn convention. Shocking. Is she the mother of one of his kids? Irrelevant.

Among the few dozen pictures, I don't see a single one of Mackenzie. I quickly debate whether I should feel enraged or relieved. It's a fleeting dilemma. The back door opens and shuts. Jarrett is on his way back.

"Hey, man, you ready to finish this shit up or what?" he jubilantly inquires.

Playing along, I tell him I can't wait to see the finished product. He slaps on another pair of latex gloves, pours some new pigments into little cups. Hesitation gets you nowhere. Assess your enemy, find your opportunity to strike, take him down. I look at his ears. The lobes are stretched wide. About the size of a quarter—the one with President Clinton, not Washington. The holes are plugged with a plastic wheel, some kind of insect inside. Like a mosquito preserved in amber.

"Wow. Hey, I just noticed your ears. Those are way cool. Are the bugs real?" I ask him, coiling back, set to strike.

"Nah, I doubt it. Looks pretty real though, huh?"

"Yeah, for sure. You mind if I take a look at those?" He's about to take one out and hand it to me. I don't give him the chance. I move in immediately, grab his ear, give it a light squeeze.

He zones out. Looks very lost. Has no idea where he is. Wasting no time, I grab the other ear, slightly lower. Jarrett drops to the floor. A few light slaps on the face. Nothing. Splash of some water . . . he's out cold. I check the pulse, he's alive.

Acting quickly, I slap on a pair of the latex gloves he keeps in a jar. I undo his belt. The pants come down. I pull the pill out of my pocket.

A suppository isn't necessary. Just figured he would hate this way more. He's already sterile, so this is purely for entertainment.

It's gonna burn when he cums.

I insert my invention, dispose of the gloves, pull his pants back up. Set him up in the chair at his drawing table, remove his gloves as well. When he wakes up, he'll think he fell asleep drawing or something. I go to the main desk, grab the waiver I signed. The photocopy of my ID as well. I leave no trace I was here. The others will remember me, but as far as Jarrett knows, I was just a dream. They must be fucking with him.

It doesn't really matter. Only a matter of time before tattooing is the last thing on his mind.

Appropriately enough, the song changes as I'm about to leave. It's Woody Guthrie. "This Land Is Your Land." A classic no doubt. I'm fond, but it's not my favorite. When his music comes on, my instant reaction is always the same.

This machine kills fascists.

That would make a great tattoo. I'll have to ask Jarrett what he thinks about that.

I turn to head out. I notice his phone has fallen to the floor. Pick it up to put it next to his resting head. The screen saver is a picture of him and a woman. It's Mackenzie. Maybe I misjudged him.

Maybe not.

So it goes.

Thanks, Kurt ;)

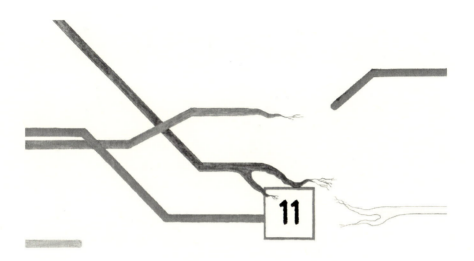

11

The weather outside Gumball Alley, absolute shit. Rain and wind somehow are coming from every direction. Good for business though. No one subjecting themselves to the outdoors longer than necessary. If you're going to kill a few hours, this is a good place to do it.

In between bites of stromboli, I explain in vivid detail the events of last night. Mackenzie smiles from start to finish. Her enthusiasm becoming more pronounced with every word that leaves my mouth. I do my best to appear neutral. Eventually, I crack; a tiny smirk flashes across my face. If you blinked, you missed it.

The place is packed. I still feel a pair of eyeballs locked on me through the mass of people. I look left, look right. Nothing. I do a second pass. That woman who skipped out on her bill last time. She's back, her gaze fixated on my every move. That explains it.

It's probably nothing, but I can't take chances. I make a mention of it to Mackenzie.

"Oh, you mean Alison? She's a regular, probably eats lunch in here an average of five times a week. She's harmless. I'll bet she's just curious who you are. Since she's been coming in for so long, we've gotten to know each other pretty well." She looks over at Alison, who is now glued to her lasagna. Her face a blank slate. Then a light bulb goes off. "Hey, I'll bet she thinks you're some guy I'm seeing or something. She knows my track record. Jarrett and all the other losers. She's probably just looking out for me is all."

I want to buy it. Reluctant at best. Something about her strikes me the wrong way. But I won't alarm Mackenzie. Yet. Play this one by ear. Keep your friends close. Enemies closer. With a stock response, I pretend to be ignorant. "Yeah, that's probably it. I'm just getting worked up over every person that looks at me these days. It's so weird being back, you know?"

She opens her mouth to respond but loses focus. Her attention drawn to something behind me. I begin to turn around, but I feel the grip before my chin moves more than two inches.

She invited Dillon.

Very promising.

Still haven't filled him in on the entirety of what's going on. Trying to reel him in slowly. Having Mackenzie on my side now, he's as good as in. A done deal. Just need to play it smooth, not force it.

Genuinely happy to see him, I stand up and give him a hug. Mackenzie does the same. Asks him if he wants any food. He signs to her that a deep-dish pepperoni and mushroom would be wonderful. She figured he'd say that, threw it in the oven thirty minutes ago. Should be out any minute now.

Facial contortions directed at me.

"What did he say?" she pleads. I'm the only one who speaks his personal language.

"You don't want to know" is all I tell her. Being on the outside looking in makes her so jumpy. A sight to see. All Dillon said was that she's a great businesswoman. Has great instincts, anticipates well in advance. His assessment spot on.

She storms into the kitchen, acting far more distraught than we know she is. A massive deep dish materializes in front of Dillon. No plates, just a fork and knife. Eats it straight out of the pan. We talk about everything, but nothing important. Within fifteen minutes, the pizza is simply a memory.

The temptation to bring up the project is strong, but I know I need to tread carefully. Alison leaves. Not without peering into my soul one last time. She's gone. In most ways, I feel relief. But something about not knowing where she's headed makes me more uncomfortable than anything. At least when she's shooting me uncomfortable looks, she's accounted for. But now, it's a crapshoot.

Push it to the back of my mind. Mackenzie takes the empty dish back to the kitchen; I head to the bathroom. First time in here. The murals are mind-blowing. Unlike anything in the MOMA. They're actually good. One wall is classic iconography paying tribute to her Japanese heritage. Most of it unabashedly stereotypical. Raised by French-Canadians, her allegiance is weak. The other is famous Chicago landmarks. Not many places can you take a piss while staring at a Dali-inspired mural of Wrigley Field.

Head back out to the dining room. Dillon has moved to the bar, drinking ginger ale. Mackenzie is running around, doing ten things at once. You'd think CNN had just announced an embargo with Italy. Today is the last day pizza will be available in the United States. Every table decorated with the tasty delicacy.

I walk up next to Dillon. He's a statue. I snap my fingers in his face, no reaction. I follow his eyes. Some guy smoking a joint. Just like that, it hits me. I know how I can pull Dillon aboard. Want to see how this plays out first.

I speak loudly into Dillon's ear. "Now I know I've been gone for a while, but isn't smoking in restaurants illegal in Illinois?" It was growing up, but things change.

Finally acknowledging me, his face twists. Tells me that smoking indoors was banned in all public places in this state. Forty-two states in fact. Recently though, an amendment passed exempting medicinal marijuana.

He wants to know what this guy is dying of. Why he can't smoke outside or wait to get home. Another thing about Dillon's reformation. He was the most liberal guy I knew. Change is the only constant. Worry less about carbon footprints, more about carbonated water. Given the circumstances, I expected him to be upset.

But he is livid. His face turning red as the sauce smudge accentuating his lips.

I glance back over. See the main source of his frustration. I missed it the first time. The guy with the joint is chatting with a pregnant lady. Every word he speaks, the cloud around her grows. With each tainted inhalation, the dreadlocks on her unborn grow longer.

Another Marley-head in waiting.

I wait to see how Dillon responds. Growing up, we both smoked pot. Not obsessively. Maybe two or three times a month. It became more habitual for him when he got to college. Then he got into porn. Swapped the bong for everything else.

He looks at me, asks me to translate for him. I suppress a smile and consent. I seem to salivate over the impending shit show.

Dillon approaches, taps the guy on the shoulder. He turns around, surprisingly irritated, given the depressant in hand.

"Yeah, what is it?"

Dillon's face tweaks as I watch.

"Hello, my friend here requests that you please put out your cigarette."

"Is that so?" He looks back and forth between Dillon and me. Back and forth, getting dizzy. Sizing him up. "Well, he looks like a big boy, why doesn't he ask me himself?"

I simply explain it's not quite that simple. "Sadly, he can no longer speak."

He thinks I'm joking. Makes a series of random hand signals, supposedly a poor attempt at ASL. Never seen *that* before.

"No, he literally cannot speak. He can *hear* you, however, so I'm just here to interpret what he says. Major accident, he doesn't like to talk about it."

Then it clicks. "Holy shit, you're that porn guy! Yeah, yeah. I know you. Oh crap, man. You're my fucking hero!"

The vein in Dillon's head pulses faster. Hates being recognized for his past. Unconvincingly, he shakes his head no.

"Sorry, man, I have no clue what you're talking about. Porn? This guy? Please. He couldn't get laid if *he* paid *them*. Forget about having it the other way around." Stoner guy buys it, pushes it aside. "Anyway, as I was saying, would you please be so kind as to put out your joint? Or at least go outside?"

"Why? I'm allowed to smoke in here, ain't I?"

I go back to Dillon for his response. "Well, the only people granted amnesty from indoor smoking laws are those with medical reasons."

"Well, no problem there, I've got a card for that," he tells us condescendingly. Pulls out a card from his wallet. "Is that good enough for you?"

Dillon wants to know why he's taking it.

"First of all, what the fuck is wrong with his face? You need to stop that shit man, because you're grossing me out." His voice growing heated. "Second of all, not that it's any of your fucking business, but I take it for nausea."

Dillon rolls his eyes. They'll write a prescription for anything. Can't sleep? Take two of these. What's that? You vomit uncontrollably every time you drink a handle of whiskey? I've got just the thing for you.

Both men growing more impatient with every breath. Dillon wants me to tell him that nausea is an excuse for the weak. We all get sick. Doesn't justify smoking pot whenever you feel like it. I relay the message, in my own words. Clean it up a bit.

He rises from his chair, barely reaching Dillon's chest. "What the fuck do you guys care anyway? This is free country, isn't it?"

Bingo. The words I longed to hear.

Pushing Dillon to the brink of animosity.

"Looks like you two could use this more than me anyway." He makes the mistake of blowing it right in Dillon's face. Icing on the cake: grabs Dillon's hand, pushes the roach into the palm. Closes the fingers tightly around it. "Not to mention, it's all natural dipshit."

If this were ten years ago, the ambulance would already be en route. I'm not so sure what Dillon's next move will be now. Fervently anticipating what will follow.

He breathes deep, takes a pen off the bar, then a napkin, begins to write. Signs to me, continues writing. Turning into a manifesto.

"He says for you to nod if you can read the napkin," I tell the guy.

"What the—?" Before he can complete the thought, his feet dangle in the air. Dillon has him by the neck, a foot off the ground. With his other hand, he puts the napkin inches from his face. No response.

"Can you read it?" I ask.

Struggling for air, he spits out "No."

Dillon puts him down, gives him the napkin, The man pounds a glass of water, catches his breath. He reads the napkin and looks at each of us. With hands suddenly weak, it flutters to the ground. He grabs the pregnant lady by the hand. Their move for the door is quickly thwarted.

"He says you should pay your bill first."

The lady throws some cash on the bar, and they're history.

He's back to his ginger ale before I can respond. I pick up the napkin. The repugnant odor of week old beer wafts. I read Dillon's potent message. Blunt to say the least.

> Well, so is my dick. If I ever catch you smoking marijuana or anything else again, ESPECIALLY around a pregnant lady, pot smoke won't be the only "all-natural" thing you find in your throat. xoxo

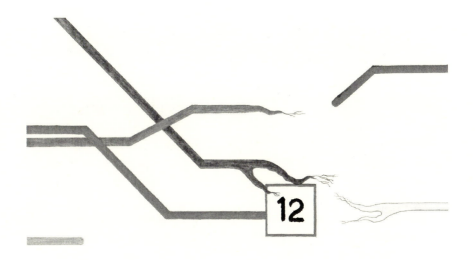

12

Measure twice, cut once—Dad's number one rule. Drilled into my head from day one. He wasn't keen on me and construction, but kids like to watch what their dads are up to. I learned from the best. His meticulous eye for detail served me well. The new floor is coming along. I ripped up the old one within a few days. Shitty craftsmanship. Mediocre material. Boring pattern. No variety.

The maple, chipped and scratched, showed signs of detriment to even the most casual observer. It's gone, every last bit.

It made way for teak and mahogany, pieces alternating. Direction, grain, color all arranged flawlessly in my parquet design. A bitch to sand and plane. But Dad taught me to always take pride in my work. The results of his labor, the work of his hands, it defined him. I suppose the same is true for me. Not so much for tangible products though.

The Blue Line train goes racing by. They must have finally gotten around to fixing the track. Last three days the CTA has been crawling along. So slowly I could read the ads on the inside of the cabins. Your breath smells awful, have some gum. Your headphones emit too much ambient noise, try these. You're ugly, aftershave will fix that dilemma. Once again, I can hear the rattle of the tracks as the train shoots by. Louder than the piercing shriek of the saw. Compound-miter, top of the line.

People are so scared of disease. With good reason; there's plenty things out there to get you. But most take effect later. Eat another cheeseburger, cholesterol won't kill you for a few decades.

Parkinson's? No one likes to shake, but it won't kill you. Public transportation, far more dangerous. One bolt—that's all that needs to snap or fall out of place. One faulty piece of hardware, that train flies off the rail and into my living room.

Swipe your card. Walking through those turnstiles at Clark and Lake is much riskier than a pound of blow. Rush hour is the best. Shoulder to shoulder, I can move undetected. It's shocking how many people don't pay attention to their beverages in a crowded public arena.

A beep comes across the room. A text from Mackenzie; she's on her way over. I'm sure she's going to lay into me for yesterday. She was so busy running a business, I don't think she saw any of what happened with Dillon. A night for her to cool down works in my favor. The backlash is always worst when the wounds are freshest.

Check the fridge—void of the essentials. I rush downstairs, grab some beers, chips, bananas. The guy who owns the bodega is a really nice guy. Has a fascinating story of his emigration from North Korea. Too bad I can't tell him about my real life. I'm sure we could go on for a while swapping stories. Instead, the exchange is a one-way street.

Back upstairs, I put the beers in the fridge then snack on some chips. I try to peel an overly green banana. Way too rigid. Need to wait a couple days. About as flavorful as tree bark.

Trying to find my pencil, I'm interrupted by a knock at the door. I check the peephole then let Mackenzie in.

"Hey there, come on in," I say while offering a hug.

Surprisingly, she graciously accepts. All smiles, in great spirits. I won't bring up yesterday if she doesn't.

"Wow, great place here, Samuel," she says, giving me a mischievous look. Emphasizing the fact that she's adjusted to my pseudonym. "I can't believe I haven't been by to see it yet." She drops her purse on the kitchen counter. Removes her jacket and throws it on the couch, which has been dragged into the kitchen. Dressed to kill, she's no stranger to seduction.

"Yeah, I would have had you over sooner, but as you can see, it's kind of a mess. I was hoping to finish the floor before entertaining any guests."

Without even asking, she opens the fridge, takes out two beers, starts digging through drawers until she finds the bottle-opener. If it was anyone else, I'd be a little annoyed, but this is tradition. We instinctively raid the other's fridge. Beer is the main objective. Certain carbonated beverages will suffice.

I offer her the bag in my hand. "Chips?"

She pulls out a small handful of the crispy snacks then makes her way through piles of wood and tools. A self-guided tour of my new place. Now out of sight, I hear her voice down the hall. Some snide comment about the size of the bathroom. Back in the main living space, she gives greater attention to the decorations on the wall. Walks up to a picture, stares at it, looks at me. "Where did you get the Modigliani replica?"

"It's not a replica," I tell her.

Another look at me then back at the drawing. "Bullshit. You probably picked it up at the Louvre or Hermitage during your travels." Almost concerned. Desperately hoping I'm pulling her chain. "Seriously. Where did you get it?"

Watching her squirm makes this all the more enjoyable. "I'm dead serious, it's the real deal. An original Modigliani." She spins around the room, questioning the authenticity of every famous work staring back at her. Her eyes light up. An overly stereotypical comparison of her face and Japanese anime cartoon characters is on the tip of my tongue. I shackle it at the last second, bite my lower lip, stifle a giggle.

Now she approaches with a furious gait. Despite my martial arts training, my fear is genuine. "Seriously, *Ted*, where did you get it?"

Amused but hoping to diffuse the situation, I concede. "Well, if you really must know, I got it through BMI."

A puzzled look. "Huh? You mean like body mass index?"

"More like black market industries." Her jaw drops. The urge to laugh is immense, but I remain collected to show her I'm serious. "Come on, I can't exactly be showing up at art auctions throwing my money around. I need to keep a low profile."

Furious, "Yeah, and buying *stolen* art is a great way to lie low. Are you out of your mind?"

Feeling I can laugh a little now. "OK, OK. Maybe 'black market' is a bit of a strong term. I hired some people to go in and bid on the pieces for me. They deal in high-priced items and auctions all the time. They're fully aware of how many people value anonymity. Plus I didn't do something absurd like purchase *David* or the *Mona Lisa*."

She calms down, just a little bit, walks around looking at all the treasures I've picked up. I grin ear to ear, watching her brain debate the question everyone wants to know.

"More than they're worth" is all I tell her. Doesn't quite satisfy her curiosity but puts it out of her mind for now at least.

She's now on her fourth trip around my "gallery" in absolute awe. Salivates over the Picasso. Knees shake upon gazing at the Kandinsky. Not a bad collection really. I also managed to acquire a Matisse, a van Gogh, two by Andy Warhol, a Monet, a Rembrandt, and a pair by Georgia O'Keefe. A small fortune. In retrospect, the look on her face is worth more than anything money could buy. Cheesy but true.

After the shock finally subsides, she's back to interrogating me. "But you hate all of these artists. Why did you spend . . ." She's at a loss for words. "I don't even want to know how much money, on all of them?"

"It's simple really." I grab a marker off the kitchen counter and walk over to the Modigliani. Title: *Kneeling Caryatid*. Medium: Blue Crayon. Seriously. Wish I were making it up. I dumped the gross domestic product of Tibet into a work children are giving to their parents for free.

She's eyeing me intently. Not sure what I'm up to. I pull the cap off the marker, draw two vertical lines. Two perpendiculars complete it.

She looks as if she's seen not just a ghost but an entire army of them. I break the silence by marking an *x* in the middle of the grid. "OK, you're turn," I say with a barely noticeable smirk. I hold the marker out for her to take and make her move.

Aghast, she refuses to play tic-tac-toe on a famous work of art. "Are you out of your mind?" Animated, her arms are flailing. "What the fuck are you thinking?"

I can only smile. It takes an intense effort to prevent all-out laughter. I tell her it's time to live. This only compounds the confusion.

"Look, it's really quite simple." With arched eyebrows, she can't wait to hear how I'm going to validate this. I continue. "I appreciate art as much as anyone else, but come on . . . millions of dollars for *that*," I say while gesturing toward the kitchen table. She didn't notice at first. Steps closer and closer. Her back is to me, but I can still see the horrific shock of recognition. Turning around, she looks like she's about to pass out. Walks back and sits down in a pile of sawdust. Mouthing words, no sound. Despite my proficiency at reading lips, I can't tell what she's saying.

But I get the idea.

"What? You don't like my tablecloth? It was a steal at fifteen million."

After a long pause, she gets up and stares at it again. "I can't believe you're using a Jackson Pollock as a tablecloth! You've gone completely insane!"

I want to object, but arguing would be futile. Look at me. Look at my plan, my mission. A rational person would not undertake what I've started. Then again, a crazy person could never pull it off. An uncharted volatile gray area—that's me.

That's kind of the point of science. Develop hypotheses, test them out. Go from there.

"But don't you see, Mackenzie? Really, it's quite intuitive. Come here, look at this," I tell her as I pull her face close to the table. "See that goop right there? Mustard. Bet you can't even tell it isn't part of the original work, huh?"

She's on the verge of losing it. Taking the painting off its frame, pulling the staples. That was condemnable in her eyes.

The mustard? In hindsight, probably shouldn't have shown it to her.

Without saying a word, she goes to the fridge, grabs another beer. Pops the top, walks back to the dusty living room. Takes a swig, but doesn't swallow. Then leaning her head back, a curveball.

She spits beer all over three of the paintings, moving her head side to side like a lawn sprinkler. Repeats the process all over the room, until the bottle is empty. The heated silicone dioxide slips from her hand. A loud thud, but it doesn't break.

I'm a little worried, unsure what's going to happen. I brace myself for an attack. You never know. A disturbing silence passes, and she laughs. It builds and builds. Starting slowly, the momentum gradually increases, until she's cackling maniacally.

I stay at a distance until the howling subsides. Approaching slowly, I ask if she's OK.

She nods, "Yeah, I'm good." Appears calm, but I can actually hear the beating of her heart. Like the ferocious pounding of a bass drum with the tempo of a hummingbird. At least she seems to be OK.

"Wow, that was awesome!" I step back, confused. "I mean, it was absolutely batshit crazy. We just took over a hundred million dollars' worth of art and made it worth less than the materials used to make them." I smile and nod. She hasn't said it specifically, but I can tell she gets it. "It's just stuff. At the end of the day, it's just stuff." It's a rather perfunctory explanation. It goes deeper than that, but she sums it up nicely.

You haven't lived until you've taken something that, for all intents and purposes, really is no big deal and defiled it beyond relevance. Because really, what has changed? No one was harmed. I didn't blow up a building. Reproductions of these pieces are still readily available. Street artists can duplicate them in a matter of hours. Minutes in some cases. You'd never know the difference. Life will go on.

Without warning, she kisses me. Not a little peck. Her tongue is so deep in my mouth, she can taste my breakfast. I don't repel her. Nor do I embrace it. After a few seconds, I back away.

"What was that?" I ask rather calmly. I know she's wanted to do that for years. It's not a surprise. But given the circumstances, I find it odd.

"Well, I just figured you'd want to thank me," she replies with a cocky demeanor.

I know she doesn't mean spitting beer on my walls. Not sure where she's going with this. I bite. "Thank you for what?"

"We really should talk about yesterday," she tells me. I agree. "You see, I was talking to Dillon online, and it sounds like he's in. Looks like my friend Rick hasn't lost a step."

Needing some clarification, I ask, "What does that mean? Who's Rick?"

Her grin is even more mischievous now. She tells me all about how the guy at the bar who went to college with her, and technically me as well, before she and Dillon went to school together. He was a theater major, did plenty of acting. "Come on, Sam, you didn't think I'd actually let someone smoke pot in my bar, did you?"

"Well, a few years ago, definitely not. But now the laws are way different. It wasn't completely insane."

So she had Rick incite Dillon, test his limits. See if she could find his breaking point. I'd say she was successful. Definitely plan to exploit his weakness.

After processing this new information, I go on. "To be honest, I'm not sure how I feel about what Dillon did. For the most part, I'm glad to see that he can still get riled up if something seriously gets under his skin. I know that his passion will be invaluable to the operation." She nods in agreement. "But I still kind of feel like he overreacted. I have to ask myself if he's a potential liability."

"Very valid point. That's certainly something to be aware of. But you have known him for a long time. He's definitely had a roller coaster of a past, but deep down, I think you know he'd do anything for you."

I definitely used to believe that. But things have changed. He's very into religion, and I'm honestly thrilled for him. Whether or not I share his beliefs is inconsequential. He is a happier person. At the end of the day though, I can't compete with that. He doesn't know the full details of my plan. Even the parts he *does* know provide monumental ethical dilemmas. Getting him on board with the story I told him was challenging enough. How would he react with full disclosure?

His hatred of smoking plays to my advantage. It led him to believe that these pills I'm distributing will curb the desire to smoke. Which is technically true. I have developed such a treatment.

But far from the primary objective.

"Oh, I know that. My main concern is will he involve himself in something that is, well, for lack of a better term . . . corrupt? He's found God. Which is great for him, but doesn't really help our cause."

A smirk slithers ear to ear. She takes a substantial pull on another beer. "Really, Samuel?" is all she says. Another swig from her bottle. "For someone as smart as you, you really are clueless, aren't you?"

Slightly offended, "How's that?"

"With the exception of maybe two or three people in the history of the world, no one is flawless." I'm about to interject, but she presses on, sarcastically. "Now I know that's hard for you to hear. You might not want to believe it, but even you, Sam, are not perfect. Mother Teresa, Gandhi, Jesus. Outside of them, even the nicest people on paper are fucked up." She walks around the room, looking at the art on the walls. Talking to me, but not facing me. "Everyone can be broken." Now her eyes lock on mine. "Everyone. We're all hypocrites, driven by our own desires."

I like where she's going with this. Yesterday was a prime example.

"When Dillon snapped yesterday, that was just a taste. We all have a breaking point. You find his, and he's your puppet. Make him dance for you."

I smile, chug the remainder of my beer, let out a small laugh. "You're good. Really good." She shrugs in agreement. "Want another one?"

I bring another beer for each of us. She pulls me closer, kisses me again. She's always been bold, but not like this. I kiss back this time, but eventually retreat.

"OK, business time," she says, pulling off her blouse.

I should be caught off guard. Learned long ago to anticipate. Expect anything, you'll never be surprised. Never underestimate those you're dealing with. My expression unchanged. "What are you doing?"

"Well, I held up my end of the bargain. Now it's time for you to deliver on your half." Before I can respond, her hand is in my pants, squeezing. The scabs on her palm chafe me. Putting her hand in the oven was a bad idea. I let out a mild groan. It hurts more than it pleases. For a girl so small, her grip should not be underestimated.

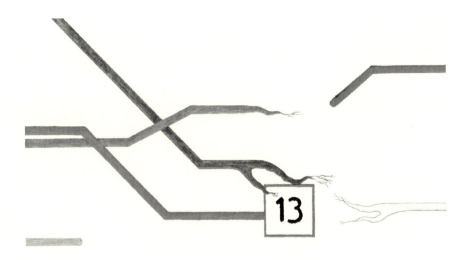

13

In the grand scheme of the universe, your life is a flash. Far more momentary than the blink of an eye. Priorities. It's all about putting things in perspective. People are looking for a legacy. To find a way to be remembered long after they die.

Truth be told, you will eventually be forgotten. No matter how kind and generous you are. Doesn't matter how great. The world will continue to turn without you. Face it. In the age of information at the press of a button, nothing lasts long. History, oddly enough, is always changing.

So the big question now: what will you do to be one of the elite? To ensure you don't fall into commonplace. What will you do in this life to make future generations thirst for your insight? To make them beg and dream you're a modern-day Lazarus?

For the overwhelming majority, the answer is simple: nothing.

Not a fucking thing.

Everyone wants to be famous. Narcissism is not a bad thing per se. I should know. In my case, it's validated. Breaking news: no one cares what you had for lunch. You had a miserable commute? Join the club. Everyone's putting their inner monologue into cyberspace. Updates every three minutes.

Just had a bowl of cereal.

I should trim my toenails.

Why are men such douche bags?

Nothing is private, yet nothing of substance ever broached. Ask someone in person about their fears. Their *real* fears. There are only bullshit excuses and myriad justifications. Not one drop of sincerity.

We're craving a juxtaposition that will never work. We want everyone to love and adore us. But we yearn for solitude. *Give me my privacy. Just be sure to think about me forever and always.* Constant contradictions rendering ourselves obsolete.

That's where I come in. My contribution.

No one ever said the world would last forever. Sorry if you thought otherwise.

Just expediting the process.

No one seems to notice. Or care.

Despite what your parents and friends might have told you, you are replaceable. Shocking, I know. You weren't meant to find out this way. Tough love.

Bastards. They're everywhere. I use the term broadly. Suffice it to say, there aren't many people I like.

But children, running wild, free from restraint. Look around, all I see is an ocean of unaccompanied toddlers.

He's my world.

She's the greatest thing that ever happened to me.

No one buys it. Be bold for once. Simply admit you wish you hadn't thrown your life away. There's merit in honesty. I used to know.

This is what I think about standing in line at Carpetbaggers. Zagat rated. I'm now in Washington, D.C., to kick my plan into high gear. Dozens of protests are up and down Pennsylvania Avenue. I make the mistake of stopping for a soda at a local burger joint. Kids everywhere. I assume the adults scattered about are their parents, but you'd never know it. Their ambivalence toward the situation dumfounds me. Guy in the jacket that says something about little league baseball is completely glued to his FlashCUBE, six sides of Internet action. When one simply isn't enough.

The couple ahead of me orders, steps aside. I approach the counter and am cut off. Some teenager who styled his hair in the dark.

"Excuse me," I say. No response. The girl behind the register ignores my plea. Kids all around stop and stare. A low chatter ensues. I let it slide and order my snack, head to the fountain drinks, fill up, find the kid. Hope his mother wasn't set on grandkids. I have a dream. Unfortunately for this kid, it involves a future without dipshits who won't wait their turn. Racial equality would be nice too.

"Excuse me," I say again, tapping his shoulder.

He spins around with fury in his eyes as if I've tried to sweep his legs from under him.

Put him in a body bag Johnny!

"What?" he shouts, not the least bit intimidated. Rather, his face doesn't indicate trepidation. Can't see his eyes, concealed by sunglasses.

"I think you owe me an apology," I tell him calmly.

He pulls his glasses up to his forehead. Bloodshot eyes. Not stoned, just tired. The look of awe tells me people don't typically approach him this way. Doesn't say a word and turns back around, whispers something to the boy and girl next to him. The boy nods.

Just as brash, he cuts to the chase. "Hey, buddy, not sure what you're talking about, but do you have any idea who that is?"

Of course I know who it is. He's the newest transmitter of my devious creation. Instead I tell him I have no clue.

"Bro, that's Micah Wells," he states as if introducing me to George Washington. I look over again. He's signing autographs, posing for a picture with a group of young girls.

Not a clue. "Who?"

His shock hits new heights. "Dude, Micah Wells! You know, number one ranked snowboarder in the world."

Never heard of him, but I recognize my chance. I play dumb, act shocked. "Oh, wow. No way! I'm sorry, I guess I just didn't recognize him in here. Sorry, it's been a long day." He's buying it. "Really, I'm a huge fan. I didn't mean any harm." He nods, accepts my display of remorse. "I'd love to buy you guys a round of beers." Micah must overhears, now looking my way.

"What was that?" Micah asks.

"Well, I was just saying that I'm a huge fan of yours, and I'm really sorry for my attitude back there. But I'd love to buy you and your friends a round of beers."

The two look at each other. No way are they old enough to drink. Doesn't stop most people. Especially celebrities. I get the feeling if he asked everyone inside to strip naked and bow down to him, they'd oblige. They accept and even utter something resembling "thank you."

Too easy. I order up a few Coronas, grab a handful of limes. I move to put the green wedges in the opening, slip in the tiny blue pills just before. Sleight of hand that would astound Copperfield. Hand them each a beer, the boys immediately begin to drink.

"I don't drink beer," the girl says. I offer to get her something else, but she declines. Oh well. My number announced, I pick up my food. On my way out the door, I notice her hand some guy her beer. He downs half of it in one gulp. Sucks to be him. Or anyone he sleeps with.

Alas. Can't make an omelet without raping a few chickens. There are bound to be some unexpected casualties. Most important thing is to push forward.

I eat my lunch on the steps of the Capitol, watch people go by, fabricating back stories for some of them. It's a fun way to pass the time. When I throw my bag in the trash, I'm met with dozens of eyes shooting daggers at me. Creepy.

Where to start? I make my way to the White House, observe my surroundings. Protests, signs, and booths overwhelm the senses. Throw on my Camelback full of coffee, saunter around. Assess the situation.

When I have more people working with me, I'll be able to hit larger areas. For now, I have to be picky.

Don't raise taxes.

Save our schools.

Equal pay for women.

Many legitimate causes, paired with plenty of the absurd. Just like that, I spot it. A group of signs to save the Bolivian River Rat. I stifle a laugh, roll my eyes, make my way over. There must be at least three hundred people. Checking my phone, I pull up a quick summary of the situation. Of all the things they could fight for or against, this is what they chose. Oh my.

I pull the paper cups out of my backpack, start pouring the coffee. "Here you go, sir. Free coffee. Completely organic, grown in upstate Oregon from fully sustainable sources." All you have to do is throw words like that at people, and they bite. Gracious acceptance. The more of them I encounter, the more conflicted I become. The plus side: it's nice to know their chromosomes end with them. The downside: they don't strike me as the kind of people who are regular patrons of fornication. Either way, it's a sad day for the Bolivian River Rat.

As devious as my actions might seem, they should really be thanking me. One of the greatest threats to their cause is humans building shit everywhere, consuming goods without analyzing the costs. Overpopulation combined with dwindling resources equals bad. I'm just doing my part. What can I say? If I'm not part of the solution, I'm part of the problem.

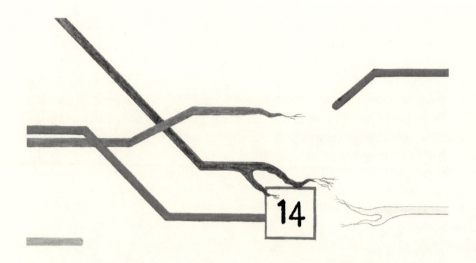

14

I'm no imperialist. Make no mistake. America flexes its muscles in unwarranted situations. I've also lived all over the world. Although riddled with flaws, there's nowhere else I'd rather live than here.

Sadly, everywhere I look, it's shrouded with contrast. People protesting anything they can, failing to realize the people they antagonize are the very people who allow them those freedoms. An ironic and vicious cycle. Never ends.

When did our country go so soft? Equality is good. Our quest for it is costing us progress. I walk by the Lincoln Memorial. Some lady wants me to sign a petition for Band-Aids.

That's right, Band-Aids. They're racist, she claims. Wants requirements placed on pharmaceutical manufacturers' practices. Caucasians are shown too much favoritism. Their wounds are easily disguised. African Americans have no such luxury. Black Band-Aids are hard to come by. Don't even try to find coffee colored. No cocoa, no mahogany, no chestnut.

I smile and nod. Her mouth is moving. Not a fucking thing is coming out.

I applaud this woman for her efforts. Equality clearly high on her list of priorities.

The blood diamond on her ring finger indicates the contrary.

Playing along, I tell her I'd love to sign. She hands me a pen and the clipboard. I ask her if she can keep a secret. She nods with anticipation. I lean in, pinch her ear.

She looks a little woozy, and I wander off. She drops.

I turn around, feigning surprise.

People are already gathering close. I shove them out of my way, check her pulse, give them the impression of aloofness. What just happened? I rub my jaw and nose, slip a capsule in. Time for mouth-to-mouth. People are watching. No hand up the ass today. Leaning over, my mouth covers hers. I pinch the nose, supply air. All for show. She's totally fine. But the panic, the urgency . . . no one notices she's breathing. They watch me operate. I spit into her mouth.

I grab the back of her neck. Slight squeeze there and she's back. Her eyes open, and people applaud. Immediately, I grab a bottle of water from a bystander, shove it to her mouth before she can spit. Too dazed to realize something is amiss.

I assess her palm and wrists. Minor scrapes from the fall.

"Oh dear, let's get you a Band-Aid," I tell her with a wink. She has one in her purse. The ever-subtle neon orange. Apply it, and I'm on my way.

Applause comes from every direction. Crowd pats me on the back. If they only knew. They offer to buy me drinks. I decline, but if they could point me to the Iwo Jima Memorial, I would be much obliged.

I've been there once in the past. It's been a while, so I take a cab. Walking up to it is OK, but sub-par. You have to drive around it for full effect. As you circle the monument, the soldiers appear to raise the flag. Your perspective changes. The memorial comes to life. I tell the cab driver to drop me off at the Smithsonian. As we pass numerous landmarks and memorials, I reflect on my favorite president.

Thomas Jefferson.

That's right. Might have had trouble comprehending the meanings of basic words, but the motherfucker could bargain. France should stick to cheese and boycotting deodorant. Real estate, not their strong suit.

#3centsperacre

He drops me off and I go for a walk. I buy a hot dog from a vendor. Got nothing on Chicago. The urge to visit the Library of Congress hits me. Not a far walk, I'm there in a few minutes. Same as always, everyone I pass stares me down. Various reasons, they all have a cause. At a crowded intersection, I wait to cross. I bump shoulders with someone, look back to apologize. He does likewise. Sporting a briefcase and a peculiar necktie. Multicolored spheres attached with sticks. Some kind of molecule. It's fleeting, but something about him is familiar. A disturbing recognition that I can't place. I brush it off and score another point for paranoia. I pass the Supreme Court then the Capitol once again. True to form, handmade signs blend together. All I see is a field of idealism expressed in poor penmanship. Clashing colors that irritate the senses.

Same as earlier. Some are germane, others validate my quest. Perhaps I'm not being harsh enough.

deMOCKracy.

Freedom for JUST US, Not All.

Question Everything.

Watch the Right, and watch your BACK.

Too many people. Not enough time, not enough pills.

A trip to our nation's capital wouldn't be complete without the requisite group saving everyone from being brainwashed. My favorite. They control us, we're all pawns, free will is a joke. You get the idea.

They're handing out copies of *1984*, *Brave New World*, *Utopia*, and countless pamphlets.

Those books take me back. Been years since I've even picked up a copy of any of them.

Just like that, it happens. A transformation of sorts. I know I just said I wasn't keen on empire. Call it a change of heart, a renaissance of sorts. Maybe I always felt it deep in my soul but refused to admit it. That's for you to decide. I also said my decisions would lack consistency.

I relish the notion of mind control. The state, the head, Big Brother. They always get a bad rap. No one tells the story from their perspective. Always the little guy being oppressed by a tyrannical system.

Give me some SOMA.

No one wants to be the guy who defends the concession of original thought. As if there were such a thing. As if "freedom" were something we could actually define. Something we could wrap our heads around.

This delusion we call freedom, it's noncircular.

First, everyone is entitled to be free. Regardless of race, religion, gender, et cetera.

Second, freedom isn't free. It comes with a cost. Sacrifices must be made.

Finally, you should never have to pay for something you are entitled to. Something that is fundamentally part of your birthright.

Freedom contradicts its very essence. So either no one enjoys freedom in any form, or whatever we currently describe as such needs a new moniker.

I'll figure it out sooner or later. First, need to shove blue pills up the butts of the group waving copies of *The Anarchist Cookbook*. Forget the fact that its own author renounced it. Everyone in the group is wearing glowing jewelry and sunglasses on an overcast day. Signs might as well read, "No one in their right mind would breed with me."

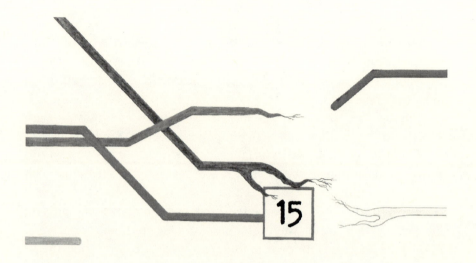

Sweet home Chicago. The plan is in full swing. Feels great to not only help humanity but to get to travel in order to do it. Great tax write-off. If I actually filed. The Dan Ryan is under construction. What else is new? Takes me an hour to get out of the city and into the suburbs, taking my new car for a drive. Just because. No one needs a car in Chicago, but I always wanted a classic.

Black,1952. Suicide doors. Eight miles to the gallon. I less-than-three pissing away natural resources.

I have no business out in Schaumburg. Just like wasting gas. Burn a full tank every other day, simply because I can. Nowhere I need to go. Just killing time. The ozone. Pavement.

There are billboards every hundred feet. Casinos, gas stations, electronics. My favorites are the series. Four of five ads until you finally get the point. Some health organization with a set promoting safe sex. Warns against STDs. Herpes, syphilis, and gonorrhea listed.

Pregnancy. They always leave that one out. Getting knocked up. Easily the worst sexually transmitted disease.

There. I said it. Gestation is a curse. One that is easily avoided at that. This is my life. You never notice how many people have the newest gadget until you're in the market for one yourself.

A world becoming quickly oversaturated with people is no secret. But now, pregnant women are everywhere I turn. Waiting to cross the street at every intersection. Sipping lattes outside every coffee shop. Getting mani-pedis inside every salon I peer into. Ubiquitous. Inescapable no matter where I go.

Suffice it to say, I'm not in the market for a kid. But ever since Mackenzie and I have been sleeping together, expectant mothers are more prevalent than usual.

She enjoys it far more than I do. Make no mistake, she's attractive. Never had a problem getting attention from guys. I simply place minimal value on intimacy.

I'm not gay.

I'm not convinced I'm straight.

Right now, I'm really into myself. Not in the way people say they're not interested in a relationship so they can focus on making themselves better. I'm already who I want to be. I'm into myself because solipsism seems to be my niche.

But a deal is a deal. Not sure what she's been saying to Dillon, but his enthusiasm grows every day. Always asking how he can help. This is about to get bigger much faster than I imagined. Naturally, I have to ask myself some questions. How do I feel about bringing a child into a world I'm trying to destroy? Wish I could say the thought troubled me. To say it didn't bother me at all would be a lie. But it's a fear quickly subdued.

I know what you're thinking. My mind will change when I see that baby smile for the first time. When he or she wraps its whole hand around my pinkie finger. Simply precious. I have no way of knowing how I'll react when and if it happens. Although I'm intelligent, I can't predict the future. But I wouldn't put money on it.

I don't even expect to be present at the birth.

Only mildly hypocritical of me.

All this is speculation right now. Of the couple dozen times we've fucked, Mackenzie hasn't been ovulating. I know because I can smell it. Women give off an odor when they're capable of conceiving. It's faint, but it's there. Most men never notice. Half a liter of whiskey will do that to your olfactory senses.

Come to think of it, I should branch out. Focus on reinstating the Eighteenth Amendment. Get rid of alcohol, curb unwanted pregnancy. Put a lot of nurses and delivery personnel out of work.

Can't win 'em all. No use crying over spilt breast milk.

The drive back from the suburbs goes by far more quickly than my excursion out. Just hit my exit, I'm over in the right lane. Doing five over in a residential near Wrigleyville. Not fast by any means. Definitely not slow. Out of nowhere, an asshole in a Smart car flies by me. Easily doing sixty. Does him no good. Foot traffic in Chicago, mixed with traffic lights and four-way stops, negates his excessive speed. I pull up behind his stopped car. Waiting to turn right on red. I creep up slowly, just inches away. I let my foot off the brake, the idling engine rolls into his back bumper.

Whoops.

We both shift to park.

He's livid. The gentle collision has caused considerable damage to his vehicle. Meanwhile, my massive Detroit icon remains unscathed after seventy years.

Now who's the smart one?

I try to calm him down, saying I'll pay for it. I have great insurance. He quickly shifts topics to my choice of transportation. Do I have any idea how much gas my car uses?

I exhibit restraint. Refuse to point out that no matter how fuel-efficient his car is, it still uses more fuel than the subways and buses he opts not to use. Brand new solar-powered buses. Even in the Windy City, they work year-round.

I could induce sleep, slip him some medication. But my gut tells me otherwise. His license plate frame claims Cal-Tech alumni status. In the unlikely event a woman wants to propagate with him, I can live with it. Uptight? Certainly. But that can be changed. There's no cure for stupid.

Simply put, I don't have the time or energy to deal with him. I pull $400 out of my wallet, stuff it into his shirt pocket along with a business card. It's just a card I pulled off a bulletin board at a coffee shop. I say nothing about who I am. Just let him draw the conclusion that I have contacts at an auto dealer.

I'm back in my car and on my way to the gym.

I could go on and on. Write a fucking dissertation on everything I hate about this place. But the worst of the worst congregate here.

Two hundred birds, one stone. Might switch tactics. One bird, ten stones. Overkill to ensure effectiveness.

This place is a textbook for poor technique. People sitting on the equipment, talking on phones, burning more brain cells than calories. Five reps in fifteen minutes. Way to push it to the limit. Dozens of dudes chugging protein shakes, comparing muscles. Homoerotic tension so thick, Excalibur couldn't cut through it.

"Seriously, bro, you're so jacked."

There are a million variations of that phrase. All from the mouths of guys who've never worked their lower body muscles a minute in their lives. Bench 225 with ease. Squat seventy-five with shitty form.

Most of the guys in here resemble potatoes perched atop a pair of toothpicks. What's worse, the women here seem enamored by it. Healthy, attractive women. On the surface, they have a lot going for them. Appearances can be deceiving.

I do some of my best work here. Just knock over some meathead's Muscle Milk, pretend he intimidates you. Cower in an illusory fear. Offer to buy him another one to smooth things over. Run to the lobby, buy a new bottle. Pop the top, slip a pill inside. Don't forget to pour some into a cup for yourself. He'll ask you why it's already open. Just say you were curious how it tasted. Obviously, it works for him. Not only does his skepticism dissipate, you're now in with his group.

So easy.

I finish up my stretches, walk over to the seated rowing machine, move the pin to ninety pounds. The handles are not fully in my grasp before a bag of grapes with Q-tips for legs interrupts. My nostrils are assaulted with the stench of creatine and date rape.

Pulling his headphones off his ears, he stares me down.

"Hey buddy. I was using that."

Still blows my mind to this day. How someone on the other side of the gym doing bicep curls manages to use the same machine as I am. I've never been humble about my achievements in science, but this guy astounds me.

Even I have difficulty grasping the workings of the space-time continuum. I really ought to pick this guy's brain.

Maybe another day. Just gonna stick with my normal plan for now.

"Excuse me?" I say. Confused. I hide my annoyance, but not entirely.

"Yeah, bro, I have three more sets. Don't worry, I'll be done soon," he says matter of fact.

I don't budge, just pick up the handles and begin my set. His jaw drops. Speechless. Static the entire time I'm lifting. Suppressing a laugh, I pick up my towel and grab the spray bottle. They tell you it's antibacterial soap. Really, it's just a bottle of peace-of-mind. So cheap, simply tap water with a splash of thrift-store perfume for smell.

Oh yeah, and my personal concoction as well. I work out just before closing time. No one around, I can put whatever I want in there. Absorbs through the skin. I spray down the bench, not without dousing my newest friend.

He's livid but utterly clueless. That's what's great about breaking social norms. He's told hundreds of people to give up the machine. Everyone obliges . . . until now.

"Hey, asshole!" I hear from behind me outside the club. Rain is pouring down.

I guess this is his idea of reaction. Showtime.

"Yeah, what's up?"

Same as before, I don't have time for this bullshit. If he wants to fight, that's fine with me. But let's do it in an alley. No need to make a scene.

He agrees. Figures the less witnesses of him kicking my ass, the better.

He figures incorrectly.

We're not fully around the corner before a cheap shot flies. Predictable. I block it, twist his arm behind him, force him into submission. He's whining, caught by surprise. Wasting no time, I pinch his neck and ear. He's out like a light.

Suppository time. My favorite. Let's see. What to prescribe?

We can't have him spreading DNA. That's a given. How about the one I gave Jarrett? One of my favorites. Not only will his swimmers be a distant memory, but it's going to hurt when he cums.

Bad. *Real bad.*

He can screw all night and day for all I care. If he's able to tolerate it, I'd be amazed. In three days tops, any ejaculation is going to feel like he's forcing a coconut through his urethra.

He's already caught in the rain.

Hope he likes what comes next.

Penile coladas. Ouch.

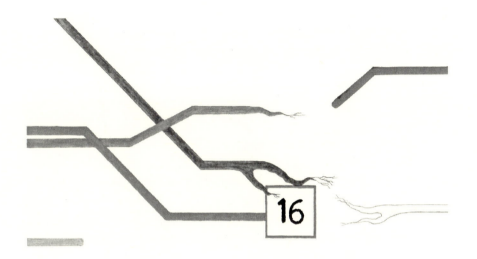

16

"Not bad, Sam, but you might not want to brag about it too much. I thought we were supposed to be discreet after all," Mackenzie chastises.

She's right though. End of story. Not that I'm bragging. Merely relaying the day's events to her.

Gumball Alley is packed, even for a Sunday. The place has a diverse clientele. Not tonight though. If I didn't know better, I'd think the sign out front said "Chuck E. Cheese." Kids everywhere. Then I remember.

Mother's Day.

This has always been a sore spot for me. Make no mistake; I adore the woman who raised me. Still, it's a tough pill to swallow. Mackenzie's doing a sub-par job of hiding her discomfort.

She wants everything parading before her. The diapers, runny noses, untied shoes. She doesn't have to say it for me to know. She dreams of sharing pizza with kids of her own. Cutting it up into several dozen tiny nibbles. Business is great, but it's only insult to injury.

I'm not all bad. Despite having given up on humanity long ago, I can make things better for her. Right then, I decide. I will get her pregnant. As you can imagine, fertility drugs aren't my specialty. I have no interest in the matter.

So why doesn't the guy who invented the sperm-killing pill take it himself? Two reasons: first, I rarely have sex. Minimal desire. It's that simple. More importantly though, my narcissism won't let me.

For the welfare of humanity, I must keep my sperm a viable option. Surely, I'd love to go around fucking every woman I encountered. Within years, my DNA would run rampant worldwide.

Easier said than done when you have misanthropic tendencies. Sex today is rarely an intimate act. Doesn't stop most people. Me on the other hand, it makes my skin crawl. No doubt a symptom of a much larger underlying issue. Oh well.

I head back to the kitchen, tell Mackenzie I'm taking her out after closing. A small smile sprawls across her face. Mitigate the pain. I'll take it. While I'm back here, figure I'll help out. For some reason, that seems to make her day. Washing silverware, carrying trays, wiping down tables. Normally a rather minimal task. Not tonight. Not with dozens of screaming kids. Surprisingly, I smile the entire night.

Like I said, consistency isn't my strength.

I wasn't all rainbows and lollipops though. I definitely slipped some pills into the refills of table fourteen. Guys with intentions far more noble than their actions could ever live up to. Bantering about how poorly dogs are treated at the pound. The oinker that fell into those pepperonis likely adored like royalty, I'm sure.

"Hey, Samuel, drop this at table nine," the cook tells me. Fortinbras, his real name. Never been much of a bardolater. But seriously, that's badass.

Side salad and a personal veggie pizza. I pick it up, look in the area. I'm fifteen feet away, and of course I see who it is.

It's *her*. What was her name? Ally? Alison? That sounds right. Oh well. Won't let it creep me out. I'm being paranoid. Just keep reminding myself.

"Here you go, dear." I hate generic terms of endearment. For some reason, it seemed like a good idea. As soon as the words left my mouth, regret takes over. "Anything else I can get for ya?"

"Just some more napkins, please," she asks in a pleasant tone.

I oblige, start clearing adjoining tables. Funny thing though. Every time I look her way, she's not staring back. Oddly enough, this upsets me more than her normal routine. All of a sudden, I become uncomfortable. Mackenzie can sense it.

"Hey, buddy, you feeling all right?" she asks, rather worried.

I need to change the subject. "Yeah, I'm fine, I just . . . hey, have you talked to Dillon lately?"

Awkward but effective. "Oh, he didn't tell you? He went to Denver," she says as if Denver were a bar around the corner.

"What in the world is he doing in Colorado?"

"Lottery." That's all she says and all I need to know.

As much as I love Dillon, one thing about him drives me fucking insane. There is no rational explanation for it, but his mastery of numbers and statistics is unreal. By my count, he has won the lottery now for the seventeenth time. I can't bring myself to believe he's psychic. But this defies simple luck.

Anyone who knows anything about math will tell you the odds of winning the lottery are slim to none. Winning twice? Forget about it. There is no possible way to predict future drawings.

Yet there's evidence to the contrary. The odds that little machine spits out 11, 25, 30, 52, 59, and 72 are the exact same as it shooting out 1, 2, 3, 4, 5, and 6. Common knowledge.

Dillon disagrees. Says the odds of six *consecutive* numbers popping up are "infinitely improbable." He reviews drawings daily. Studies past results like an archaeologist studies artifacts. Analyzing every detail, looking for any connection.

It blows my mind.

Even more shocking? What he does with the winning ticket. Doesn't throw it away. He doesn't win simply to validate his intelligence. He gives the winning ticket to a charity.

Why not just write a big check? If you won *anything* that many times, you'd arouse suspicion. He kept the first payday. Combined with his porn royalties, he's set for life. The mail isn't safe enough. It could get lost, fall into the wrong hands.

So he picks a cause, locates them, and flies in for a visit. He walks into their office, large manila envelope in hand. Asks to speak with whoever is in charge. They chat for a while. He types away on his FlashPAD. He never mentions money, just wants to make sure they're legit.

He stands up to leave; they shake hands. Dillon says, "This is for you." He's out the door before the glue is ripped apart. An angel come and gone.

His only caveat, that they use the donation for charity. He'll know if they cash in the ticket for themselves. People are stupid with money.

Despite his daunting stature, not everyone heeds his conditions. "I've taken care of it" is all he says in a few facial contortions.

The frustration his power with numbers brings me is outrageous. No time to dwell on it though. Alison's eyes all of a sudden are burning a hole in me. Back to normal. A weird kind of normal. Not sure if I have a choice.

I bring her the bill. Her credit card is already out. I run the card, bring her a pen. She signs, looks right at me. "Excuse me, but you look very familiar. Do I know you from somewhere?"

Fuck. If she knows anything about Ted Watts, this could get ugly.

Calm down. I do kind of look like the Cubs' center fielder. People ask me that all the time.

"Oh, I'm not Jason Randall."

"I know that, silly." Her tone is eerily friendly.

I have to get out of here. "Well, my friend owns the place. I spend a lot of time in here, so you've probably seen me around."

"No, no." Shakes her head. Uncomfortable silence. Suddenly, she lights up. "I know! Yes, how did I not see it sooner?" I shrug. "I was close with your mother. We spent a lot of time together."

I breathe a sigh of relief. My mother had a couple of very close friends. This lady wasn't one of them. She thinks I'm someone else.

"Sorry," I tell her. "I don't remember you. My mother only had a couple of friends that I ever met."

Shooting me an unnerving smile, "No, silly. I'm not talking about Josephine Watts. I'm talking about Penelope Strickland, the woman who gave birth to you." I do a shitty job of concealing my shock. "I met you the day you were born. She was my sister."

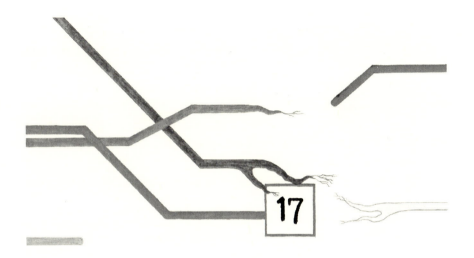

17

My alcohol consumption is cyclical. There are times when I'll drink a liter of whiskey every night for a week. Next thing you know, I'm eight months sober. Usually, I'm somewhere in between.

Not tonight.

The Warning Track is approaching vacancy. Doesn't stop me from keeping the bartender Kim running around all night. Great name for a bar. Funny thing about the warning track in baseball. The fine line between heroism and mediocrity. A few inches means the difference between an out and a trip around the bases. Thoughts of baseball help ease the tension.

Three fingers of whiskey, keep 'em coming. None of those little girl fingers either. How would you pour a drink for King Kong? Pour it like that.

I'll probably feel it in the morning. But right now, I'm convinced she's serving me straight ginger ale.

Mackenzie and I sit silently, watching the TV at the bar. I told Alison to meet us here later, that I needed to help Mackenzie close down the restaurant. I really just didn't want to deal with her. I want so badly to believe she's crazy. But curiosity is getting the best of me.

"I'm gonna pick out some songs on the jukebox. Any requests?" Mackenzie asks, getting off her stool.

"Lawrence Arms," is all I tell her. She nods accompanied by a smirk and wink. We must have seen those guys over thirty times growing up. Local favorites.

Over at the machine, she's hitting buttons. Not really browsing; she knows what she's going to play. She always knows. No, she's just giving me time to think. I filled her in. Her reaction was telling. As if months and months of her most loyal customer was suddenly explained.

Most of the monitors are sports related. The one just off to my left is news. No sound. The captions are on. A recent string of vandalism to expensive cars. Not the typical keying of paint. Someone has been drilling quarter-inch holes in the body of flashy automobiles.

Actually, it was 5/16″.

I may or may not have had everything to do with that. Again, purely aesthetic. Doesn't affect performance. It's not like I cut the brakes.

Don't make the assumption that I did this as an act of revolt against the wealthy.

But people with lots of money tend to buy expensive cars. People with expensive cars typically park like shit. Your Audi is great. Not so great it deserves two spots. If you can't live with your Porsche getting dinged, park it in the Sticks and walk.

Hondas and Subarus have felt the wrath too.

Equal opportunity.

I stare down, stirring my drink, looking for patterns, images in the quickly melting ice. It wasn't packed when we arrived. My demeanor partially explains the desolation. So I tell myself. Seeing my reflection in the mirror behind the top shelf, I can't describe what I look like. No one can. They've never seen anything like it.

A Gaslight Anthem song comes on over the speakers, which helps. Mackenzie is still hitting buttons but pauses to acknowledge me. My favorite song. She knows me too well. My first smile in a long time. Certainly ephemeral. But it's a start.

A slurping sound resonates from my glass. There's another one sitting in front of my face before my lips part with the straw.

A perfunctory nod is all I can manage as a show of thanks. Another sip, I feel a squeeze on my shoulders.

"Wow! You are so tense, man," Mackenzie says after giving me a brief massage. My expression tells her what she already senses. *You were expecting me to be relaxed?*

After a long silence, I look at her and say, "Thanks for coming with me. I really have no idea what to think. You know her way better than I do. She seems crazy, right?" Mackenzie nods. "But there's just something about her that is so sincere. Plus, she said she has proof."

We drink in silence for another twenty minutes, listening to her musical selections. Smiling at familiar verses. Exchanging knowing glances as we both reminisce. Replaying events of our past. Times these tunes have become the soundtrack for.

The drinks are finally kicking in. Hitting me hard. Not nearly as hard as anticipated. I shouldn't know which planet I'm on. Never mind which bar. I look at Mackenzie. For a moment, I feel human. It lasts no longer than a camera shutter, but it's unmistakable. There's a part of me that wants what she wants. Marriage, kids, soccer practice.

It takes more than a few drinks to erase decades of cynicism. You don't convert to romanticism after a little whiskey (or a lot, as the case may be).

"Well, I guess she's not coming," I tell her. She nods, says she's going to the bathroom while I pay my tab. I flag down Kim. She's giving me a peculiar look. Like she can't believe I'm not only conscious but actually standing unassisted.

Mackenzie's back, we head for the door.

"Can we get burritos?" I ask her.

"Of course," she tells me with a smile.

We're not even ten paces out the door when Alison starts calling my name. I turn around, not recognizing her face, but knowing exactly who she is. She's fifty feet the other direction. Running late.

"Let's get this over with" is all I mumble to Mackenzie as I pull her back into the bar. Alison following seconds behind.

This time, we grab at a table in the corner.

We sit at a stalemate. Getting frustrated, I look at Alison and say, "Well? I'm here. Your punctuality is greatly appreciated, by the way."

"Benjamin, please don't act surly with me. I'm sorry I'm late," she tells me, offering no explanation.

"My name is not Benjamin. It's Sam." Sharp and concise. "You're either out of your mind or need to do your homework before you make these claims, lady," I say, standing up.

"Sam, Ted, Benjamin. Whatever. Please just sit down and listen to what I have to tell you." *Ted*. That's the clincher. Where did she get that? How does she know? *What* does she know? I do my best to keep a poker face. Miserable failure. Shock is now my quiddity.

"Who is Ted?" I object, but she cuts me off.

"Benjamin is your real name. Or at least, that's the name you were given at birth," she begins. Just then, she glances at Mackenzie. "Would you mind if the two of us—"

I return the favor. "She stays," I say without looking away. She nods, unhappy about it. Oh well.

"Very well. As I was saying, your birth mother named you Benjamin. When you were found and adopted by the Watts, they obviously had no idea, given the circumstances." She goes on to explain in great detail the dumpster story and my struggle to survive. I sit, listen, and blink. That's all. Probing for holes in her story. I don't find a single one.

I let it sink in. Give my mind time to process. She knows what she's talking about. But I'm not convinced. Back before I was exiled, every pharmaceutical company on the planet knew my entire life story. Not sure why, but that didn't even occur to me until just now. Someone, maybe lots of people, know I'm back. They want something.

My help with a new disease. Monetary reparation. My head in a noose.

The possibilities are infinite. Few, if any, are favorable.

Finally I feel composed. "I hate to break it to you, lady, but you've got the wrong guy. It's a fascinating story. No doubt that if what you're talking about really happened—a baby abandoned in a dumpster, adopted by an amazing couple—it made headlines. It's a story that people eat up. Reciting a bunch of stuff you read in the papers, or on the Internet, doesn't make me your guy." The smugness has returned. Almost to the point I genuinely believe I'm not who she thinks I am.

Silence, no reaction at all. Slowly, she reaches into her purse. "Funny you should mention the newspapers. I happen to have one you might like to read." Cockiness is all over her face. Like I fell for a trick she didn't expect to work. She throws down a dirty and faded copy of the *Chicago Tribune*.

Fuck me. Where did she get this?

"I apologize, it's a little faded. A few decades will do that though," she says with a chuckle. The most hideous laugh. Approaching insult status. "Now, I know it's been a while since you were a baby, so obviously that infant could be just about anyone." She opens the folded paper completely. Covers the entire table. "But do *they* look familiar?" Her tone grows more cryptic with each syllable. I must make her stop. "That's Paul and Josephine Watts."

The precipice of losing my cool is now at arm's length. I barely stop myself from shouting *I know who they are!* Managing to cool myself somehow, I say, "They look nice. What have they got to do with me?"

"You can stop playing dumb, Benjamin. You know very well who they are."

I am sick and tired. Desperately wanting to get some sleep. Just forget tonight in the wake of tomorrow's impending hangover. This never happened. "OK, fine, you got me. I had a rather unusual youth. This paper doesn't prove that you know who my mother is. So let's cut the bullshit. Why are you here? Do you want money? Who do you work for?"

She stifles a small laugh and reaches back into her purse. "Well, since we've finally agreed that the baby in the paper is in fact you, maybe this will help." She lays an actual photograph in front of me. A woman holding a baby. The same baby in the newspaper. Both mother and child appear healthy. Small exception being the scar on her abdomen exposed due to an untucked shirt. I once read C-section babies are predisposed to cynical behavior.

Or maybe they're prone to making up their own statistics.

For how old it is, the photo is nearly mint condition. A small bend in the upper right corner, but that's it. I pick it up. Examine it more closely. No sooner is it near my face that my hands convulse. I drop it as if molten lava.

Her demeanor is now calm and comforting. "The woman holding you in this picture is Penelope Strickland, your mother. It was taken just days after you were born, when she was finally able to bring you home from the hospital." My tremors grow worse.

Mackenzie attempts to diffuse the tension. "I'm gonna grab a beer. You want some water or something?" A single nod is all I can muster.

I'm sold. The resemblance is ridiculous. Funny thing, genetics. I always laughed when people would say a boy has "his mother's eyes." Time to eat my words. Still, this is too much to digest.

With no resolve, I retort, "Alison, I will certainly concede that this baby is me. But this woman here, holding me. She could be anyone."

So many things she could say. She knows I'm full of shit. I'm a dead giveaway. The resemblance is unreal. She knows that I know.

#Indisputable

One more picture materializes from her purse. A photo of Alison and my mom, hugging. "Take a look at her eyes. What do you see?"

I pull the photo close for intense scrutiny. Somehow, I manage to hold on to this one. She said look at the eyes. I look at everything else, fearing where this is going. I accept the inevitability and finally acknowledge her ocular cavities.

My heart nearly erupts through my throat. Just as I expected.

"It's a rare condition, called—"

"Heterochromia Iridum," I finish. I have it too. My last-ditch effort, I tell Alison, "I know what it is. What's it got to do with me?"

"Your mother was always a terrible liar," she says with a cheerful smile. "How long have you been wearing contacts?"

"I don't. My vision is fine. I have a pair of prescription glasses that I wear on rare occasions, but I've always been fine without them."

"Well, good for you. You must have inherited *that* from your father then. Our side of the family wasn't so lucky. We've all had glasses, contacts, Lasik. You name it, we've had it. But I'm talking about the contacts you wear to make your eyes the same color." I squint. A weak attempt to conceal my secret. Apparently, it isn't much of a secret. "Even in this dark bar, I can tell," she tells me.

I crumble. She's got me. There's no avoiding it. "Since I was eight," my simple answer.

She nods. "It's a rare condition. Your mom was even more of an anomaly."

Shit. Don't tell me.

"Most of the people who do have it, their irises are two different colors. Maybe one brown, one blue."

I nod. Know how it works. Like I said, I have it too.

"But your mom, she was even more rare. Hers changed color, kind of like a chameleon."

Same with me. I've never told anyone, not even Mackenzie. I chug the water she brought back for me. Not enough. I finish her beer too. Run my hands through my hair. I resemble a horse cadaver dismembered by a speeding train. A complete mess.

No choices here. I surrender. Not sure how to react as I never expected this day to come. Certainly never played out like this in my mind.

So many questions. But what little I've learned about my mother tonight is more than I've known about her all my life. Do I push my luck?

"What about my father?" I ask. Instantly wishing I hadn't.

"Good question," she says. Glances at something behind me. A weird cringe. "You want to know about your father? Take a look at the TV above the pool table."

I look back, confused at first. It's a commercial. For condoms.

Just then, a million scenarios rush through my head. None of them good. All the possibilities considered, I know the reality. I don't even have to ask. My dad is Nicky Salcedo.

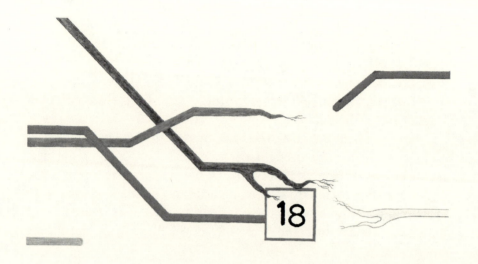

18

Familiar with the story of Oedipus? Quick recap. Laius was king, Jocasta the queen. No children. The oracle of Apollo said any child born to the king would kill him.

Funny thing about fate. You can't escape it. No matter how big your ego, it will find you. Lauis didn't get that. Sent his son off in the hands of a servant. Abandon the boy on a mountain. His feet were fettered, couldn't crawl.

Laius was in the clear.

Except not even close.

The servant couldn't do it. Couldn't leave an infant to die. He gave it to a shepherd.

The kid grew up. Ran and scraped his knees. Got on a chariot. So did Lauis. Their paths crossed. They fought. Oedipus the victor, killing his father. Not that he knew who he was at the time.

I was never really big on that story. Until last night. The night I discovered it effectively *was* my life.

Nicky Salcedo. "The Sauce."

Everything in the room you're in, look at it. Chances are, Nicky Salcedo had something to do with it. CEO, president, CFO, the list goes on. He's been on the board of just about every corporation within the last fifty years.

Most notably, Prolific Prophylactics.

What a catchy name. So much fun to say. Too bad the founders didn't own a dictionary. Effectively foreshadowing their demise. To their credit, only a handful of people know what that word means. But still.

They were one of many. One of the dozens of companies who put a bounty on my head. Not necessarily to kill me. They wanted me to fix the mess I'd put them in. Threw insane dollar amounts at me. Create a disease ten times more devastating. Their absurd proposition dismissed within seconds.

At the time I had morals. I had a soul. I said no.

The result? Phony passports and IDs in eight languages. Money stored in bank accounts on four continents. Most importantly, the steady decline of the condom industry.

But far from absolute annihilation. They're still around. Thanks in no small part to my dear old dad.

How do I know I'm his spawn? Sometimes you just know.

Alison's testimony was rather compelling.

So Nicky Salcedo, Wall Street's golden boy, a pillar of the community. Beautiful wife. Four kids now grown up.

Oh yeah, and countless mistresses. My mother being one of them.

So I ask you, how would it look if the man who made millions pushing condoms cheated on his wife?

Pretty bad. Made much worse considering he didn't have enough common sense (or confidence in his product) to shrink-wrap his rod. Or worse. He used one, and it failed.

Shit, the guy did what he had to do.

I was a threat to his entire livelihood. He did everything in his power to have me aborted. Mom wasn't having it. She hid out for a while. But when you wield his kind of power, you find who and what you're looking for.

Chased up and down the Windy City, she dropped me in a dumpster. A slim-to-none shot. Still, better than being caught with me.

You know the rest.

I drank more last night than in the last three years combined. It doesn't show. Fully functional, I could run a marathon. A bastion of strength. Pinnacle of health.

I lie here in bed, Mackenzie at my side. I must have been an awful fuck last night. Thinking about everything *but* the task at hand. But now I look at her and hope my swimmers are hitting the mark. Make no mistake. I'm a sperm donor, not a father. Yes, it's shitty and hypocritical. It has also always been part of the deal.

I look at her, look out my window, replay last night over and over. Every single time my resolve grows. Determination amplified. I know what I have to do.

I head downstairs to grab some breakfast for Mackenzie. Who should be on the cover of *The Tribune* but the ball-sack that created me.

He's hit another home run. They've created a lubricant that protects against STDs transmitted via skin. Coats the penis, no condom required. At least they've finally accepted that condoms are the VHS tapes of this generation. An obsolete invention.

This lube, it's made with Kevlar. He's actually guaranteeing its effectiveness. He might be the biggest piece of shit on the planet, but I believe him.

How do I know it will work?

Simple. I invented it around the time I cured AIDS.

Oh, Nicky. So cute. You keep at it there, maybe one day you'll do something impressive. But you better do it soon.

How do I know? It's simple.

I have to eliminate Nicky Salcedo.

Do unto others, before they do it to you first.

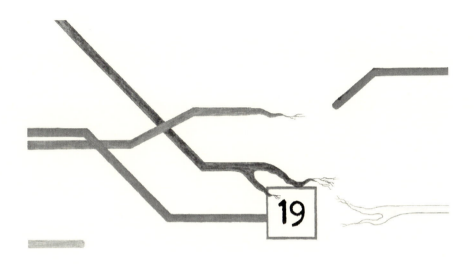

19

It's an odd look, mixing confusion and eagerness. "Las Vegas? Are you out of your mind?"

This question. Getting kind of old.

"Mackenzie, I'm absolutely serious. It's the perfect place to take this plan to the next level. Not only is there tons of booze and casual sex, it's filled with tourists. They show up, get the disease, and take it back home. Soon enough, it's all over the country. Eventually the world. Besides, I need time away from Chicago until I figure out how to deal with The Sauce."

She knew Nicky Salcedo was a big name in business. But had no clue he was one of the people who wanted me dead. Definitely puts a new twist on things. It doesn't take much to convince her that leaving town for a bit is in my best interest. She's a bit hesitant about Sin City though.

I saw resistance a light-year away. Lay out my argument, thoughtfully, with precision. So many positives. Far away. Copious drugs and alcohol. Hedonism served for breakfast on a golden platter. Too easy. The clincher?

Dillon *hates* smoke. Cigarettes, pot, cigars. You name it, he hates it.

Las Vegas, the only major city in America living in the 1900s. Smoking in public buildings? Condoned and encouraged. As tough as it's been getting him on board, I knew Las Vegas was the linchpin. Come to think of it, Nicky Salcedo has a lot of friends in big tobacco.

That settles it.

I'm hitting the lab tonight. Not wasting any time. A food additive that curbs the desire to smoke . . . maybe if the body reacts with the tar . . . furious headaches when you smoke? Induces vomiting? I've already got something. Just need to perfect it. Another plus? I'm not totally lying to Dillon.

Sure, the greater good . . . all that fun stuff. It benefits public health. I don't care. Twofold purpose: get Dillon on board and hit The Sauce hard.

"I've already booked flights for the three of us," I tell Mackenzie.

Doesn't look shocked in the least. "Well, I've always wanted to see if counting cards was as easy as they make it look in the movies," she says. Very sly. You can see the wheels turning. She's planning something. I like it.

"I'll see you and Dillon at O'Hare in eight days."

Taken aback, she says, "What? I can't leave in a week. I have a business to run."

I'm not buying her act. She's resourceful, she'll handle it. "I have the utmost confidence in you." Let's push her buttons. "Hey, why don't you have Alison run the place? She spends almost as much time there as you do." I'm met by a playful punch in the arm. Only wish she'd hit me harder. Anything to take my mind off the pain in my balls. Not sure what she and I did when I was drunk. My gonads aren't a fan. "But seriously, you'll be fine. You have a pretty solid staff and a loyal clientele. Oh yeah, the pizza is pretty good too."

That gets a small chuckle. Every year, some local publication votes Gumball Alley best pizza in the Chicago-land area.

"OK, fine." With a deep breath, she's still taking all this in. "I guess I'd better get home and start packing." A kiss on the cheek and she's out the door.

I walk her to her L stop, pick up some supplies. Miracle medicines don't just grow on trees. I stop for lunch. A new place. New to me, anyways.

Some bar in The Loop. TVs floor to ceiling. I order an ahi tuna steak, side salad. Above average. Jury still out on the service. Some girl with big tits and a gallon of peroxide in her hair, massive throat tattoo, spends her time laughing at what I assume are supposed to be jokes. There are three guys oozing immaturity. Dwelling on all the things they *should* have done. My favorite, the guy in the middle. Lecturing his companions about the merits of free-range chicken. Organic food, no more pesticides. How soda is poisoning us. Agricultural giants have the FDA in their pocket. Apparently, the hand-rolled smokes in his shirt pocket are high in fiber too.

He's about to start another round of passing judgment when something on TV grabs me. Every screen but two shows sports. One of the two with news is right in front of me. No sound though. No captions. But he's at it again. Nicky Salcedo surrounded by the press.

Flashbulbs going crazy. Microphones in his face from every direction. Looks like a porn star at a cock buffet.

That tie. I've seen it before. Not The Sauce's. The guy next to him.

His lawyer? Maybe. But he's wearing a tie covered in molecules. Probably some guy who helped with the Kevlar cream. R&D, something like that.

Then it clicks. The guy I saw in DC. My stomach churns. Don't know what the connection is. I don't like it. Looks like I have some research on my calendar.

Jugs comes over, offers me a refill. I accept, ask for my check.

"What do you want to do with your life?" My query seemingly coming from outer space.

"Excuse me?"

"I said what do you want to do with your life? I get the feeling you don't get asked that a lot," I smile jokingly.

"Seriously?" I nod. "I'm going to finish up school in less than a year, and I'd like to run my own PR firm. But hopefully travel the world for a year or two first. I have some pretty big plans, but more than anything, I want to be a mom." I am blown away by her candidness. I like this girl. Not in that way. If I had any kind of libido, I'd make a half-assed attempt to fuck her.

But no, something about her is refreshing.

"Good answer. Do a shot with me?" I ask. She pours two glasses full of whiskey, puts her chaser next to them. I knock mine over. Pretend it's an accident. I slip a pill in her drink. A vaccine. I hope she does become a mom some day. Not sure why. There are few people in this world I like. Attractive women are sparse on the list.

It's bitter and juvenile.

No shit. Are you seeing a theme?

We put back the shots, she chases. I leave her $200 for a tip and head out the door.

Seconds later, the Doppler Effect is in full swing. The sound of shoes slapping the pavement steadily increases in volume.

"Hey, what's this?"

"It's your tip. What does it look like?"

"You're sure?" Skepticism is heavy.

"I'm in a giving mood today," I tell her deadpan.

Her eyes light up, she hugs me. More emphatically than I like. Personal space. Maybe I'll write a blog about it. "Thank you. Seriously, thank you." Awkward pause. "I'm Kendall by the way."

"Samuel."

"Nice to meet you."

"Same here. Oh hey, you know those guys at the end of the bar?"

"Yeah." Rolling her eyes. The tone and expression say it all. She can't stand them either.

"I'll give you $100 each if you slip one of these in their drinks." I hand her a few blue pills. "I'll give you another $200 each if you find a way to piss in their next drink." That part, just for my own sick amusement.

She's trying hard not to laugh. Her efforts fail. "Wow. You're serious? Um, okay." She laughs again. "I probably shouldn't ask, but why? Did those guys do something to you?"

"No, I've never met them before in my life. Let's just say, sometimes people rub you the wrong way. Just a gut feeling. Are you cool with that?"

Her smile now big and genuine. "Totally cool."

"Great. I'll come back tomorrow with the money. You tell me how much I owe you. Do a good job, you might be opening up that PR firm sooner than you thought." I turn and hop in a cab.

Time to visit Mom and Dad. Paul and Josephine.

The driver drops me off at the cemetery. Step by step, I take the painful walk. So many thoughts flood my mind. I don't stay long. But this is something I needed to do. The walk back out is surprisingly calm. There are a few people paying their respects in the distance. An elderly man, probably visiting his wife. Some guy drops flowers on a grave. Down on one knee, one hand on the tombstone, I pass behind him.

His concentration broken by a noise behind him, he turns around. I catch a glimpse of his face.

Defeated and worn. I know his pain. Even worse, I know his face. He's the guy from DC. The kid next to The Sauce on TV. Apparently not a live feed. Either that or H. G. Wells just creamed his pants.

He turns back around, doesn't appear to recognize me. Not that he has a reason to.

I catch a glimpse of the name on the grave. My eyes bulge. Like I've seen a ghost. This isn't happening. But there it is. Undeniable. Carved in stone.

Very familiar name. Haven't heard it in forever. It's not one you forget.

KRYSTAL MADIGAN.

My first time.

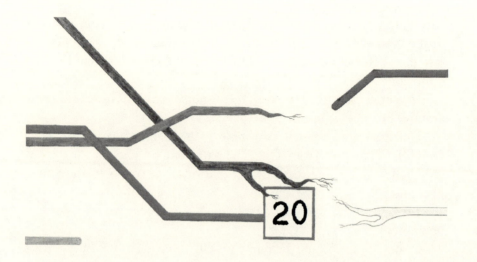

20

I love the Windy City. It's not without flaws though. The stretch of the Blue Line from Clark/Lake to O'Hare being one of them. I am tempted to get out and walk. Might literally be faster. Traffic on the Dan Ryan is backed up to Indiana, so a cab won't do.

"Attention: we are stalled waiting for signals ahead. We will proceed shortly." That recorded announcement, taking its toll on your sanity without fail. Each time you hear it, the agony compounds.

Construction on the track. Can't think of a time when the Blue Line *wasn't* under repair.

Maybe Dillon and Mackenzie found a faster way.

Unlikely.

Knowing Dillon, he's been there since last night. A very casual and tranquil individual. Aside from secondhand smoke, he hates being late. A dinner reservation or a movie, not so much.

But a flight? Forget about it. I doubt he's ever arrived at check-in within the four-hour window. He's always early. Too early.

As frustrating as this is, I accept what minimal control I have over the situation. Listen to my iPod, read *The Girl with the Dragon Tattoo*. Twice in three months. In Swedish this time. No, I don't speak it. What better way to learn though?

The train arrives at Montrose. A few leave, a few enter. Nothing strange. Inevitably, you get the one guy who walks from car to car as the train is moving. The door opens. You hear the vibrations of the track and buzzing of the wind as you race by. Just sit the fuck down, buddy. Plenty of seats in this car.

Most of them aren't even covered in puke for a change.

Your tax dollars at work.

Jefferson Park. No one gets off, two get on. A lady in a suit, some dude with a turban, talking way too loud on his phone.

Racism is a peculiar thing. Odds are high that he's going to the airport. I see a guy dressed like this, speaking Farsi. My brain goes to red alert.

Whatever. Lisbeth Salander is way more interesting than whatever he's yapping about.

Eventually we get to ORD. I begin the mile-long trek to ticketing. Waiting in line, I get a text. Time-stamped twenty minutes ago. Finally in an area with service. It's Dillon. As expected, he's waiting at the gate. No word on Mackenzie.

Boarding pass in hand, I go through security. Pockets empty, shoes off, you know the drill. Somehow, people still manage to prolong this process. Turn it into an entire production. They make me do a body scan. Three women with massive racks are told to do the same. All very flirtatious with security. With everyone in line for that matter.

How convenient. Once through, I observe. Sure enough, most of the people they make do the "random" scans are women. Attractive and highly Caucasian. I say most, as I was clearly an exception.

Whatever. I head toward the gate, grab a coffee on the way. Not surprisingly, Dillon is there, reading. He sees me, signs hello. I ask him if he's seen Mackenzie. He tells me she's on her way.

He sees my latte, decides he wants one too. I tell him I'll get it. For a mute, ordering food is rarely a simple task.

Cream, three Splendas, please, he winks to me.

"Sure thing, buddy."

I'm still drinking mine when I order again. Back at the gate, Mackenzie is seated next to Dillon and some other chick. If the gates were busy, it wouldn't be so weird. But half the seats are vacant. If this were Europe, that might fly. Why is she sitting next to someone?

She sees me, stands up, and smiles. I give Dillon his coffee.

"Ooh, that smells good," the girl next to her says. "Hey, M, I'm gonna grab one. You want anything?"

"Ooh, I'd love a cappuccino. Thanks, babe," Mackenzie tells her. Once the weird coffee girl is gone, I cut to the chase.

"Who the fuck is that, Mackenzie?" More defensively than necessary.

Taken aback, she's confused. Looks at me as if I didn't recognize the Bears' starting quarterback. "Who, Daivey? I thought you two met a while back."

Then it clicks. The bartender from a while ago. Where I met Jarrett.

"Wasn't she blonde?"

She laughs. "Who, Daivey?" As if I'd be talking about someone else. "It seems like she's changing her hair color every other week."

"Right, I remember her. But *why* is she here?" A million thoughts stampede my brain. Paranoia. How much does she know? Anything at all? Wouldn't be here if she was completely clueless. Who else has Mackenzie told? Fuck.

Not fully comprehending the gravity of the situation, she chuckles again. The answer is obvious. "Duh, she's coming to Las Vegas with us."

"I got that part Mackenzie." Bite my tongue. Don't cause a scene. "Let me rephrase." Deep breath. "Why. The fuck. Is that bubbly girl. Flying. To Las Vegas. With us?" The last few words escape through clenched teeth. Barely audible. Luckily my point is made.

She opens her mouth to respond. I don't want to hear the answer. I pick up my carry-on, prepared to call the whole thing off. Not the start I wanted. Mimicking my tone, she says, "Well. She's. A. Bartender. Sam. I thought she might be helpful to the cause."

Not the answer I wanted. Dig what nails I have into my forehead. Stare at her. Not a word comes out. She knows what I'm thinking.

Finally she drops the oblivious act. "Look. I know you're some big shot who knows more than Einstein about science and genetics and all that shit. But for someone so smart, you overlooked *a lot* of important details." I say nothing. Curious where this is going, I nod, tell her to begin her list of grievances. "First of all, Vegas isn't a town you just show up in and get a job. At least not at any place worth working. Any place that draws a large crowd, the kind you're looking for, they're all in mega resorts. The hiring process is intense. They background check and drug-test everybody." I'm well aware. I've already created false profiles for all of us if necessary. The drug test won't be a problem. Dillon's been clean for years.

Mackenzie goes on. "Now you might be smart. For all I know, you've already concocted a way to reverse global warming. Maybe you've figured out a way to control weather patterns. But Vegas doesn't care about that. They don't look at resumes for awards and achievements. A Nobel Prize is worth as much as the material it's made of." She steps in a little closer. Stares up at me. Holds my attention with her gaze. "There are only two things that town is interested in when it comes to hiring." Right then, she grabs my hands. Places them firmly on her chest.

Just like that, her point is made. She's right.

I nod, conceding.

The tension subsides. We're returning to a state of calm. "Look, all I'm saying is that it's never a bad thing to have an attractive woman with you in that town. Daivey has worked in bars all over the country. When I mentioned Las Vegas, she rattled off a name of at least eight people she knows working there. Connections, man. You can't deny that it's a huge help to have connections."

I'm too proud to admit the flaws in my plan. Background checks are no big deal. It's been so long since I held a typical job. Clearly, I've forgotten just how tedious the process is. She sees I'm calming down. Can tell I'm not completely settled.

"Baby, I know you're stressed that telling more people will blow the plan to shit. I get that." She looks around. Wonders if Daivey is approaching with coffee. Coast is clear. "But you are aware of how she and I know each other, right?"

Not sure of the specifics. I know it involves Jarrett. I nod yes.

"OK, so you know that she and I, and several other women"—the last words are under her breath—"are members of what is basically an anti-Jarrett club."

My head still hurts. Too much to process. Just make the announcement to board already.

I turn around, and Daivey is approaching. Two cups in hand. Calmly, "We'll finish this conversation later," I tell Mackenzie.

I sit back down next to Dillon. Make small talk. Tell him all about the improved concoction. How it curbs the urge to smoke. Still in the dark about my whole plan to eradicate the population.

#Details

He goes back to his book. I sit and wait to board. Tap my foot in a sporadic pattern. Fuck this. What do I have to be anxious about? I look around, nerves are calmed. Everyone is busy on a laptop or cell phone. I could whip it out right now. Start to piss and spin in circles. No way I don't hit at least five mobile devices. People have no idea who they are. What they want. A purpose? Forget it. The years are short, the days are long. Always in a rush to get to the next place. Why sit and do nothing here? I'd rather sit and do nothing over there. Get me to my destination now. I've got texts to send. Brain cells to kill.

Shit people are stupid. I smile for the first time in a while. It's fleeting. Before I know it, a voice on the PA sounds. Our flight is boarding. Daivey and Mackenzie are lined up. I waste no time. Get me there first, so we can all get there together. Dillon stands up, a curious look in his eyes.

Let's do this, man.

I share his enthusiasm. To a smaller degree. "Yeah, buddy, let's go put big tobacco out of business," I say. A firm pat on his massive back to keep him fired up.

Not that, Sam. I mean eventually yeah. But right now, we've got bigger things to deal with.

Rather ominous. "How so?"

Did you wake up today knowing that you were going stop this plane from going down?

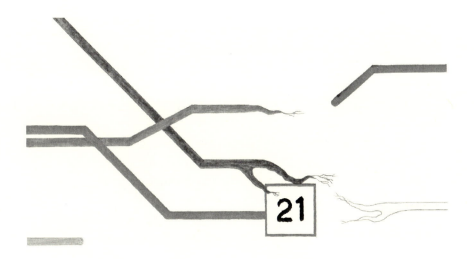

21

I hate flying. It's safer than driving. But safety doesn't factor into my opinion. Middle seats. Enough said. Few things worse than being elbowed by a sleeping stranger for countless hours. They smell. Spill drinks on you. Step on your toes to use the bathroom. Smack the back of your head when they return. What a treat.

Top it off, they read tabloids.

Jenna got a boob job. Denies it.

April cheated on Joey with the roadies on his band's tour.

Monica's dress is ugly.

Sorry Monica, it's not the dress. No fabric or pattern in the world can reverse ugly.

If Jean-Paul Sartre made me a character in a play, this would be it.

An announcement tells us the flight is full. As of now, half the seats are empty. There's a line out the door. Probably up the jet way too. Dillon gets out of his palatial aisle seat, not that he has anywhere to go. Eventually squeezes his way near the big door. Despite his stature, he disappears behind people stuffing bags overhead.

I look to my right to the window seat intended for Mackenzie. Managed to switch for a seat next to Daivey. Lucky day. Her replacement? Some sweaty guy intently studying a book on card counting. Not sure who makes more. Casinos or the publishers of such literature. Every asshole that ever shuffled a deck thinks they're going to get rich quick. I'm not a betting man, but I'm confident this guy won't break the mold. Plus he smells like elephant fart. I've been to India, I know.

With only a few stragglers looking for their seats, Dillon makes his way back to our row.

Signing this time, *Let's go.* I shoot him a quizzical look. *I got us some better seats.*

"Better? Like first class?" Unlikely, but worth a shot.

No, not quite. I got two people up in the front of coach to switch with us. He starts grabbing our luggage out of the bin. *Let's go, buddy. Oh, and grab my duffel bag on the floor, would ya?*

My agitation compounds, mostly due to the card counter but also at Dillon. "What are you talking about? How is up front better?" Not that it could be any worse. Still, in a row of three, I'm automatically relegated to the middle seat. Particularly if the other is Dillon. "Please sit back down," I plead and close my eyes.

Immediately, my sleep façade is interrupted. Dillon doesn't budge. Points at his crotch then makes a motion with his arm. He's hit me over the head with his cock before. I rub my head while reliving painful memories. Dillon wins this round. I grab our stuff and make for the front. Let's just get this over with.

The couple that has agreed to switch places with us arrives, and we make our way past them. I'm not sure what Dillon wrote down or managed to tell them. I don't really want to know. Just get me to my middle seat and get this plane in the air.

Our bags go up top once again. I greet our newest window seat companion and move for the middle. I am about to sit down when Dillon grabs my shoulder. Before I realize it, he's on the other side of me. Sitting in the middle. Leaving no room for anyone else.

"Come on man, move over." I'm groveling like a kid. Not becoming whatsoever. Just want to be on the way.

Now he's blinking and flaring his nostrils. *No, you take the aisle this time. I don't mind. In fact, I insist.*

I'm too tired to object or even care. Way out of character for him. Finally, we get situated. The door shuts, and we're on the runway. Unsure of when I'll see Chicago again. *If* I'll see Chicago again. Don't have time to dwell on it. We speed down the runway and climb into the sky. Five minutes later, I'm asleep.

Wish I had some profound dream. Wish I could wake up and tell them all I've got it. A revelation. Epiphany. Not the case.

Just a sex fantasy. Involving Daivey. Not sure what to make of it. Attractive no doubt. Not my type. Must have something to do with Mackenzie's sudden affinity for her.

My time to ponder it ends abruptly. We're caught in the most violent turbulence I've ever encountered. Not your typical bumpy ride. Literally feels like a rollercoaster. Ups and downs are expected. The plane is thrown side to side. Thirty feet to the right without warning. As if this 747 were a plastic model in the hands of a toddler. He's whipping us around, no regard for those with motion sickness.

Plastic cups and aluminum cans are falling everywhere. Ice bounces around like lottery balls. Clutter in the aisle accumulates with every drop and shift. Of course my nerves are a wreck, but it will pass. The other hundred-plus passengers aren't so collected. Somehow, Dillon is sleeping through this. That can't be. He must have taken something. Then it hits me. What Dillon said to me right before we boarded.

Did you wake up today knowing that you were going stop this plane from going down?

It defies all logic, the guy just *knows* stuff. Not sure how he does it. I'll never admit it, but it drives me fucking crazy. Suddenly, my neutral demeanor begins to race. What if this is it? Are we going to be headline news? His words roll around in my mind. I soak them in. My hands are twitching, but he did say I was going to save this plane. Makes no sense. While I understand the physics of aviation, I have no control over the weather. I might understand how planes fly. Doesn't mean I can land one. It's eating away at me. Oxygen bags drop from the ceiling. Deep breath. Cool yourself. I look back for Mackenzie. Don't see her. People are holding hands across the aisle. With people in front of them. I give Dillon a steady shove. Tell him to put on his mask. Just looks around, shrugs, and signs to me.

No worries, man. We're good.

I'm seconds away from punching him, when the plane calms itself. Just like that, we're flying straight and steady. Tension is still high. Everyone braces for more jarring. It never comes. We sit for the next half hour shrouded in paranoia. Knowing that the choppy air is waiting for us to get comfortable just to shake us when we least expect it. But that never happens. The rest of the ride is smooth. I look across Dillon and out the window. See the Grand Canyon. Estimate we're about thirty minutes out.

On the verge of napping again, commotion in first class catches my ear. The curtain blocks my vision, but I can hear them just fine.

"Excuse me sir, but you are *not* allowed to have that on. Cellular phones are forbidden until we've landed and the captain approves it."

Slowly leaning forward, I peak inside the curtain. It can't be him. But sure enough, there he is. Standing, not sitting, less than five feet away. The dude from the Blue Line. He's not alone. There are two other guys standing in the aisle, punching away on mobiles.

Back to my seat, I look at Dillon. His expression stoic. As if practicing for the poker room. He grabs my hands, looks at the bumps on my fingers. Gives me a thumbs-up.

You don't have to be a scientific mastermind to guess what happens next.

This plane is about to use Las Vegas Boulevard as a landing strip.

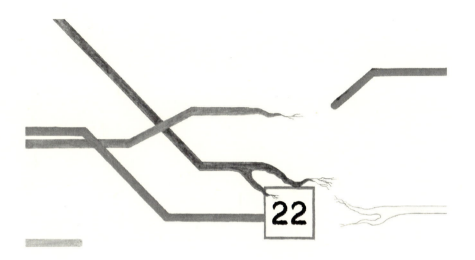

You play these scenarios out in your mind. Over and over again. Knowing that when and if the opportunity arises, you're prepared. You will be ready for anything. Everything that can and will go wrong. If situation A occurs, you come back with response B. If X then Y.

That's all well and good. But life is never like that. Not some algebraic equation that plays itself out the same way every time. Sure, you can make some educated guesses. Your predictions can hold true for a while. But you can never account for everything.

Variables. Always variables.

Everyone dreams of being a hero. Don't deny it. You've been on a plane, looked at the stranger a few rows up, concocted a plan. What you'll do when they lose control? Most people never get the opportunity. Good thing. But here we are. Las Vegas bound. Nearly two hundred people have the chance to be a hero. Several problems though. One major one. By the time they realize what's going on, it will be too late.

I know I'm supposed to want to be a hero. This is the point where I'm supposed to step up huge. Save a bunch of lives. Not only the passengers on the plane, also the people in cars on The Strip. The pedestrians, the people in the hotels gambling, drinking, sleeping, fucking, whatever.

These people are relying on me to save them.

So we've come full circle.

The couple thousand lives I'm about to save? Nothing compared to the millions I saved years ago. Where did that get me?

This is the part where I'm the bigger man. Rise above my ego. Forget all the trouble I've endured in the past. Focus on what I'm called to do right now.

So what? Maybe all I want to do is sip a martini and watch this debacle unfold. Truth be told, most of the people I'd be helping, they don't need it. I'd just be delaying the inevitable. Everyone is born, everyone dies. Cliché, but given. For an overwhelming majority, everything in between is mere formality.

Biding time.

But who am I fooling? Ignoring the obvious fact that I'm too vain to die today, I could never sit idly by in a situation like this. Despite my approval rating for humanity plummeting to unthinkable lows, I still cured AIDS.

Somewhere inside—very, *very*, deep inside of me—there is something good. Something that believes people aren't all bad. Something that wants to help once again. It was a fire that burned deep inside of me for years. I know it's there. The flame didn't fully extinguish. Contrary to what was previously thought.

It's just a pilot light. But it's there.

If Anne Frank can say people are good, maybe I can too.

Or maybe this is me, afraid that I've reached the end.

A deathbed repentance of sorts.

Maybe Dillon is blowing this way out of proportion. We're getting worked up over nothing. We'll land in thirty minutes. Laugh at irrational fears. Then give Las Vegas a complete makeover.

Funny how all these thoughts, we spend a lifetime debating them. Are we good? Are we evil? What do we value? But put your back against the wall. You condense thousands of years of philosophy into a matter of seconds. Because seconds is all I have.

I unbuckle my seatbelt, casually walk into first class. Assess the situation. That's all.

My hand is on the curtain when one of the men asks, "How much longer until we land?" Not an unusual question.

Once.

They've asked five times since the turbulence. Not sure how many before. The flight attendant is pleading with them to sit down. Informing them it is illegal to have their mobile devices turned on.

Just like that, one of them starts talking into the box in his hand. Someone says something back in Farsi.

I have no clue what's going on. Simply put: I don't care.

The thirty-second hesitation I've taken is twenty-nine too many. I rip the curtain open. A series of quick moves. My hand squeezes their necks and ears. Before anyone has time to question what is happening, they lay on the ground.

"Handcuffs. Now," I tell the plane's crew. They have heavy-duty zip-ties for situations involving rowdy passengers. I grab a handful, secure each man's right arm to left ankle. Repeat with the other side. They're lying facedown, limbs making an awkward X. Out of nowhere, Dillon hands me three gags.

I'm not sure what's more alarming: the fact he had these in his carry-on, or that I reach out as if expecting them all along. Don't want to use them unless absolutely necessary. Curious what they have to say. Maybe they'll come clean.

The three men are flailing and screaming. Denying any wrongdoing. Apologizing for using their phones during flight.

I unwrap the turban from the guy on the train. Little bags of powder and liquid. I do a quick check of color, smell, and texture. Hard to say, but my guess is grain dust, nitroglycerin, and flash powder. I lay it out on the floor. They all deny ever having seen it before. Clearly the intent was some kind of explosion. Not necessarily too big. Maybe just enough to blow the lock off the cockpit door. I start searching their pockets for more clues.

Dillon taps me. Look back, he's making the letters *CO* with his hands. Not sure why he's focusing on Colorado. We passed it during the rough atmosphere. But then it clicks.

Carbon monoxide.

Tasteless. Odorless. It will knock you out. Intense rush. I remain calm enough to gently set down the chemicals. Don't want to know what happens if they mix.

I immediately grab bags from overhead bins, demanding to know who owns what. When no one speaks up, I search it all. Furiously tearing apart purses, duffle bags, briefcases. Anything in my path gets shredded.

Sure enough, gas masks. Knock everyone out, blow the lock off the door, crash the plane.

Expressions of terror consume the faces of those around me.

Disaster averted. Barely.

Feeling like a trophy detective, rather proud of myself, my bravado quickly dissipates as I look at the luggage tag.

Leanne Marlow from West Palm Beach.

Odd name for a man. Especially one allegedly from the Middle East.

Sweating bullets sitting in the second-row window in first class, the big-tittied platinum blonde from security. The one that no doubt created a diversion with her rack. Like David Copperfield. A master of misdirection. Probably great at sleight of hand too.

Intuition kicks in.

I scan first class. Another Barbie doll.

My eyes dart back to coach. Sure enough, first row behind the partition. Aisle. One more.

The three gags are not for the men on the floor. Meant for the broads who skated security by batting their eyes.

Your tax dollars at work.

I look at Dillon absolutely dumbfounded. Shoot him a stare of improbability.

He merely nods, calls me a racist.

Leanne, likely a phony identity, is on the verge of tears. There's nowhere to hide. Not waiting for the flight attendants to bring me more zip-ties, with blood boiling hotter than magma, I punch her in the face. Absolutely livid that the Swedish bikini team tried to kill us. No clue why. Don't really care.

But now I'm going to look like a racist. All over the news.

Then the chatter comes out of nowhere. All at once. People explaining to those around them what just happened. By the time the story reaches the back of the plane, the account is so twisted, I want to laugh. I prefer it this way. The fewer people who know the truth, the better.

Had I thought of it earlier, I might have sat idly by. Now my cover is blown. People are going to want me on talk shows. They'll want to know what the bumps on my fingers are. How did I knock out three men in a matter of seconds? Why did I punch a lady?

I clench my fists in frustration, admittedly feeling pretty amazing for what I just did. Might have just screwed the whole mission in the process.

The pilot announces we're about to land. Seatbelts on. Seats and tray-tables up. As soon as he's done, I'm on the PA, saying the only thing that comes to mind. My one desperate attempt to mitigate a potentially volatile situation.

"Ladies and gentlemen, I'd like to say something." Silence. The crowd is mine. I pause for effect. Going for patriotic, with a touch of cryptic, I continue, "What just happened is something I know you will all talk about for a very long time. I hope you live to tell this story for decades to come. It's rather tasteless for someone to ask for something in return in a situation like this. But I feel I have little alternative. Simply put, I just saved your lives." Another long pause. "You never saw me."

On cue. As if every passenger is a marionette. The strings dance, they nod in unison.

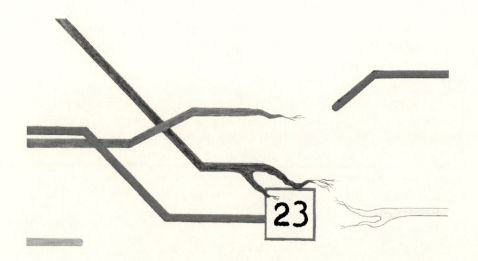

23

I'm the first off the plane. Don't know where I'm going. Doesn't matter, so long as it's anywhere else. Media and police are already flying by me. I expect some of them to question me. Associate me with recent events. So far so good. Dillon's grabbing my stuff from baggage claim. Me, I'm not hanging around one second longer than necessary.

Outside, an infinite line of people. Waiting for taxis. The sun is setting, but the heat is unrelenting. There's a guy eating a Kit-Kat; it's melted. I watched him grab it from the gift shop inside. His fingers already stained in chocolate.

Must get out of here. Far away. *Now.*

I open my wallet, remove every last bit of cash. The front of the cab line is beckoning. A young couple loading their bags. Before the driver packs the last set of golf clubs, I interrupt. "I think this one is a bit too small for you guys. Take the next one." I slap the cash in his hand. Not subtle. They get it, no objections. Just a pair of smiles, dreaming of the numerous ways they can lose that money. The bags are out, and I hop in.

I grab the handle to close the door but encounter resistance. It's Mackenzie. I wave her in. No sign of Daivey; don't have the time to wait.

The wheels begin rolling. The driver asks, "Where to?" I'm not sure what to tell him. Before I can utter so much as an "um," Mackenzie says, "Madera Roja apartments in Summerlin. Hualapai and Charleston." Then she throws him a wad of crumpled cash.

Unsure why, I say, "You don't know how much it's going to be yet—" and before I can finish, her tongue is in my mouth.

She comes up for air, makes eye contact with the driver via the rearview. "There's $200 there for you to drive. *Just drive.* Nothing. Else. Got it?" He must because before I know it, Mackenzie has my cock out.

Not a typical day. Not even for me. Calmly I ask, "What are you doing?" Instantly, she's got her finger over my lips, telling me not to talk.

Softly she whispers in my ear, "What you did back there. That was the hottest thing I've ever seen." Now she's tonguing my ear, stroking my shaft. A seductive whisper, "I've never wanted you more than I do right now." Just like that, I'm inside her. Twenty minutes later, the driver pulls up to some apartment complex. Safe to assume this is where Mackenzie and Daivey will be living. I had arranged a place farther south. Planned on staying in a cheap motel for a few days first. Change of plans. Getting used to improvising.

We step out of the cab and into the front office. She tells some dude inside who she is. They've been expecting her. A few signatures and they hand her some keys. I'm dragged by my right hand outside to apartment 314.

"Like pi," I chuckle to myself.

Mackenzie hears it though. "Almost like that. Except pi is never-ending." She doesn't need to finish that thought. Her look says it all. *Never-ending, like all the sex we're about to have.* The weirdest thing? I'm thrilled by the prospect.

For the next four hours, we fuck in every room of a nearly empty apartment. It's furnished with a couch, coffee table, pair of end tables, and a TV stand.

We do it in the kitchen, living room, bathroom, both bedrooms. Even the closet. I love every second of it. For the first time in my life, I'm not tolerating sex.

I'm loving the shit out of it.

So much sex, we're both about ten pounds lighter. Sweat it all out in water-weight alone. She's on top of me, appearing to enjoy it more than is humanly possible. There's a sharp pain in my groin. Always with the ball squeezing. Not sure what it is about crushing my scrotum, but Mackenzie loves to do it.

"Easy!" I yell. More ferociously than intended.

She doesn't get defensive. Doesn't say a word. Just stops what she's doing, gets off, lies next to me. With a quick kiss on the cheek, she wraps her arms around me, catches her breath, and looks me in the eye. Very sullen. "Ted?"

"Yeah?"

"I think I just felt a lump."

Her expression is all business. I nod. "OK, well first thing tomorrow, we'll get you a mammogram. I'll go with you."

Even more morose. "Not my boobs, Ted. Your balls."

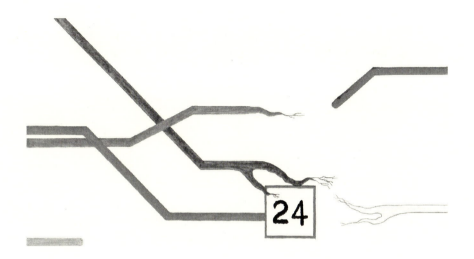

24

Manifestation.

Take a moment. Consider that word.

Does simply being in Las Vegas cause one to sin? Does this town take otherwise pious people and corrupt them? Or are sinful people drawn here? Some kind of hedonist magnet?

We've all heard the criticisms. Fake people. All about image. No substance. The list goes on. Be honest, similar words have left your mouth. Or at least floated around inside your head.

But most of the people in this club are from everywhere but here.

Call it fake. I say this is the most honest place I've ever been. Doesn't force anyone to do anything they don't crave deep down inside. Don't like alcohol? Simple. Don't drink. Think the dancers with the fake tits are compensating for various deficiencies? Then why are you wearing a dress three sizes too small? Face layered with more goop than a Betty Crocker recipe.

This town doesn't create anything false. Anything that rises to the surface while you're here, it was inside you all along. The catalyst to manifest it was simply never present.

Like surfing. Living in a desert, don't really get the chance. To the naked eye, you could say I hate it. Or maybe I never surf because I don't have an ocean.

Drop me near the Pacific, see how long I stay off a board.

Merely refraining from gambling because you live in Des Moines doesn't certify your proclaimed self-discipline. Only means there are no casinos.

So what brings you here?

You can tell me, it's OK. You love everything about it here. The booze. Gambling. Sex. You couldn't forget the sex if you tried.

Ubiquitous.

Overstating the obvious, but Las Vegas is full of attractive women. Most of whom you'll never sleep with.

Sorry. Did I shatter the illusion?

That's not to say none of the women here will fuck you in exchange for a cocktail and stock compliment. But it's atypical. Contrary to popular belief.

Just listen to some guys talk. Taking their word as bond, I'd say the average woman in Las Vegas has slept with well over four hundred men. Sure, some of them have. Suffice it to say, these numbers seem a bit skewed.

But they provide job security, so what do I care? Far from the best part though. They're so drunk, so pussy-whipped. Bastions of obliviousness. Makes my job super easy. Not my glorified busboy position. The term is *runner*, thank you. Of course I'm referring to slipping shit in their drinks.

No one notices anything. They set a glass down, I slip a pill in while picking it up. "Hey, I'm not done with that." Feign ignorance and give it back. If they get really pissed, I just get them another one from the bar. Even easier.

Candy from a baby.

Then there are the drugs.

Don't get me started on the drugs. Literally everywhere. Do you know how easy it is to slip foreign chemicals into some dude's coke? The white shit. Although the cola is easy too. At this rate, human life will cease to exist by Friday.

We've been here for three months now. Feels like three years. Feels like three minutes. That's how things work here. Time is irrelevant.

Daivey and Mackenzie make a killing at the bar. The plan is going far better than it should. Almost concerned. Murphy's law waiting to deliver a very rude awakening.

Mackenzie wasn't exaggerating when she said Daivey had connections. She seemed to know everyone here before we'd clocked in for our first shift. A charmer that one.

Our hotel is only a year old. New, even by Vegas standards. One grievance though. The restaurants. Likely delicious. Amazing cuisine. But the names—something's gotta be done about the names. There's Finestra . . . $$, Capelli Biondi . . . $$$, Cavallo Vecchio . . . $$$, and my favorite, Tavolo Ventotto . . . $$$$$ It's literally as if someone with a very basic Italian vocabulary named them. Just wrote a bunch of words on a wall and threw darts. Tavolo Ventotto means table twenty-eight.

Arguably the nicest restaurant in the country, it makes tons of money. Hand over fist. Reservations are booked eight months out. Minimum. The name is misleading. Despite having "table" in the title, there are actually only twenty-eight seats.

Very exclusive.

No one I've spoken with remembers the last time a tab came in under four digits. Worth every penny I've been told.

Sign me up.

Dillon doesn't work in the hotel, so he eats there all the time. Not because he's a celebrity from his porn days. He's a big-time gambler.

Let me rephrase.

He plays a lot of card games. "Gamble" actually implies some kind of risk on his behalf. I've literally seen him turn $5 into $10,000 in an hour. Local charities have never been so excited.

Defies logic. A sight to see. Funny thing is watching him lose on purpose. Doesn't want to arouse too much suspicion. No one is that good. He was once as arrogant as they come. A poster boy. No longer the case.

Dillon knows this town runs on arrogance. Most people think it's greed. Sure, the two are linked. They're not the same. People profit off greed anywhere you go. But arrogant people lose the most money gambling. For unknown reasons, they think odds don't apply to them. Think the house won't always win in the end.

They will. Without remorse.

You've got to be some kind of special dispshit to think the rules of mathematics don't apply to you. But I never tell anyone this. Bad for business. Just smile and nod. Tell them what they want to hear.

I've been doing an abnormally high amount of flattering for a Tuesday night. The place is packed. Sure, always busy. Not like this. Shoulder to shoulder. It's because Dwight Cumberland is the guest of honor.

Three months ago, he's just an average Joe. Then flight 194 came into the picture. Dwight is the guy who single-handedly prevented a terrorist attack. Saved the people on the plane and thousands more on The Strip. Remember, he knocked out those guys in the turbans? Put them to sleep. Restrained them. What a guy.

Funny how the blondes behind it all quickly became a footnote. Sure, they're in jail. Obstruction of justice. two thousand counts of attempted murder, plotting, etc. Sad thing, prison is an improvement to their standard of living. Having been bought and sold in the sex trade most of their lives, that plot was their ticket out. Some loaded dude from Georgia (the one by Russia) who hates America is behind it all. Promised them enough money to buy their freedom if they pulled this off.

As for the guys I falsely arrested, they're in the software business. Pretty loaded. Just closed some deal in Chicago, ready to celebrate in Sin City. Seems the three blondes seduced them at the airport, slipped all kinds of drugs and chemicals into their headgear. If they make it through security, their plan goes ahead. They get busted? Oh well. Back to turning tricks. Only way to go is up.

Pretty sure Dwight still thinks the Taliban was behind it. A good ol' boy if ever there was one. But truth be told, I owe him a great deal of gratitude.

He took any potential pressure off me. I went on with my plan. He ended up on every talk show in America.

A book deal too.

I'm not jealous. Just a bit annoyed. He's milking this a bit much. Tonight being the third blowout party in his honor in as many weeks. Dwight's a looker. Helps with marketing. He's got that going for him. Nice enough guy. But enough is enough. He's had his time in the spotlight.

In the future, everyone will be famous for fifteen minutes. And obsolete every second after that.

Oh well. Did you really think the guy who painted soup cans was that reliable?

Dwight and his entourage occupy most of the second floor. He's the one smothered in tits. Time to make my rounds. I grab empty glasses. Wine, shot, pint—you name it, they're drinking it. Delicately balanced, I carry them away like it's an act in the circus. I head back immediately; the glasses keep piling up. No rest for the wicked. Or their livers.

I pick up some random trash. Napkins, straws, limes and lemons. Lucky day, plenty of syringes everywhere. Needles are the new must-have accoutrement. Douchebag is the new black.

Reaching for an empty ice bucket, the melted water contains a prize. A pair of used condoms. Not sure how to react. Disgusted is one thought. Confusion sets in though. Didn't know people still used these things. Must be collectors' items by now.

For a fraction of a second, I'm almost tempted to slip them the vaccine. Reward them for a sliver of responsible behavior. But where's the fun in that? This Dwight guy shoots me a knowing wink. Drunk as shit but coherent enough to know who I am. I can't out him without putting myself in the spotlight. He knows this. Taking full advantage, sounds like now is the perfect time for that complimentary bottle of the most expensive champagne in the house. You know, the one reserved for honored guests? Fortified with "vitamins."

I drop off the trash and empty glassware. Return with a magnum of BonSoir, already opened and laced with my handiwork. No one seems to notice. One of the well-endowed cocktail waitresses shows. Starts pouring flutes, I pass them out. Give Dwight the first glass.

"Here you are, sir. Just our way of saying thank you."

Barely acknowledging me, too focused on the three backsides in his face, he downs the drink in one gulp.

I hope the classy dame with the velvet thong doesn't dream of motherhood. Attempting to blend in, I pop a fresh beer in the middle of the crowd. Can't let Dwight have all the fun.

How does that phrase go?

When in Rome. Go for the jugular.

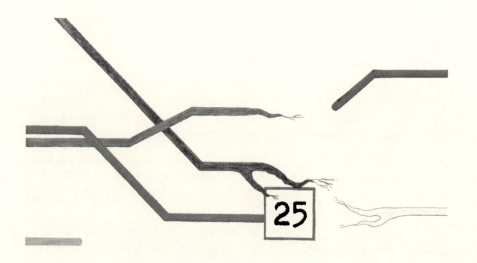

No one likes gridlock. Even on a good day, a rational man is driven to madness stuck on the freeway. Today doesn't fall under "good" days. Just left the urologist. Biopsy results are in.

Testicular cancer.

The great ironies of life. Funny, aren't they?

Most people pray for world peace. An end to hunger. Relief for flood victims.

Me, I prayed for cancer. A few decades ago, but still.

Good things come to those who wait. If I wait too long, my cum's no good. The guy behind me is laying on his horn. Oddly enough, it's endearing. Reminds me of Chicago. Useless honking capital of the world. You'd expect NYC to have a claim. Thing is, their infrastructure is solid. Things get done. Cars move.

No idea behind the reason for the delay here. Road construction on I-15, always a safe bet. Lane restriction? I could only hope to be so lucky.

Honking that obnoxious horn, it's like a yawn. Contagious for no apparent reason. Everyone around me joins in the act. The guy in the Honda to my left, windows rolled up, but his lips are moving. Screaming at no one and everyone. Punching the horn. Literally. Smashing his fist into the steering wheel.

But for some reason, this does it. Thousandth time's the charm. It's like he's Moses, parting the Red Sea. Instantaneously, the road transforms from a parking lot to a . . . . wait. Never mind. False alarm.

He's still an idiot.

Not enough honks in the world to cure stupid.

Until now, I keep my cool, handling this rather well. The cancer. The traffic. Things could be worse. A lot worse. I could be the jackass in the car next to me. But then I look at him, and something snaps. I know nothing about him. He might be a great guy. A true intellect. Maybe he helps numerous charities.

No clue.

What I do know: I don't like him.

I flip on my turn signal. A complete formality. If anything, it stacks the odds against me. No one's letting me over. So I squeeze in. The wailing horns that ensue, they make the past ten minutes seem like yoga on the beach. Mr. Honda hates me. Sucks to be him. I've saved the best for last.

I pull my car a few feet into his lane. The tail of my car still hanging into the former pathway. The middle lane, my favorite. I creep halfway into the far left lane. Not all the way in, but far enough. Leave only three feet between my left headlight and the divider.

I put the car in park, kill the ignition, walk away. Very tempted to leave the keys on the seat. Wouldn't matter. No one's going to move it. Decide against it. To everyone looking on, I shrug and say I'm out of gas. No one's buying it. Oh well. What do they expect from me? I'm from Chicago. Get a fucking subway system and this wouldn't be an issue.

The guy in the Honda, his window is down, yelling at me. The obscenities blend together. Somehow, his voice gets louder the farther away I walk. Definitely the kind of guy who justifies rape based on a woman's outfit. Across three lanes, walking down an exit ramp, I can still hear him screaming.

I shake my head and laugh for the first time all day.

A bus stop sits at the base of the exit ramp. After a ten-minute wait, I get on the first one that comes. Ride it for fifteen minutes. Traffic flows better. Not by much. I get off the bus after covering three miles and change. Call Mackenzie, tell her where I am. Ask for a ride.

Her attention is divided. The mixture of a hair dryer and pop music combine forces to make her impossible to hear. Must be getting ready for work.

"I can't come and get you right now. I just got out of the shower, then I've gotta do my makeup." Her tone shifts. Frustrated to bubbly. "Hey, are you working tonight? It's gonna be pretty nuts. Some company bought out like half the club. You know that anyone who can afford that is gonna be dropping some major cash . . ." All I want is a ride. Doesn't look promising. I guess I'll just have to play the card.

Feigning stress, speaking very softly, I begin. "Um, yeah. I'm, yeah, I'll be at work tonight. Don't worry about the ride. It's just, you know, I just left the doctor." Mackenzie gives an audible gasp as it registers. "Just as we thought. It's cancer." Pause for effect. "But hey, I'll see you tonight. I'll just take a cab home and get a ride to the club." I hang up before she can respond.

Not more than ten seconds after the phone goes silent, I get a text from her. Says to meet her in front of the 7-11 on Sahara and Arville in fifteen minutes.

Works for me.

This isn't about getting a ride. I could take a cab. I could have Dillon pick me up. No, it's bigger than that. It's time for a conversation I've been dreading.

I make it to the convenience store in five minutes. Hop inside, grab a bottle of water. A bag of Skittles too. Mackenzie loves to taste the rainbow. Should diffuse her frustration with me just a bit.

Her car pulls into the lot promptly. Parks at the pump, says she needs gas. I put my hand up, stop her from paying. Use my card instead, hand her the Skittles. She wants to be upset. Does a good job at first, but can't hide it. Gives me a big hug. I think the word cancer scares her more than it does me. This isn't any big surprise. But still, just hearing it from a doctor's mouth—terrifying. Nothing can fully prepare you.

We're on the road. She's like a loving mother now. The rigid façade a distant memory. Asking me every other minute if there's anything I need. Anywhere I need to stop. Am I too cold? Should she turn up the A/C?

Come to think of it, there is something I've been meaning to do.

"Can we go to In-N-Out Burger?" Seems like everyone in the world worships this place. Claim they can do no wrong. I'll be the judge of that. Been in town for a while now, still haven't been. I'd say now is a pretty good occasion.

"No way!"

Taken aback. Her eager-to-appease attitude is short-lived. "What do you mean? You can't say no to me, remember?"

"Look, if you want some food, that's one thing. And I don't mean to overstate the obvious, but you have cancer. *Cancer*. We're not talking about some stupid head cold. You're a smart guy. With all of your scientific knowledge, you of all people should know how important your dietary choices are going to be in the coming months." I arch my eyebrows, but she goes on. "From here on out, it's spinach and okra. Cauliflower and eggplant. No dairy. No meat. That sure as shit means no In-N-Out Burger."

The thing is, I completely agree with her. I fully plan on shifting to a raw vegan diet.

After tonight.

I just want one cheeseburger. Or two, if they're as good as everyone says. I'm able to convince her. Not trying to put a morbid spin on it, but of course I compare it to a dying wish. Mackenzie is totally right. I tell her as much. Her genuine concern quite evident.

Just like that, it clicks. This woman is going to be a phenomenal mother. Certainly, I always knew that. Never doubted it for a second. Makes the looming conversation much more ominous, my stomach turning more knots than a bowl of pretzels.

This double-double and fries isn't doing much to help that. Definitely shouldn't have gone with the large shake. I'll be paying for that one later.

But it's so worth it.

Mackenzie sits there, sipping lemonade. Occasionally stealing a fry from my tray. Half my food eaten in utter silence. A standoff. See who will break. Who mentions the pink elephant in the room.

"How's the shake?" Mackenzie asks.

Guess I'll be the one to cave. "It's excellent. You want some?" I point the straw at her face. Shakes her head no. "Thanks for bringing me here. For picking me up too. And well, thanks for everything I guess." Am I scared? Absolutely. But really I'm more uncomfortable than anything. Hoping my melodramatic demeanor will put me at ease. I'm attempting to appear more distraught than I really am.

Her eyes start to water. Not what I was going for.

"OK, let's just talk about it." She raises her brow, wonders what exactly "it" is. Dropping my tone to just above a whisper. "Our deal, Mackenzie."

Her face has taken on a comical nature. She's chosen humor and sarcasm as her way to deal with this. An excellent foil for my histrionic approach. "What was our *deal,* Sam?" Her words nearly rip my head off. Without provocation. My pain is apparent. "Sorry, that was harsh."

"It's fine. Let's just start again, OK?" She nods. "What I mean is I know I promised to help get you pregnant. In the simplest terms, losing an entire testicle might complicate that." I judge her reaction. Unaffected. This is kind of common knowledge. I continue. "*But* the odds are still very good that it won't have a negative impact on my reproductive abilities. Honestly, we won't know for a while. The doctor says I could freeze some sperm. Not sure what good that would do. Either way, I just thought you should know."

Mackenzie's a smart woman. She knows all of this, is well prepared. Still, I expect some kind of reaction. But nothing. No way to judge her right now.

She scratches her head, cracks a sly smile. "Don't worry about it."

Her nonchalance is very unsettling.

"What do you mean by that? I'm telling you that I'm not up to the task at hand, which is kind of a big deal for me. I'm not exactly what you would call modest, and you're being very blasé about this whole thing."

She breaks out into laughter. Not hysterical fits, but loud enough to be heard across the room. Loud enough to piss me off. I get up, storming out. But she grabs my arm and sits me down next to her. "OK, OK. You're right. I'm sorry about that. But what I meant was, you don't need to worry about our arrangement anymore. I'm pregnant."

Just like that, everything is a blur. Images of me coaching baseball. Helping with homework. Making PB&J sandwiches. The next twenty years of my life condensed into a millisecond.

I'm terrified. I'm thrilled. Excited, nervous, annoyed. You name it, I'm feeling it. The one thing I'm not?

Apathetic.

Always assumed when Mackenzie gets pregnant, I would congratulate her. Give her a gift card at the shower, and that would be that. Now I'm not so sure. What is my role here?

"You mean I'm going to be a dad?" Looking at her stomach, I hug her. A genuine, comforting embrace. "Congratulations! This is awesome!"

She averts her eyes. Her discomfort has finally broken through. "Thanks! I owe you so much. I'm finally going to be a mom." Not full-on waterworks, but her eyes are tearing up. I hug her again. Can't help but feel slighted. She said nothing in response to me being a dad. Never part of the plan, but still.

Something feels off.

"Come on, let's get you to work," I say while gathering the trash.

She smiles at me, stands up, and lets out a groan.

"What's the matter? I thought we were cool."

"Not that. You and I are fine. It's just those kids over there," she nods to the back corner. Four kids with skateboards and clear cups. "They asked for water cups, but keep taking soda from the fountain."

She makes a valid point. As a restaurant owner, people doing this must make her irate. For all intents and purposes, it's stealing money right out of her pocket.

We head out; I hold the door for her, both sucking the last few ounces from our cups. That we paid for.

They're kids. Just being kids.

You're starting to sound like them.

Can't pay two bucks for a drink? Don't spend $400 on a phone.

Just then, I see it, and I snap. A kid their age, sitting outside, slurping on a cup he paid for. Shoes with holes. Probably hasn't bathed in days. Might be by choice. Hard to say with teenagers.

Mackenzie is getting in her car, putting on her seatbelt. Without uttering a word, I head back inside. She's calling after me. I remain silent. One quick movement, I'm inside, grab two skateboards in stride, and am back outside. Smash the first one over a metal railing. Set the second one on adjacent benches, straddling it. The kids are outside, pissed off but silent. Mouths wide open. Eye contact. I stare the tall one closest to me right in the eyes as I chop the board in two.

I walk up to them. They were annoyed at first. Now simply terrified. Open my wallet, throw fifty dollars at them.

"Here's some money for the boards. I know that won't buy you two complete decks, but just use the cash you saved not paying for soda to cover the difference."

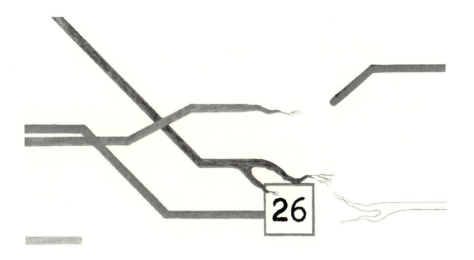

26

Disagree with me all you like. Some things are irrefutable.

Whatever anyone tells you. No matter the size of your paycheck. One axiom remains.

You. Are. Dispensable.

No matter what you do for a living. No matter how difficult or important you think you are to your job. I assure you, you're not. You can be replaced. The world will not stop spinning without you. Don't cry. Of course your family and friends will miss you. They will mourn your passing. Deservedly so.

But your job. This career you consider to be your essence. That you feel entitles you to more than everyone else. That you assume no one else can perform to your level. Think again.

Ancient cultures accomplished far more than you will ever comprehend, with much less technology. Who you are. What you have. The resources available to you, all the result of several thousand years of human innovation. Sure, you created some fancy computer program that simplifies doing your taxes. Not brand-new technology, but the best there is. Congratulations. You're the first person in the history of the third millennium to excel with computers. But you want your payday.

You deserve it. You worked hard. Put in the hours. What you've done will help people. Never stopping to trace the origins of their accomplishments. So you're good with technology. But computers needed Internet, which needed phone lines, who needed Alexander Graham Bell, who really just improved on the telegraph. Samuel

Morse, he was just tired of waiting for the mail to arrive. Pony Express my ass. Horses are majestic creatures, but grace can't compete with speed. The Postal Service thrived from a need to communicate across large distances. If everyone lived in walking distance, they fold. Thank you, Andrew Jackson and Westward Expansion. A new frontier. Thank you Christopher Columbus for having horrible navigation skills. Without you, Sitting Bull and company might have just played lacrosse all day. He needed boats. Vessels don't build themselves. The product of thousands of hours of sweat and manual labor. A combination of innovation and exploitation.

You get the point. Trace anything you've ever done back far enough, you arrive at day one. Cavemen, dinosaurs, Adam and Eve. Whatever you believe. That's up to you.

What do I believe? Simple. I'm far superior.

Disagree all you like. Names and insults are rolling around in your head. Therein lies your problem. All words. No action. At least there's unity in numbers. But remember this: the demented actions of one are far more powerful than the righteous intentions of an overwhelming majority.

So after all that's been left for you, what will you leave for the generations to follow?

If you answered "Uh" to the previous question, it's a miracle you've made it this far.

I'm finishing up my Coke and orange, ready to clock-in and prepare for the night ahead. Push in my chair, startled by a loud cheer behind me. Soccer game on the television. More than twenty people nearby watching the match. Roughly the same amount watching basketball on the opposite side of the room.

The soccer side full of people in light green shirts. The other side, the basketball side—everyone else. Bellmen. Valets. The guys complaining that $750 a day is "scraping by."

Oh, the workforce.

Can only dwell on it so long. Can't be late for work. Not just anyone can do what I do. Stanchion placement is an exact science after all. Not meant for the weak of heart. More importantly, there's some big party tonight. Mackenzie says it's a huge deal. The launch of a new energy drink. I toss my trash and leave.

The walk down the hallway is quick. There in no time. Everyone huddled around, waiting for assignments and general notes for the day. More of us than usual. Our managers Miguel and Naomi arrive. The chatter subsides. I get assigned to Kylie's section. Could be worse. She's never happy to be here. Overcompensates with a smile so wide it must hurt. Been avoiding it, but tonight I'll have to slip something in her energy drink. Way too tense. Coming from me, that's saying something.

Miguel says that half the tables have been reserved by some corporation for a huge party. Confirms the event is to promote some new trendy beverage. The company name sounds familiar, but doesn't stick. Dollar signs sparkle in everyone's eyes

Finally, Naomi asks all the girls to assemble for a picture. They fall in line without question. Do this all the time. Usually spontaneous. Not sure why our boss asked them.

The flash goes off; they take another. Naomi says, "Mackenzie, come here and gimme a hug, girl. We're gonna miss you so much!" They embrace. All the other girls join in. Eventually, Mackenzie emerges from the pile. Her gaze catches mine. Shoots me a weird glance and quickly walks away.

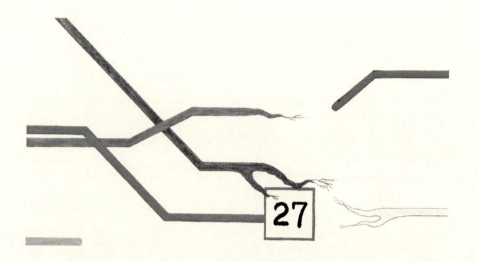

27

The doors open at ten. At 10:01 p.m., I can tell this night will be a thorn in my side. The chances of getting some one-on-one time with Mackenzie are slim at best. People slowly trickle in. Not for lack of interest. The doormen are taking their sweet-ass time. Checking IDs takes a matter of seconds. A task elongated by the endless parade of tits. Distractions at every turn. The first patron is through the door, every waitress plasters on a smile. Kylie's in her element. How do people do this night in, night out?

Within an hour, it's wall-to-wall with people. Breathing proves to be a chore in itself. Never mind just moving around. Forget it. If they're bothered by it, they hide it well. The stock room is flooded by voiced frustrations about the dickheads at table 9. Complaints that quickly go by the wayside. Three hundred percent gratuity will have that effect. We've still got six more hours.

#hooray

All the girls are great at putting on a show. Most hate their jobs but love the money. Some actually adore everything about this place. See Daivey. Tonight at least, Mackenzie is neither. Seen her for thirty seconds. Cumulatively. Something's eating her up. I try not to jump to conclusions.

The DJ takes a break from doing whatever they do. Spinning? Shuffling? His index finger needs to rest.

No one seems to notice. The music goes on. Pretty sure the same song has been playing all night. Or some variation of it.

I grab empty glasses, none of which stack. All different shapes and sizes. Some covered in smudged lipstick. No condoms—yet. I find a rare walkway and dart for the kitchen. So close. Out of nowhere, I'm bumped from the right. Knocked right into some guy. Spills wine all over his suit and shirt.

I am expecting a verbal onslaught.

"Oh shit! I am *so* sorry dude," I explain. I might hate being here, but even I can appreciate a finely crafted suit.

Gives me a stern look like he's about to flip out. But just like that, he shrugs and laughs. Turns back to his friends.

I breathe out. Relieved. Continue on toward the kitchen. After two steps in, someone grabs my shoulder. I turn around to face him. My eyes can't meet his. They're drawn to that shirt. And that tie. With massive stain covering the front. Beet red. On the verge of a second apology, I'm interrupted as my mouth begins to form the words.

"Just don't let it happen again. Got it?"

His words. His tone. They cut me down. He's drunk. I get it. People exaggerate and magnify their emotions. But something about his tone. It's chilling. This time my eyes meet his. My jaw drops. Frozen in terror. I simply nod, mouth a very quiet "Got it," and race for the kitchen. Feeling like Moses, people step aside. They're instincts reading my mind. Sensing the urgency.

A momentary blackout, and I'm in the kitchen. Cups in the dishwasher. A pair of barbacks stares at me. Freaked out like they've just seen a ghost. Can only imagine what I must look like. They shrug and turn away. Just another guy having a rough night. Nothing they haven't seen a million times before. Nothing vital enough to distract them from their lines of blow. Sucks to be them. Hope they never dreamed of being parents. Fuck away young ones. Consequences are so 2010.

"You guys should probably wait until you get home for that," I tell them. Not because I really care. If they want to destroy their brains, fine with me. More validation for my cause. Really, I just want to be alone. Collect my thoughts. Composure is key. They leave. Those kegs can't change themselves.

Or maybe they can.

Is there an app for that?

I eventually return to normal. The panting and palpitations subside. Five minutes of solitude is interrupted by someone stomping in. It's Daivey; she looks pissed.

"Seriously. How fucking hard is it to grab a bottle of Johnnie Walker Blue Label?" She notices me, tones it down a touch. "Oh hey, Samuel. Sorry about that." I nod. It happens. "But I sent Todd in here for it. He didn't show up, so I sent in Jenny, and now I can't find either of them."

I say nothing. Just put my finger to my nose and sniff. She gets it. Not surprised at all. "Shocking," she says. Excessive sarcasm. Just can't get enough. Daivey grabs the pricey whiskey as well as a bottle of well vodka. As she makes for the club, she stops in front of me. "You OK?" she asks with great concern. "You don't look so good."

Too exhausted to pretend nothing is wrong. "It's a long story," I tell her. She must sense the gravity of the situation.

"OK, let me go drop these off. I'll have Michelle cover me for a bit, and I'll be back in a few, OK?" I nod. "Ok. Be back in a minute." She rushes out the door.

I pour myself some tap water. Surprisingly, it helps a lot. Gradually, I calm down. Ready to head back to work, I check myself in the mirror. With a deep breath, I reach for the door. Had I been any closer, I would have a broken nose. Luckily, the distance was precise, as if calibrated. I'm able to react and block the door.

"Oh, wow. Babe, are you OK? I can't believe I just did that. I am so, so, soooo sorry, Samuel." It's Daivey, obviously in a rush.

I'm shaken up yet again. "It's fine, Daivey. It was a close one though. I should probably ask you if *you're* doing all right now. You seem a bit flustered."

Her eyes, big and shiny. Like the disco balls above the dance floor. She's stunned. In a good way.

In a daze, she says, "Yeah, I'm fine." Shakes her head. "Actually, I'm better than fine. Some guy just ordered a bottle of Henri IV Dudognon Heritage." She says this like it's standard. Happens every day. Sure, selling a bottle of the most expensive cognac in the world is status quo. Another day at the office. I don't like where this is going.

"Bullshit" is all that comes out.

"No, I'm serious! Can you believe it?" she screams, jumping up and down.

"Really? You mean someone ordered a bottle of alcohol that *retails* for TWO. MILLION. DOLLARS? I don't even want to know what the markup on it is."

"I know! I didn't believe it at first either. I looked at him and laughed. Just thought he was being a smartass. He didn't budge. Just handed me his credit card. AMEX Black. I ran it, and it cleared."

"Well then, I guess you better get going. If I were dropping that kind of money on anything, well, I wouldn't like to be kept waiting." She nods, agreeing. "I hope he tipped you well," I add jokingly.

Her eyes get even bigger. Tell me all I need to know. "Oh yeah, I might just retire off this night alone. But that was the weirdest thing. I mean, I know this place is full of loaded corporate types. But he looked so sloppy."

"How do you mean?"

"Well, obviously I get a lot of drunk people ordering from me. I've developed a thick skin for that. But the way he carried himself. And his tie was so weird. Here's this guy with a $7,000 suit, and he's wearing a necktie with a DNA helix on it, and there's little microscopes scattered around it." On the verge of vomiting, my worst fears substantiated. I don't even bother correcting her. DNA is a double helix. Even at my worst, I'm a perfectionist. She goes on, paying no attention to my lack of pigment. "But the worst part was his shirt." Here we go. "It had a huge wine stain on it. Now granted, lots of drunk people gathered together in a crowded place, these things are bound to happen. But he didn't even seem to care. I don't think he even tried to clean it up."

I rush to the trashcan. Too far, so I puke in the sink. Much worse. No desire to clean that up. Oh well. I purge my system, drink more water. I find some air-freshener. Short-term solution, long-term problem.

Awkward silence. Daivey breaks it. "Wow, are you OK?"

I shoot her a wicked glance. "What do you think?" Immediately, I feel bad and apologize. She understands. "I guess this whole Mackenzie thing is really taking its toll, huh?"

I feel like an idiot. How did I not consider that possibility? Surely, on some level, that's affecting me. Subconsciously, this contributes. But it's not the main cause. "Well, that's *part* of it."

She expects me to continue. That's all that comes out. Eventually, Daivey breaks the silence. "Umm, so, what is the real problem?"

I spit in the sink. Trying to get the taste out of my mouth. Another deep breath. "You know that guy who just bought the $7,000,000 bottle of cognac?" She takes her thumb, points upward. More than that? Oh my. "Anyway, that guy. I think he's my son."

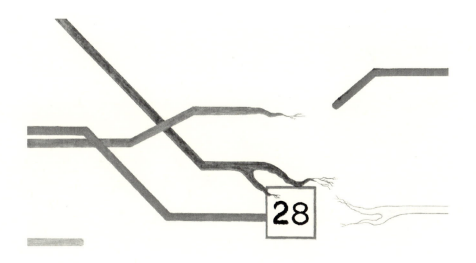

28

My life is quickly becoming a shit-storm. You put so much stock in knowing everything. Having all the answers. Never fully equipped to handle the variables. Confusion. Uncertainty. As I said: life will go on.

Put an asterisk next to this moment. The one that will make or break me. Do I go all-in or simply crawl away? Forget everything I worked for up until this moment?

My Achilles heel, also my greatest asset. That which shackles me also fuels my fire. My priorities now divided. Processing the information recently thrust into my life. Mackenzie is back in Chicago. Still haven't spoken to her. Businesses don't run themselves. I get it. The timing of her departure is still peculiar.

I still have Dillon. A ladies' man in every sense of the word. Even without the ability to talk, women are drawn to him. He'll gladly chat with all of them. Never sleeping with any. Not sure when the last time he got laid was. He's really into his faith now. Who knew that in the middle of this den of iniquity stood a massive Catholic church? Dillon goes at least twice a week.

Then he comes to the club and helps me with my dirty work. Gonna make a pretty great Catholic after all. He can get those women to do anything.

He buys them a drink. Quickly adds the magic. Repeat. Still thinks my main objective is to shut down cigarette companies. At least he shows no indication of questioning my objectives. I'm all for shutting down big tobacco. Though it's not high on my list of priorities. His passion certainly works to my advantage. I have no problem using that.

Sadie on the other hand, might. Dillon flipped out at Gumball Alley when that actor was smoking a joint next to a pregnant woman. Imagine how he feels about the fact that one of the club's cocktail waitresses is pregnant.

Not like a little bump. Like thirty-two weeks.

Turns him red with rage when he sees her walking around the smoky club. Not an issue of morality. He doesn't care if she's married and planned it or got knocked up from a one-night stand. Just doesn't approve of all the secondhand smoke.

Seeing her makes me uncomfortable, too. Just different reasons.

Pregnant women have no business in food service. The only thing worse might be a gestating stripper.

They might serve alcohol, but they're selling fantasy. Men tip them absurd amounts of money on the slimmest chance they *might* sleep with them. No one is attracted to damaged goods. I find their exchanges hilarious. Dillon does have a great heart. Looking out for her best interest. A crusade to stomp out smoking. Good for him.

But I know Dillon. He's the smartest man the world has seen in a long time. Didn't put it to the best use. But a genius nonetheless.

He might be on to me. My real motives. With the way he just knows everything, I wouldn't doubt it. Conceals it well. But in his mind, he owes me. I saved his life, gave him a second chance. If only everyone else saw it that way.

Daivey seems to view it that way, at least. Her help invaluable. After serving up that absurd bottle of cognac, she came back and calmed me down. Helped me clean up the puke. I laid out the cause of my frustration. Told me she wanted to help.

She went above and beyond. A guy leaves a $100 tip on a glass of wine, feels he deserves to get laid. Imagine what a guy who tips seven figures feels entitled too. She fucked him that night. Can't say I blame her. As weird as I find that, it needed to happen. The things she learned as a result of his drunken logic are huge.

Game-changing. Stomach-turning. Life-threatening. Seriously.

When I looked into his eyes, panic consumed me. They didn't change color like mine do. It was a gut instinct. Something I can't explain. A striking resemblance to Krystal Madigan. The girl I lost my virginity to. A one-time thing so long ago. Unpleasant and awkward. You never forget your first time.

And then I replay that night in my head again. Fumbling with the condom, starting to put it on backwards. A bead of cum gave signs of what's to follow. I got my head on right, put the rubber on correctly. Was there spermicide on it? Was that little drop of knob sauce all it took to make me a father? The odds? Staggeringly small.

But as Mom and Dad always said, nothing is impossible. It gets worse.

Get enough drinks in a guy, he starts talking. Put a naked chick on his cock, he practically gives up his identity. But he knew better. Didn't answer all of Daivey's questions. Said enough to make me worry.

Most importantly, his name is Cooper Madigan. So yes, the odds that he is Krystal's son are high. Desperately hoping he's a nephew, but I know better. The math works out too. She and I were kids. So young. Even though Cooper could pass as a high school student, he's twenty-three. Daivey's seen his ID. I'm thirty-eight. I was fourteen when Krystal and I slept together. The nine months for pregnancy fills in the gap.

But that's all boring exposition. Shit you can find on the Internet. I wanted to know what this guy has to do with some new energy drink. According to Daivey, he's got quite a bit of clout at Inizia.

A small offshoot of one of Nicky Salcedo's moneymaking machines. The plot thickens. Before I fled the States, energy drinks were everywhere. Then they got a lot of bad press. Too many college kids mixing them with alcohol and cough syrup. Reports which conveniently failed to mention that LSD and cocaine were often part of the equation. Either way, the FDA cracked down.

Daivey said Cooper wasn't too vocal about the specifics but said he bragged about getting around some red tape. Never made a specific reference to who, where, or when. But at some point in their conversation, he spoke of the Smithsonian.

As in Washington, D.C.

My mind races back to my visit. When we bumped shoulders on the street.

What was he doing there? Immediately, I assumed he was bribing people. Get this drink approved and on the market. Not out of the question. The jury's still out.

The final gem, icing on the cake. A nice little ribbon to complete this awesome little present. After they finished screwing, Daivey laid down to fall asleep. Cooper told her to leave. He'd paid her, gotten what he wanted.

She wasn't exactly heartbroken. Not like she even liked the guy. But she was tired. Just wanted to sleep. Told him she wasn't some hooker. He couldn't treat her like that.

A drunken slur, as it was relayed to me, "Darling, I might not have paid you directly to sleep with me. But we both know what this was. I gave you a massive tip, and you fucked me. Sugarcoat it all you want, but you're a whore." Daivey was fuming, got dressed as fast as she could. Just wanted to get out, get home, and shower off the filth.

She flung the door open, ready to storm out. Cooper interjected. "Babe, don't worry about it. Prostitution is gonna be the norm anyways. In a few months, it'll just be a normal job like bartender, or one of those guys who dresses up like Santa Clause at the malls around Christmas time."

Her first instinct: get pissed off. Be offended at his casual attitude. His poor humor. But she told me something about his tone; it was off. Like what he was saying wasn't a joke.

No clue what to make of that. He was a drunk dude who'd fucked some girl he just met and wanted to get rid of her. Hardly a first. Not exactly a guy whose state of mind can be given too much credibility.

I head to the coffee shop down the street. Need something strong. I down the espresso in seconds. Order another along with a latte. Pound the second espresso, grab a seat on a couch. Slowing my pace, sipping the latte.

Some guy comes in, orders, sits across from me. Opens up a newspaper. Initial reaction is shock. They still print newspapers. They're antiques. Thought they'd gone the way of the walkman and proper grammar. But here one is, right in front of me.

Business section.

Sports.

Food and entertainment.

He folds it up, lays it on the table between us. Heads through the door without it. I'm about to do the same, but I pick up the paper just for fun. Like I'm holding an ancient relic. I flip through it casually. Nothing too interesting happening.

Grab the main section. Front page. It's not the headline, but still major news. There at the bottom, the heading sheds some light on what Cooper said. Read through the article once for general comprehension. Then again for the fine points. One final time for good measure.

Heart beating faster, I try to digest what I'm reading. Surely my assumptions and accusations don't have lots of backing yet. Just met the guy. But this article, it changes things.

I sit for another twenty minutes. Pondering. Debating. Try to make sense of it all. I want to know why and how, with the most overwhelming dominance the Republican Party has enjoyed since the end of the Civil War, they are on the verge of passing a bill limiting the number of children a mother is permitted to birth.

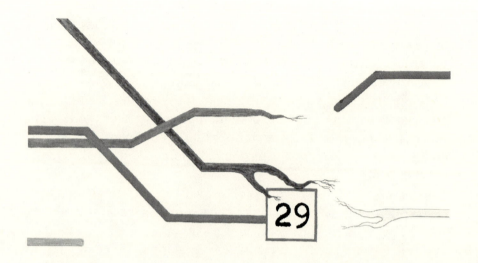

29

The bone-chilling winter Chicago wind has never felt so nice. By my estimate, Mackenzie is six months pregnant. Haven't spoken to her since Las Vegas. Our time out there was productive, but it's time to get back. Fingers crossed, she'll be at Gumball Alley when Dillon and I are done with confessions.

Even without the ability to speak, Dillon has a way with words. Somehow convinced me to go to church with him. Fact of the matter is I have plenty of reasons I *should* feel remorseful. I'm not sure which is worse. The things I've done or the fact that I don't feel bad about them. Almost as if the demon inside started as a seed. Each deviant act I commit is like water and sunlight. Making the seed grow. Bigger. Stronger. Past the point of no return.

I should feel bad. I want to feel bad. I just don't feel.

Whether or not I agree with Dillon in matters of faith and the ethereal, church has an undeniable calming effect on me. Puts things in perspective. I question my motives, put my ego on trial.

But in the end, I always acquit.

A man who represents himself has a fool for a client . . . unless you're me. Gotta love life's little caveats.

I finally understand why people in power go overboard. Once you get a taste, you're hooked more than any drug ever made. It's only the people who have never felt control that blaspheme it. Put in a position to exploit, they'd do the same thing. Turn down every dream and thing you've ever wanted, then we'll talk. Of course you can lecture me about the banality of things like power. You want what I have. Until you've given and saved life, as well as taken it, you will never understand me.

Not proud of it. A definite last resort. If there were one thing I would confess, that would be it. Up in the air.

Did I enjoy it? No.

Did I feel a rush unlike anything I've ever experienced? Absolutely.

Are the two one and the same? Possibly.

Surely there are things you've wanted to do. Things you'd never have the bravado to attempt. But in your mind, you pull it off flawlessly.

Robbing a bank. A bit extreme, but you've thought about it.

Hopping a turn-style on the subway. A little more your pace. Hardly a felony. But enough to make you feel like a cheater.

Ordered the most expensive bottle of wine on the menu, tasted it, and sent it back. Adrenaline coursing through your veins.

You're at a movie theater. The dude three rows down won't shut up. Never-ending commentary you could do without. You grin and bear. Perhaps make a shushing sound. I dump the largest soda I can find on his head.

Ever parked in a handicap spot just because? OK, even I won't do that. But I'll bet it's a rush.

The list goes on and on.

Add to the list "killed a man."

Must reiterate. I didn't do it just to know what it felt like. But yes, I've wondered for a long time what kind of sensation it would ignite.

It all started when I spilled a soda in this guy's lap. Purely accidental this time. The guy at the movies decked me. Completely unrelated. I was working a day job at a Taco Bell drive-through. Seems weird, right? My only regret is that I didn't think of it sooner. I have access to people's beverages. They don't see me prepare them. They come in a cup, not a bottle. Most importantly, people who use drive-throughs annoy the shit out of me.

Global warming and depleting fuel sources don't concern me. My carbon footprint would put Shaq to shame. People never shut up about how expensive gas is. Their solution? To use as much of it as possible for the most mundane activities possible. Some cities need them. Not Vegas. Their three largest cash crops are sand, strippers, and parking lots. An average of seventeen asphalt slots per capita.

Suffice it to say, the world of the future needs people who don't mind walking a few extra feet and standing in line. Relax, I didn't slip the pill to everyone. Just most of them.

But I digress.

So I accidentally spilled a soda on this guy. He flips out, says he'll come back later to talk to my manager. I tried to look concerned. The Emmy goes to…not me. Gave him some napkins, he was on his way. Tires squealing.

Never heard from my manager. But, two nights later, at the club. Who should I run into but angry soda-pants. Three sheets to the wind. So drunk he doesn't notice me. The night goes on. He dances. Drinks. Slurs random pickup lines to anything with two X chromosomes. Strike 15. Admire his persistence I guess.

A normal night at work. Picking up glasses. Mopping spills. The sun is peaking out over the mountains. People slowly trickle out, but the place is still packed. He's on a couch. Awake, but barely. Doing my rounds, a drunken bachelorette party knocks me to the side. I step on his shoes. It gets his attention, and he's fully awake.

Looks down at his shoes. A pristine pair of white Nikes. Well, except for the desecration I just stamped on his kicks. I apologize, to no avail. His eyes are wide with rage. Then it clicks. Recognizes me from Taco Bell. Winds up to take a swing. I dodge it enough to avoid a hit to the face, but I drop everything. Shattered glass goes everywhere. Security is on him before the last shard stops bouncing. He's out the door, sent on his way. A smart person would sleep it off, maybe buy a new pair of shoes.

He never struck me as the logical type. Waits for me to leave work. I'm sure in his inebriated state he was very stealth. Not quite. I knew he was there the whole time. Followed me to the garage. Either too drunk to drive, or to find his car, I'm tailed in a cab all the way home. I park, get out, go inside. Less than two minutes later I'm startled by a pounding on the door I knew was inevitable. Fight or flight I guess.

Initial reaction, call the cops. Maybe grab a kitchen knife. Fuck that. Run to the door, throw it open, pull the dude inside. So drunk he can barely stand, falls immediately to the floor. I would love to paint an image of some amazing action film fight sequence. It was nothing like that.

Before he can react, I pull him off the floor. Position myself behind him, sedate him using proper pressure points on the earlobe. No resistance. I snap his neck.

Grab a shower, a sandwich, and call a cab to take me back to work. Scour the garage up and down until I find his car. Black BMW. 2019 model. Middle console still sticky with soda. Drive back home, throw the dead man in the trunk.

Cruise downtown, quarter-mile from the Palomino Club. Park it in the dodgiest place I can find, careful no one sees me abandon it. The sun now fully above the horizon. The only people awake at this hour are too drunk or high to credibly recount anything suspicious. Or they run bakeries.

Leave the door unlocked, but bring the keys with me. Find a spot to ditch them later. Regardless, this ride will be in a chop shop by lunchtime. Would love to see the reactions of the miscreant mechanics when they pop the trunk. Alas, my imagination will have to suffice. Walk two miles back the way I came, catch a bus.

Not pretty, but necessary.

Dillon pops out of the confessional, notepad and pen in hand. Nods his head at me, signals it's my turn. With great reluctance, I oblige him. Can't remember the last time I was in one of these.

The priest is behind a partition in the small room. I can kneel by it for privacy, or walk around for face-to-face interaction. Prefer to remain inconspicuous. Must hear my breathing, he encourages me, "Whenever you're ready, please begin."

I'm not telling him anything specific. I know they're bound to secrecy by their vows. Still, I'm skeptical.

After a long pause, I begin, "Um, bless me father for I have sinned. It's been over a decade since my last confession." I pause. Allow time for him to ask why the prodigal son has returned. Must be reserving comments for the end. I continue, "Um, so it's been a long time since my last confession. You're probably wondering why I've come back after all this time. I mean, ten or more years is plenty of time to rack up quite the list of grievances." Another uncomfortable pause. Met not with words, but the sound of his breath. A different approach. "You know, this is kind of weird isn't it? Kind of like giving a physics lesson to Albert Einstein."

"I'm sorry?"

"What I mean is, don't you find it odd? Listening to a confession from God?"

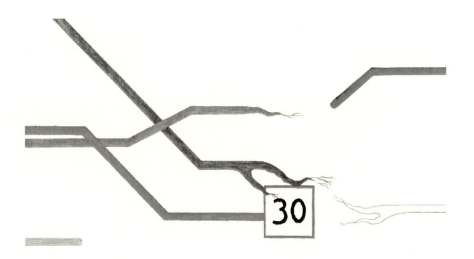

30

Gumball Alley looks just like I remember it. With minor exceptions. A couple of the sculptures and paintings are gone. Not enough to be considered a remodel. She does this a lot. Must have a gallery opening or exhibit to go to. Shows some of her work off, maybe get new clients. Everyone there is giving me the runaround. Like they've never heard of Mackenzie Desjardins.

I'm about to order a pizza when I see a poster for an exhibit at Navy Pier. It opened yesterday. Goes on for the next three days. Bingo. I'm out the door and in a cab to Navy Pier with a rare smile on my face. Lake Shore Drive is a virtual parking lot. Not in the mood to be patient, I tell the driver I'll give him $50 for every minute before 5:00 he gets me there. I tell him this at 4:42. At 4:48, I hand him $600. Not sure which tally is higher. The cab fare or number of traffic laws he broke. Ride the shoulder for miles. Put it on the list of things I've always wanted to do.

I follow the signs all the way to the end of the pier. The gallery is upstairs in convention hall B. Mom and Dad took me here years ago for some science exhibit. Always seem to come full circle.

I pay my entrance fee and head up the stairs. The room is twice as big as I remember it. Paintings, photographs, and sculptures seem to stretch for miles. A collection of countless hours that will lead to nothing. Not fame. Certainly not fortune. Rationalizations like "I do it because I love it," or "art is good for the soul." They can lecture me all they want about how art gives meaning to life. Provides inspiration. Soothes the soul.

That's all well and good. So why does the guy selling an aluminum cast sculpture for $125,000 not strike me as someone whose soul thirsts for pursuits majestic? The craftsmanship is solid. The body of a horse with the head of a chicken. Don't make the mistake of asking him to explain it. What took him thirty-seconds to conceive in a drunken stupor will evolve into a twenty-minute diatribe.

Aluminum is pricey, I'll give him that. We're talking maybe $4,000 worth of materials. The hours and labor involved? Give or take 140. Plus or minus a few minutes. By those calculations, he's charging around $860/hour for his labor. So tell me why so many artists haven't showered in months.

Most of the people here will ramble about saving art programs in schools. Lecture your ear off for buying from corporations when so many creative and talented people can make you something unique.

Eye roll.

One more time for effect.

Evil corporations and government. Raking in the dough, not providing for citizens. Making health care so expensive. How dare they take a fundamental human right and make it virtually inaccessible to most.

Look in the mirror.

This art you have anointed. It's no different. The horse/chicken carver wonders why more people don't have art in their homes. The concept that most people don't make $860/hour is far beyond his comprehension. He and his colleagues are to blame. Taking something so allegedly precious, something they consider essential. Turning it into that which is virtually unobtainable.

But alas, I digress.

I consult the map and index. Mackenzie's booth is up three rows and to the left. I take my time. I've waited this long, no need to storm in like a lunatic. Peruse the work on display. Some if it's great. Most of it isn't.

Turning left, I immediately know where to go. It's a new piece I've never seen, but the style is blatantly hers. I walk slowly. No surprise, her stall is rather crowded. Not NYSE crowded, but certainly popular.

I stop a kid passing by in a Bears cap. "Kid, I'll give you twenty bucks for that hat." Looks at me like I'm speaking Dutch. "Thirty bucks for the hat," I tell him. I don't wait for a response, just take the hat and stick the cash in his palm. Looks at the cash like it's a bar of gold.

Very snug fit, but it will do. Just enough to disguise me from afar. I approach her booth slowly. Through the crowd, I see her seated on a chair. High backed, upholstered in red velvet. Wearing a sports bra, her baby bump is proudly on display. I get closer and see what the commotion is all about. Mackenzie is using her large belly as a canvas. Painting an image on herself. Even more impressive, the work is inverted from her perspective. The audience sees it conventionally.

A small smile slithers across my face, knowing that she's going to be a phenomenal mother. I squeeze between a few people to get a better look. Upon closer inspection, I recognize the facsimile. Everyone does. *The Creation of Adam*. God and Adam, fingers on the verge of touching. One of Michelangelo's most famous works from the Sistine Chapel.

Simply amazing. If I had a soul to soothe, this would do the trick. Can't get sentimental. Not now. Cautiously nudge my way to the front, head down. Very slowly, I begin to raise my head. Eyes just barely catch her face under the brim of my new hat. Minutes go by, I remain unacknowledged. She washes her brush out. Prepares to change colors, but drops it on the floor. She bends over to retrieve it. On the way up, her gaze meets mine. Gone in an instant, but I see the look of fear in her eyes. Still not sure what I did. But I'm here to find out. She goes on painting. Now noticeably distracted. Her eloquent demeanor replaced by stuttered sentence fragments. It goes on like this for a few more minutes until she needs a break. Tells everyone thanks for watching, she'll continue in half an hour or so.

Clumsily organizes her supplies. Not making a big deal, I slowly walk by her. Don't even look her in the eye. "Brewery downstairs. Twenty minutes."

"Forty," she says without missing a beat.

No point countering. A futile endeavor.

My eyes shifting constantly from the clock on the wall down to my phone. Back up at the wall. The longest forty-four minutes of my life. She's doing this on purpose. Making me squirm. Despite the fact it's driving me insane, I applaud her approach. So far I've been well behaved, downing bottles of water and Arnold Palmers. Obviously I'm not in her good graces. Greeting her in an inebriated state wouldn't help.

Finally, she arrives at last. Sweatpants and a hoodie. Total "I don't give a fuck what anyone thinks" outfit. Somehow she pulls it off. Pregnancy is a good look for her.

"Can we sit at a table instead of the bar?" That's her greeting. Didn't think hi was too much to ask for. Clearly, we're off to a great start. I oblige, and we take a table in the back corner. Isolated and poorly lit. Probably a good idea. The second I sit down, she heads back to the bar and orders orange juice.

Sits down, slurps half the glass through a straw in a matter of seconds. Staring at me. Burning a hole in my head with her stare. I want to brush it off. Laugh an uncomfortable laugh. Awkward smile. But she's a juijitsu master. I could probably take her. Stress on the "probably." But even without the baby, I wouldn't dream of harming here. So yes, I'm a little afraid of what she might do to me. Tread carefully.

"Well?" Tapping her fingers on the table.

"Well what?" Trying to diffuse the tension.

"What do you want?"

No use being coy. "Truthfully? I want an explanation. I haven't heard a word from you in months. You just left Vegas for no reason, as far as I could tell. I don't know what I did to make you this upset. I would love a chance to make things right, but I seriously have no fucking clue what is going on inside your head."

"I'm not upset." Downs the rest of her juice. Stirs the ice with her straw. "One minute," she says while getting up, returning to the bar. This time it's milk. Absolute torture. She sits back down, takes a small sip. Wipes her mouth with a cocktail napkin. This whole ordeal feels like some kind of acting exercise. Get a reaction without words. Somewhere out there, Sanford Meisner has a massive boner.

"I'm not upset with you, Sam." I wait for her to elaborate. Shocking, but she doesn't say another word.

"Well, um, OK. But if you're not upset with me, why haven't I heard from you in forever? Why are you practically ignoring me right now? I mean, we're about to have a fucking child together, and I feel like a stranger right now."

A vein twitches in her neck. It's instantaneous; she restrains herself. But there was a glimpse of a verbal lashing waiting to be unleashed. "Sam, I appreciate everything you've done for me." Looks me square in the eye, her demeanor finally softening. "Words cannot express how excited I am to finally become a mother. But you don't need to do this."

A conundrum wrapped in an enigma. "What do you mean I don't 'need to do this?' What exactly is 'this?'"

Another sip of milk. "What is that?" pointing at my glass.

"Arnold Palmer. There's no booze in it if you'd like some." She nods. Something dawns on her face that appears to not be outright angst. Mackenzie quickly downs the rest of it.

"Ted. I'm sorry, but for this conversation I'm going to call you by your real name." I don't interject, just nod. "We've been through a lot of shit together. I love you more than you'll probably ever understand. But you held up your end of the bargain. You knocked me up. Your DNA will carry on in this world. And you don't have to change a single diaper. You've done your job." Something about hearing the word "job" cuts deep. I've never been known as overly sentimental, but this hurts. Mackenzie continues. "I'd be lying through my teeth if I told you I didn't dream of us together. House in the suburbs. Raising a family. Christmas cards with hideous matching sweaters." We both shift uncomfortably in our chairs. "Look, I get it. You were never going to feel the way about me that I felt about you. It's taken me years to come to terms with that fact. I still have moments of weakness where I wish that could be the case. But I'm gonna be a mom soon, Ted. I have to think about *my* child." The stress on "my" stings more than expected. It must show. "Ted, come on. You never wanted this. I so desperately wanted you to want it, but I've got to face reality. You've gone your way, and I need to go mine. So long story short, that's why I left Vegas so abruptly. That's why you haven't heard from me in so long. I need to forget about you, and that seemed like the only way."

"So that's what you want? To never see me again? You're not even going to let me see a child that is also part *mine*?"

"You never wanted this!" Her voice instantly rises, but just as quickly calms itself. "You never wanted to be a dad, Ted."

Not my eloquent self, "Things change, Mackenzie."

"OK, let's just pretend for a minute you wanted to be a dad. Do you honestly think you're the kind of role model I would want influencing the upbringing of the child I gave birth to? Seriously, think about that. You hate people, Ted. You're trying to wipe out the human race. You believe there are few things worth saving. Make no mistake, I'll never forget all the amazing things you've done. But I want the Ted who saved lives, not destroys them." About to open my mouth to defend myself, I'm interrupted. She's on a roll. "I mean, I know you had a rough upbringing, and the whole deal with your aunt showing up unannounced. Shit is really rough for you. I haven't forgotten that. But that's not enough. You walk around like curing AIDS entitles you to do whatever you fucking want. Being a genius is a blessing and a curse. You deserve praise and all the accolades. But you also have a gift, and with that gift come the responsibility to help people. Not walk around like you're better than everyone else."

There it is. The phrase I wholeheartedly despise. Nothing infuriates me more than being asked or accused of thinking I'm better than everyone else. A purely loaded question. Can't win in this scenario. If I say I don't think I'm better than everyone else, I'm lying. If I tell them the truth, admit my egomaniacal leanings, I'm an asshole.

Just sit there, it's all I can do. Any response fuels the fire. But I'm dying to defend myself, and she can tell. Deriving immense pleasure watching me squirm. I don't blame her. I absolutely exploited her affections for me to advance my cause. I deserve this.

Getting up to leave, she says, "Are we done?"

If I were a romantic, had the soul of a poet, not a scientist, I'd grab her. Kiss her, never let her go. Tell her I'll change. That I can find the man she used to know. Give her everything she's ever wanted. The house. Soccer van. Fifteen-piece place settings. But I'm not that guy. Never will be. So I nod. We're done here.

"Let me walk you out." At the door, she turns, hugs me tighter than I've ever felt. Pulls back, kisses me one last time. Passionate. Insult to injury. Mouths, "Good-bye Ted," and walks away. Ten steps later, she stops on a dime. Turns back.

"Oh, Ted, how's your um, your . . . you know?" Points at her groin.

"Oh, been better. But I'm getting it removed in three days."

"*Getting* it removed? You still have it?" She's incredulous.

No good excuse for this. "I've had a lot on my mind" is all I can come up with.

One last time, she hugs me. No kiss. Whispers in my ear, "Speedy recovery. I'll be praying for you." Turns and walks away. Again, I should run after her. Epitomize every pop-culture cliché. But I don't.

I sit down at the bar. "Another Arnold Palmer, buddy?" the bartender asks.

"No, thanks. I'll take a Goose 312 and a shot of Bushmill's." Pours the beer. I drink half before he's even opened a brand-new bottle of Irish whiskey. Slides that my way. It's down my throat in the blink of an eye.

#Liversareoverrated.

Unfazed, he asks, "Want another one?"

"Yeah, make it a double. And you might as well just glue that fucking bottle to your hand. I'm gonna be here a while."

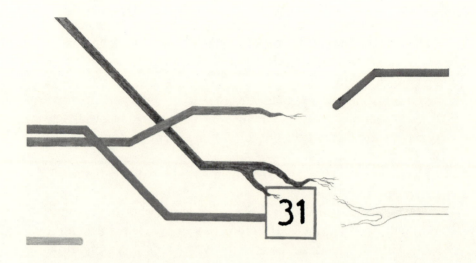

31

Slowly, her eyes open. The lids separating reluctantly, as if held together by rubber cement. I say nothing, just let her come to on her own. Takes longer than expected. Finally, she appears aware of her surroundings. But still very confused. Here's the thing: I remember every detail of last night.

This woman tied to a chair in my hotel room on the other hand, she has no recollection of the last sixteen hours or so.

You probably want me to rewind a bit.

That's fair.

Where to start?

Mackenzie walked away. With good reason. No argument there. But even those of us who avoid emoting at all costs still feel from time to time. I did nothing to stop her. Honestly, had I been able to change her mind, I would have lost respect for her. It pained me deeply to watch her go.

I'm far more comforted knowing my child is in good hands.

There. My sentimental bullshit for the day.

My emotional quota filled, I still left room for plenty of booze. I might have pissed upward of eight liters of urine out last night. Could still walk a tightrope without fail. Ever tried one of those "hangover prevention" pills? Most people have. Ever met anyone who said it actually worked? Didn't think so.

Not only am I not hung over, I barely felt a buzz. Alcohol distributors would either want me dead or make me king of the universe. My latest creation really could go either way.

Not exactly capable of handling the situation like an adult, I compounded my rage by drinking heavily. A boatless booze cruise for one. The ports of call: the Cubby Bear in Wrigleyville, JP's on Donleavy, the Goat Den on Belmont, and finally some place in Wicker Park called Pockets.

Yes, they have pool tables. But its name comes from the clientele. The guys who go there, very wealthy. Deep pockets. The women on their laps expect nothing less.

Not in the best of moods, I decided to play.

Martini in hand, I sit on a couch in the back corner. Low lit, but not clandestine. Anyone who spends $29 on a martini must have some extra cash. Maggie wanted to know just how much she could squeeze out of me.

"Hey, cutie, want a dance?" She manages to spit this out with a straight face. Impressive.

"I'm sorry, I had no idea this was a strip club."

Sitting next to me, she says, "Oh, it's not, sugar. You just looked like you could use a friend. Rough night?"

"You could say that. No offense, but I really don't want to talk about it with anyone. Definitely not a stripper."

She laughs it off. "Darlin', I'm not a stripper."

This leaves few options. Playing dumb. "So why did you offer me a dance?"

Once more, she giggles. "You are just too cute. This must be your first time in here, huh?" I nod. "See, we're not exactly allowed to say what we can and will do for you. It's just kind of implied. 'Dance' is code for . . . well, every guy is different. Oddly enough, blowjobs are the most popular. Watching us masturbate is gaining ground though. But some guys are just lonely. They just want to talk."

"Well, I appreciate the offer, but I'm not paying you to listen to my problems." I'm not sure what her rate is, but I feel confident it's substantially higher than any licensed therapist.

This time, she actually looks offended. Like she might actually cry. "OK, I get it. It's just that, I got a kid on the way, and my rent went up, and I don't know how much longer I can do this." The floodgates are opened. Either an excellent actor or this girl is far more disturbed than the stereotype implies.

As she sobs, I hand her a napkin to dry her eyes. "How much for a hand job?"

"What?" A glimmer of hope in her eyes.

"Go get cleaned up, and meet me back here in ten minutes. I wouldn't mind a tugger."

Just like that, the tears stop. She's good. A master manipulator. I can use a woman like this. The ethics of what are about to transpire don't bother me. Paying for something I can do myself. That unnerves me. Like hiring a world-renown chef to come to your house and microwave a frozen dinner.

Maggie is back, looking good as new. Sits down next to me, licks my ear, and puts her hand in my pants. Still, one thing eats away at me. "So, um, is your kid a boy or a girl?"

"Huh?"

"The kid you're working so diligently to care for. Is it going to be a boy or a girl?"

"Oh, um, I'm waiting for it to be a surprise." The lies pile up. I like it. But just then, I see a woman who is most definitely very pregnant approach a man at the bar. I squirm, for various reasons. Still can't get Mackenzie's belly out of my mind. More specifically, the intricate painting from earlier in the day.

Michelangelo. Master artist. Funded by the de' Medicis.

Most importantly, a thorough examiner of cadavers.

You will hate me for what I do next.

I pull her hand out of my pants. Place it back on her lap. Zip back up.

"Did you cum already?" she asks with surprise.

"No, but I was thinking we'd have a lot more fun alone. Like in a hotel room." She smiles. Dollar signs flashing in her eyes. "Meet me in the lobby of the Elysian Hotel in one hour."

Flirtatious, she says, "Why can't we just go across the street, baby? Don't make me wait so long." The act is getting annoying. Should have asked for two hours. Just to get away for a bit.

"I need to get some cash." Her eyebrows go up. "OK, I need to get *a lot* of cash." She winks in agreement, telling me that's more like it. "Great, well then I'll see you in one hour. Don't be late."

"Wouldn't dream of it, baby."

Out the door, I breathe in the crisp Chicago air. Refreshing is an understatement. I take a taxi back to my place, grab a wad of cash from my safe, throw some supplies in a bag, pull up to the lobby of the Elysian with ten minutes to spare. No sign of Maggie. I pay for a room under John Simon Ritchie. You might not mind the Bollocks, but I do. I sit and wait. Just when I think she's bailed, she struts through the door. Right on time. Very efficient businesswoman. She and I are going to get along just fine.

"I've already checked in. Shall we?" I ask while offering my arm.

"Absolutely," she replies, a hint of excitement in her voice.

We step into the elevator, insert my key, and push the button for Penthouse. I see her nostrils flare out of the corner of my eye. If she wasn't wet before, she is now. The doors open, revealing an assortment of couches, a wet bar, hot tub, and an amazing view of the most breathtaking skyline the world has to offer.

"Grab a seat, I'll pour you a drink," I say, walking her to the couch. "What would you like?"

Her all-business demeanor has vanished. She's like a kid in a candy store. The fervor in her voice betrays her. Whatever rigid exterior she had is now gone. "I'd love a glass of champagne. If you have it, of course."

"Please. If this bar doesn't come with at least a dozen bottles of Dom Pérignon, I'm demanding a refund." Open the fridge, pull out a bottle. Take two glasses hanging from above. Pop the cork and pour. "There you go, sweetheart."

She takes the glass and sips it. Attempting to look like she's done this millions of times. Any acting skills she had at the beginning of the night seem to have gone by the wayside. We'll work on that. We begin kissing. She grabs my head. "So what did you have in mind for tonight?"

"Oh, let's just play it by ear," I say with a wink. My tongue in her right ear, a hand on her left ear, the teasing begins. I'm either really good at this, or she's channeled her inner Laurence Olivier.

"Baby, that tickles." I continue. She giggles and moans. We switch sides; symmetry is important. A few minutes pass, and she puts her hand on my cock. I pull away. "Is something wrong?"

"Oh no, not at all. But I completely forget to ask you something earlier." My right hand now firmly caressing her left ear. Already, she's woozy.

"What was . . . what was that baby?"

"Oh, I just need to know if you have any prior medical conditions or allergies." Right on cue, she's fast asleep.

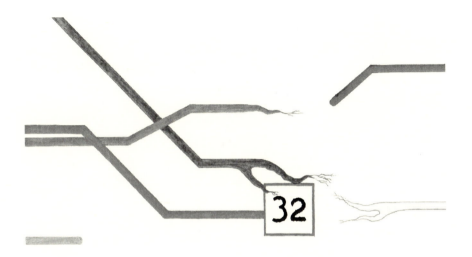

The unbearable heat of Las Vegas is now a distant memory. I embrace the chilly Chicago air. Way too early in the morning. Slept pretty well after surgery. Early bird gets the worm. In this case, the worm is a pair of cappuccinos and apricot flaxseed muffins. It'll take a lot more than a continental breakfast to persuade Maggie, but it's a start. Enter the hotel. Something about revolving doors just get the adrenaline flowing. Alone in the elevator, doors open to the penthouse. I put her breakfast on the counter, finish mine. Play the Alkaline Trio omnibus at a low volume. Cajoling her awake.

Slowly, her eyes open. The lids separating reluctantly as if held together with rubber cement. I say nothing, just let her come to on her own. Takes longer than expected. Finally, she appears aware of her surroundings but still very confused. Here's the thing: I remember every detail of last night.

This woman tied to a chair in my hotel room, on the other hand, she has no recollection of the last sixteen hours or so.

Her eyes now fully open, she looks around. Panic sets in. Understandable. Looks at the ropes binding her arms and legs. Tries to scream, but it's muffled by the gag. Even if she could scream, no one would hear her. I rented out the top three floors of the hotel. Not to mention guests here like their privacy. The soundproofing is excellent.

"I bought you some breakfast, but you probably want to know what the fuck is going on. Am I right?"

She nods vigorously.

"That's fair. I'm going to explain in great detail what happened last night. Do you remember *anything* about last night? About meeting me at Pockets? Anything?" Shakes her head side to side. "I thought not. Now, before I tell you about what we did last night, and what I hope we can do together in the future, I want you to take a good look at your chest and stomach." She does this. Pure terror in her eyes. Most likely residual effects from waking up in a strange place. Not so much displeasure at the new modifications I've performed on her. "Do you like your new boobs?" I ask.

"You see, Maggie, I have no desire to hurt you in any way. Believe it or not, I want your help. The more cooperative you are, the better it will be for both of us. I enlarged your breasts just a bit, as well as performed minor abdominoplasty. What most people call tummy tucks. I did these not because I think you need them. You're quite attractive. That's not the point. But I need you to understand that if I really want to make your life difficult, I can. You've seen what I can do when I'm 'helping' you out. Imagine what I can do with malicious intentions." She's gone pale. "OK, you need to eat something. I'm going to undo your gag. But don't scream. No one will hear you. All that it will accomplish is you getting on my nerves."

I approach her. Expecting her to bite me, I do it quickly. But she remains calm, at least on the surface. I hold a bottle of water with a straw in it up to her mouth. Gulps the entire thing down in seconds. I remove the bottle, she spits on me.

To say I deserved that would be putting it mildly. But no screaming, so I'm OK with it. Blatant signs of nausea. She's going to puke. The vile sounds of hacking and wheezing are empty threats. Nothing to vomit up. "Here," I say, breaking off pieces of the muffin. She chews. Nearly takes my finger in the process. Her hunger, not her rage, being the reason.

"I'm going to untie your hands now. But for your own sake, don't try anything irrational. Most importantly, you need to rest. Surgeries like these require several weeks to fully heal. Oh, you'll be feeling normal in a matter of days, maybe even hours, but rest is still by far the most effective medicine. That being said, don't be foolish because you really don't want to complicate your life more than it already is."

She nods slowly, taking a deep breath.

I undo the restraints, minus the belt securing her to the chair. Hand her the cappuccino. By now room temperature, she drinks it anyway.

Suddenly, the tears she's been holding back come rushing out. "Please don't kill me," she pleads. Momentarily, I feel awful. The thought is fleeting. A cardinal rule of manipulation is to never underestimate your opponent. The moment I empathize with her is when I discover she's a trained assassin. No, thank you.

Again, I reiterate she is in no danger. In fact, I'm trying to help her. Give me a few minutes. She'll have a case of Stockholm syndrome before you know it.

"Maggie. I know you are going to find this virtually impossible to believe, given the circumstances. But I am on your side. I want to help you." A picture might be worth a thousand words, but the look she's giving me carries only three: *You're fucking crazy.*

Brevity. Once such a beautiful art form. Then came the LOLs. Game over.

"Yeah, I'm well aware that you would love to bash my brains in right now. You're envisioning torturing me with who knows what kind of contraption. Whatever rage you're feeling right now, I've felt it too." She rolls her eyes. "I don't expect you to believe me. All I can do is reiterate the fact that I have no intention to hurt you."

She sighs deeply, trying to force back tears. "Look, if you really want to help me, let me go. I swear I won't call the cops. You'll never hear from me again. *Please*, just let me leave now!"

I massage my head. Pause for dramatic effect. Deep sigh. "Maggie, do you make good money turning tricks?"

Unlike last night, she's a terrible liar. "What are you talking about? Turning tricks? I bartend a couple nights a week to pay for school."

"Right. Only a few more credits and you'll have your degrees in English literature and psychology." Not a question. Stated as fact.

A look of shock on her face. "How did you . . . ?"

"Let's just say I'm a pretty smart guy. But part of being smart is knowing when to ask for help. That's where you come in."

Her tears have subsided. Her voice still trembles. "You need help all right. But the best doctors in the world couldn't treat whatever fucked-up shit you've got going on up here," she says, pointing at her own head. Instantly, regret is evident. Insulting the crazy guy, bad idea.

"Since you're majoring in English, I'm going to go out on a limb and say you read a lot. Am I correct?"

"Yeah, so?"

"Just books or do you read periodicals too?"

She's offended. "Yeah I read tons of books. And no, I don't read those stupid gossip rags. Just because I'm some 'dumb whore' doesn't mean I spend all my time reading up on the lives of celebrities."

Clearly, she hopes for more of a reaction out of me. Sorry to disappoint. "What about newspapers?"

Dripping with scorn. "Yeah. I read the paper from time to time."

"Wonderful." I hold an old issue of the *Wall Street Journal* for her to see. One with an article about pregnancy limits. "How about this? Have you been keeping up to speed on this? Looks like someone is poking the hornets' nest."

Her eyes scan the page, nostrils flare. "Yeah, big deal. I know some whacko senator proposed some bill to limit the number of children parents can have. Personally, I think it sounds great. But it'll never pass. Way too extreme."

"You see, that's what I thought. So many Republicans in Congress. If this law goes into effect, the annual number of abortions will eventually skyrocket. Not to mention the fact that foster homes are already far too crowded as it is. Pass this, and any woman with the maximum number of kids will have to give one up. I don't see the government killing off any children. Liberals or conservatives, that's a stretch."

Suddenly, as if all my recent transgressions against her never happened, she's immersed in the enigma. "True, but maybe people are finally coming around to gay marriage. Maybe this will open the door and make it easier for gay couples to adopt."

"Possibly, but despite all the progress made in recent years by the gay community, I think it's safe to say that kind of equality is a while away. And even if that were the case, it would probably make child abandonment more socially acceptable. At least on paper, the right wing doesn't endorse behavior like that."

Pondering, her eyes whipping back and forth across the print. Scanning it to refresh her mind. Searching for answers. Appearing stumped, she brushes the issue aside. "Well, either way, I don't think it's such a bad thing. Let's be honest, the last thing this world needs is more people. Resources are strained as it is. Maybe they're just trying to salvage what's left of this planet."

"A valid theory. I would buy it if the left were in charge. But typically speaking, the people in question aren't known for conservation of resources." I sip a glass of water, give some to my guest. "Something just doesn't add up. You see, there's a saying in science: once you eliminate the impossible, whatever remains, no matter how improbable, must be the truth. I have a feeling that the answer here is something so diabolical, so corrupt, it will make you cringe."

A long pause. She soaks it in. "That's not science."

"Excuse me?"

"That quote. It's Sir Arthur Conan Doyle."

"As in *Sherlock Holmes*?"

"Yeah. While that philosophy works for science, that quote is still from a work of literature."

Interesting. Take a step back. "I'm impressed. You really do read a lot."

She gets defensive once again. "Yeah, well, like I said, we're not all just a bunch of *dumb whores*." Excessive sarcasm on the last two words.

Wheels are turning. "Agreed. However, am I wrong in assuming you're the exception to the rule?" She begins to interject, but I continue. "We're all aware of the stereotypes. Obviously, not all strippers and prostitutes are illiterate, image-obsessed heroin addicts. But be honest. Are you an accurate representation of your colleagues?"

She scowls at me. Planning her attack against me when I eventually free her. I grab a photo from the counter.

"Have you ever seen this man?" I hold it inches from her face. She studies it intensely. Shakes her head.

Even being restrained, her body language gives her away. This girl displays glimpses of being an excellent actor, but she's lying.

"Bullshit. I'll say it again. I'm not going to hurt you. But if you don't cooperate with me, well, I have no problem leaving you here for days. Longer if necessary."

Fatigue and fear now controlling her decisions, she concedes. "Yes."

"Yes, what?"

"Yes, I've seen him."

Long pause. "Well?"

"Well what? You only asked me if I've ever seen him. I said yes."

Oh boy. This is how we're going to play this. I don't say a word. Move closer, untie her restraints. Even she is in disbelief. Thinking this is a trap. "Better?"

She stands up, stretching her arms. Bends down to touch her toes. Comes closer, attempts to gouge my eyes and kick me. Times like these make me thankful for all the instances Dillon kicked the shit out of me. Sharp reflexes.

I restrain her. Gently sit her on the couch. Remain calm. Remind myself I deserved that.

"Look, I promise you'll have your chance to hurt me as much as you want soon enough. But right now, I need your help."

Dismayed, she says "My help? You're fucking insane! Even if I could help you, there's no way I would after what you've put me through. All that aside, how in the world could I possibly be of any service to you?"

Pick up the picture of my son once again. "This man, whom you've seen." She nods. "I'm going to guess that you've seen him at your establishment on several occasions." Nods again. "And he probably showed up with this guy at least once or twice," I say, this time holding up a picture of The Sauce.

Her eyes go wide. "Yeah, what about it?"

"What do you know about them?"

"Not much except that they're both fucking loaded. They're good customers, don't get me wrong. But the way they talk to me, you'd think I was a billionaire."

"How so?"

"They keep telling all the girls that soon enough we're going to be loaded. Like filthy rich. They're always saying that we'll be able to retire in five years and shit like that."

Not good.

"Hmm. That is a little odd." Actually it's not. Only adding credibility to my theory.

"But it's really strange. They come in every once in a while, throw money around like it's plain paper, and leave. No dances, no fooling around. They talk to every girl there at least once every time they come in. At first it was nice, but now it's just weird. Honestly, what guy spends that kind of money on a woman, several women really, and doesn't expect anything in return?"

Oh, honey, they expect more in return than you could possibly know.

"So you know who they are? I mean, how powerful they are in the business world?"

"Well yeah, Nicky Salcedo is kind of a big deal around here. The younger guy, Madigan, well his name is Cooper, but he goes by Madigan. He's some scientific prodigy."

No surprise there.

"Exactly."

"So are you going to tell me what all this is about?"

"Soon. For now, be very careful what you say and do around these guys or anyone you see them with." I'm met with a mixed look of concern and skepticism. "I will know more soon, but I have every reason to believe these guys are up to something extremely dangerous." Her look shifts slightly toward concern. "Admittedly, this next part is going to sound very sanctimonious given the source, but please listen carefully. The worst part is I think they're planning on using sex workers as their disposable chattel to carry out their plan."

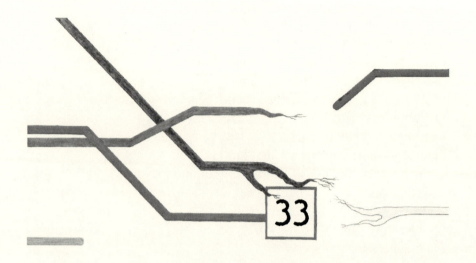

33

I'm so groggy, barely aware of my surroundings. The cabbie shouts some number at me. Points at the red digital display. All a blur. Probably around a $12 fare. Pull my wallet out, grab three bills. Could be $3, could be $300. I think it was $45. No objection on his part.

Surgery, drastically prolonged, is finally done. Walking around with 50 percent of my testicles doesn't feel any different. Because I can't feel a thing right now. The drugs wearing off with incomparable sluggishness. Stumble through the entrance to my building, eventually find my door.

Really wish I hadn't installed this new lock. Keypad with five-digit code. Five minutes later, I'm through the door and passing out on my bed.

When I finally come to, I feel pretty good. About as good as one would expect. Still a little numb down south, but not in pain. I rub my balls. To the touch, they feel the same. If I didn't actually have one removed, I might not know which is the fake. To my surprise, I've been in bed a mere two hours. Then I check a calendar.

Make that twenty-six hours. Healthy, wealthy, wise.
#Dick'sAlmanac
Deep breath. Stretch it out.

I undress, take a shower. Feeling much more like myself. Perfection still a while away. Throw on sweatpants, no underwear, ratty Northwestern T-shirt. Head for the kitchen. Pretty sure I have orange juice. Which side of the expiration date it's on, that's another story.

I open the fridge. Instantly, I know something is amiss. I have milk. Eggs. Cheese. All things I eat. Haven't purchased them in a while though. Dillon must be fucking with me. Push my nerves aside, pull out a frying pan. Light the stove. A nicely refurbished apartment, but still uses a pilot light. Vintage is the new black.

I crack a couple eggs. The instantaneous hissing is strangely soothing. Reminds me of my youth. Hated eggs as a kid. Dad loved them. Mom made him omelets and scrambles all the time.

Today, I'm in an over-easy kind of mood. Never prepared an egg this way. Haven't eaten one in years. But now, I'm one ball lighter. Change is afoot. Embrace it.

Wait for the whites to set then flip.

#LookseasieronFoodNetwork

Fuck me. Scrambled it is.

I run around looking for towels to clean the mess. Nothing is ever where I left it. Check the bathroom. Nope. Hallway closet. Nothing. Run into my bedroom, grab a dirty undershirt. Put paper towels on the shopping list.

I head back to the kitchen floor. Start wiping it up.

"Are you sure there isn't an original Salvador Dali you'd rather use?"

My nerves rattle me with such fervor I whack my head on the oven handle. That wasn't Dillon. Even if he regained the ability to speak, that was most definitely the voice of a woman. Shift my gaze toward the source of my panic.

It's Alison. My aunt.

Not exactly in the mood to have company, especially unannounced intruders. For lack of a better word. She might be a relative, but I hardly know her.

Head still throbbing, ignoring any impulse for decorum. "What the fuck are you doing here? How did you get in?" I move closer to the set of knives next to the fridge. Not that I need them. Just need her to know I'm not in a good mood.

"Relax, sweetie. I'm just here to see how you're doing. I figured you could probably use someone to take care of you after your surgery. Or at least lend you a helping hand."

"How did you know about my surgery?" I shout, overly defensive.

"Mackenzie told me." My skepticism grows.

"Bullshit."

"Look, you don't have to be Sigmund Freud to know there is tension between you two. She was a little reluctant to talk to me about you at first. But perseverance pays off. Whatever you two are going through, that's none of my business. Just know that she seemed genuinely concerned for your health. She told me to make sure I reported back to her on how your recovery is coming along."

I want to feel moved. I want to reminisce. I would love to be the guy who takes this information and uses it as fuel to win her affections. But I'm not. All I want is an Advil (my ears can only numb the pain for so long) and a working lock on my door. My agitation quite evident. No effort on my behalf to conceal it. "Well, tell her I'm great. A little sore, but otherwise feeling fine. Now, getting back to *my* questions. How the fuck did you get in the door?"

A sly smile. Maybe this would work had I spent more than a couple hours with her. Had she been at my birthday parties, taking me to parks, that kind of shit. Then maybe I'd be moved by her affections. Instead, all I see is an interloper. "Dillon told me the combo. He said you wouldn't mind if I stopped by."

"Once again, that's bullshit. No one knows the combination except me. One last chance, lady. How. Did you. Get in the door?"

Her smirk quickly dissipates. She senses my sincerity. "Look, darlin', Dillon really told me the code. He went on some really long explanation as to how he knew it. He's really good with numbers and stuff like that, isn't he? He was drawing all kinds of diagrams. Charts and graphs spread out all over the place. All I wanted was a simple number, but he went on for what felt like forever. But he's such a sweet guy, I didn't have the heart to cut him off. And his voice, the poor thing. I just can't imagine not being able to talk."

It can be arranged. Keep it up.

"So he's going on and on, and I'm not the smartest, so I only got the basics, but he basically said that you're very predictable in your choices of passwords. He said when most people set codes on this kind of keypad, they use famous numbers. Ones they won't forget very easily. A birth date maybe. Or that song about

Jenny: 8-6-7-5-3-0-9. Something like that. So he eliminated a few possibilities that way." An awkward pause, and she goes on. "Then he said people also use words, kind of like on a phone pad. Like the word D-U-C-K would be 3-8-2-5."

I'm not a fucking idiot, I know how this works. "Yes, I get that. Could you please cut to the chase? I'm not exactly feeling well. Surely you can respect that," I say, pointing at my ball.

Recognition finally shows on her face. "Oh, I'm so sorry. But honestly, I don't know how he knew. That's kind of where he lost me. You'll just have to ask him yourself. But that is the honest truth. Dillon told me the code, and he made it seem like it wouldn't be a big deal. If you want me to leave, I will."

She shoots me those puppy dog eyes. So predictable. Too tired to fight. "Whatever. You came all this way. Am I correct in assuming you're the one who stocked my fridge with food?"

She nods, biting her lip. A poor job of repressing a smile she doesn't want me to see. "Well, thank you. I was making breakfast. Not off to a good start."

This time, her laugh is acceptable. I've never cared much for eggs.

Ovaries kind of freak me out.

"Well, don't worry about that. I'll finish cleaning up, and then I'll make you a nice big breakfast. Why don't you just go rest for a bit, take another shower, something like that?"

I'm not in the mood for visitors. But I will admit, her offer is tempting. At the very least, maybe I can get some more info about my mom and The Sauce. "Thanks, Alison, that sounds great. I'll be in my room. Just give a yell when you're done."

"You got it. Just glad to help. If there's anything you need, anything at all, don't hesitate to ask. And please, call me Aunt Alison."

More coarse than necessary, "I don't think so." The pain on her face shows. Even I know that was a dick move. Remorse. A feeling I'm not familiar with. "I'm sorry, Alison. All I mean is that, although I do genuinely appreciate your generosity, I only met you a few months ago. I barely know you. It's just really weird. To suddenly have a close family member show up out of nowhere. This is going to take some time for me to get used to."

A succession of quick nods ensues. "OK. I understand. Now go get some rest."

I head back to my room, throw myself on the bed. Grab my phone, send Dillon a quick text. Chastise him for breaking into my apartment then giving the code to a stranger.

> Thanks for giving out my door code, fuckface :P I think my aunt has a crush on you BTW.

Just typing the emoticon makes me want to shower. People like that deserve to lose testicles. I hit Send and pass out with no hesitation.

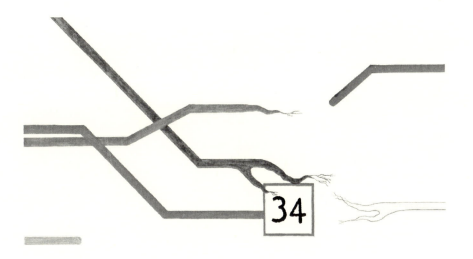

34

I wake up to the familiar sounds of a passing train. Rattling steel. Maintenance long neglected, will have to wait longer. Tax money vanishing faster than collective common sense. The mayor drives a Bugatti. Truth be told, not sure I could sleep if that thing ran smoothly.

My nap quickly evolved into another long slumber. Alison didn't bother to wake me up. I head to the kitchen. Table with a plate of cold food. Take a seat, grab a fork. About to chow down, interrupted by Alison storming out of the bathroom.

"No, no, no!" she yells as she snatches the plate of cold pancakes from me and dumps them in the trash.

Not really sure what is going on, I ask. "Are you OK? I would have eaten those."

"Don't be silly, darlin', I'll make you some fresh ones."

"I have a microwave." She rolls her eyes. The absurdity of my suggestion. An insult to everything she stands for. "Well, thank you" is all I manage. Trying to mitigate the damage my rudimentary idea may have had on her psyche. "I'll be right back." Head back to my room to check messages.

Nothing. Battery is spent. Plug it in to charge, head back to the kitchen.

"Sorry, I slept so long, Alison. You really don't have to stick around you know. Just buying me food and stocking the fridge is already above and beyond."

"Oh please. It's the least I can do. We're family. And after all you've been through, a home-cooked meal is just what you need."

Her enthusiasm is infectious. Not necessarily in a good way. Feeling more cynical than usual. What does she mean by "all I've been through"? She barely knows me. I sit in silence, study her movements. Take in her mannerisms. Watch her chop veggies. Slice thin strips of some kind of meat. Most likely a salad, but not sure. Minutes later, the smell hits me.

"Is that ahi tuna?"

She lights up like Times Square on New Year's Eve. "It sure is! Do you like ahi?"

"Absolutely. Haven't had it in a while though."

"Well, you're in for a treat. I got this recipe from your mother. Ahi was her favorite. Any kind of fish really, but especially seared ahi."

Momentarily, I feel a connection with this woman. But it's fleeting. Something about her seems so contrived. Is she putting on an act? Why? My stomach rumbles. Part hunger, part nerves. Need to dive deeper.

"So tell me about her."

"What was that?" A mix of confusion and trepidation.

Her reaction, not what I envisioned. Looks at me like this is the last question she expected. As if I asked her how much money she made, or how many sexual partners she's had.

"What do you want to know?"

"What do you mean? Anything. Everything. I don't know anything about her. Was she smart? Was she nice? What kind of music did she listen to?" Really don't care. Inane questions to buy time. Nothing against my birth mother. She had reasons for doing what she did. But biology does not beget parenthood. Despite what you've been told. Anyone can shoot a kid out of their snatch. Not just anyone can love unconditionally.

That's what Paul and Josephine Watts did for me.

When I'm thinking rationally, my judgments not driven by impulse, I have no ill will towards my birth mother. But I also have no desire to learn anything about her. I ask questions to gauge Alison's response.

"OK, I know her favorite food. What was her favorite band?"

"Oh, well she liked rock music mainly. She was always stealing my CDs. You're probably too young to know what those are." I feign amusement. Partially at the comment about compact discs, partly at watching her squirm. "But she loved a band called The Misfits." Even I have to applaud that one. My birth mom was a real badass. Why didn't she fuck Glenn Danzig instead of Nicky Salcedo? Maybe she did. But you get the point.

"Were you guys close?"

Puts the finishing touches on my ahi salad. My jaw drops, mouth begins to water. Before her hand is off the bowl, my mouth is stuffed.

No hesitation this time. Her eyes actually begin to tear up. "Absolutely. We did everything together. We talked about boys, clothes, the normal stuff. But we were so much more than sisters. We were best friends."

Heartstrings officially tugged.

"So what happened to her?"

She has reached a new level of discomfort. Wipes her eyes. The waterworks have stopped. Her demeanor now bordering on anger. "She got what she deserved."

Oh shit.

"Excuse me?"

"She was a fucking dirty slut. She stuck her nose in other peoples' business. Oh, she was smart, all right. So smart. But book smart you know? Never knew when to leave well enough alone."

This conversation, ominous at best. Fearing the worst, I desperately attempt to ease the tension. "Um, Alison, this is delicious. I'm totally going to finish it, but I need to run to my room and grab my painkillers. I'll be right back."

I'm not a betting man. But I know this won't end well. She is crazy. Who is she? What do I really know about her? Are we even related?

I grab my pills next to the phone. Notice a new text message. From Dillon. My heart nearly barrels through my rib cage. Eyeballs not far from emancipating themselves either.

Haha dude LOL. Your aunt is hot and all, but I don't think it would work. JK☺ But what are you talking about? Door Code? I haven't seen your aunt in months. How are the balls BTW?

OK. Calm down. Collect your thoughts. There's a crazy woman in your kitchen. Need to get out. Fire escape access is in the living room. Next to the Monet. Fuck. Full panic mode. What do I do? Where do I go?

A shout from down the hall. "Benjamin, I've gotta run. I cleaned up everything in the kitchen, but left your salad on the table for you to eat. I hope you finish it all. You need all the nourishment you can get." The tenderness in her voice. Disturbing. Minutes ago, this same woman called her own sister a slut. A sister whose demise appears rather inconsequential to her. So many questions. Worry about that later. Just leave me alone, crazy lady.

"Oh, I will. It's delicious. I'm gonna finish it up in just a minute. Thank you so much once again, Aunt Alison." Not sure why I picked now to act like family. Fight or flight response makes you do weird things.

"Bye, sweetie!" followed by the closing of my front door.

Breathe deep, fall on my bed. First thing in the morning, getting the door code changed. Add a few more deadbolts. Lie there for a solid fifteen minutes. I finally calm down. Head into the kitchen to finish my salad. She might be neurotic, but the bitch can cook.

I walk down the hall. Enter the open space connecting the kitchen and living room. Eyeing that salad. Don't make it that far. Struck from behind, spun around, and kicked in the groin. I drop to the ground faster than gravity necessitates. Not enough painkillers in the world to help me now. Coughing up blood, I reach for my right ear, try to alleviate the pain.

A kick to my wrist. "Get your hand away from your ear, asshole!" she screams. "I know what you're trying to do. I might not be a genius who cured AIDS, but I know the basics of acupuncture."

Mouth moves to form a response. Words replaced by hacking coughs.

On my hands and knees, struggling to breathe properly. Alison walks up to me, takes my chin in her hand. With the most cryptic tone I never thought possible, she tells me, "You ruined my life. Now I'm going to ruin yours."

I want to protest. Not only can I not form the words, but it would be pointless. She's already succeeded at her goal. My biggest fear is what else she is capable of. I force myself to my knees. Hands down by my side. Nearly ready to stand up and fight her. Irrelevant. Before I even begin to stand up, she pulls a gun out of her purse. Without hesitation, points it at my side, fires a shot into my right hand. Middle three fingers gone. Blood flooding my floor. Without looking back, she's out the door. Losing blood at a fatal rate, I pass out on the pristine parquet masterpiece, for what I assume will be the last time.

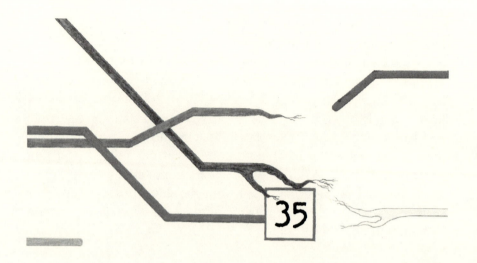

35

I wake up in my second home. Room is different, but it's all the same. White walls. Curtains. Monitors. Drab clothing. Some of the nurses I've seen. Two guys, three women I don't recognize. Missed out on the pleasure of my testicular extraction. The place smells like shit. Not a metaphor or exaggeration. There are bedpans as far as the eye can see.

I look at my hand, survey the damage. Not surprisingly, it's bandaged. Looks like my arm is the stem of a carnival serving of cotton candy.

Being here, it's odd. Consider myself an eloquent man. But at the moment, "odd" is a sufficient description. My history with the medical community is conflicted at best. Obviously, I believe pharmacology has the power to save lives. But just like anything, abuse it, and its powers can destroy.

Doctor shopping. Enough said.

They'll never tell you this, but most medicines: serendipity. Completely random and, well, lucky. That dude who made great advancements toward curing schizophrenia? Trying to cure Parkinson's syndrome. You know that woman who saved the lives of countless diabetics? Wanted to develop antiaging pills.

#Betterluckythangood.

The list goes on, but you get the point.

Suffice it to say, anything a doctor tells me, I overanalyze. Fine-tooth comb. Put their every word under a microscope. Make no mistake. I like doctors. Probably be dead right now without them. I like whatever's in the bag hooked up to my arm even more though.

God saves lives, doctors collect the bill. Who said that? Lincoln? Alexander Graham Bell? Fuck if I know. So out of it right now. Sure, they make tons of money, not sure if I could do what they do. Not the pressure. Bend don't break. I guess they get respect, but not enough.

Thanks to the Internet, everyone's a doctor. That sore jaw you've got? Most likely it's TMJ. Not fun, but not uncommon. But you read on the Internet it could be tetanus.

Lockjaw. Maybe you should read the part that says most people are immunized against it.

Why spend eight years in med school when you can spend eight minutes online?

Take the chick in the bed next to me. Injured her leg surfing in Bali. Bruises and swelling for weeks. Stopped at a pharmacy for some Tylenol. Asked the pharmacist what he recommends for the bruises.

"I recommend you see a doctor."

She'll be fine with the pills, she told him.

Now it's getting amputated.

If you can afford to go surfing in Bali, you can afford to see a doctor.

Priorities.

The moment I can leave this bed, I've got a special prescription just for her. Oh, the plans I have. Time to step up my efforts. Not until I was on the verge of death did I recognize my nonchalance. No time to waste.

"Hey there, mister. How ya feeling?" inquires another nurse I don't recognize. She looks at clipboards. Writing, doodling, drawing. The pen moves. Left to right, up and down. Across the page, repeat. Might as well be hieroglyphics. No clue what she's scribbling.

Trying to be calm, I say, "Well, given the circumstances, I'm feeling pretty good." Holding up my hand. What does it look like under the dressing? How many fingers did I lose? Did they cut off the whole hand? Did they put the severed digits on ice, reattach them? Don't want to know right now.

"There's someone here to see you. He's been waiting for hours. We didn't want you being disturbed while you recovered and slept. But now that you're awake, would you like to see him?"

First instinct, Alison has sent a man to finish what she started. Calming down, I know it's Dillon. Hiding any trace of emotion. "Yeah, send him in."

I should know better than to ever be surprised by him. After all these years, I should expect the unexpected. I'm still caught off-guard when in walks a giant sporting a hospital gown. Likely the largest one they carry. He's still stretching the seams.

"Hey, buddy, great to see you." He nods back. "What's with the getup?" Scanning him over, he looks fine. "Did you get attacked too?" I sign the question after the verbal version. As best I can with one hand.

Attacking Dillon is tantamount to fighting a grizzly bear on steroids. Meant to be a joke, his demeanor remains neutral. Looking around, he doesn't trust anyone here. Can't say I blame him. Not too keen on trust right now. He decides to use the patented facial twitch/Morse code method. *My clothes are covered in blood.*

I sign. My body and face too sore to handle that much activity. *What are you talking about?*

Holds up a finger, he'll be right back. Goes into the hall, returns with a backpack. Pulls out a notepad and pen. I shake my head no. I don't feel like writing. Without hesitation or contest, he pulls out an electronic tablet. I sigh. Not up for this right now. But I can tell he's serious. Doesn't want to chance anyone intercepting our conversation.

Puts the tab in my hand, his face goes to work. *I didn't have time to go home and change. This was all they had for me to wear.*

Trying to save keystrokes, I type, **But WHY?**

The shock on his face is genuine. He thought I knew. Goes on to tell me how he found me in my apartment, gushing blood like a fountain.

What were you doing in the area? Asking, pure formality. I know the answer.

When I got your texts, I knew something was up. Your aunt, or whoever that lady is, she's weird. I never really trusted her. But then when you said she was in your apartment because I told her how to get in, that sealed it for me. Obviously, she was lying, and I knew you were in trouble. Sorry, I didn't make it sooner, buddy. His eyes water. Not full tears, but definite moisture.

About to respond, surfer chick catches my eye. She looks thoroughly freaked out. A common reaction. People always stare at us this way. Dillon's facial twitches, me typing on a pad. An entire conversation without words, mere feet apart. Oh, to be a fly on the wall of her inner monologue.

I smile. **Dillon, don't apologize. You saved my life!** As I type that, I wonder if he actually did me a favor. Conveying an attitude of appreciation. Really, I'm just confused. Trying to lighten the mood, I type some more. **I guess we're even now, huh? I saved you, you saved me. We're square.** Instant regret. Wish I could take that back. His pain evident. Typing fast in an attempt to backtrack, **Dillon, Ims' sorry, I'm kinod of out of it right now . . . tha'ts now thwat I meant.**

He reads my attempt at an apology and chuckles. *I know, buddy. Lucky for you, I don't consider this some kind of debt I had to repay. If that were the case, I would walk out that door and let you get your ass kicked some more. But you're my friend, and something tells me you're going to need my help in the near future.*

Hate when he does this. His cryptic foreshadowing. As if he knows something you don't. Something you should know. Something you *must* know. But he just shrugs his shoulders, pretends it's no big deal.

Just then, a screaming lady wheeled down the hall. Pregnant and sweaty. Instinctively, I shout, "Abortion! You don't want to deal with that for the next eighteen years! It's only a matter of time before it's mandatory! There's a great dry cleaner three blocks from here. All the wire hangers you could ever want!"

The surfer chick gives me a death stare. Dillon slaps me hard. Aside from that, it's as if it didn't happen. The hallway is far too noisy. Fortunately, people have more important things to do than listen to the rants of a madman.

Dillon goes down the hall, returns with a soda from the vending machine. I'm not sure where he is keeping his money. If you fear the answer, don't ask the question. He takes a sip, puts the cap on, and slaps me again. *What the fuck is wrong with you?*

Typing again, **Look, that was messed up. I know. I don't want to use this incident as an excuse, but I'm not feeling well**

right now. And I don't just mean physically. I'm talking about my head. I'm screwed up. I can't think straight. I'm confusing simple facts. I think I might have hit my head when I fell.

One of my nurses returns. Looks at a clipboard, writes some stuff. Starts to leave. I interject. "Excuse me." She turns around.

"Yes?"

I rattle off questions without taking a breath. Sounding like a lunatic. "Um, how much longer do you think I need to be here? How many fingers did I lose? Did you sew them back on? Did you have to cut the whole thing off?"

She appears oddly unscathed by my brash attitude. "I'll get the doctor, and she can answer all your questions."

Before the nurse is even out the door, another woman enters. "Hi there, Sam. I'm Doctor Higgins."

"Hi."

She turns to Dillon, "Hi there, Dillon. How have you been?" Must know ASL. He moves his hands around. Tells her he's fine, been dating a nice woman lately.

"Oh, good for you. I hope that works out for you." Turning her attention back to me. "Sam, how are you feeling?"

Dillon looks at me, mouths the words "sexual addict support group," points at Dr. Higgins.

"Well, I'd give you two thumbs up, but that would be a lie." Not even sure if it would be possible.

"Understandable. I overheard you saying you weren't aware of the nature of your injuries."

I nod. "Correct."

Cutting to the chase, she says, "Well, you lost a lot of blood, but thanks to your friend here, you'll be fine. As for your hand, you lost three fingers. The middle three."

Look at my good hand, curl the middle three down. Extend my thumb and pinkie. "Well, I guess I should move to Hawaii." No one laughs. Lighten up, people. It's called a coping mechanism.

"Dillon recovered the fingers and put them on ice. Unfortunately, despite all the medical expertise within these walls, no one here is skilled enough to attempt a surgery this delicate."

Not exactly shocked, it's what I expected.

"But," she continues, "there is a clinic in Santa Monica, California, that specializes in reconstructive hand surgery. Doctor

Chirag Jayaraman is the best surgeon in the world at this kind of procedure. We can have you on a plane tomorrow, and you should be . . . I don't want to say 'good as new,' but you should have excellent mobility in your hand in almost no time."

Pondering, I close my eyes, take deep breaths.

"Um, thank you for all of your help, Doctor. Please pass my appreciation on to your staff as well. I owe you a huge debt of gratitude. But I think I'm going to pass on the surgery option. I know these procedures are very delicate, and even though you say this guy in Santa Monica is the best in the world, I'm skeptical."

"I understand. We're still going to keep you overnight. Let me know if you change your mind." Pats Dillon on the shoulder and leaves the room.

He shoots me a quizzical look. Confused as to why I don't want the surgery.

Grabbing the tablet, I type. **Look, it's a risky procedure. The success rate on things of this nature is incredibly low. The upsides are obvious, but the risks are pretty substantial too, believe it or not.**

He doesn't believe me but nods and accepts it.

Plus, there's a far more pressing issue at hand here.

Holds up his hand, stops me from continuing. *Mackenzie is fine. She's in Calgary visiting her stepsisters. When I got your text about your aunt, I immediately wrote her to stay there indefinitely, not to ask any questions. I haven't told her anything yet. I wanted to discuss with you what we should do about this mess.*

I'm a vessel. An empty shell. Going through the motions. Dillon catches me staring off into space. Starts snapping his fingers. Finally gets my attention. *Did you catch anything I just told you?*

I nod. I must be pale as alabaster. Nicky Salcedo. This woman claiming to be my aunt. It's one thing to come after me. I deserve it.

But to endanger Mackenzie. And my child. Unraveling. Too much for me to handle.

Typing, **I caught it. And thank you. Thank you a million times for taking care of Mackenzie. I can handle her never speaking to me again. But if anything were to happen to her** or her kid, I'd lose it. **Look at me, I'm already losing it. I don't know how much more I can handle Dillon.**

He sits on my bed, careful not to squash me. *Get some rest, buddy. We'll discuss this in more detail when you're feeling better.* Looks around, nods at the surfer girl. *And when we've got some privacy. I'm gonna take off, buddy, but definitely call me if you need anything.*

Speaking now, I say, "Will do. Thanks, Dillon."

Take care, and at least think about that surgery, OK?

Back to typing. **All right, but only because you saved my life. But the odds are slim.**

He winks at me, pats my shoulder, and leaves.

I lean my head back on the pillows. Seconds before I doze off, a thought comes to me. I do need two good hands. But if I'm going to get a new one, I'm going to perform the surgery myself.

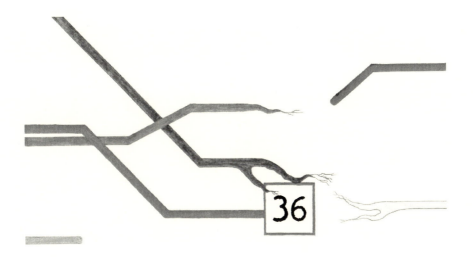

36

Sitting on a rooftop with a bag of Chicago hot dogs. Brown paper soaked through with grease. Random entrails providing a literal window into the contents of the sack. A perfect companion for tonight. An event so rare. To say "once in a lifetime" isn't close enough. Scientists dream of witnessing what I just saw. Certainly, I wasn't the only one. But truthfully, how many who actually saw it know just how spectacular that was? How rare?

Epsilon Orionis has burnt out. Alnilam. The middle star of Orion's belt. Gone. Supernova.

Not sure of the exact dates. A supernova hasn't been witnessed in over four hundred years. Give or take.

And it just happened. "Just" being a relative term. Given the distance, from earth, this took place several million years ago.

I sit and ponder this for a minute. Alnilam, one of the (former) brightest stars in the Milky Way. Keystone of one of the most famous constellations. Critical in celestial navigation. The guiding light, a prime reference point. Erased. For thousands of years, explorers stared in awe. Fully vested in Alnilam's reliability.

And it was never really there.

A myth. Holographic farce.

I look across the sky. Which of you other great big balls of gas are long gone? North Star, I'm looking at you. Ursa Minor, you always made me skeptical. Never fully content in the proverbial shadow of the Big Dipper. Cracked under the pressure.

Of all the times this could have happened. Of all the places I could have been. I see it live. A sinister chuckle is all I can manage.

Like this is some great metaphor. Something is long gone. Has been for a while. We're clueless at best.

I sit here on the cusp of a major decision. To be the man my parents wanted me to be. That Mackenzie wants me to be. The guy who saved millions of lives. Gave hope to so many.

Or to be the person I want to be. Asshole extraordinaire.

It's a ball of gas. Has nothing to do with anything in my life. Can't help but wonder if it has some deeper meaning. Ten years either way, early or late, I could have been anywhere else in the world. Oblivious. A decade in the vast life of a celestial body that old. Like a single heartbeat for a human. Less than a second for us. Of the billions of years it had to burn out, it chose a precise second to call it quits. The odds are staggering. To put it lightly.

Neil Young, your thoughts? Kurt Cobain, how 'bout you? Is it better to burn out or fade away?

Not ready to settle that debate just yet. In time, perhaps. But I sit here, staring at the gap in Orion's belt. Now just two outer dots in the sky. I think. Reflect. I disgust myself. Here I am. A shell. A physical, living, breathing man, sure. Constantly projecting the illusion of worth. Holding on to some kind of value.

I'm up then down. I want to save the world. Create a panacea for any conceivable woe. Real or fictional. Past, present, future.

But then I look down. The alley between apartment buildings lined with dumpsters. Not unlike the one I was abandoned in so many years ago. A man digs through it. Maybe it's a woman. Skin so dirty, covered in layers of clothes brought over on the Mayflower. The noble thing, go down there. Give them some food.

My tunnel vision won't allow it.

Nicky Salcedo. That bat-shit crazy lady who claims to be my aunt. My theoretical son. They have to go. Am I jumping to conclusions? Too many assumptions? Probably. But last time I wavered, I lost a hand.

A costly mistake I clearly can't afford to make a second time. My enemies. Much like Alnilam, their time was over long ago.

They just don't know it yet.

I might not save the world. But I can at least make it better for my child. The one I'll never know. Never hold.

Crying. A rare show of emotion infiltrates my face. No one around to see it. Deep breaths, I compose myself.

There, that's better. Ready to do this.

I head down to bed. Third night in the new apartment. First one isn't safe. Not that this one is any better. They found me once, they can find me again. Hooray for fleeting psychological victories. But this one is bare bones. A bed, fridge, couch. Essentials. Gets the job done.

Rest. Much-needed, glorious rest.

Long days of scouting for donors ahead of me.

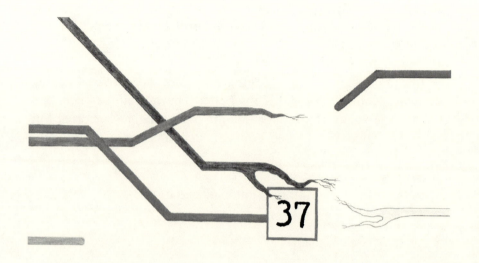

37

My mind officially blown, I thought I'd seen it all. So proud of myself. Just took a shit. One long continuous snake, easily twenty inches. Coiled around in a perfect circle. With a corkscrew too. Making a marvelous Möbius Strip.

Even my shit is smart.

Many ups and downs over the past months. Especially these last few days. But it's come to this: analyzing my stool samples. It's stories like mine that inspire people. On the verge of death, life in shambles. Given another chance. Then comes redemption. Do something heroic.

Me, I'm going in reverse.

True, I *should* want to help people. But why? Look where it got me. Sure, it's not all about me. I've done more living in the last month than most people will do in ten years. Not an exaggeration. Everyone is stuck behind a computer, cell phone, virtual reality sex simulator. If people are so deserving of life, why aren't they *living* it?

This whole debacle with my hand confirms something I am dreading. Past the point of no return. Any hope I had for retrieving a shred of my former, noble self: gone.

Strangely fine with that.

Sure, I've degenerated into the pinnacle of despair. Never felt so alive. So fresh. Defies logic.

So I ask the obvious: if I'm so despicable, why is no one doing a thing about it? I gave humanity a fresh start. A chance for other people to live long, healthy lives. Cure other hideous diseases. Discover new elements. Eradicate poverty. Grand tasks for sure. But there was a time when a cure for AIDS was considered nonviable.

Instead, we got soda-flavored toothpaste and twelve-thousand-calorie burritos.

Perhaps it's time to accept the harsh reality: humanity has peaked. No longer capable of greatness. If we ever were. We had a good run. But we've run our course. Accomplished all we're going to. This is as good as it gets. Now it's time to embrace our demise.

If at first you don't succeed, you're probably not very talented.

About to finish photographing my epic turd, it's time for my new favorite activity. I get dressed, hop on the Blue Line, transfer to the Orange, get off in the Loop. Time to go where all the smokers hang out.

Get off the train, through the rusty turn-style. Likely the original gate installed several decades ago. Down the creaky wooden stairs, every instant of pressure applied by my feet hints at collapse. Ralph Macchio could shatter these planks by snapping his fingers.

Down on street level, I head to Mackenzie's favorite deli. As good as her food is, even she concedes their Reuben can't be topped. I opt for meatball. Messy as ever. Stain both sleeves. Totally worth it.

People are staring. To be expected. My hand is different. Plain and simple. But it still feels weird. Thought I was ready for it. Guess not. Something I'll say with less frequency than Haley's comet. Not so much the staring that bothers me. The really bad attempts to hide it, that's what gets me.

Look or don't look. I know you're staring. You know that I know.

Not as if I have spinach stuck in my teeth. A booger in my nose. I'm well aware of my condition. You're doing no one any favors.

Try being adopted. The looks I got when people found that out, those hurt. Helped me develop thick skin for a while. Not long enough I guess. But Mom, that was the worst. The way it affected her. Seeing the pain on her face was way worse than the way anyone looked at me. Their comments and looks made her feel broken. Dysfunctional.

She was the greatest woman I have ever known. Redundant. I know. Not possible to overstate her generosity.

And now, these stares. Old feelings flooding back. That look in her eyes stirs a rage inside me. All the positive, wonderful memories of her. But these are the ones resurfacing from my subconscious.

Enough is enough.

"Hey, asshole. What are you looking at?" Apparently a BLT. His eyes immediately dart down, focused on a basket of fries. I stand up, walk over slowly. "I said what are you looking at?"

His trepidation obvious. "Nothing, man, sorry."

"Yeah, I'll bet you are. Listen here, buddy. If you ever look at me like that again, I will rip your heart out through your urethra. Got it?"

Says nothing, just nods. Eyes still locked on his food. Everyone else staring, for different reasons now. Not just the guy with the weird hand. Now I'm the crazy motherfucker so close to snapping. Who also has a weird hand.

I throw away my trash, step outside. It's gonna be a good day. That felt good. Got the sardonic juices flowing. Plenty more where that came from.

Just looking to pick a fight? You bet your ass.

Before the bars close, I will have my ass kicked three times. Maybe more.

What better place to start than Millennium Park? The assholes outnumber the blades of grass. Cross the street, head straight to "the bean." That big silver shiny smooth reflective thing. Just a skid mark on the underpants of a great city.

#LaundryDay

I approach the silver monstrosity. Cameras are snapping like paparazzi. Will I take your picture? With resistance and chagrin, yes.

I walk a few laps around it. Looking for the perfect target. A few more laps. Take a few more pictures. People on vacation from Toronto. Tokyo. Los Angeles. Cairo. Paris.

Forget New York.

The Bean is the new melting pot.

A few more laps. Then perfection.

Some lady is standing by a stroller. An infant inside. Little boy, maybe age three, holds on to her leg. Her right hand on the push bar, typing on a gadget perched atop. Left hand holding a cigarette. But it's cool, she's holding it away from the baby.

Game time.

Walk in her direction, I stop about ten feet away. Reach inside my messenger bag, pull out a white canister. Attach the red funnel, push down on the top. The piercing shriek wastes no time. Babies are crying and screaming instantly. A couple kids are laughing, asking their parents if they can have one.

Mom with the stroller drops her nicotine craving. Gives me a contemptuous stare, moves around to check on her infant. Pulls out a baby girl, cradles it. Several minutes later, she is back in the stroller. Time to light up another. She pulls a lighter out of her right pocket, ignites another stick of tar and ammonia. More cyanide for the rest of us.

She dials her phone, still staring me down. I walk to the other side of the bean, countdown from ten like it's New Year's Eve. Get to zero, run full speed back toward negligent mom. Finger pressing firmly on the horn the whole time. Circle the plaza a couple times, drop the horn, and come to rest a couple feet from the mom and her children.

Puts her phone in her pocket. "Are you fucking crazy?" True or false: I will hear this question (or some variation) more than once today?

"I'm sorry, miss, what are you talking about? I'm simply enjoying a lovely day in the park. And it just so happens I'm a big fan of science. So I was also demonstrating the Doppler effect for everyone in the area. You're welcome, by the way."

Looks at me like I'm speaking Mandarin. "That, stupid air horn you were blowing. You're annoying everyone here, not to mention scaring my children out of their minds. You're going to damage their ears with that thing. Do that one more time and I'm gonna call the cops."

"So let me get this straight. It's OK for you to annoy me with your cigarette smoke, but my ambient noise is unacceptable?"

Her eloquent rebuttal: "It's a free country. If you don't like my smoking, you can go somewhere else."

Ah, the "free country" excuse. Desperate last resort of a deficient argument.

"The same can be said for my air horn. More importantly, why does your right to smoke cigarettes trump my right to breathe clean air?"

Immediately I regret using the word "trump." Already this debate is way over her head. Her response, a simple blank stare. Defiantly, she takes a deep puff, blows it toward me. Not directly in my face, but close.

I spit out the taste of stale smoke. "As for the health of your kids, I find it odd that the woman blowing secondhand smoke into her young children's still-developing lungs is lecturing me on the health and well-being of kids. Do I have that correct?"

A picture might be worth a thousand words. I'd gladly pay a million bucks for a framed print of her reaction. Absolute shock. How dare I. Might as well spring for the matte and glossy finish while I'm at it.

"Don't tell me how to raise my kids."

Once again, she and I disagree. "Someone has to."

More shock. Followed by a slap. I repulse her. That makes two of us. We're now at the point of making a scene. Most had their eyes on me already, thanks to the air horn fiasco. Now almost everyone is focused on our exchange.

Normally, I'd grab her by the ear. Shove a couple pills down her throat. Too many witnesses. Get out now, or I never will. Instead, I lean in close to her. "Your children are going to be deadbeats. Turning tricks to put Happy Meals in the mouths of your illegitimate grandchildren."

This time, a punch in the nose. A little blood, nothing crazy. She punches like the poor excuse of a mother she is.

I begin my walk of shame. People slowly part, making a path for my exit. The stares continue. If I had two good hands, I might care. Even then. Unlikely. Thirty paces away, I turn back.

"Do the world a favor. Get your tubes tied, bitch."

Shock and dismay, cries of "How dare he?" and the like ensue. I can feel the disdain. The judgment. Hotter than a thousand suns. Once more, I stop and shout, "Do it! Hit the crazy motherfucker with the fucked-up hand! Go ahead!" I sprint toward the L, dodging traffic, ignoring the blaring horns and middle fingers.

I hop the turnstile. More of the same. People judge silently to themselves. Not so much upset that I'm a criminal. More mad at themselves for not having the balls to do likewise.

Down the stairs, a train is approaching. Slowing down, all cars are packed. A common occurrence. No seats anywhere. This train is barely SRO. I learned long ago, look for the crazy person. Every train has one. Even during rush hour, there's a small halo around them. No one wants to be next to the crazy person.

My lucky day. The crazy person can be spotted immediately. He is me. I am him. Oh boy, oh boy. Always dreamed of this moment. Not really, but here I am. Might as well embrace it.

Shove my way through the double doors. Stay calm until they shut and we're on our way.

Showtime.

Start slowly, softly. Not too loud at first. Let their discomfort sink in. Don't freak them out all at once. "Colostomy bag. Colostomy bag. Colostomy bag." Eyes begin darting back and forth. "Colostomy bag. Colostomy bag. Shit in a bag. Colostomy bag. Shit in a bag." Passengers growing visibly uncomfortable.

Shouldn't have waited this long to try this. Perfect solution for those with personal space issues. Amp it up a bit. "Colostomy bag. Shit in a bag." Once elbow-to-elbow, I can now stretch my arms out in front of me without interference. Train stops. Some get off, some get on. More or less an even exchange.

Adams/Wabash to Madison/Wabash, it's "Colostomy Bag."

From there until State/Lake, it's "supersonic dildo."

Transfer to the Red Line. Until Grand it's "Sodomy and Justice for All."

Until Clark/Division, I simply state a fact. "I cured AIDS." No one believes me. Not that I blame them. I'm a mess. Aware that I'm falling, no clue where rock bottom is. But this is my stop. I get off and walk the streets, pass the hair salons and convenience stores. Hop in real quick. Grab a Coke and pack of smokes.

After the debacle in the park, I need a cigarette. Still hate the taste. Nothing fuels rage and resentment like blatant hypocrisy.

And nicotine. Don't forget nicotine.

Benson & Hedges, you still taste like shit. But moral superiority quickly washes that away. Sip of Coke, take a puff. Back and forth until the soda is gone, and half the pack empty. Three or four puffs on each, toss it to the curb. When all is said and done, I've probably got three sticks in my system. Throw the rest in the gutter. The sounds of sewer rats rejoicing on the receiving end already audible.

I keep walking. No particular place in mind.

Pick up the pace. The guy behind me, he wants me dead. One of Salcedo's goons. The mom with two kids folding granny panties at the laundromat. Been on my trail for weeks. Gotta get outta here.

Turning around, I head back toward the train. Speed up even more, walking with a purpose. Looking left, looking right. Up, down, everywhere in between. Just like that, I hear it. Unmistakable.

Drumsticks and paint buckets. The sound of home.

Make no mistake. Quality music requires quality instruments. Recording studios. Mix and master; do it again. Which requires money.

Except for these guys. The exception to the rule.

Each step brings me closer to serenity. The unified beating grows increasingly louder in my ears. Sending signals to my distraught and fragile brain.

For right now, none of that matters. I could stand here for hours. Or until the police or local shopkeepers come and kick them out. No encores or grand finales. Instead of a final bow, the show ends with a collective scramble to grab everything and get out.

The Miracle Mile, the shops on Michigan Avenue near the Hancock building. The Water Tower. For many years, a reliable stomping-ground where street musicians flocked. All hours of the day. Too much of a hassle now. Most of them have migrated. Just a few stops up the Red Line. Truth be told, I hardly recognize the place. Once a massive taboo, it now glows with the neon lights of coffee shops and furniture stores. Cabrini Greens—only a couple decades ago, the most dangerous housing development in America. Now, much nicer. Don't go thinking it's done a complete 180. No high-rise condos selling for seven figures. Still, a much safer place to live. Much more chance of prosperity for the working class.

#HoorayForGentrification

A group of eight kids sits before me. Milk crates and shine boxes make great seats, double as storage space. By my guess, the age range goes from around nine up to seventeen.

But they're so crisp, so on-point. Sound as if they've been playing for decades. Slowly, a crowd gathers. Song after song, people surround them to listen. A cop walks by, shoots them a look. Nothing more. No frantic scramble, no threatening words. An unheard-of scenario a few years ago.

The beats continue. A large hat taken from a Kentucky Derby reject bin slowly piles up with money. Not as much as they deserve. I step inside the nearest shop with an ATM, grab some cash. Crumple it up and throw it in. Let them be surprised later. Some passerby sees that kind of money sitting on the sidewalk; it's gone and spent before the resonations subside.

I'm not even ten feet away before I know they've opened up my contribution.

"Nigga, check this shit out!"

"Oooh yeah, boy. Damn nigga, time to buy them Jordan's I been eyein' for real nigga."

Et cetera, et cetera.

I make my way back to the Red Line. Thinking of Miracle Mile reminds me of Christmas time. Mom and Dad would always take me down there in December to look at decorations. I hop the turnstile again. No resistance, just looks of indignation. The ride that normally takes three minutes stretches into an eight-minute trek.

"Please excuse the delay. We are waiting for signals ahead. We will be moving again shortly." Hope the lady who recorded that doesn't get a residual. Tax revenue would vanish like an ice cube in a frying pan.

I exit at Grand. Take the stairs to street level. Scaffolding casts a veil over three of the four corners. One less obstructed building than usual. People shuffle back and forth, shopping bags and briefcases in hand. I pass a guy smoking a cigarette, regret tossing my pack away earlier. *Slaughterhouse V* catchphrase.

I take the stairs up to Michigan Avenue. Stare up at the Digital Playground building. Formerly the Wrigley building.

Head left, away from the river. People hustle by against the grain and flying past from behind. A never-ending rush to get somewhere that isn't where they are. A fate worse than Sisyphus.

A group of young men shuffle around like a rabid swarm of bees. Constant movement I can't keep track. The distance between us constantly decreases. Eventually, one from the group approaches me, something small and plastic in hand.

"Hey, homie, you like hip-hop, dawg?"

"Huh?"

"Yo, check it, me and my boys are trying to get our sound out there, know what I'm sayin'?" Technically yes, but not really. He waves this piece of plastic at me. "So how 'bout it?"

Was there an offer that I missed? "How about what?"

"Check out our album. It's sick man. Do you like the Maulratz? Compozit? Ramen Thief?"

Never heard of any of them. Shocking, I know.

If their talent for naming bands is indicative of musical ability, fairly certain I'd like to keep it that way. "Not really."

Clearly not paying attention to my demeanor. "OK, cool, well, check out our record. Ten bucks."

Ten bucks for this guy to leave me alone?

Deal of the century.

"OK yeah, give me one." I pull out my wallet. "Can you break a twenty?" Stares at it like it's a baby Pegasus. Then he laughs.

"Man, where'd you get that? Shit, son, you must be a lot older than you look. Only old people use cash."

Feeling confrontational, just want to get this over with. "Well, how about you just give me two copies of your CD then?"

Another laugh, this one more hysterical. "CD?" Yelling at his friends. "Nigga, you hear that. Homie wants a CD." Laughter ensues all around. Eventually subsiding, they carry about their business. The urge for confrontation grows. "Sorry, man, that shit was funny though. No one uses CDs anymore, son."

"So how do you expect me to listen to your album?"

"You got a phone on you?" I nod yes. "Well, I just plug this little thing in, and voila, you've got the album in seconds."

"Fine." I pull out my phone. He plugs it in. Give him my twenty, tell him to keep the change.

"There you go, boy. Make sure you tell everyone to buy it. Tweet that shit, son."

"Yeah, no problem. Take care, man, good luck."

Sticks out his fist for some kind of handshake. Never been big on this crap, but whatever. "Keep it real, son. Thanks for the support."

"You're welcome. Good luck selling albums. See ya 'round, nigga." His eyes go big. It just slipped out. Like I said, feeling confrontational. Subconsciously, I've been waiting for a fight. Safe to say, there's a storm on the horizon.

From ten feet away, I hear, "Yo, Payday, what'd this cracker say?"

My new friend, apparently named after a candy bar, does his best to cover for me. "Yo, D-Frost, chill man. He didn't mean nothin' by it."

"Bullshit, nigga! What'd you fuckin' say, boy?"

About time. Been looking for a fight for a while now. "Well, I bought this album, then I told him I'd see him 'round. Look, it's just a figure of speech. I know I probably won't see him around. I didn't literally mean that—"

Cuts me off. "Not that shit! After that!"

"Oh, I said nigga. But it's no big deal. I said the one that ended with a *ga* not an *er*."

"I heard what you said, and I don't give a fuck what it ended with. *Why* did you say it?"

"Well, you guys were all saying it. I thought it sounded like a pretty cool word. Just seemed like fun." I was right, this is fun. The veins pulsing in his neck, a topographer's crowning glory.

"Just cuz *we* were sayin' it, doesn't mean you can say it!"

"Why not?"

"Cuz, you can't! Motherfucker, gimme a reason not to kick your ass right now!"

"OK, first of all, you mean I *shouldn't*. 'Can't' implies a lack of ability. You really meant to say that I'm not *supposed* to say it. Clearly, I've demonstrated an aptitude for saying it." Too much fun. So many years wasted not being an asshole.

"Bitch, knock it off with that big-word suit-and-tie bullshit! You can't say that word. That's *our* word!"

"You mean your rap group invented that word?"

A knife materializes in his hand. Waves it around, points it at me. "Mothafucka, listen close. African Americans. Blacks. *Us*. That is *our* word!" Steps closer. "Now getch yo hate-crime, slave-drivin' bitch-ass outta my face before I cut you up!"

Game over. Quicker than I've been in a month, I grab his ear with my injured hand. Only need two fingers to pinch, drop him to the ground. The knife falls free. Pick it up with my good hand. Press the blade flat against his throat. His friends stare in disbelief. People shuffle by. A crowd wants to gather. Commotion draws them in like moths to a flame. The shiny blade repels them just as quickly.

I whisper in my companion's ear, "Listen closely while I make this short and sweet. If I really hated black people, then why did I spend the better part of three years saving lives in Africa? A continent most people have written off. I've been all over South Africa. The Congo. Sudan. Can you even find those places on a map?" A bus rolls by. "If I were a racist, I would drag you on to that bus and make you stand in the back, even if we were the only two people on it. See, when you tell me I can't do something because of the color of my skin, you're no better than the person you're accusing me of being. If I kill you right now, it would be a hate crime. But epidermis has nothing to do with it. All crimes are hate crimes. I hate you because you're intellectually deficient, and you're ruining the world. So I'm going to go now. If you see me, any time, anywhere, turn around. Don't let me see you because next time I won't be so gracious." I put the knife in my pocket, hail a cab.

Cabbie must be oblivious to what just happened. In awe, he actually stopped. "Where to?" he wants to know.

"That computer store near the Water Tower. I want to pick up one of those fancy new fun pads or whatever they're called."

His eyes grow large. "You mean a FlashPAD? Good luck, buddy. There's a line wrapped around the corner halfway to Lakeshore Drive."

"Even better. Just drive."

He shrugs, pulls away, drops me off minutes later. He wasn't kidding. The line must have three hundred people or more. A clock in the window of the building counts down.

14:29:13.
14:29:12.
14:29:11.
You get the idea.

More than half a day remains. I head into the store. People are shopping for less popular items. Old versions of this gadget on clearance.

I find a clerk. "Excuse me there, young lady."

"Yes, how may I help you?" Service with a smile.

"I was just curious, how long have people been waiting out front for this new thing?"

She attempts to conceal her dismay. Almost works, but her eyes betray her. Wants to make it seem like no big deal. Underneath, it's obvious she thinks they're bigger idiots than I do. "Well, most of the people in that line showed up within the last four hours, but the first three people showed up as a group five days ago."

Nearly a week of your life. Is there anything you want so badly you would throw away a week of your life to get it? Something that will be there days later? Something in abundance.

If your answer to that question is no, you obviously didn't read this far. You learned to spot a waste of time when you see one.

If you answered yes, pay close attention. Look out for assholes like me when waiting in line.

I walk up and down Michigan Avenue. Scanning the crowd. All their eyes glued to devices soon to be rendered obsolete. The final moments until technology becomes antiquity. I circle the block twice, soak up the beautiful Chicago air.

Round the corner, approach the front of the line. Making my way over, I pull out my FlashPAD. The old model, of course.

Quick Internet search for Dillon Pulaski, millions of results. The man is a porn legend. So many choices. No desire to see him in that pumpkin head for the thousandth time. Scroll up and down. Page over. Skip to a random number: 29.

Scrolling again. *Slut Fest 33. Back Door Summer Lovin' 12. Asian Fixation 20.* The list goes on and on. Then I see it.

Dillon's Cherry Poppin' Fiasco 3.

A very early and out-of-date collection.

When Mackenzie screwed Dillon on film. Not a secret. I've known about it for years. Suddenly, it bothers me. Too little too late. But now, annoying and underachieving twenty-somethings get to bare the brunt of my rage.

Scrolling down, I click on *Cocktoberfest*. Dillon and two other guys, going to town on some chick. Grunts and moans ensue. I put on my glasses so only I can see the footage. No headphones though. I blast the volume for all to hear. The honking cabs and ambient noise can't drown out the "ughs" and "ooooh yeahs" surging out of this technological wonder.

Bees to pollen. All eyes in the vicinity immediately cut me down. So far so good. The murmurs begin to fly. Everyone expressing their distaste to their friends. To anyone who will listen. Anyone but me.

A couple women whisper in the ears of the guys next to them. Husbands and boyfriends.

A few minutes pass. The discomfort grows. I can feel eyes all over me. Burning holes in my clothes. A small chuckle to myself. I crank the volume up even more. Step closer to the people in line. Begin pacing. Up and down. From Huron St. to Ontario. Back again. The murmurs grow louder. Ready to bust. Scan the crowd. Which one of you? Who will be the first to snap?

"Hey, asshole! Turn that shit off already!"

Finally. Stroll toward the voice. Time to face my accuser. A line packed shoulder to shoulder with people, they've created space for her. She stands alone, ready to take me down.

I walk slowly toward some girl with a big grin, standing like she's queen bee. Looks vaguely familiar.

"Hey, fucker, where have you been?" Her demeanor disconcertingly playful. I stare blankly. She goes serious. Must know me, can tell I'm drawing a blank with her. "Wow, you really don't remember me do you?"

"I'm sorry, it's been a long week."

"Wow, you sure know how to make a girl feel special."

"Excuse me?"

Leans in close. "I know there are guys out there who sleep with so many women they lose track. But I was kind of under the impression that I was the only woman you'd ever knocked unconscious and stuffed with silicone."

Takes a minute, but it comes to me. "Maggie."

"Oh, so you *do* remember." Steps out of line, grabs me by the hand. "Do you have a favorite bar in the area?"

"Not really, why?"

"Because I need a drink. And when you hear what I have to tell you, you're gonna want one too."

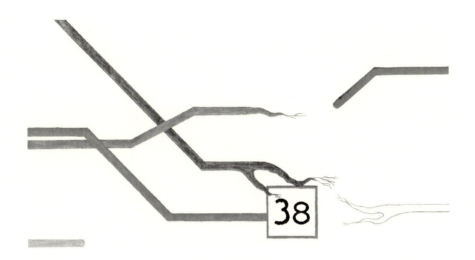

38

Somehow we end up in Lincoln Park. I protested the entire way. What do you expect? That's what happens when you drink with kids. Not literally. She's old enough to drink. But she could slip into a high school algebra class, no one would question her presence.

Lincoln fucking Park. The second we leave the L station, my nostrils are bombarded with myriad stenches. Mainly body spray and desperation. Still, a sacrifice I'm willing to make if she has anything remotely useful to tell me.

She asks me which bar I prefer. Inner monologue says none of them, my tongue tells her to choose. Twenty or so to pick from. All of them interchangeable. She decides on one with a coat-of-arms above the door. Tell her to grab a seat in the back corner, I'll get the drinks. Manhattan for me, Midori-sour for her.

"There you go."

"Thanks."

Cutting to the chase, I say, "So what did you find out?"

Exaggerating her surprise, "Whoa there, buddy. Slow down. Can I at least take a sip first? Sheesh."

Impatience evident on my face. No attempt to disguise it. Put back half my Manhattan before she's two sips in. Fingers tapping the table, I sit and wait. She's quite amused. At least one of us is.

"Oh, before I begin, I wanted to say thank you."

"You already thanked me for the drink."

Chuckling, "Not that. Well yes, thank you for the drink, but I meant these," she looks down. "These puppies are great. Business has never been better."

Dryly, I reply, "So glad I could help. Now, with all due respect, I'm not exactly in the best of shape. I'm literally losing my mind. Any information you have for me would be greatly appreciated."

Sly smile. "Oh, I don't doubt that." Her delays, beyond cryptic. Takes me back to the last time I saw Mackenzie. My eyes start to water. Ever so briefly, but it shows. "Hey, are you OK?"

"Yeah, I'm fine. Allergies." She can tell I'm full of it, lets it slide. A gesture for which I'm internally grateful.

"Well, long story short, your suspicions were justified." I nod. "It's been a while since we spoke, so I'm not exactly sure what you thought they were up to, so I'll just tell you what I know. Sorry if I repeat some stuff."

"Not a problem. Please, continue."

"Well, first of all, those guys don't like to talk. It was a full-time job getting them to open up about anything." Another strategically placed pause.

"Is that a prompt for me to ask you how you got the info?" Smile blazes a trail wide across her face. "OK, how did you get them to talk?"

"Oh, you know, feminine charm. Men are so simple. Tits and ass is all it takes. Some more than others, but at their core, you're all just wastes of DNA."

I'll drink to that.

"So a couple lap dances were all it took? I find that hard to believe."

"Well that, and a couple of those pills I swiped from the counter before I left. You know, when you abducted me?"

Wait. Did I hear her correctly? "How did you know what those were for?"

Laughing. "I didn't. But you had just knocked me out the night before, so I don't think it was too much of a stretch to assume they were some kind of sedative."

Logical assumption, although not entirely correct. Do I divulge the ear pinch, the beads in my fingertips?

She continues, "So anyway, I got them very relaxed. Eventually, they just wouldn't shut up about it. You were right, they want to legalize prostitution. At first I thought it was a great idea. You know, less legal restrictions means more business for me—"

Interrupting her, "Not exactly. See, when that happens, more competition enters the marketplace. Part of the appeal of what you do is that it's forbidden. That's why you're able to charge so much. High risk on your part, so in the long run, it probably hurts you."

Smiling. "Well, thank you, Warren Buffett, but had you let me finish, I would have said that after considering it, I realized it wasn't such a good thing after all. Of course the guys were selling this idea like it was going to make us filthy rich. After all, we're just a bunch of dumb sluts. We don't know anything about economics."

Reductive judgmental logic. The apple apparently didn't fall off the tree at all.

Hoping she'll elaborate, I press, "But why? I mean sure, if they control it, they stand to make a great deal of profit because they'll have more employees. But this can't just be about money. There's got to be more to it."

"Oh, there is. Much more. So I get Madigan in the back room alone. Give him a few dances. Generic conversation at first. But eventually, we start talking about my 'future' once this all goes into effect. I've slipped him three pills at this point." My eyes nearly pop out of my head. Highly dangerous. One is bad, three is nearly fatal. "So eventually, the floodgates open. He won't shut up, spouting off about how he and Nicky are gonna run the world. 'We've got plans. Oh, baby, have we got plans!' he kept saying. I didn't want to sound too intrigued or interested, so I played dumb. Just asked him aloofly what kind of plans. So he tells me that he's been back and forth between here and Washington DC, finalizing some kind of deal."

Our nation's capital. Keep coming back to it. Suddenly, I'm on the edge of my seat. "Go on." Trying diligently not to sound desperate for information this time.

"Well, when I found out, I thought I was some kind of super sleuth, but apparently, it's been in the news for a while. Basically, Congress is very close to passing a law that is going to limit the number of children a woman can give birth to."

I conceal my eagerness. "It sounds vaguely familiar."

"But it just doesn't make sense."

"How so?" Please tell me what I want to hear.

"Well, this is obviously going to increase the number of abortions. And with so many Republicans in Congress, it just doesn't fit." I knew I picked the right woman for the job.

Challenging her, I agree, but can't leave any stone unturned. "Right, but it's also going to result in more condom and birth control sales, which Salcedo will profit from greatly."

Nodding. "Very true. But how much does he stand to make on the sale of pharmaceuticals with competitors entering the fold every day? A couple hundred million? Billions? Certainly a lot, but think about this: would he be able to sell enough pills and rubbers to erase the national deficit?"

A curveball. "Excuse me? You lost me." I shudder instantaneously as those words leave my mouth.

"Right now, the United States is indebted to China for a great deal of money. Probably a one followed by so many zeros it could wrap around the Equator twice."

I applaud her hyperbole. Liking this girl more by the second. Still dreading where this is going.

"So, hypothetically, if one were able to get this number back down to a manageable number, or even create a surplus, they stand to gain a lot, right? I'm not talking monetarily, but more like power. Prestige."

I finish off my Manhattan. Stare off into space. Cycling through the potential ramifications.

She cuts to the chase. "We owe China a lot of money. But we have something they need."

Grasping the magnitude of what she's telling me, I say, "Women."

Somberly, she agrees. "Exactly. For decades, they restricted births, even killed off female babies because they were considered inferior. So now they have the largest country on the planet overcrowded by a predominantly male population. They need females."

Shit. I rub my face. Feeling nauseous. Pinch my ear, attempt to calm my nerves. Nothing works.

"Basically, as far as I can tell, Nicky Salcedo wants to sell children to China at a hefty price. Then he can run for president on the platform that he saved the American economy."

On this point, I'll contest her. "Not Nicky. Cooper. This plan will take a couple decades to go into effect. The law isn't even official yet. But thirty years from now, Cooper will be in prime position to run this country."

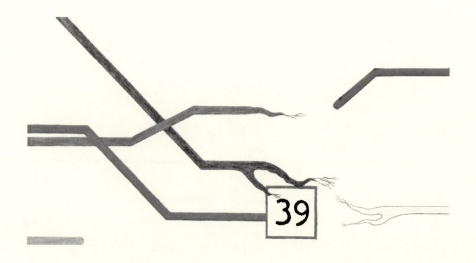

Thirty minutes pass like that. Practically time traveling. Three shots go by even more quickly. Time I spent challenging everything she said. Contesting every word, everything she *thinks* she heard. Things she hypothetically saw.

Maybe she was wasted. Those clubs are kind of loud after all.

Her conviction unwavering. Fully convincing, not that I wasn't already decided. Never truly doubted her. Just wishing it not to be true.

Shit in one hand, wish in the other.

Speaking of hands, she hasn't mentioned mine. I've caught her glancing once or twice. Overall, she's been casual about it.

Both concede it's been a long day. Information overload. Time to head home, get some rest. Regroup and reconvene at Pick Me Up Café tomorrow at noon.

"Are you headed back to the L, or do you want me to hail a cab?"

Small chuckle. "Nah, I'm good. I live really close to here actually."

#Shocking

"Well, let me walk you home at least. Lead the way."

Catches her off guard. "Um, well"—thinking—"it's no big deal. I'm really not too far. I'll be fine." Her cynicism justified. Last time we were in a room alone together . . . well, you know.

"Oh, no, it's not what you're thinking. I don't want to come inside or anything like that. Just want to make sure you get home safely. Believe it or not, I am actually capable of doing nice things from time to time."

The muscles on her face twitch. A series of squints and puckers. Pondering. "Not."

"Excuse me?"

"You said, 'believe it or not,' and I choose to *not* believe you." Awkward pause. Busts out laughing, "Dude, I'm fucking with you. Sure, you can walk me home. But if you touch me, your balls might look like your hand."

Oh my. Should I be consoled that only one of them is real? At least the elephant in the room has been acknowledged. My hand now fair game.

"That sounds reasonable," I tell her. "After you."

Thirty minutes later, we're in Boystown.

Time to speak up. "I thought you said you lived really close to Lincoln Park."

"What? It's like two miles. That's nothing when you live in the city." Her level of sincerity is nearly impossible to gauge. True, two miles isn't far if you live in Chicago. Don't think most people would file it under "really close." Just what I need. A "partner" pushing my already fragile mind closer to the edge of insanity.

Pedestrian traffic increases. Everyone is out for a night on the town. Most of the two miles is void of human interaction. Passed eight or nine people the entire way. Virtual abandonment given the area. But alas, Boystown is as busy as ever.

"OK, in all seriousness though, I am getting pretty tired. I'm stressed as shit, and I really do think it's only a matter of time before my brain disintegrates. I'm going home to get some rest. Are you good to make it home from here? I can have my cab drop you off if you'd like."

Silence. Long, excruciating silence. In reality, I'm well aware of the horns blaring around me. The roar of shitty music and people laughing. I know it's there but not a single decibel registers.

"Hello? Did you hear me? Are you good to make it home from here?"

Terrifying maniacal grin spreads ear to ear. Finally she speaks, "Follow me." Grabs me by the arm, drags me down the street. We approach and stop in front of some bar with a flashing green neon sign.

Purple. That's the name of the bar.

Not really sure I get it. The word "purple" written in bright green letters. This is why I hate art. People think this is clever. Like they're the first to do this. All bow before the visionaries.

"What are we doing here?"

Turns face-to-face, looks me right in the eye. The smile from a minute ago remains, refusing to subside.

"Throwing a wrench in the gears." A nefarious look consumes her eyes. My heart skips a beat, goose bumps on my arms. Walks up to the bouncer, he waves her through. From the threshold, she yells, "Hey, jackass, are you coming or what?" I follow her inside with reluctance. Can't ignore the adrenaline pumping though. Curiosities peaked, I really want to know what's going on inside her brain.

Shouting above the loud music, "What are we doing in here?"

Grabbing me by the neck, she pulls me down, shouts in my ear, "Do you know who that is?" She points to a group of women in the back. All wearing bright pink dresses. Accoutrements include sashes, tiaras, various penis-shaped medallions.

"Well, I assume it's some kind of bachelorette party. But if you're asking me if I know any of them personally, I don't."

Eyes go wide. Pauses. Assumes my ignorance is an act. Gives me time to break character. "Really?" Still nothing on my face resembling familiarity. "Oh wow, you really don't know who that is. The one with the white veil, the bride-to-be . . . that's Nadira Madani."

That first one meant nothing. Madani, however, that's familiar. "As in Amir Madani? The guy who owns the Bulls."

The relief on her face blatant. "Yes! Thank you! For a second, I thought you grew up in a cave or on another planet or something." Not recognizing Nadira Madani in her world is tantamount to not knowing who Michael Jordan was when I was younger.

I pause, expecting her to elaborate. Can't wait forever, so I watch Nadira dance with her friends. Ponder why they chose a gay club for their celebration. Maggie interjects, "Well?"

"Well, what?"

"Dumbass, that girl dancing over there is the daughter of one of the wealthiest men in Chicago. Do something."

Can't stifle my laugh. "I've got plenty of my own money, but thanks for the advice."

Her jaw drops to the floor. My ignorance stretching out far beyond her perceived acceptable limits. Sounding more like a teenager with every word out of her mouth, "Wow, you really are a lot dumber than I thought. Listen closely." Last two words drawn out for emphasis. The following sentences roll off her tongue and move through a field of molasses. "Nadira Madani is engaged to marry Cooper Madigan. They are getting married in a few weeks. As in she might have some information that's valuable to us."

I let this sink in. Possibilities. They move around like bingo balls, popping in my head. So many to choose from. Which one finds its way to the top first? Lost in thought, my blank stare registers as lack of comprehension.

She lightly slaps my face. Grabs my chin, forces my eyes to meet hers. "Listen, Sammy, I know you're supposed to be the fucking genius here, but you don't seem to be grasping the bigger picture. She's a bombshell, no doubt about it. She might even be really smart. No one gives a shit. This marriage is all about status and power. Uniting Nicky Salcedo and his crew with another major player in Chicago."

Being contrary because that's what I do. "That makes perfect sense, but Cooper is a good-looking guy with a lot going for him. Based on what you've told me, they seem to make a great couple. Maybe they're actually a good match."

Her deep heavy breath scoffs at my ignorance. "Seriously, if it weren't for the fact that I know what you're capable of"—looks at her boobs—"I would never believe you could tell left from right. I see Cooper and Nicky all the time at various clubs. I think I've told you before, they never used to sleep with the women there. Well apparently, I was misinformed. I've certainly never been with either of them, but they've had their way with their share of my coworkers."

"So? He was young and irresponsible. Maybe he's a changed man."

"This was three nights ago." Long pause. "Look, I get it, this whole situation is fucked up. You're terrified. I am too. But pretending something sinister isn't happening will only make matters worse."

I hold up a finger, tell her I'll be back soon. Beeline for the bar, order two Long Islands. Never been served so quickly in a crowded bar. Need to drink at gay clubs more often. "Here you go, I thought you might want this."

She takes a sip followed by a strange face. "Wow, that shit is strong. But I like it. I think I need to get drunk tonight." I nod. "You, however, need to watch yourself." I raise my eyebrows. "You need to keep a level head if you're going to take advantage of that woman tonight." Look of shock shrouds my face. "Oh, come on, don't feel bad about it. She cheats on Cooper just as much as he cheats on her. They both know about it. Like I said, this is a marriage of status."

"You really don't understand. I am horrible with women."

Yet another deviant grin creeps towards her ears like the shadows falling over Chicago at sunset. "Oh, believe me. I understand. That's why I'm here."

What a confidence boost.

"OK then, Goose, show Ice Man how it's done."

"WTF?" Look of total confusion. *Top Gun* reference misses by a mile.

"Never mind. Just tell me what I need to do."

The obvious tension in her shoulders eases slightly. My willingness to take a proactive approach relaxes her. For now.

"OK, well, first and foremost, we're going to wait until they leave the gay club. If you start talking to her now, she'll never take you seriously as a potential hookup."

"What if they stay here all night?"

Her eyes roll; physically causes me pain.

"You really need to get out more. They're young women, bar hopping is what they do. Plus, they won't get nearly as many free drinks at a gay club."

Confused as to why a wealthy socialite needs free drinks. Don't bother letting that thought leave my mouth. Everything else I've said has been a mistake.

"How am I even going to get close to her? She's got two bodyguards that I see. Maybe more outside."

Doesn't miss a beat. "Easy. We're going to knock them out just like you did to me."

"It's really not that easy."

Her look calls my bluff. "Bullshit. Now what kind of pills do you have for me?"

The last time I let my guard down, I lost three fingers. I'm usually good at learning from my mistakes, as few and far between as they are. Apparently, this isn't one of those times. "I didn't knock you out with pills."

She's intrigued. "What do you mean? Those pills I took from you worked on Cooper."

Internal debate gives me pause. Don't tell her yet another secret. But for some reason, I can't help it. I look at her, feel something I haven't felt in a long time. Maybe ever. Attraction for another person. Male or female.

"Put your glass down."

"Huh?"

"Just put it down on the counter." She obliges me. I move my good hand slowly toward the back of her neck, pinch the right spots. Her mouth drops wide open. Eyes begin to roll back then the lids shut. Throws her hand up to her mouth to cover the scream.

"How? Did you? What just happened?"

"Not bad, huh?"

"How did you do that?" I shrug. "Seriously? I haven't cum like that in years. What did you do?"

Grab her small fingers with my injured hand. Place them over the good one. Move it around slowly, back and forth. "Do you feel those bumps?" She nods. "Long story short, there are numerous pressure points all over the body that control various nerves and therefore generate different responses. I just showed you one on the back of your neck. Most of them are actually in the ear. That's how I knocked you out a while ago."

Pure fascination. Intrigue and awe like I've never seen on anyone when explaining anything vaguely scientific.

"Perfect!"

Not quite the reaction I was expecting. Better than the alternative.

"What do you mean?"

"Well, the pill thing is great, but it's not going to work on her guards. You won't see them touch a drink all night. And if they do, it will be a bottle of water that you won't get close to."

I agree. "So what's your plan?"

Looks away from me toward the group of girls. Now gathering their purses and toys. "I'm not exactly sure, but we have the rest of the night to figure it out. Come on, they're getting ready to go to another bar." She downs the rest of her drink in one breathless slurp. Before I know it, we're out the door, trailing the loudest group of women I've ever witnessed toward Wrigleyville. A few minutes later they enter the Cubby Bear without even showing ID. Now out of sight. She grabs my bad hand and drags me to the door. Excitement glowing across her face. I don't like it. Not at all. Not because it hurts. Quite the opposite.

This rush that courses through my veins. When she touches me, I've never felt anything like it. Not even close.

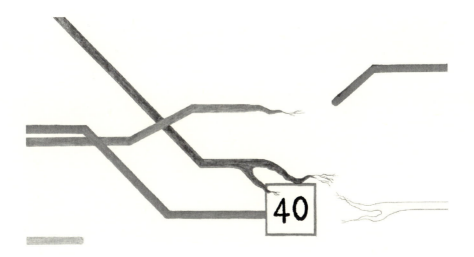

40

Today's the big day. My little boy is getting married. Pains me greatly that I won't be there to witness this momentous occasion. Something tells me there will be other opportunities. If there's one thing the men in my gene pool know, it's functional relationships.

Can't even think that with a straight face.

I've been waiting for this day for three weeks now. Ever since the epic bachelorette party. What a night.

I grab my FlashPAD. The new version. Didn't even have to wait. Got one for Maggie too. Felt bad for pulling her out of line that night. Turn it on, check some e-mails. Typing is so much easier with two good hands.

Do you need that repeated?

Correct. I have two good hands. I'll get to that, don't worry. First I want to enjoy my breakfast bowl of Cap'n Crunch. Soymilk in the cereal. Bit of rum on the side. Captain 'n Cap'n. Breakfast of dipshits.

I surf the Web. Chat with Maggie on IM for a bit. Check scores and the market. Pause to look at the rock on my finger. Shines like a Harley headlight on a dark city street. Alone at night, it stares you right in the eye. Freezing you, captivating.

Easily worth two million. Could pawn it for $50,000 or so. Not about money though. A badge of pride.

The upsides to having ten fingers are obvious. The drawbacks, minimal but present nonetheless. My typing skills, not what they used to be. Adjusting to life with hands of different sizes is harder than you'd think. Makes my dick look massive when I pee, which is nice I guess. Buying gloves sucks. Gotta buy two pairs. Not to mention the stares. Nothing compared to when I had seven fingers, but still annoying. They don't say anything, but you can tell. You know what they're thinking. *Look at that dude. The guy with one normal hand, and one tiny girly hand. So feminine.* The color is off too. I've tried self-tanner. Can't lighten the skin tone of the addition. Instead, now I go spray tanning once a week. Match my body to the new extremity.

I put my bowl in the sink, pour another cocktail. The wedding is about to begin. Can't wait to see the bride on her day. I heard all about her dress. Handmade by Henri Chevalier himself. Nothing like it in the world.

Where's Billy Idol when you need him?

Hope the designer is a fan of décolletage. Anything to take focus off the poor girl's man hand.

By now I really hope you've put the pieces together.

Merely wanted to get a little bit of information. Maggie took the guards out of the equation flawlessly. They might be big and strong. But a man's libido will always reign victorious over the part of his brain affecting logical behavior. Some take longer than others. But they all crumble eventually.

Once Marco and Rodney (names I gave them) were out of the way, it was clear sailing. A couple drinks go a long way. Got her friends tired, put them in cabs home. Didn't take much convincing to go to a hotel with me. By "me" I mean Charles Dodgson.

So long, Wonderland. Tonight, we're going through the looking glass.

Didn't need any pills. Maggie's powers of suggestion, far more potent than I gave them credit for. Girl has the gift of gab. Normally hate people who talk more than necessary.

Back on track. Nadira was oblivious. Didn't have a fucking clue what Cooper, Nicky, and possibly her dad are up to. She just wants to drink and party. Listening to her talk was death by the slowest torture. Heard every word she said, understood not a thing. Purses and shoes. Made her suck my dick literally to stop her from talking.

Deep-throats like a champ. Wish I could say she swallows. No idea though. Made her work so long she passed out. I went to work. Sedated her just in case she awoke during the procedure.

Have you ever tried to transplant a hand after a few cocktails? Rhetorical question.

It went flawlessly. Minimal blood. As far as I can tell, virtually no scarring or complications on either of us. Took pictures after she awoke. Used her phone. Can't have that traced back to me. Sent them to Nicky and Cooper. Along with the name of that surgeon in Santa Monica.

So now I'm waiting to see just how good he is. I happen to think I set the bar pretty high. Guess those extra nights spent molding clay came in handy. Don't forget jewelry making. Soft hands. Precise, delicate movements.

All of Nicky's money might be able to buy the best doctors in the world. But it will never buy him peace of mind. Not even close.

The best part? He has no idea who is screwing with him. Sure, Nadira will tell them Charles Dodgson. No record will be found. They'll check the surveillance tapes at the hotel. Won't matter. It's already been hacked and erased. Irrelevant even if they saw the footage. I look nothing like I used to.

The webcast of the wedding opens up on my screen. Palm trees and rolling waves. One of the many beaches in Maui. Probably rented out the entire island. To control everyone who comes in and out. Make it as exclusive as possible. To get a chair in the crowd harder ticket than the Super Bowl.

A quick pan over the guests. By my estimate, five hundred in attendance. Could be way more. Cameras only do a partial scan. Doesn't really matter. There are only two faces I'm interested in.

Cooper heads down the aisle. Takes his place near the minister. I grab a drink from the fridge. An IM from Maggie pops up.

> **dudeMAGnet27:** Ready for this?
> **BigBother1984:** You have no idea.
> **dudeMAGnet27:** How's the hand?
> **BigBother1984:** Feeling great. Better dexterity every day.
> **dudeMAGnet27:** Sweeeeet!!!

The processional music begins. Bridesmaids and groomsmen flock to the front.

BigBother1984: Showtime!
dudeMAGnet27: Ick! Those bridesmaids' dresses are hideous.
BigBother1984: Hadn't noticed.
dudeMAGnet27: Yeah, whatever. I know you're secretly a diehard Vanity Fair fanatic.
BigBother1984: Busted. Secret's out.

It's just like any wedding—uneventful. Nadira looks striking. My fist time seeing her in natural light. Her skin, a dermatologist's wet dream. Flawless. Smooth and soft. The color, simply perplexing. A natural tone making her a racial chameleon. One of those pinnacles of feminine beauty that could be any nationality. Dark enough to be African American, light enough to be Native American. East Indian, Spanish, Hawaiian. Take your pick. Her last name indicates Middle Eastern. Doesn't seem to count for much these days. My dad is Italian. As Guido as Guido gets.

Salcedo. Spanish.

My skin tone, more formaggio than tapas.

Nevertheless, she is a knockout. Cooper knows what he's doing. They'll make the perfect power couple. Beauty and power. A virtually unstoppable force. Not to mention the fiscal support.

dudeMAGnet27: This is kinda boring, huh? I thought they'd make a bigger deal out of her hand.
BigBother1984: Yeah, me too. Not surprised though. They've got an amazing PR team. They had a couple weeks to get their shit together. Not to mention, that doctor in Santa Monica is supposed to be amazing.
dudeMAGnet27: True. Either way, I think they got the message.

BigBother1984:	Exactly. I must say though, even with that cast on, she is drop-dead gorgeous in that dress.
dudeMAGnet27:	Eh. She's ok.

I stifle a smile, not that she can see it. Not my area of expertise. But that seems like jealousy.

dudeMAGnet27:	I mean, anyone is gonna look good in a $25,000 custom designer gown. Athena, on the other hand, she looks incredible. Probably had a few surgeries, but doesn't look anywhere near her age.
BigBother1984:	Who is Athena?
dudeMAGnet27:	Oh, I don't know her real name. That's just what I call her because I think she's gorgeous. Not exactly sure what her job title is. Personal assistant maybe? I don't think it really matters. I'm pretty sure he doesn't keep her around for her typing skills, if you catch my drift :P
BigBother1984:	I think I can put 2 and 2 together.
dudeMAGnet27:	Smart boy . . . cute too ☺

Every time you type an emoticon, a puppy falls in a blender.

BigBother1984:	Yeah, yeah, whatever. So which one is she?
dudeMAGnet27:	Tight white dress with red trim. Like three rows behind Nicky.

I start scanning the crowd. Interactive feature lets me control the view. Zoom in on Nicky. Pan up, viewing the people behind him. Look around. Everyone is in a white dress. Only one with red trim though. Zoom in closer. Nearly spit my drink across the room. Coughing so violently, tears form in my eyes. Regain my composure, clear my vision. Back to the screen, I sit locked in a trance. With each blink, I hope what I see will change.

Five times. Then ten. Even twenty isn't enough.

No matter how many times I blink or rub my eyes, she's still sitting there. Taking down The Sauce is going to be more difficult than originally planned. For some reason, my aunt is working for him.

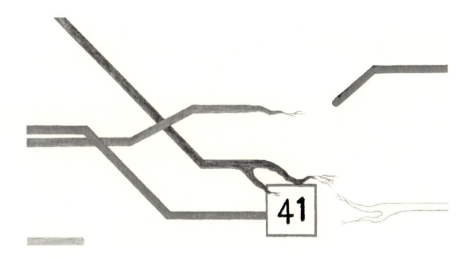

41

Teenagers throw parties. Mom and Dad leave town for the weekend. Like a right of passage, invite a few friends over. Never intending it to escalate to Mardi Gras status. Harboring a hope that it would, nevertheless.

Welcome to my world. Every sip I take. Every bite of food. Expecting it to be tainted, laced with poison. Like Nicky and Cooper know about me. Every corner I round, I flinch and brace for an attack.

Nothing comes. They're either clueless or holding their cards close to the vest. Days pass after the wedding. Then weeks. Now approaching a month and a half. Most would think they're in the clear. That's why most people will never run the world.

Assumptions lead to demise.

Nicky and crew are just waiting for me to let down my guard.

Not gonna happen.

Suddenly, my phone beeps at me. Jump more than I should. Equally as paranoid as I am prepared. Not a good combination.

Half expecting a threat from The Sauce, my reaction to every IM, e-mail, text, and phone call these days. Part of me longs for it. Just get this over with.

Throw into the mix my aunt. Or whoever the fuck she is. Can't find anything on her. More secretive than I am. Not good.

I pick up the phone, open the message. It's a picture from Dillon. Simple tagline reads, "It's a girl!" Open the image. A sonogram. Black, white, and gray pixels. Seemingly scattered, organizing themselves at random. Yet flowing together so gracefully. It's fleeting, but I'm touched. To see the daughter I'll never know. At the bottom of the image, Dillon has written, "You didn't get this from me."

How awful am I? With this shit storm of a life I've been leading, I completely forget about Mackenzie and her baby. Which is likely how she wants it. Still, that Dillon did this for me, it's huge. Momentarily sentimental. Resolve and determination grows.

A girl.

I remind myself most of what I'm accusing Nicky of. It's hypothetical. Basing lots of it on speculation. But waiting for confirmation isn't an option. By then, it will be too late. Mackenzie's little girl could end up turning tricks in China for egg rolls. Sure, even if these preposterous ideas become law, it wouldn't impact her.

But if it starts at all, where does it end?

Can't have that.

Would like to say I'm doing this for humanity. So future generations, especially women, can thrive and be prosperous. Which is partially true. But no matter how you slice it, my motives are self-serving. With potential trickle-down positive side effects for a few of my friends. Not exactly worthy of a Nobel Peace prize. And I'm OK with that.

Tenacity mounting. Like water through a busted dam. Slow at first, gaining momentum. Eventually resulting in pure chaos. If Nicky and Cooper want to stop me, they'll have to kill me. Anything short of that, tantamount to plugging the dam with chewing gum.

I look up the address of Doctor Jayaraman. Verify the phone number for his office. Hop on travel sites, looking for hotels and flights.

Shortly after, I pick up my phone, call Maggie.

Answers almost immediately. "Hey, you, what's up?"

"Not much, just screwing around on the Internet. Hey, I was wondering if you felt like getting out of town early next week."

Excitement in her voice. "Yeah, that sounds great. I haven't been to Madison in a while. Or were you thinking somewhere else?"

Depraved grin. "I was actually thinking somewhere a bit sunnier, with a beach."

"Oh, like Milwaukee?" Slight chuckle at her own joke.

"Not quite. I was thinking West Coast. Have you ever been to California? The Pacific Ocean is absolutely gorgeous. Especially when you watch the sunset over it from the Santa Monica Pier."

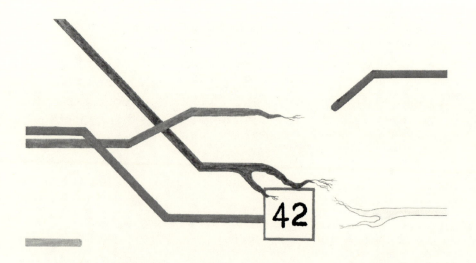

42

She's a smart one. Convinces me to take a ride on a Ferris wheel. Doesn't broach the topic until we're in motion. Can't ignore it now. Either face the conversation, or jump. Can't be more than fifty feet. Lost in thought. Plotting a route to the bottom where I could break my fall, I'm interrupted.

"Hello? Are you listening to me?"

"What? Yeah, yeah. Sorry, I was just a little distracted. Go on."

She sits there and stares. Somewhat incredulous. Can tell I'm avoiding the issue. Agitated, she goes on. "OK, let's start over." I nod, facing her this time. "I think it's fair to say that I've been rather helpful to your 'cause,' or whatever you call it." No disagreement from me. "And I'd love to keep helping you. But I don't think I'm being irrational by making a few demands of my own."

"Sounds fair. What were you thinking?"

"I want you to take me on a date. Somewhere nice. Like really nice."

I tear a huge chunk of cotton candy. Stuff my mouth full of pink and blue. Anything to delay the inevitable awkwardness. Finish chewing. "You're kidding, right?"

"No, I'm not kidding. Why is that such a stretch? You think I'm just some dumb whore? Like because I screw for a living, I don't want to be treated like a lady?"

Instinct says exactly that. Mouth says nothing. Shrug the shoulders, feign ignorance.

"Look, when you do what I do, and I'm not saying I'm proud of it. I'm not saying I'm ashamed either. It's a means to an end. It is what it is. But when you sleep with men for money, well, suffice it to say, there isn't much romance involved."

No surprise there. She's definitely barking up the wrong tree. "OK, I see your point. I can kind of see how over time that would weigh on your mind. But let me ask you something. Do you really think I'm the best candidate for this?" Rolls her eyes. Dead serious, I stare right into her soul. "No, honestly. I knocked you unconscious and performed surgery on you without your consent. I cut off a young woman's hand and replaced it with my own mangled digits. I'm being sincere here. What makes you think I have the capacity to be romantic in any way whatsoever?"

Can't gauge her reaction. She just sits there and smiles. Annoying at first. Slowly becomes endearing. Out of nowhere, she grabs me and kisses me. Not a full-on tongue thrashing. Soft, gentle. But passionate.

Pulls away, smiles at me some more. Breaks the silence with a giggle. "You don't see it, but I do."

"See what?"

"Exactly. You've got so much love inside of you. You don't even realize it. You might say you're doing all this for revenge or because you have some kind of egomaniacal complex. But I see through you. Deep down, you're just a hopeless romantic. An eternal optimist with such lofty expectations, you just find it easier to expect the worst in humanity."

Well, fuck me. I've got a big-boobied Confucius on my hands.

The wheel comes to a stop. Our turn to get out. Not a moment too soon. I'm out of the gate like a steed at Churchill Downs. A mint julep would be nice right now. Walking so quickly, Maggie can barely keep up. The end of the pier thwarts any potential for escape. I lean against the railing, stare at the sunset. Wait for Maggie to catch up. Joins me at the fence, mimics my pose. Silence for a couple minutes. Just observing the beauty before us.

"I'm nearly twice your age. You know that, right?"

"Come on, you're not *that* much older. Plus, your years have made you wiser than the boys my age. You have life experience."

Can't help but laugh at that. I might have life experience. Definitely lack the experience she's more familiar with. "Don't be so sure. For a guy my age, I haven't been with very many women. I don't even particularly like sex."

Not just a chuckle, a full-out laugh. Everyone within a hundred-foot radius turns and stares. "First, why is it always about sex with guys?" Bite my tongue. She would know better than I would. "And more importantly, that's only because you haven't tried it with me."

She's serious. I wait and wait. Knowing that any second, she's going to break into a hysterical fit of laughter. Her best hyena impression. No such luck. Just a stern yet somehow comforting look. Her nostrils do this weird flare. Really cute actually. Makes my good ball tingle. Have to look away. Can't let emotion interfere. We stare out across the water, watching the sun drop out of view.

"Come on" is all she says. Takes my good hand, leads me back toward the parking lot. Tension runs up my arm. Very uncomfortable right now. But I know if she lets go, I'll be disappointed.

We get to the car. She moves around to the passenger side. About to get in, I interrupt her. She's barely tall enough to see over the top. Stands on her toes to meet my gaze. "What did you have in mind?"

Playing dumb, she knows she's got me. "What do you mean?"

"For our date. Where did you want to go? I've never had an actual girlfriend. I have one good testicle. You're gonna have to coach me through this."

Licks her lips. Tries to suppress a smirk. Fails miserably. "I've got a few places in mind. Most likely somewhere in Beverly Hills. Somewhere really expensive. That takes reservations. And you're gonna wear a suit." Finally satisfied that she's got me where she wants me, she ducks down to get in the car. I don't follow. Simply stay put, staring at the void where she just stood. Notices I haven't moved, she steps back out. "What's the matter?"

"Fuck that."

"Huh?"

"It's not a money thing. I'm not a cheap guy. I have no problem spending money on a date. But if you're really serious about being treated like a lady and not just some whore, we're going to do this differently than you're used to."

Her eyebrows raise. "Interesting. So what were you thinking?"

"Fish tacos. I know a place. Best guacamole you'll ever eat. Margaritas that will knock you on your ass. And if you're lucky, you might get me to dance." I wink, feeling almost like a normal person.

It's hard to read her. "Sounds like a plan, asshole." Just like that, she's in the car with her seatbelt fastened.

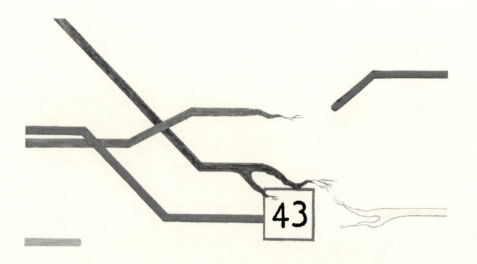

43

A rush of adrenaline coupled with an increasing sense of infallibility. Squeezing his neck so tightly, pushing him closer to the brink of death with every attempted inhalation. The look of fear in his eyes. Knowing you have the option to end a life. A sick, depraved feeling. Incomparable nonetheless.

My eyes move up and down. I meet his gaze then stare at my hand. He can't say a word. The look he's giving me says enough. Pleading with me. Begging me to ease my grip. I can see the gears turning in his head. Desperately hoping my arm grows weak. That I'll lower him just enough. He can almost feel the ground. The carpet barely kissing the tips of his loafers. Inside his mind, just another half-inch. That's all he wants. Just enough to transfer some of the weight to his legs. To ease the pain.

My eyes drift back to my hand. My diamond ring shines bright against his dark skin. Like a train approaching, heading your way down a dark tunnel. A welcome sight to anyone who has ever waited for the L in Chicago.

I ease my grip. Even with a complexion darker than straight coffee, I can see him growing pale. Lower him, his feet flat on the ground. Hand still wrapped around his neck. Not squeezing. Simply preventing him from leaving.

"Like I was saying, Doctor, I transplanted this hand myself." My thoughts interrupted momentarily by heavy breathing. "I don't doubt that you're the best in the world at what you do. But with all due respect, it doesn't really seem to be as difficult as you're making it out to be." He looks to his office door. Maggie stands in front of it. Her small stature far more imposing than one would expect. Arms crossed, the message is clear. No one comes in. You don't get out.

I let go completely. Point to his chair. "Have a seat. We have some things we need to discuss." He quickly obliges. While he loosens his tie, I pour him a glass of water from a cooler in the corner. He downs it with the enthusiasm of someone lost in the Sahara for the last week. Take a seat opposite him across his desk. Wait for him to regain his composure. Offer him more water. I've made my point. I'm not in any rush.

He walks over to the cooler, fills a large thermos to the top. With great anxiety, he sits back down behind his desk. Shoots me a vicious look. One that tells me to get on with whatever it is that brought me here.

Works for me. "Several weeks ago, my hand was severely damaged by a gunshot wound. I lost three fingers. My attending physician in Chicago referred me to you."

"And who might that be?" he asks. No effort to hide his resentment.

"Irrelevant." That's all the info he gets. "Point being I took matters into my own hands. No pun intended. I'll spare you the details, but I have a strenuous history with the medical community. Doctors make me skeptical."

Gives me another look from his arsenal of rage. One that says this isn't the most effective way to ask for help.

Point taken.

"That being said, I have a rather intrinsic understanding of the medical world. And I had to do something."

Furious, he says, "So you kidnapped a young woman and cut off her hand?"

I give a sly smile. The kind where one side of the mouth stays still. The other draws closer and closer to the ear. "She was quite willing to come with me. Obviously, the surgery is a different story. But sometimes you have to do what you have to do."

His fury and fear still obvious. "Can we please just cut to the chase? What do you want with me?" As he speaks, he can't take his eyes off my hand. Or the ring. Likely a combination of both. Might play naïve, but he knows better.

I pause for dramatic effect. "OK, Doc, I'll give it to you straight. Nadira Madani. She was here a couple weeks ago. You repaired her hand. I don't know what or how you did it since I left you a complete mess to work with." I hold up her hand, validating what he already suspected. I pause again, observe his countless degrees and credentials. "I have to say, I'm impressed. Putting her hand on my arm was difficult, but it was a simple cut-and-paste procedure. Did you use a cadaver or something?"

Maintains his calm to a degree, but internally, he's boiling. Makes a mild attempt to appear composed. "I can't talk about other patients with you. Confidentiality," he says. Stress on the sarcasm. What strikes me most about this man, his accent. Dark skin, obviously of East Indian descent. Not a trace of it in his voice.

"That's fine. Just making small talk. I could care less how you did it. What I really want is for you to get her back in this office."

"I'm afraid that would be unethical."

My diabolical smirk shifts to the other side. "Why is that? Surely you must need to see her for a checkup. See how her recovery is coming along?"

"Yes, that *would* be standard procedure. But given the circumstances, I—"

I cut him off. "But what? You think I have some kind of heinous motive? Some desire to hurt her?" Says nothing. Of course that's what he thinks. Only a fool would think otherwise. "Well, despite my track record"—hold up her hand,—"my business is finished with her. I want Nicky Salcedo."

He recognizes the name. Needs me to elaborate.

"This guy," I say, slapping news clipping and articles I printed off the Internet. "He's up to no good. Read up on him and you'll see." Maggie coughs, grabs my attention. Nods her head at a picture on the wall. Doctor Jayaraman's family. I get out of my seat, move toward the picture. "You have a daughter." I say it as fact, not inquisitively.

His eyes bulge. "If you lay a finger on them—"

Cut him off again, "Relax, relax. My point is that if we don't stop Nicky Salcedo, children born in this country over the coming decades, primarily the daughters, don't have much of a future."

He relaxes. Just slightly but enough to know I'm not entirely crazy. I go on. Explain to him Cooper and Nicky's plans. Placing limits on the number of children a mother will be permitted to birth. Potentially banning abortions. Not because of a moral dilemma. Simply to force women who are pregnant to give up extra children to the state. Increasing sales of his birth control drugs. Making money off prostitution. Men who've maxed out their wives will seek release elsewhere. Gross, but plausible.

"I will admit I'm basing this on a lot of speculation. But I know Nicky Salcedo better than most people. He is quite capable of impropriety. Especially when it comes to children."

Doesn't look at me the entire time. He's locked into the literature I've presented him. His mind's a sponge. Soaks it all in.

"What if I refuse?" His voice cloaked with terror. No attempt to hide it.

"Doc, do whatever you want. One way or another, I will get to Nicky Salcedo. You can either sleep better knowing you've helped a worthy cause. Or you can lie awake every night. Sweating. Checking the locks. Constantly wondering if I'm coming for you. Because even though I'll tell you right now I will never harm you, I'm smart enough to know you will never believe me. Which makes sense. I cut off a young woman's hand. So I know you're asking yourself what else I'm capable of. How far will this sick lunatic go? The short answer to that is: as far as necessary."

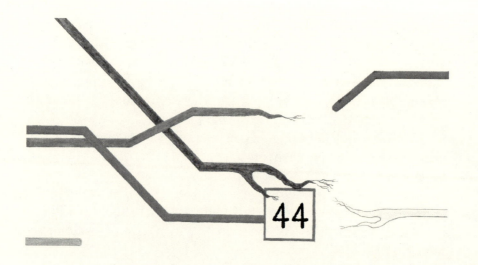

44

"I think you might be more deranged than I am." Maggie laughs. Her naked back pressed against me. My good hand cupping her breast.

"Probably. But what makes you say that?" she wonders.

So many possible replies.

"Where to start? I think it goes without saying that what I did to you and Nadira Madani was insane at best. Add to it threatening Dr. Jayaraman to convince The Sauce, Cooper, and Nadira to meet him across the country."

"I thought that was pretty clever," she says. I agree. After chatting with the doctor and reviewing the articles I gave him, he agreed to ask Nicky to come along with Cooper and his wife. Going to sell him some story about how he has a colleague from medical school developing a new drug. One that messes with Xs and Ys. Exponentially increases the odds of birthing a girl over a boy. If my suspicions are right, he'll bite in no time.

"Well, thanks, I guess. But you have no idea about all the other crazy shit I've done. Just last week, I overheard some guy ranting about his tax dollars at work. How enraged he was that 'all of his hard-earned money' was going to all the freeloaders on welfare and food stamps. Mind you, I've met plenty of people in my day who exploit the system. Still, the guy wouldn't shut up. So I literally started throwing silver dollars at him. Told him that should cover his share. When it all breaks down, that's about how much he contributed."

She's still not looking at me. "That's not fucked up. That's funny."

"Well, how about a few months ago? I found some protest. A bunch of people yapping about free-speech violations. Something like a group of guys out for a night of drinking got a little out of control. They pissed on some statues in a park or something. See, if they do it on a wall or the side of a building, it's reprehensible. If the target is an effigy of a political figure or idea, then it's freedom of speech."

"So what did you do? Pee on them?"

I wince. "No, that would have been awesome though. Instead I pulled out a gun."

Immediately, she turns around and faces me. "What?"

"It's not quite as bad as it sounds. It was empty. I showed them the thing didn't even have a clip in it. I pulled the trigger with the thing pointed at my foot. But it's funny, people still freaked out."

She challenges me. "Well, I don't blame them."

"True, but I made my point."

"Which was?"

"Here's the thing. I disagree with almost everyone. I like to be difficult. I contradict people just because I'm an asshole."

"No argument here," she laughs.

"Exactly. But I just find it so odd that people are willing to defend with unbridled conviction the First Amendment. Citing it's in the Constitution. But the instant a weapon enters the picture, it's as if Alexander Hamilton and company never existed. They're called *amendments* for a reason. By definition, they can be altered. Should be altered. But both sides don't want to budge."

"Hmm. Well, I guess when you put it like that, it makes sense." Rolls on to her back, stares at the ceiling. "I think it's funny that of all the founding fathers, you chose Hamilton as your example."

"Why is that? He did it all. Soldier, philosopher, economist. A true Renaissance man."

"True. Most people say Jefferson or Franklin though. I just found it, I don't know . . . cute." Turns to me and smiles.

Cute. Not an adjective typically affiliated with me. First time for everything. Or so they say. "I suppose so. I've never been much of a fan of Jefferson. The guy owned slaves. The guy most synonymous with 'all men are created equal' didn't really see it that way."

"What is your deal?"

"Huh? Look, I'm sorry if you're a big history fan. I know the guy did a lot of great things for this country. But like I said, my default mode is antithetical."

"I'm not talking about politics. I was trying to give you a compliment, and you just completely ignored it."

Scylla and Charybdis. What to do here? Feel like this is a trap. No right answer to avoid an argument. Gotta say something. "I'm sorry, I didn't realize it was a compliment. I'm not exactly the world's most affectionate person. I've never really been one for dating and relationships. Not to mention—"

Cuts me off, finishes my thought, "Let me guess. You're *literally losing your mind*." Her inflection cuts deep. Must admit, I'm impressed. Rolls away from me, gets out of bed to use the bathroom. She returns, doesn't get back in. Just stands at the foot of the bed. A dark silhouette barely made visible by moonlight seeping in. The shades drawn, but not completely.

"OK, OK. I get it. I don't know what you want from me." If her face contorts to show a reaction, I can't tell.

Her response says enough. "I want you to stop playing the pity card. From what I know about you, yes, your life has been abnormally difficult. I wouldn't wish most of what you've been through on anyone. With that being said, you've also been given opportunities most people don't even have the resources to *fathom*, let alone actually participate in." Her lecture, reminiscent of my last night with Mackenzie. As intolerable as this is, it's exactly what I need. Mackenzie told me things I didn't want to hear all the time. Dillon does, but not often enough.

My hamartia. Ignoring valuable advice.

Yes. That's correct. I admitted a flaw.

For some reason, Maggie does something to me. She has this pull. Her words excite me. Incite me. Motivate and degrade me. I equally love and hate this quality about her.

"Thank you."

Even in the dark, her confusion is obvious. "Excuse me?"

"You heard me. Thanks."

"For what?"

"For calling me out. It's not often I admit I'm wrong. But I needed to hear that."

"You're welcome." With no effort to be sensual, she crawls next to me. "And believe me, there's plenty more where that came from. But for now, can we finally make love?"

Confused. "I'm sorry, what were we just doing for the last hour?"

She turns on a bedside lamp. Bright enough to force me to squint. My eyes take a moment to adjust. Finally, they focus on her. Seduction all over her face.

"That? That was fucking. I want you to make love to me."

I'm still confused. "What's the difference?"

She laughs. A laugh that gets caught in her throat. More like a snort. The kind of laugh that has an entire room laughing at your expense. "Oh, babe. There is so much I'm gonna teach you." She moves for my neck. Kisses me all over, tongue in my ear. I want so badly to be into this. Something isn't right. Instantly she can tell. "What's wrong?"

"Nothing really. Just, this whole thing with Nicky. It's stressing me out. This has potential to blow up in my face. I'm not talking some minor setback, but something—"

She pinches my lips shut. "First off, it could blow up in *our* faces. We're a team. Second, we'll be fine."

A team? Claustrophobia sets in.

Old habits die-hard.

She has no clue what she's getting herself into.

"Maggie, listen to me." I grab her cheeks, force her eyes to lock with mine. "This is no joke. Just knowing me could get you killed. You don't want to think about what those guys are capable of if they find out you're turning against them. Get out now while you still can." I go on. Variations of the same warning. Empty deterrents.

Which am I more afraid of? Her well-being or the potential of splitting the glory?

She knows what I'm thinking. Scares me beyond words.

"You're incredible." Her tone is clear. That was not a compliment. "You'll do anything to push people away, won't you?"

Going back to exhibit A.

"Maggie! Think about it. The night we met, I performed surgery on you." Pause for effect. "I knocked you out against your will, and cut you open. I don't want to think about how many laws I broke. And if by some divine intervention I was ever able to regain a sense of morality, I'm sure my ethical standards would guilt me forever."

Without warning, she leaps up. Smashes her fist into my groin.

The light in the room flashes every color of the spectrum. Me wailing in pain is an understatement.

"Fine. You don't want my help. Fuck you." Storming around the room, she begins getting dressed. I think. Not entirely sure where I am. "Now we're even. You keep bringing up the night we met, well there you go. You hurt me, now I've hurt you."

Any attempt to respond is instantly terminated. The blow she's delivered might stifle me for a month. If I'm lucky.

With somewhat calmer demeanor, she continues. "I get that you're screwed up. In case you forgot, I'm the *dumb whore* here, not you. I'm pretty fucking messed up too. But you know what? At least I've learned about forgiveness. Sure, I don't always practice it. But I know it exists. You should try it sometime." Now fully dressed, her clothes a mess, but covering the necessary parts, she looks at me with disgust. Or pity. Take your pick. Putting an end to her dramatic pause. "You should especially try forgiving yourself. It's not as bad as you might think." She storms out. I scream in pain. The door opens instantly. Maggie throws a bag of ice at me. "Hope this helps." Slowly, she sits on the bed, leans in close. I brace for the worst.

She kisses me. Nothing seductive. Just plants her lips on my forehead, whispers in my ear. "Good luck with Nicky."

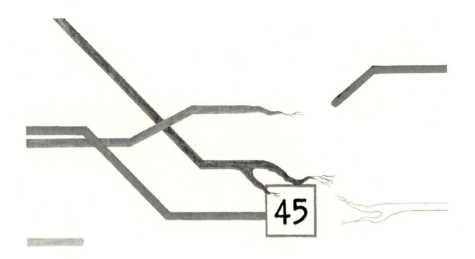

45

So it comes down to this. We all have dreams. Those moments we play over in our heads. Again and again. We run through multiple scenarios. If A causes B, how will I react if C becomes G? After we've cycled through the nearly infinite possibilities, the loop starts over.

That first at bat in the big leagues. Walking down the aisle at your wedding. Winning the lottery.

We all value things differently. But ultimately, we all value something. I peaked early. Effectively saving millions of lives. Hard to top. My goals, reprehensible at best. To my credit, I follow through. Set my sights, slit throats to get there.

Figuratively and literally.

Will I regret my actions? Perhaps. But a large part of me regrets saving the world. Doubtful most people would like to undo that feat.

Regret.

I'm watering it down here. When people say they never regret anything. Say that everything they did wrong has led them to this point. As if it could lead you anywhere else. No matter what you do, who you are, you are on a collision course with the next instant. Then the one after that. And so on.

Just once, say you fucked up. Far more liberating. To look yourself in the mirror and know you could be better. The poets and hippies will tell you, it's part of a process. Part of growing up.

The choice is yours. Just remember this advice. Recall it when you haven't showered in a month. Clutching to the ramblings of a fragile pedagogue. That person raving about the process. End results are worthless. It's what you learn along the way. Let me know how that works out for you. When the guy you despise is kissing the girl of your dreams, the girl you were too scared to talk to, tell me how it's no big deal. You were a billboard pussy. Why regret it? You'll do better next time.

Newsflash: eventually, there is no next time.

Take the chances you have when you have them. One opportunity is all you need. And more than most people get.

Looking out the window, I play one of the myriad versions of this scenario over in my mind. Nicky gets out of his limo escorted by some muscle.

They were there in my dream. Everything about this moment, I've seen it before. I look at Nicky again. He's wearing a purple tie. In my dream it was red. Close enough.

Cooper has been in the building for an hour or so. The checkup with Dr. Jayaraman is coming to a close. The elevator doors slowly spread open. Nicky and his bodyguards step out, approach the receptionist.

This feeling in my throat. No matter how many times I've thought about this moment, there's no preparation. A combination of rage and anticipation floods my senses. Lips are moving, words exchanged. All I see is a Dali painting. People and images stretching and swirling.

You ruined my life. Now I'm going to ruin yours.

Her voice. My aunt. Or the woman who claims to be. Nowhere to be seen. But the sound resonates with disturbing clarity.

"Did you hear that?" I ask. More paranoia in my voice than I would like. If I'm to be a believable colleague of Dr. Jayaraman, I need to get my shit together.

Nicky looks at me, responds without a hint of sarcasm or mockery. "Probably just another earthquake. You should be used to them by now though, right, Doctor?"

My blood boils. Not a fucking clue who I am.

Ultimately, that's how I want it. But still.

I guess all Nicky Salcedo's bastard children look just like everyone else.

He and his crew march right by me toward the conference room. The doctor will be with them soon. Nadira's extraneous checkup almost complete. They proceed through the door, take their seats around a large table. The open blinds are quickly drawn shut. The door remains open.

My palms and armpits are sweating profusely. I rush to the elevator, push the button for the ground floor. Then the >|< button. Hit it faster than a Japanese businessman on a vacation he'd rather not be taking. When they reopen, I dart outside. Fresh air, my temporary saving grace. Beautiful weather. A crew of five men performs various acts of horticulture. The lawnmower. So shrill. Piercing my eardrums like glass shards from a cannon.

Not until the guy pours gas into its tank do I realize it's not even on. This doesn't bode well. At least I'm composed enough to know I'm crazy.

Joseph Heller, thanks for that.

I pace back and forth for a bit. Make my way around the side of the building. In the shade, out of sight. Pull it out, let it rip.

The landscapers don't take too kindly to it.

No use delaying the inevitable. I start that awkward walk past them. How I imagine a "walk of shame" feels. If I wasn't seeing Santa Claus riding a unicorn, I might care.

#BiggerFishToFry

Back in Dr. Jayaraman's office, the door to the conference room is nearly shut. A small gap, though, big enough to fit my fist through. I open it just wide enough and squeeze through. I take a seat next to my "colleague." Scan the cast of characters. Nicky and his guards plus another man and woman I don't recognize.

I assume the room is dim as a large projection screen displays a generic screensaver. But to me, I'm staring at the surface of the sun. Fiery halos surround everyone.

"Excuse me," I say to no one in particular. "I left something in your office." I grab a fistful of the first sedatives I can find. Rush to the sink, wash them down. Like putting a Band-Aid on a gunshot wound. Better than nothing. Something to be said for psychosomatic effects.

When I return, the door is fully closed. No use knocking. I open and enter, taking my seat as inconspicuously as possible.

Quite relieved that the glow around the guests has subsided, there's still a shred of hope for this after all. I reach for the pitcher of water just to my left. And there he is.

Cooper Madigan.

My first attempt to see if he recognizes me: a subtle cough.

Nothing.

I just stare at him. Wait for him to sense my gaze.

He remains stoic.

I knock the water container over. Nothing subtle about it to anyone paying attention. Luckily, everyone is focused on the glow in front of them. Superfluous screens display the same information on the wall.

Dr. Jayaraman notices my strategy immediately. Throws his white coat on the table to mitigate the spill.

Not my finest moment. But I have Cooper's attention. Mission accomplished. Yet disappointing. No recognition whatsoever.

Sudden realization. Three generations of a single DNA strand in one room. Most of which have no fucking clue what's going on.

So it continues. Dr. Chirag convincingly spits out the info we went over. There's no pill for chromosome alterations. He knows that. I know that. Nicky and Cooper—not so much. It dawns on me, those people I don't recognize. Probably pharmacologists of some kind. Consultants if you will.

Whoever they are, they're buying it. Before I know it, he's calling me to speak. Now it's my turn to sell them on something that doesn't exist.

I should run for office.

Hope my son is taking notes. He'll need it if he's going to be president one day.

Except he won't. Not a fucking chance.

I'm instantly snapped out of my daze. The last twenty minutes flew by like seconds. Hands buried in my pockets, I trade places with Dr. Jayaraman.

Clear my throat, drink more water. Deep breaths. I've got this.

A surge of confidence sweeps over me. I pick up where my colleague left off. Next projection appears. Then another. And so it goes for fifteen minutes. A vague collection of fancy words spews from my mouth.

If you can't dazzle 'em with brilliance, baffle 'em with bullshit.

Not a problem.

Only now do I notice a critical mistake. I've been waving around Nadira's hand for at least half my presentation. Surprisingly, no one seems to notice. Just to be safe, I tuck it back in. Prepare to wrap this up.

I bring the lights up in the room a touch, let their eyes adjust. Most of them furiously type notes. Cooper appears bored to tears. Nicky initiates a small conference with the two I've never seen. Then he looks at Cooper, gives small shake of the head. Intended to go unnoticed. Should have tried harder.

And now Nicky, primarily inanimate until this point, assumes his tough persona. Looks right at me. "I'm sorry, Doctor. What did you say your name was again?"

Chills.

The only appropriate way to describe what his voice does to me. Swallow a little, calm my nerves.

"My name is Dr. Poquelin, Mr. Salcedo. But please, just call me JB."

He shifts in his chair. Pondering.

No one recognizes my most recent pseudonym. Except him. Something about his face tells me he knows more than he's trying to show.

"Well JB, I have to say, I'm impressed."

"Thank you, sir. I think you'll find it to be a worthy investment." Try to nudge him some more. Not sure why. This fictitious pill, irrelevant. It's served its purpose. Now it's time to capitalize. "FDA approval is less than six months away."

Everyone in his party laughs, especially Cooper. The Sauce shoots me a look that says I should let him worry about the FDA. Then another that says he *is* the FDA.

Whatever is intended by his reaction, I can tell he likes what he hears.

He straightens his tie, gaze locked on me. Trying to weaken me. Not this time. Still focused on me, he says, "I'd like to have a word with Dr. Poquelin in private, please." His people obey without hesitation. The guards require an extra nod on his behalf, but even they acquiesce without much resistance. He has them trained well.

Despite being a brilliant surgeon, Dr. Jayaraman doesn't get the hint. I lean in and tell him to get out, thank him for his help. Next thought is to tell him it's been nice knowing him.

But that's a flash in a pan. Can't afford to think like that. A defeatist attitude will do just that.

Tortoise and the hare motherfucker. Never give up.

Chirag leaves. Nicky follows close behind and locks the door. Walks back to his chair, instructs me to move closer.

"I'm fine where I am."

A simple nod is the only reply I get.

A smirk on his face is growing bigger by the second. "So, JB, please tell me more about yourself. We're going to be partners after all. I like to have an intimate knowledge of the people I do business with."

So many thoughts race through my mind. Intentionally delaying my response.

"We've met before, haven't we?" His inflection implies a question. His face says he's stating a fact.

Choose your words carefully.

"You do realize I'm going to kill you, don't you?"

A barely noticeable upward curl of the lips. The only reaction I receive. "I expect nothing less. But before you do, would you mind telling me who the fuck you are? I know that you're not really Molière."

"I'll get to that." I pull out a picture of my mom and aunt. Not mincing words. "I wanna know everything about the women in this picture."

Slide the photo across the desk. He picks it up, puts on his eyeglasses. Immediate recognition crosses his face. Sets the photo down, glasses back in his jacket pocket. This time the gun holstered near his chest catches what minimal light swirls throughout the room. Another trademark shit-eating grin from The Sauce. His go-to reaction. Can't find a way to mask his shock. How surreal this is.

His face straightens, looks at me deadpan. With a cryptic timbre, "You should get comfortable. This could take a while."

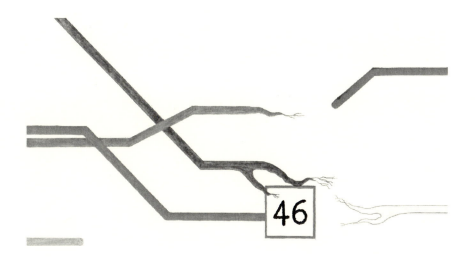

46

By now nothing should shock me. I've traveled the world. Been places seen by no more than a few dozen. Witnessed acts of incomparable generosity. Stared into the eyes of unspeakable depravity. These days, a glance in the mirror is all it takes. I've given people a second chance at life. And taken away several options from those I deemed unworthy. I have studied with some of the greatest minds the twenty-first century—possibly the world—has ever known.

Never let down your guard. Assumptions will be your downfall. Never underestimate your opponent.

A million other clichés that could easily be substituted. Yet again, I'm reminded of my fallibility. A bitter pill to swallow. Right now, using every muscle in my face to prevent my jaw from falling into my lap.

The only real wisdom is in knowing, that you know . . . how's the rest of that go? I liked Socrates better when he was just a character in *Bill & Ted's Excellent Adventure*.

It doesn't take long for him to drop the first bomb on me. Never thought I'd be happy that Alison left me something. This is an exception. She gave me a copy of the picture of me as a baby. Along with her and my mother.

Or so I thought.

"You're not a doctor at all, are you?" Simply shake my head. I'm not looking for some sentimental reunion. This man next to me, he's pushing eighty. We know nothing about each other on a personal level. In an hour or so, he will simply be a memory. I will continue on the downward spiral of my shattered existence.

But still. Is some fucking recognition too much to ask? The man is no idiot. Not every day a stranger shows up with a picture like this. Clearly he's making the connection. Causing him great anxiety. He's blatantly flustered.

"Do I know you from somewhere else?" he asks. Voice trembling.

"Yes." Simple and sweet. Not here to catch up on the last four decades. "Tell me about the picture. This woman"—pointing at Alison—"she works for you?"

He's growing paler by the second. A glass of milk has a better complexion than he does right now.

"It's complicated" is all he can manage to spit out.

"What does that mean?" I try to calm myself. My agitation only compounds his discomfort. A much longer pause. "What else, Nicky? Please, this is very important."

Looking straight ahead, emits a barely audible murmur. "She's your mother."

The plus side: he has some kind of understanding of who I am. The down side: he can't differentiate between the two women in the picture. I remove his glasses from his jacket. Brush the gun but leave it be. This man, so fragile and nervous, poses no threat. He couldn't muster the strength to pull the trigger. Put the frames on for him.

Pointing at my mother, I say, "No, Nicky, *that's* my mother. The other woman is her sister, my aunt." Infuriating myself. Shouldn't have let that slip. No need to admit any relation to anyone in the picture. Rather, a *presumed* relation.

He shakes his head. "No" trickles from his lips, lacking conviction.

"What do you mean no? You mean these women aren't sisters?" My composure wears thin. Patience being tested. Pushing me to the brink of fury.

Another long pause and he finally commences. "No, they were sisters. *This* one, the one who you know works for me, her name is Penelope."

And the saga continues. According to "Alison," Penelope is the name of my mother. So she's mostly full of crap. But not entirely. No help whatsoever.

Leading him, prying for more information, I want to hear him speak from his own lips what I already suspect. "OK, but what makes you so sure that Penelope is my mother? Have you met my father?"

This pushes him over the edge. Complete meltdown. Unlike anything I've ever seen. Despite his age, Nicky exudes power. A bastion of control and dominance. But not here, not in front of me. So weak and defeated. Nothing like the man strutting around television. Flashing that priceless smile. Forcing his teeth to show through lips so full of botox. Skin pulled so tight it's a wonder he can chew his food.

Not sure how to react. Compassion isn't exactly my nom de plume. I stand over the hunched shoulders of a man I've been waiting to kill. I have my chance. No need to wait. Take care of business, get on with my life. So easy.

Or is it?

Killing Nicky Salcedo is not a challenge. Getting more than five feet outside the door however, different story. Massive guards flank my only exit. My thought process interrupted by his response.

"Because I'm your father."

Now we're getting somewhere. I breathe a sigh of relief. He does too. Much more apparent than mine. The tension in the room subsides. More than ready to snap at him. Unleash the rage I've suppressed for longer than I can remember. But something tells me I want to know what else he has to say.

I make my way to a fridge in the corner. Grab a bottle of water for each of us. Open his for him. His stamina in rapid decline with each tick of the clock. I circle back to the other side of the table, make myself comfortable, simply staring and waiting. I drink my water, set it on the table, swivel side to side. Another sip, repeat the cycle.

After a few minutes, he's ready to go on.

Wiping his eyes, he says, "I haven't seen that picture in nearly forty years."

Not budging an inch, I offer no sympathy. "Nicky, I'm gonna need a little more exposition. I think we've established that *one* of the women in this photograph is my mother, although after what I've been through, I think a few DNA tests will be in order. But let's presume that, as you claim, Penelope is my mother. What makes you so sure you're the father?" Digging deeper, the gloves come off. "Let's be real here. For almost five decades, you've been one of the most powerful men in Chicago. Arguably the world. How many times have you been married?" The implications of my tone affect him severely.

He holds up a hand, extending all five fingers. "But I never loved anyone more than I loved her." If I had a soul, it would be moved. His inflection is on point. Could sway the hardest of hearts. Alas, his cries fall on deaf ears.

Laughing, I say, "Nicky, give me a fucking break. I did a little research. At the time all of this went down, you were married to Norah Blanton. A swimsuit model and actress. There wasn't a man alive who wouldn't have killed to be in your shoes. So please, explain to me how you were so in love with, as far as I can tell, a lowly pedestrian."

For a split second, something appears in his eyes. As if insulting Penelope rekindled a fading fire buried deep in his heart. Quietly, but with assertion, "Watch what you say about her. That's the woman who gave birth to you."

Clench my fist. The temptation to smash it across his plastic face, so intense. Admittedly, I'm impressed by my restraint. "Wow. Well, OK, if that's the angle you want your argument to take, I can play that game." Pause for effect. "This woman, the love of your life as you claim, left me in a *fucking dumpster*."

Catharsis.

Decades of aggression purging itself from my mind in controlled chaos.

"She might have shot me out of her snatch, but my mother is Josephine Watts." Recognition on his behalf at that last name. "She raised me. Taught me how to read. Cared for me when I was sick. Most importantly, she didn't abandon me when times got rough!" I turn away, fighting back tears. Don't expose your weaknesses, for they will be exploited.

Staring at a painting on the wall, a pleasant surprise at last. A bottle of water smashes against the frame, splashing me slightly. About time The Sauce lives up to his billing. Turn to meet his gaze, his face bright red. "For someone of your caliber of intelligence, you're not very bright."

Interesting. Proceed.

"I would think that the prodigy who cured AIDS would be wise enough not to make assumptions. But that's irony for ya. I assumed too much myself."

The plot thickens.

"Cured AIDS? What in the world are you talking about?" Emotions running high, I can't even keep a straight face. Cover blown, and I couldn't be happier.

"Well, I can only assume that if your mother was Josephine Watts, by default you would be Ted Watts. *The* Ted Watts."

"Well played, sir. Glad to see your mind is sharper than your sense of style." Brown shoes with a black suit. Are you fucking serious? "Oh, I've been meaning to tell you, I didn't really appreciate you trying to kill me all those years ago. I mean, I get it. You had investors and all that stuff. And even though this will stay between you, me, and probably a handful of other people, you're always going to be the guy who attempted to kill the guy who saved millions of lives around the world."

He jumps out of his seat to object. I shove him back down. Doesn't require much force. Don't want to hurt the guy, not yet. Need to draw this out.

"But please. You were saying something about my assumptions. I want to hear more about that." Shit-eating grin plastered ear to ear across my face. Hitting my stride. Feeling inexorable.

Nicky can sense his time is almost up. The years have finally caught up with him. He's growing weaker by the second. I might not even get a chance to do what I came to do. Mother Nature might beat me to it. His discomfort isn't lost on me. I replace his bottle of water. Almost like a last meal. By no means am I fulfilling a dying wish. But for some illogical reason, even I want his last few minutes on earth to be less stressful than this.

Will I still snap his neck?

Absolutely. Hypocrisy runs in our family.

He can sense the tension in the room tapering off. After a few sips, he goes back to the topic at hand. "First off, yes, she did put you in that dumpster. And yes, I was married to a very famous woman. No, Norah was not at all happy about it. But you are very clearly under the impression that she put you in that dumpster because she didn't want you."

This should be rich. "Please, enlighten me." Nicky opens his mouth to reply. As the first words leave his mouth, I cringe.

You ruined my life.

As if it was pumped into the room through the highest quality surround sound speakers.

"Is everything OK?" Nicky asks, alarmed, confused.

Pointless asking if he heard that. "I'm fine. Continue."

Suddenly, Nicky resumes his powerful demeanor. His posture perfect. Shoulders no longer slouched. Voice resolute. "For obvious reasons, dumpsters are associated with trash. Did you ever consider the possibility that she put you in there because it offered sanctuary?"

A laughable concept. But not completely void of merit. "Naturally. Of course I assumed her motive was to get rid of me. But over the years, I've toyed with the idea, and I do mean very briefly, that she did it in hopes someone would find me. And it just so happens that's how it turned out. But it's going to be a hard sell convincing me those were her motives all along."

Not wavering for a second, he rises from his chair. More animated than I've ever seen him on television. "Believe whatever the fuck you want. That's exactly what she did. She never planned for you to end up with the Watts—"

Taking great offense to this, I threaten, "Say one bad thing about them. See what happens."

Pushing back, he says, "Let me finish for fuck's sake. Penelope lived a few blocks away from that donut shop. It was where I met her. She would grab her morning cup of coffee there."

"What were you doing in a shithole like that? Kind of beneath a man of your stature."

He shoots me a smirk. "Indeed. But there are a few things you don't mess with." Holds up a single finger. "One, hot dogs. You grew up here, you know exactly what I mean." No argument here. Making a peace sign, "Two. As I'm sure you know, I'm Italian." Another nod on my behalf. The Colosseum, Sistine Chapel, and bear claws. The first things that come to mind when thinking of Italy.

"We take our food very seriously. And there ain't one thing I love more in this world than a fuckin' cannoli." He's gone straight *Godfather* on me. This thick accent descending upon him from the heavens. "It don't make no sense, but this donut shop. They made the best damn cannolis in the States. No way can they compete with the stuff you can get in Italy. But damn, these were close."

"A donut shop? Served cannolis?" I momentarily forget there's a point to this story. He might be crazier than I am.

"I didn't believe it myself when I heard it. So I had one of my drivers pick up a few one day. It was love at first bite."

I'm ready to get on with the story. Time to concede. "OK, so you went in one day to get a cannoli, and she was in there drinking coffee. You obviously hit it off and had me."

"I tell ya. You ain't never seen nothin' more beautiful. She was a knockout."

Irate. "Nicky! I don't have time for a fucking romance novel. Get to the fucking point!"

Met with a look that says, *You're my kid all right.*

"She and I were having an affair."

No surprise there. "Obviously, you were married to Norah. What about her?"

He nods. "Yes, she was married. Only a few months. Not that it made it right. She was just a kid."

"How old is Penelope now?"

Doing the math in his head. Needs to recall his age first. "By my count, she should be fifty-nine."

"Which would mean she was around twenty-one when she gave birth to me. Does that sound about right?"

He nods.

"OK, so she was young and stupid. Undoubtedly impressed by your wealth and power." He goes red at the insinuation. The thought that she didn't actually love him causes his veins to bulge. "Maybe marriage wasn't all it was cracked up to be. Cold feet a few weeks too late? This is all well and good, but it's irrelevant. Just a fun little subplot. So please, get to the point. Because I find it nearly impossible to believe that she didn't throw me in there because you threatened her. You obviously had so much more to lose than she did. She threw me in there to spare herself, and maybe you. But get real, my well-being had nothing to do with it."

He takes off his jacket, his pistol clearly visible. "Kid, say one more bad thing about her, and I'm gonna do to your other hand what she did to the first."

Excuse me? I gather my resolve, straight-faced. Holding up Nadira's hand, "I was helping someone change a flat. The jack was placed incorrectly. Smashed it to shreds."

Nicky isn't buying it. "Kid, I know all about it. The broad might be batshit crazy. Most of the things that come out of her mouth are pure fantasy. But seeing you here in front of me. I got no choice."

Pure fantasy. Understatement of the year. "Crazy how?"

"The less you talk, the faster I get through my fucking story. The sooner you'll see what I'm talking 'bout."

So I got my mother's eyes, father's chin. Both contributed equally to the crazy.

"So we'd been having an affair for about four months. She says the husband never suspected a thing. Norah knew, but she didn't really care. She was fooling around too. As you know, our marriage was mainly about status. But a few weeks into our thing, I was genuinely falling for her. I talked of divorcing my wife, marrying Penelope. I could tell that in the back of her mind, she thought about it. Part of her really wanted to. But she said she just couldn't do it. Said she knows that cheating on her husband doesn't really show it, but she loved him."

Yawn. Stretch. My agitation shows. Nothing compared to Nicky's.

"*Anyway*, one day, she breaks it off. This was way back before cell phones. She dropped off a handwritten note at my office. Long story short, she was pregnant. Said it really put things in perspective, that what we were doing wasn't right. Said she wanted to raise the kid right with her husband. Things weren't perfect between them, but she wanted to make them work. I literally cried for days. I was heartbroken."

"Why? She was offering you a free pass. If word got out that you knocked up someone who wasn't your wife, you were fucked. I'm sure you considered the ramifications of the CEO of a condom company not using his own product. Or even worse, using it and having it fail."

Shoots me yet another *No shit* look.

"For the last time, I loved her. It was the hardest thing I ever did, but I respected her decision. First off, she wasn't sure it was mine. We had weeks where we wouldn't meet at all. Said in the letter that the timing was about right that the kid belonged to her husband. So I figured that was that. Slowly but surely, I went on with my life."

So I'm finally intrigued. I know how the story ends. Still, a few essential details remain.

"So reading about me in the newspaper when Paul Watts found me, that's when you thought I might have been your kid?"

"Not at all. About a week after you were born, she contacted me. Via phone this time. Crying hysterically. Said she knows for sure the kid is mine."

I raise my eyebrows. Want to know how she knew.

"I never met the guy, but she said her husband was a very dark-skinned Polynesian man named Rangi." Despite my spray tan, I know how pale I am. White as paste. "The lights might be dim in here, kid, but I know you're about as cracker as they come."

OK, *that* is the understatement of the year.

"She calls me, super fucking early in the morning. The sun wasn't even out yet. She asks if we can meet somewhere. Says her husband is flipping out. She tried to calm him down, convince him it's really his. That some people have really light complexions. The guy knows better, but they run a DNA test. No surprise there, it wasn't his."

I feel like I'm finally getting somewhere in this story. Brevity might be the soul of wit, but verbosity can numb your enemies into submission.

"She says she's really afraid. Mainly for the kid but for herself too. I tell her not to worry. I tell her to meet me at the donut shop. I'll be there as soon as possible. I drive myself down there faster than I've ever driven before. I park illegally in front of the shop, and she's nowhere to be seen. I wait a few minutes. I am sweating even though it's like fifteen fuckin' degrees outside. After ten minutes I can't take it anymore. I'm walking all over the place. Up and down every block within a mile radius."

Could this be it? The pot of gold at the end of the longest rainbow? A minimal amount of consolation after so many years of wondering?

"I was panicking so much, I was about to call the police." It's obvious it pains him to admit that. "Can you believe it? The fucking fuzz? But what can I say, I was losing my mind."

"OK, but you said 'about to.' So you found her by yourself?" I ask with genuine intrigue.

"Yeah. After half-a-fucking hour. About three blocks from the donut shop in a small alley behind some apartments. She was lying on the ground. I thought she was dead. Bruises all over her face. So when I get to her, she's barely awake." His eyes start tearing up. Remembers it like it was yesterday. A painful clarity. "But she is breathing and awake, and she recognizes me, so I've got some hope. I need to get her to a hospital, ya know? I mean, she looks like she's on the edge of death, and I am freaking out. I don't want to leave her side, but I got no choice. I run back to my car, drive it close as I can, and help her inside. Floor it to the hospital. All the way there I am asking questions. Way too many for her to understand. I am going nuts, which is only making her more uncomfortable. But she tells me her husband beat her pretty badly. Like no shit he beat you. But don't worry, I'll take care of him later." Quick tangent as he recalls another memory. "Try and find anything you can about the guy. You won't be able to. No news coverage, no newspapers. Like he never existed. I made sure he paid for what he did."

Tempted to interject. Would love to remind him that he *thought* his men had killed me. Something tells me this guy wasn't as cunning or lucky.

He refocuses. "But I tell her that I'll make sure he never sees the kid again, but right there, I just wanna make sure she's OK. She tells me not to worry about her, says she wants me to turn around and go back for the kid. I tell her over and over that I'll go back and get him, but I need to get her to a hospital immediately. Poor thing, she has no strength to fight me. Sure, she objects, but not like she could physically force me to do anything. So we pull up to the hospital, but before I head back, she tells me she left the kid in a dumpster behind the donut shop. Said she didn't want her husband to find him, cuz she had no idea what he might to do him."

This time, he's actually moved to full-out tears. I remain solid as stone on the surface. The man is good. Can't tell if it's an act or if it really went down like this. Nicky Salcedo has made a living for a long time putting on a good show. I would love to be moved by his words. Can't allow it. I've come too far to crumble now.

He calms his nerves. Composed, he says, "The rest you pretty much know. I went back, but you were gone."

Very interesting. Certainly feasible, although still somewhat difficult to buy into. "So why didn't you get me back for her? Surely a man of your influence could have approached the Watts and made them an offer they couldn't refuse."

"No shit, kid. Believe me, I thought about it. But as you've already figured out, it wouldn't have been good for business. I had an image to protect. But yeah, I thought about it. Anyway, when I couldn't find you, I went back to the hospital. Stormed in there demanding to see Penelope, but they wouldn't let me. Wasn't fuckin' family. I sat in that fucking waiting room for an eternity. Her sister showed up right after I returned, and I gave her the rundown. The lady went white as a ghost kid. She said she never really trusted Rangi. As if she saw this coming. But the whole time I see through her. There's something she's not telling me, but I'm too tired to argue. She gets to go in and see her sister, and I don't try and stop her because I'd do the same thing—"

Interrupting, I say, "So this sister that came to visit, is it the same woman with her in this picture?"

Gives me the biggest *How much of a fuckin' moron can you be, of course it's the same woman* look. Strange. Given how many falsities Penelope has already given me, I don't find it outrageous to ask.

"Well, you know that Penelope told me my mother was the other woman, her sister. And that instead of being my mom, she led me to believe that she was my aunt."

He starts coughing violently. We've been in here a while. A thunderous knock on the door is barely audible over his hacking. He continues a few seconds longer then shouts, "I'm good Max. We're almost done in here."

I beg to differ. "Hold on a minute. Why would she go through all the trouble of tracking me down after all these years, lie about our relationship to each other, then blow my hand to bits?"

"Kid, you just don't get it, do ya?" Still noticeably dejected. "She'd been beaten within an inch of her life. She was in a coma for three weeks. When she came out of it, she was never the same."

Once again, it makes sense on the surface. Still skeptical taking it as axiomatic. "Does she know who you are? That the two of you were intimate? I'm guessing that since she doesn't even recall giving birth to me, her knowledge of you is vague as well."

Moisture still evident in his eyes. "Yeah, kid, she knows a lot of that stuff. But it comes and goes. And most of what she knows is only because she's been around me regularly for almost forty years."

Things just don't add up. The Sauce didn't get to the top via philanthropy. The guy is as cutthroat as they come. I could ask him why he gave her a job. He'd just say it was a sense of obligation. Take care of the love of his life. There's got to be more to it than that.

Reflections abruptly cut short. Another piercing howl outside. The walls begin to melt. The audible pain quickly subsides. The visual effects, however, not so much. I can hear Nicky clearly. The tone in his voice lets me know he's grinning like a madman.

"Looks like it worked."

Blinking and squinting, I inquire, "What worked?"

"Maggie Delaney. You know she works for me, right? What am I saying? Of course you knew that. You're a fucking genius." He begins strutting around the room. All I see is a fuzzy blur. "You see, when you kidnap one of the broads who works for me, I'm gonna find out about it." The blur slowly subsides. His face comes into focus. Now looking me square in the eyes. "That's right asshole. She told us all about it." I cough. A reaction to betrayal. Not even close. I deserved this. Another wonderful reminder that I didn't consider everything. "This bitch, she comes in asking a million fucking questions. That tipped us off right away. Like what is this whore doing being all inquisitive and shit? Then of course she's got the boobs"—pats me on the cheek—"good work by the way. Anyway, some time went by, and one day Penelope was ranting like crazy about how she "found our kid." And she says something about shooting off his fingers. Crazy stuff, but I've learned to tune it out. You have no idea how many times over the years I've had to listen to this shit. But for once, I'm thinking maybe she's not full of it."

He keeps talking. My focus drifts away quickly. A slip on Nicky's part. Did he not just acknowledge that Penelope referred to me as "their kid?" She knows more than he's willing to admit.

"We knew you'd be looking for a new hand. So Cooper comes to me with this idea. Says let's inject Nadira with Composition V. That's what we were calling it at the time. It has a much fancier name the science freaks call it by. But that works for me. Can you believe that? It took 'em five fuckin' tries to get it right. A bunch of shitheads, I tell ya." My vision nearly back to normal, I don't recognize the man strutting around the room. So full of energy.

This can't be happening. Only dwell momentarily. Interjecting, "That's not what that means."

He's looking at me like I'm crazy. Like a heavyweight champion who's knocked his opponent down a dozen times. But just keeps coming back for more.

"Oh really? Well then, wise guy. Tell me, what *does* it mean?"

Shake off the cobwebs. Back to normal. For now. "Wassily Kandinsky. Russian abstract painter. Many of his works had titles, but a large number were simply called *Composition* followed by a number."

Stares at me menacingly. The kind of look you get when you step in dog shit. "So?"

"So Bing his paintings. They're kind of out there. Not so crazy that they don't look like anything. But most of the images are blurred or distorted. I'm guessing that whatever this intravenous substance is, the side effects include dizziness, blurred vision, maybe even delusional thoughts."

Nefarious laugh. "Kid, those aren't the side effects. That's what it does. It slowly makes you go out of your fucking mind."

Don't like where this is going. "Well, if you're implying that I've contracted some kind of mental illness via blood-borne pathogens, that's absurd."

He's mildly offended, but more amused. "Is that so? By all means, please explain to me how you're so sure."

Another sudden realization. Terrifying. Because I'm *not* sure. My instincts tell me that most of what this man creates is pure garbage. The first few installments at least. His track record, pure shit. But the signs are there.

"Because I ran every test possible before I did the transplant." I have my Finnish mentor to thank for that. Results ready in twenty minutes. Highly expensive, but impressive. Saving lives around the world.

Small snort. "Oh, you ran some tests? Well, problem solved. I guess I have no clue what I'm talking about. And, kid, even if you did run every test possible, as you presume, new diseases are starting all the time. There's no such thing as testing for everything possible. Because no one, not even science, knows what is possible."

I swallow painfully. Like forcing a tennis ball down my throat. Because he's right. The first sensible thing I've ever heard the man say. No matter what, you cannot prepare for everything. You can take precautions. Plan ahead. Calculate risk and minimize it. But no matter what, you can never eliminate it. A crushing blow to my ego. Humility, until now, a stranger. Suddenly wanting to make up for all the years lost.

"So you and Cooper basically sacrificed Nadira's sanity to get back at me?" I want to be appalled. More frustrated than anything. Should have been more precautious. His strategy worked. They've won this round. That's what bothers me the most.

"Don't act surprised, kid. I know a lot more than you think I know." A cryptic implication. He doesn't come out and say it, but he hints at something greater. As if he's known of my whereabouts not only since I've been back in Chicago but around the world as well. "And don't pretend like you care about her well-being. It's not like she and Cooper were in love."

This time, it actually does offend me. Because one image stands out from the crowd in my mind. A sonogram of the daughter I'll never know. A virtual deathbed repentance on my part. Likely too little too late. But suddenly, I care about the fate of the world.

For her. For Mackenzie.

Indignation. Never been a fan of hiding it. Now is no different. My temper flares. Without warning, I smash Nicky across the face. It's an understatement to say I could never deliver a beating that would undo all the pain he's caused me.

But it feels fucking good.

His nose bleeding, I throw him a box of tissue. After he cleans up what he can, he looks at me. Not with fear. Almost pleading. As if he knows his time has come. That he's content with his fate. "Are you going to kill me now?" is all he says. A rather serene tone.

"No, Nicky, not quite yet. Because I have a few more things I need to know. For starters, why are you behind this movement in Congress to limit the number of children people can raise? Why do you want to sell unwanted kids to China? Why are you trying to legalize prostitution?" So many more things to add to the list. But this is a good start.

Pure silence. He just stares at me. Stunned. Eyes as wide as high beams. "I have no idea what you're talking about," he tells me. Not convincing at all. For once, the master con man can't bullshit himself out of a situation. His act is weak, but it confirms my fears. Until now, it was primarily speculation. But that look of panic speaks volumes.

"Look, Nicky, I know what you're up to. Truth be told, I'm not exactly interested in stopping you. That's not to say that I won't see to it that other people don't shut it down, but I'm exhausted. Physically sure, I've had some rough weeks." I hold up my hand. "But mentally, I am so psychologically drained I can't even begin to explain it. Truthfully, I just want this to be over." Whatever "this" is I'm not exactly sure. One of those things you just know when it happens.

I walk behind him, he crouches in fear. Temptation runs strong, but I resist. I simply remove his gun, empty the clip. Stand behind him like a cop in a movie. Arms spread wide. Interrogation style.

And it works. He bursts into tears once again. "I never wanted to give you up!" he yells. The man has always been a performer. "It was the biggest mistake I ever made. All I want is to prevent anyone else from going through what I went through." So confused. His situation was extreme indeed. Where is he going with this? "So many women are getting pregnant by men who will be horrible fathers, assuming they're even present at all. I was hoping that by legalizing prostitution, more men would seek that avenue to relieve their sexual tension. And by limiting the number of babies a woman can bring to term, well, anytime you put a limit on something, people become more selective. Women would pick their partners with greater care. They'd use more protection."

The cynic in me interrupts, "So you can sell more birth control. Your sentiment is very sweet, Nicky, but I'm having a hard time believing that your motivations weren't primarily financial."

He doesn't deny it but looks at me. I can tell he's sincere. His intentions completely irrational. But if I said what he's done is wrong, pure hypocrisy.

Coal. Kettle. Black.

I'm sterilizing the human race. Little room to judge.

Then again, I've always been a fan of double standards.

Hypocrisy it is.

Now he's practically begging me. Looks at me, implores me to end his misery.

"Nicky, you have no idea how long I've dreamt of doing just that. But I don't think the timing is right."

Looks at me shocked. Like I'm fucking with him. Like any second now, I'm going to pull out a sword and sever his head.

"I'll tell you what. Get me a copy of your last will and testament. I have a feeling I'm going to need to make some revisions." His eyes bug out. "When it's all final and official, then I'll end you."

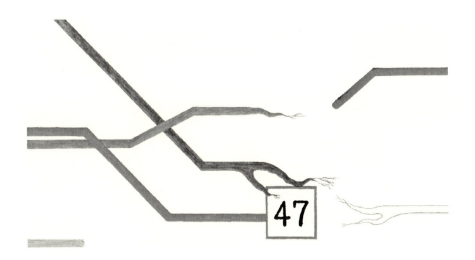

47

Four hours of my life. Normally followed by "that I'll never get back." Not this time. Very interesting. It took forever to get in touch with his lawyer. Finally got it sent over. Read through it a dozen times. A rather short document in general. But as far as wills go, the thing is a dictionary. The guy has a lot of stuff. And I say "has" because I guess technically it's still his. He might be dead. But possession hasn't been transferred yet.

Satisfying, yes. But the buildup was too much. No way after all these years it could live up to the hype.

So just like that, I did what I came to do. One problem gone, another dozen arise.

Very tempting to watch him die a slow and agonizing death. Only get one shot, so make it count. I just went with a classic neck snap.

The escape wasn't easy. His two guards ever so faithful. Never left their posts outside the door. The building had no doubt been vacant for hours. But they stood their ground until I left.

Killing Nicky simply teased the palate. Gave me a taste for blood. With Nicky down, the second I walked out, I was a goner. Let the fun begin.

Grab his gun, lock, and load.

What a stupid fucking phrase. Like putting underwear on last.

Unless this is the age of ramrods and bayonets.

I throw the door open, shove the pistol under the jaw of the guy on my left. Blood and brains paint the wall. Hope Dr. Jayaraman has an excellent cleaning crew. Drop the pistol, thwart the attack of the other guard. Pinch his ear to stifle his movement. Drive Nadira's fist right into his throat. Her ring—maybe a wedding ring, maybe engagement, maybe just a flashy rock (no clue, either way)—cuts through flesh like nothing. Jugular vein spurting blood. A ruthless cascade reminiscent of a fire hydrant.

Wash my hands, go find a car.

Hot-wire the most blasé vehicle in sight. Try to keep a low profile.

Gotta get back to Chicago. Grab an umbrella cuz shit is about to hit the fan. Flying down the highway toward LAX. Shocking, given the fact that all Los Angeles roads are merely taxpayer-funded parking lots. The engine has some juice for a hippie, fuel-efficient lunchbox on wheels.

A green sign overhead says the airport is seven miles away. Cell phone beeps and vibrates in my back pocket. About to pull it out and check it. California won't have it. Big Brother is watching. Flashing signs and billboards warn against the dangers of texting and driving.

But they never apply to me. Other people sure. Never to me.

Airport exit in five miles.

I pull the phone out, check the text. A photo of a hand. A woman's hand. Small, light brown complexion. Massive shiny ring on it. Simple caption reads, "She said YESSS!!!"

Mackenzie's hand. I throw the phone over my shoulder. Hits the backseat, falls to the floor. Not my finest moment.

Doing a modest ten over. Make that fifteen. Why not twenty? Black Audi cruises by and slows down with nowhere to pass the car in front. Eventually pull even. Just a kid. Not literally. Probably nineteen or twenty.

A radio commercial warns of the dangers of drinking and driving. Followed immediately by an announcement stating the same for texting while driving.

Still even with the black Audi.

The kid is texting. What else? Or checking his parent's bank account. Looks up at the road. Back at his phone—3:1 ratio. Three seconds staring at the screen. One second on the road.

The announcement drawing to a close. States that one in three people will be severely injured due to an accident involving text chats while operating a vehicle.

Dillon and Mackenzie. That cocksucker.

Three miles to LAX.

Kid looks down.

Looks up.

I'm no better. Staring at him with condescension. Judging him endlessly. All the while leaving my eyes everywhere but where they belong.

Focus.

Hypocrisy is fun. High-speed collisions are not.

Two miles. Traffic condenses. Should probably start moving over. Prepare to exit.

But that would be too easy. Notice blood on my clothes. Custom tailored, not cheap. Guess I'll have to go to Italy again. Simply reminds me of the rage inside. Not yet fully discharged. Need to purge my system. Mackenzie marrying Dillon isn't helping calm my nerves.

Look at the kid once again. Three seconds down, one second up. Honk my horn, draw his attention to me. No dice. Honk again.

One mile.

Not like I even have a flight booked. I can't miss my flight if I'm not scheduled to be on one. I've got time to waste.

The kid is tailing the minivan in front of him. Honk once again. Finally get him to glance. Point my finger down. He doesn't get the memo.

I tried.

Gradually steer my stolen car into his. Just a tap. Definitely have his undivided attention. Thoroughly freaked out. Justifiably so.

Another small tap. Panic blankets his face. Phone nowhere in sight, two hands on the wheel. Can't speed up. The minivan isn't paying any attention. Hits the breaks, tries to drop farther back.

Big mistake.

Without hesitation, I swerve hard, clip the nose of the Audi with my tail. Send the kid into the barricade. Right into the carpool lane divider. Splits his ride in half. Not exactly a picnic for me. Takes everything I have to correct my car. Focus isn't coming in spades right now, but I rally enough to get the job done.

His family and friends will say how tragic this was.

On the contrary. He's a hero.

He just saved two lives.

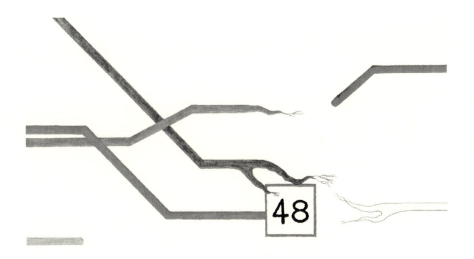

48

Most people dream of dying as heroes. Going out in a blaze of glory. Saving a life. Preventing a tragedy. Reality: most of us pass on under ordinary circumstances. That doesn't stop us from fantasizing. Believing we'll be different.

A rare occasion where I follow the trend. Never thought I'd bow out in a most cowardly fashion.

But what a view. The last thing I'll see before taking the plunge. Chicago sky is clear. Crisp, cool, far from cold. The view goes on for miles from the Hancock Observatory. I still remember the first time Mom and Dad took me here. Breathtaking. Most kids wanted baseball games and movie theatres. Those were fine, just not my preference. This is where I got my start in the arts. Opened my mind to the unrelenting power of imagery.

Never underestimate it.

Fitting that this is where it will end.

I'm back in town a full month since killing Nicky. Still haven't heard from my aunt. Alison. Or Penelope. Whoever that psycho bitch is. Whatever Nicky's chefs cooked up in that lab, whatever they did to Nadira, it works. Never been this depressed. Not just that. Everything is distorted. Sights and sounds. Likely that I can only enjoy this view so much because I have it committed to memory. Maybe those in the real world inhabit a world of gray skies and rain. Maybe I'm soaking wet. All I see is Wrigley Field.

Approach the edge. No one suspects anything. Confirming everyone's greatest fear. When we die, do we become obsolete? Just asked my Magic 8 Ball.

All signs point to yes.

I step up on the ledge. Hands on the fence, start my climb. Seven feet up, 1,134 feet down.

My hand grips the top of the chain-link cage followed by Nadira's. Now people are chattering. Just a bunch of mumbling to me.

They talk, but no one does anything about it.

Out of nowhere, I'm pulled down. Flung to the ground by someone kind enough to step in.

Bruised shoulder, a few scrapes and bruises. Nothing compared to ball cancer. Or plummeting nearly a quarter-mile at 9.86 m/s^2.

Look up to face my Good Samaritan.

It's Dillon.

Well, slap me across the face with rotten pancakes, this guy is everywhere. He stands over me, furious. Slowly helps me back up. I brush the dirt off my shoulders.

#99Problems

Temptation runs rampant, desperate to knock him out. Instead, I simply turn around. Casually walk back to the fence. Slowly attempt another ascent. Dillon pulls me back down. He responds with less desperation this time. More like he's handling a toddler at the playground who refuses to leave the sandbox.

He stands there, staring at me. A look unabashedly projecting annoyance. Fuck this. I saved him. Time to end him. Lean back, wind up, drive my fist right at his jaw.

The shattering sound can be heard above the ambient noise of honking cabs. Not his face.

My hand.

Metacarpals crumple like aluminum foil.

As if he's not even human. Made of some element not yet known to science. His jaw so hard, I stand a better chance beating my fist against a wall of tungsten carbide.

No point pretending it didn't hurt. Let out a scream so distressing, it causes parents to take their children inside.

Make yet another trip to the fence. Dillon doesn't bother following me. He knows I won't be able to climb now. My hand trembling. Just stands back and watches me further humiliate myself.

Goes on for at least two minutes. Finally, he interjects from afar.

"Are you done yet?"

I keep trying, ignoring him. So consumed by indignation coupled with my deteriorating mind. Now I *know* I'm hearing things. Dillon's voice. Haven't heard it in years. But sounds so real to me.

Block it out. Just another effect of Nadira's hand. No matter how hard I try, her hand alone can't pull me to the top.

"Ted. Seriously, you can knock it off now. You know that even if you were capable of climbing that fence, I would never let it happen. So come on back here, we've got a lot to talk about."

Stumble back over, squeezing my hand. About to pinch my ear. Not gonna happen. Not nearly strong enough to force the fingers shut. Noticing my pain, Dillon reads my mind. Grabs a ballpoint pen from his pocket. Examines my ear, drives it into the exact spot.

Instantaneous relief.

I catch my breath. Always the anticipatory perfectionist, Dillon produces a bottle of water from his coat. "Here, drink up."

Conceding the fact he will have his way, I accept.

I gulp half the bottle in seconds. Catch my breath. "Where did you learn about the pressure points in the ear?"

A little caught off guard. Certainly expecting my first question to be along the lines of *When did you get your voice back?*

"Come on, Ted. That's like basic stuff. I thought everyone knew how to relieve joint pain via acupuncture meridians."

Typical response from him. So arrogant. As if he knows everything there is to know.

"Don't give me that look, Ted." Must have seen me rolling my eyes. "Yeah, I saw it. So I guess you're going to keep strutting around like the brainchild of Einstein and Isaac Newton?"

Actually flattered by the comparison, I don't let it show. "That's funny. Coming from the spawn of Nostradamus and Buddha."

Merely responds with a shrug, as if to say, *You got me there.*

Pushing the adulations aside, I get to the real point. Gulp down more water. "So please forgive me, as you can see, my mind isn't quite right." An almost undetectable display of agreement on his part. "I don't know what Nicky did to me or what kinds of drugs I've been slipped, but right now, you can fucking talk." Burst out in a fit of laughter. Overly hysterical. Truly looking like a madman, I'm now rolling on the ground. Collecting filth from the shoes of tourists, ejected lunches of birds flown by.

Waits for me to calm down. Gently guides me to sit up straight. Takes a seat next to me, close enough to embrace me if need be. Or maybe restrain me.

"Are you good now?" I nod. Then start laughing again. Dillon grabs my injured hand, places it on the ground. My resistance is futile. He will win this battle every time. Still, I haven't completely given up. Removes one of his shoes. Raises it high above his head, and lowers it with a thunderous smash. I scream loud enough for the people at street level to hear. Very out of character for him. But then again, I'm only dreaming. Or drunk. Likely, reality does not coincide with my perspective.

He stabs me in the ear again. Doesn't hit the right spot though. Just leaves a blue mark mixed with blood. On the cusp of screaming again until I realize Dillon isn't joking. Always the pacifist, he isn't letting me leave simply because I'm acting childish. He commands my undivided attention.

"I'll ask again. Are you good now?"

Much more austere in my demeanor now. Hoping to avoid further physical pain. Also realizing that he and I have unfinished business.

"Yes, I'm good now. Go on. As you can see, I've got some business to attend to," I say, making a dipping motion with my finger. Climbing up, falling down.

"Would you knock that off?" He swats my hand away. More a playful approach, no violence involved. "You're not going to kill yourself."

"Yeah, we'll see about that."

Responds with one of those deep breaths. The kind a fed-up girlfriend gives her sugar daddy that recently cancelled the credit cards.

"This is what she was talking about," says under his breath. Barely audible, but loud enough it's obvious he intended me to hear.

Quick on the defensive, I say, "What the fuck is that supposed to mean?"

Another deep breath from Dillon. Not quite as melodramatic. "What do you think it means? Mackenzie. For months, well years actually, but especially over the last couple months, she says you've been really"—pauses to find the perfect adjective, settles on—"complicated."

About to lash out, I remain silent. Not wanting to validate the claims. "Explain" is all that leaves my mouth. Forced to exit through clenched jaw, lips barely agape. Dillon, on the brink of response, his mouth opens. I interrupt. "Hold that thought. Let's forget about that for a minute. When and how did you get your voice back?"

Deadpan, "I've always been able to talk, Ted."

Don't even bother keeping up the Samuel Clemens charade. "Impossible. You expect me to believe that you've simply kept your mouth shut or at least your vocal chords silent all these years?"

"Well, technically, there were a couple months where I couldn't speak. But that was simply because my jaw was so badly damaged that it hurt to move it. I'm sure you remember my injury." I nod. Despite my impaired frame of mind, you don't forget something like that. "Well, I had a lot of time to reflect on my life. Weeks in the hospital. Seeing and hearing that man's reaction in court. And of course all I went through with AIDS. It took a while, but eventually, it all started weighing on me. Really started to sink in, you know?"

I feel I'm in for a parable. Some kind of born-again lecture.

"Well, it was a while before I could even make any sounds, let alone fully enunciate words. But eventually, over time, I regained control of my speech."

Fully listening but staring off into space. Giving the illusion of indifference, I finally direct my attention to him. "That doesn't make any sense."

Cutting to the chase, he says, "Look, Ted, it's no secret that my life has taken a very spiritual path over the years. I'm a lot different than I used to be."

#Overstatingtheobvious

He senses me on the verge of another smart-ass comment. "Anyway, after I recovered, I made the decision to live my life differently. No more sleeping around. No more drugs or alcohol. I resolved to help those in need, do more charity." He's running down this list as if I just met him.

"I'm aware of your pending sainthood, Dillon." I make no attempt to hide my contempt.

He ignores my snide remark. "But I decided in addition to all of those things, that I was going to take a vow of silence."

Never understood that one. Might work fine in Nepal, on the top of a mountain surrounded by nothing but clouds and monks. Not in America though. Not in a land so dependent on free speech. Whatever that implies.

"I know it sounds crazy, but I told myself that I wouldn't speak a word to anyone, under one condition."

Slightly intrigued. I'll bite. "Which is?"

"Will you marry me?"

This explains a lot. Most people would be shocked. Yes, we live in a progressive society. Homosexual couples are much more common than they were only a couple decades ago. But they still surprise people.

Not me. Always suspected Dillon had a thing for me. Add to that the symptoms of Nightingale syndrome, when I saved his life. It all adds up.

Not really sure how to respond. "Um, well Dillon, I'm not really sure what to say. Basically, I don't want to get married. I don't mean that just about you. I mean I really detest the institution of marriage. I have no desire to marry anyone. But"—hoping to ease the blow—"I'm flattered you think so highly of me."

He's rubbing his temples. "That's not what I meant."

Oh. I knew that.

He elaborates. "What I meant was I made a personal vow not to speak to anyone unless I was ready to at least *ask* them to marry me. I wanted to make sure I was truly in love. That I had the right intentions. That I had finally put my past behind me and was really ready to start a new life with someone."

"OK, but why not just ask some random girl you fucked on camera to marry you?" Right as it comes out, I realize how foolish it sounds.

Rolling with it, "Because, Ted, that would defeat the entire purpose of my vow."

"OK, so you're speaking to me." Just then, I remember the text, *She said YESSS!!!* driving to LAX. "I got your message." Playing aloof. Want to hear it from his mouth. With obvious resentment, I ask, "Who's the lucky girl?"

Whatever saltiness my tone exudes, he ignores it. Or possibly doesn't detect it at all. So in love, nothing can bring him down. Even the way he says her name, you can tell he feels invincible.

"Mackenzie," he utters calmly. Obviously forcing back the excitement, unsure how I will react.

My actual response is far more civilized than the one in my mind. "Good for you."

He stands up, clearly bothered. "You see! That's exactly what she was talking about."

"Huh? What?"

His tone firm. "Ted, I just told you I'm marrying Mackenzie. The woman who is about to give birth to a child. A child fathered by you. A woman who has been in love with you for over twenty years."

"I don't see what—"

Cuts me off. "You're so fucking arrogant. Why can't you just admit this bothers you? Don't get me wrong. Obviously, I wish we lived in a world where everyone got the girl. Where no one ended up alone. But life isn't a rom-com. It doesn't always work out for everyone in the romance department. So I don't expect you to be thrilled for us."

"It doesn't bother me. 'Everyone gets the girl.' What are you talking about?" Can't even look him in the eye when I say it.

"Bullshit! That's exactly why you're miserable. The second Mackenzie walked out of your life, *that* was when you wanted her. You never fully appreciated her." He's going on. I'm trying to drown him out, not in the mood for this. "Sure, you always liked having her around. But you craved her reliance on you. You do this with everyone. You're so fucking narcissistic, it's ridiculous."

Not up for a debate. "Says the guy who's fucked, what is it now? Two thousand women on camera? Three thousand?"

Hooray for cheap shots.

"Fine. You know what? Jump. Go ahead, Ted. That's what you need anyways. But I got news for you. No one is really going to miss you."

Where is this all coming from? Never seen anything like it. So unprepared for this side of him. My rebuttals consist of one or two syllable words.

Uh-huh. Yep. Got it.

"Just jump already because that's exactly what you need to fulfill your legacy. You need everyone to swoon over you. You want a big elaborate funeral, your face plastered all over the news. Everyone will finally know that you survived Nicky Salcedo's goons years ago. Your vanity knows no bounds. In your mind, you're so important that you can't stand the thought of anything, or anyone, being the cause of your downfall other than you."

My tone thick with agitation. As if his presence is an extreme burden on my existence. Throwing everything he said right back at him. "Dillon, you have no idea what you're talking about."

Irate. Ludicrous. Preposterous in his view. "You know what, you're right. I'm completely off base. This whole thing you've been doing, running around the world, slipping people pills. Sterilizing the population. Your lame attempt to play god. It was cute at first. You'd been through a lot. Now it's just pathetic."

My arrogance breaking through. "Are you done?" Says nothing. His face red, breathing heavily. Can't recall a time I've seen him this animated. Terrifying, yet still invigorating. "That's convenient. It's easy to talk shit about all the things wrong with me. But let's evaluate you for a minute."

Gives me a look that says, *Gimme what you got.*

"The fact of the matter is that whether or not what I'm doing is ethical, at least I'm doing *something* with my talents. Whereas you just fucking run around acting like life is so peachy. Like everyone has so much potential just waiting to flow forth."

"And what's so bad about that?"

"Because you're so focused on bringing out potential in everyone else, helping them convert their lives that you've completely disregarded your own talents. What about your potential?"

The defensive mind-set shifts to him.

The clear sky darkening. Clouds moving in. Wind picking up. Looks like rain. A family of five comes out of the door. Look around, notice only two men on the roof. The dad senses something's not right. Directs his wife and kids back inside.

Light drops begin to fall.

"What about my potential?" Dillon demands.

Rolling my eyes. This time, justifiably frustrated. "Dillon, you are one of the smartest people the world has ever known. You could be curing diseases. Solving major crises of the world. Eradicating poverty. But no, you just sit around like everything is so dandy and fine."

Scratches his head. "Well, I will certainly admit, I haven't always lived up to my potential. And although I haven't done all that I should, or at least could, to erase poverty," he pauses to think. He hates bragging about his good deeds.

I finish for him. He takes great pride in not being proud. "The lottery tickets."

Gives me a smile. The first one on this roof since we were alone. "Exactly."

How could I forget that? Dillon, personally responsible for millions of dollars distributed to local charities. No small feat.

Awkward silence. Dillon is the first to break it. "I don't think everything is all wonderful and lovely. I'm just, ya know, optimistic."

The tension in the air is still present. But mitigated with each passing moment.

"I've known you for so long, and I love you to death, man, but that's one thing I'll never understand about you."

Genuinely shocked, almost offended. "How do you mean?"

"Look around, Dillon," speaking rhetorically, he turns his head side to side anyway. "Things are falling apart. The world is going to shit. And all you can focus on is the 'good inside people.'"

So much more calm this time around. Displaying his sympathy for my alleged arrogance. Finally, I'm not cowering in fear. "Ted, you just don't get it. Of course things aren't perfect. But that's what makes life so incredible."

Super. Another one of his "imperfections are beautiful" pep talks.

"Ted, I know you're a smart dude. And deep down, I know you have a good heart, with wonderful intentions. But you're not seeing the bigger picture."

I wait, assuming he's about to follow up. No such luck. "Which is?"

"There will *always* be problems in the world. Disease. Crime. Class warfare." Feeling insulted. He's stating the obvious. "You cured AIDS. Think about that, man."

Don't need to. I was there.

"That is something so astounding, there aren't enough trees in the world to make all the thank-you cards people would love to write you."

"Dillon, that's all well and good. I know most people were thrilled by my discovery. But look what they did with it." Gives me a blank look. Just doesn't get it. "I gave millions of people a second shot at life, and they wasted it."

Looks disturbed. "How so?"

"They do nothing with their lives. Video games. Television. Porn," that last one slips out. Touchy subject for him. "Point being, they are wasting their lives."

His sympathy for me extremely blatant. Like he pities me. "No offense, buddy, but what they do with their lives isn't really up to you. People fuck up. Some of them will learn from their mistakes. Others will suffer because of them. But ultimately, you have to stop trying to control everything. Focus on what you *can* control."

Now he's my fucking therapist.

Jack Avalanche, PhD.

He's right. Stings so bad, but he's right. Still a bitter pill to swallow. Can't help but taking another jab at him. "I mean, I guess I'll just pray for a better world, and everything will be rainbows and bunny hugs."

He just shakes his head. Very accustomed to attacks on his faith. To his credit, he's made quite the conversion. Very devout. "So you're saying prayer doesn't work?"

Snarky, "I never said that."

"Right. But you implied it."

"I'm a scientist, Dillon. It doesn't fit with my worldview."

"You got cancer."

"Thanks for the reminder. Why are you bringing that up?"

"True or false: when you were a child you used to pray you would get cancer?"

Never ceases to amaze me. He literally knows *everything*. "I never told that to anyone." A perfunctory shrug, his response. Despite being deranged, I see the wheels turning in his head. When you know someone as long as I've known Dillon, well, you tend to know what they're thinking. He's staring at me, very disconcerting. Cut him off right now. "Oh no, if you're going to tell me that there's a correlation between praying for and actually getting cancer, you're out of your mind. In no way does that prove the existence of God."

Gives me one of those smirks I would love to erase with a Louisville Slugger. Which still might not be strong enough. "I never said it did."

Now he's the one implying things. Neither one of us speaking in subtle subtext right now. "Just checking."

"But"—here comes the fine print—"it also wouldn't be very rational to rule it out completely."

His Herculean stature is the only thing preventing me from a violent rampage. My composure nearly sucked dry to the last drop, sanity following suit. "Dillon, I'm not shitting on your beliefs. I don't try and stop you from believing what you want to believe or how you want to practice your faith. I've even gone to church with you a few times. I'm not denying the existence of God. Honestly, my brain's gas tank has been running on E for months now. So no matter what I do or do not believe, it's probably best to not take me too seriously. Either way, please stop trying to force your beliefs on me." Intended to be firm but constructive. You never know how Dillon will react.

Long pause. He's very clearly replaying in his mind what I just said. Deconstructing it. Finding flaws as well as valid points. Always fair in his assessments. One of his many admirable traits. Definitely factored into Mackenzie's decision to marry him. Will he be raising my child? Stupid question. The answer seems rather obvious. He finally responds. "OK, look. You're a grown man. I think it's fair to assume that at this point in our lives, we're not going to change the other's mind on religion. So I apologize if I come off that way. But what you're accusing me of, somewhat hypocritical of you, don't you think?"

It takes a lot to blow my mind. To literally make me think I misunderstood. "Excuse me?" Sarcasm building.

"Look, buddy, I'll say this one last time. Ever." Gets into a kneeling position, hands overhead, bends at the waist. Begins an overly facetious worship bow. "You cured AIDS. That's a *big* fucking deal. Amazing. One of the greatest moments in the history of mankind. But that doesn't make you impeccable. You are still human, and therefore not immune to making mistakes. I'm not talking original sin and the fall of man, this is just basic stuff. But you're walking around this life like you own the world and everyone who lives in it. I know that people who sit there on the Internet all day and claim to know how to fix the government, everyone who throws in their two cents, I know they annoy you to no end. Believe me, I'm right there with you. And sure, you might not get on television, or write a blog, and literally tell everyone how to live. But when you effectively make lifestyle choices for people without their consent, without even discussing your perceived errors of their ways, then yes, you are most definitely forcing your beliefs on them."

Not in the mood to argue.

Less interested in backing down.

"Dillon, what I'm doing . . . rather, what *we're* doing. Don't forget, you helped out in Las Vegas. But what I started, it's making a better world. Sure, we probably won't live long enough to see the results. But isn't that what people are always yapping about? Future generations. Save the trees so our kids will have them to climb on. Don't deplete the ozone so future generations won't get sunburn after thirty seconds outside. Sure, I'm unconventional. But you've got to understand that the endgame is ultimately a good thing."

Sees he's getting nowhere with me. Using his own chess analogy, "Well, I guess we're kind of at a stalemate. Neither one of us really willing to concede the other being right." He stands up from his kneeling posture. "But please, just think about this: is the world you're creating really the kind of future you want for her?" Removes an envelope from his jacket pocket. Attached by paperclip, a photograph. I remove it and peruse. Revision. Not a photograph. The most recent ultrasound.

Of the daughter I'll never know.

I sit there, weak. On the verge of tears. Dillon turns and walks away. Reaches the door to access the elevator. Begins to open, but returns to me. "By the way, you're not going crazy. Whatever was in Nadira's blood stream, it's nothing. Completely psychosomatic."

Again with his omniscience. Never ceases to amaze me. Past the point of asking where he heard about that. I just accept that he knows whatever he knows, lacking the energy to contest too much. "Dillon, whatever it is that's wrong with me, it's been going on long before I got tangled up in that web. But whatever Nicky's scientists did to her, it's definitely taking its toll on me."

Trying to conceal his amusement. "Ted, listen to what you just said. You said Nicky Salcedo's corporation actually set an objective and accomplished it. They are the most incompetent bunch of hacks, and you know that." Can't argue with that. "Like I said, it's totally in your head. Metaphorically, I mean. You've always had a strong need for attention. And yes, I'm not exactly one to talk, given my"—pauses for a euphemism—"history in cinema."

Impressive.

"But you're just being melodramatic because Mackenzie is totally right. You are so vain, it's destroying you."

Closed lips are my only reply. My silence is my consent.

Sensing I'm not planning on being difficult, he elaborates. Steps even closer, places his massive paw on my shoulder. "Ted, your mom and dad were amazing people. Two of the most incredible people I've ever had the pleasure of knowing. And for the most part, I'd like to say they did a good job raising you. But once again, do you think they'd honestly be proud of you now?" The rain comes harder. Our feud has simmered down. A handful of people enter the viewing area holding umbrellas.

Reminisce.

Mom and Dad. Paul and Josephine. My heroes in more ways than one. I should want to make them proud. They would want me to be a better man. I want so badly to *want* to change. Ultimately, I'm in the wrong. But sometimes, you cross a threshold. A point where you simply stop caring. Check the rearview. That place is nowhere to be seen. Buried beneath a mound of dust. So long ago, so ancient. Archaeologists might be studying this very moment.

Right on cue, Dillon continues. Seemingly reading my mind. Scratch that. I'm certain he's inside my head.

"I know you miss them, buddy. They were incredible people. And if they were still here, I'm fairly confident you wouldn't be acting this way. And please understand that I'm in no way saying you don't love them dearly. I know you do. And I know that deep down inside, there's a part of you that truly believes you're making them proud. But they always wanted the best for you. So I'm sorry to be so blunt, but effectively, you're shitting on their memory. I know that's not your intention, but that's what's happening. And yes, it drives me crazy to see you this way." He takes a long dramatic pause. Locking eyes with me, making sure he has my attention. "But you're also demonstrating a fact of life: It. Goes. On."

The man can give a speech. But I wonder. Do his words carry so much weight simply because they've lain dormant so long?

"You're trying to leave your legacy as if curing AIDS wasn't enough. But the fact of the matter is people will forget you. You will still matter, and people will cry when it's your time to go. But in the grand scheme of things, you're not even a blip on the radar."

Love that he's reciting my personal philosophy to me. Using it against me. Excellent tactic. Hard to argue against.

Oh wait, he's not done. "For the longest time, AIDS looked like it would never be cured. Obviously that changed, thanks to you. And I hate to say this, but something else will take its place. Possibly whatever sterility drug you've introduced. Maybe that's the next pandemic."

That's the idea.

"But eventually, someone will cure that. And another disease will take its place." Looks at me, about to drop the hammer. "The same goes for people. Your greatness will live on for a while. But eventually, someone else will take your place." Squeezes my shoulder. Gives me a weird look. His internal debate concludes. Decides to give me a hug. Embraces me so firmly, oxygen now hard to come by. On the verge of fainting. He releases just in time. "Now I could go into detail about how in heaven your greatness will live forever, that everything on earth is just temporary, and all that good stuff. But I know you're not interested in that."

Maybe one day. But not today.

For the second time, he walks away. Just as quickly turns back to face me. Switching to his cryptic voice. The prophetic one you know not to ignore. "Oh, have you been to visit your mother's grave lately?"

Shrug of my shoulders tells him not recently enough.

"Maybe you should do that soon."

His tone makes me apprehensive. Trying to downplay my discomfort, I make a joke. "Well, if she's risen from the dead, it's gonna make Jesus's three days look rather rudimentary."

He doesn't laugh. "Just go. Something strange is afoot."

Only Dillon could do that. Only he could terrify me to my core by quoting *Bill & Ted's Excellent Adventure*. What I wouldn't give to be back in my living room, watching that with him. Brings a smile to my face. Only momentarily. Because I open the envelope. A wedding announcement.

Visions of their perfect day vivid in my mind.

They're going to make each other so happy. A beautiful ceremony followed by a beautiful reception. Beautiful lovemaking on a beautiful honeymoon. Their collective life growing more beautiful with every passing day.

Everything is going to be simply amazing for them from here on out.

So I have to wonder . . .

Why would they jeopardize that by inviting me?

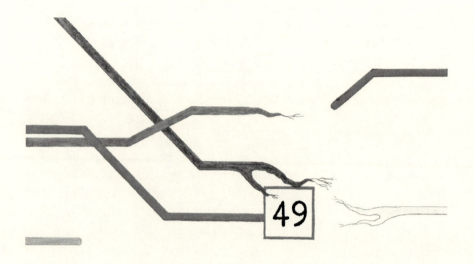

49

Two months pass in an instant. Like I slept through it all. Wishing I was waking from a horrific dream. All the while knowing it's more real than anything imaginable. Dillon and Mackenzie, tying the knot.

Stepping up to the open doors, we find our way into the nave. That's right, I brought dates.

Plural.

Completely unsure to head left or right. Groom side or bride?

I ask the girls. They say groom, since they've worked with Dillon in the past. One hooked around each arm, we stroll near the front. Eyes follow like magnets. Every head on a swivel as we pass by. Gawking and stares all of us accustomed to.

"Ladies, you look lovely this afternoon," I tell them for the third time in as many hours. Pretending to be flattered, flashing plastic smiles shiny enough to see your reflection.

The minutes tick by, music continues to play. I look around, admire the fabulous architecture. The stained glass. Sculptures. Not my favorite place to spend an afternoon. Majestic nonetheless.

Chateau uncrosses her legs. Crosses them the other way. Adjusts her short yellow skirt. Pulls it down, now only fourteen inches above her knees. Chateau, as in Chateau Chase. She and Dillon go way back. Filmed over thirty scenes together. Sounds like a lot. Until you realize my other date, Ambrosia Austin, is just shy of triple digits in such a feat.

The stares continue. Being a white male, it's difficult to fully understand prejudice. Rarely on the receiving end. But now, we are the pariahs. How it goes when you bring porn stars to a wedding. Can't help but laugh to myself. Chateau leans into my ear. I move in to meet her halfway. Expecting a sensual female voice. Caught off guard by an abrasive male tone, paired with a firm grip on my shoulder.

"Ted. May I have a word with you?"

Dillon is beet red. After years of horseplay and "boys will be boys" fights between friends, I genuinely believe he will kill me.

His long legs carry him outside from near the altar in a matter of seconds. Not exactly dawdling, I'm behind him by twenty feet in no time.

Interjecting before he can chew my head off. "Dillon, I'm so sorry. I told Chateau yellow was a really tacky color to wear to a wedding. But you know women, they're just so unpredictable."

Not paying attention to anything I say or do. His tone forceful. Yet aware of his surroundings. Keeping himself relatively calm, so as to not scare those entering the church. "I don't care about the color of her dress! Are you out of your fucking mind?"

Clearly he's not acting. But his mannerisms. His flailing about. Looks like a college botany major auditioning for *West Side Story*. Every movement exaggerated. Hard to take him seriously.

But I know better.

His subdued rampage continues. "What in the world possessed you to bring two porn stars to *my wedding?*"

Really?

Oh, cognitive dissonance. You tricky bastard.

"Dillon, Chateau and Ambrosia are people just like you and me. I don't think it's fair for you to judge them based on their profession. I hate to remind you, but you used to work with them, remember?" My tone playful, hoping to diffuse the bomb I intentionally lit.

Irritation escalation. His initial response impulsive. Lashing out, "Their names are Amanda and Denise!" A littler cooler, appreciating the environment. "I'm not judging them for how they make their living." He totally is. "But I know it's going to make Mackenzie uncomfortable. Having women at our wedding that I used to"—choosing his words carefully—"work with." The man sure can own a euphemism.

Fuel to the fire. "Dillon, don't worry about it. Mackenzie and I used to bone on the regular back in Las Vegas." Eyes nearly pop out of his head. Veins in his neck. Look like garden snakes crawling up toward his face. Thick as a cigarette. "Besides, I wanted to bring a woman you hadn't slept with. But do you know how arduous of a task that is? I think the nearest one was in Morocco. Or maybe it was Monaco."

Guests passing by, saying nothing out loud. Their looks expressing enough concern. Pass by uncomfortably, pretending everything is in order.

"Look, just get them out of here. I'm sure they'll understand."

My best over-the-top look of shock. Taking sarcasm to plateaus never before seen. "Dillon, how could you? This is God's house after all. Everyone is welcome here. In fact, these are Jesus's people. Didn't he save a prostitute from being stoned to death? You know he wouldn't discriminate, and you shouldn't either." Steam spews out of his ears. Looks as though he spent a week in the Bahamas without sun block. His face like a tomato. Clearly livid I'm using his beliefs against him.

Simply put, I'm fueled by spite. You expected something else?

But as my contempt and mockery manifest themselves, I calm myself. My initial motives entirely juvenile and self-serving. Not for long. As I replay what I've just said over in my head, it makes sense.

Jesus. Whoever he was . . . is . . . whether you believe him to be the Son of God or not, no denying his impact on the world. A true humanitarian. A revolutionary.

A momentary blow to my solipsistic worldview.

Hold that thought. Let's revisit when I'm not so pissed at Dillon.

My dates now in earshot out of curiosity. Overhear one of them say something about the bride. My attention darts away from the fuming behemoth casting a shadow over me.

Twenty yards away, taking pictures with family and friends, she looks to be ten months pregnant. The bulge in her belly nearly doubling her body mass. While most weddings feature a pregnant bride, never seen one this far along. Her immaculate dress undoubtedly altered so many times she put the seamstress on the fast track to retirement.

Suddenly. Finally. After all these years, my brain finally relents. Allows my heart to triumph. Admit to myself what I've suppressed for so long.

I've always been in love with Mackenzie Desjardin.

Would love to strangle Dillon. For taking my woman. For not asking me to be his best man. Not that I deserved it.

But whether or not I agree with Dillon's view of religion, the teachings of Jesus, this is a place of peace. A time for celebration. Not even I'm cruel enough to unleash the monster raging inside.

Turning back, I say, "Ladies, let's go. I'll call the limo." They exchange anxious glances, unsure how to respond. Not wanting to add to the tension, my request meets no resistance. Dillon begins to return to his regular complexion. I walk by him, say nothing. The ladies finally feel comfortable enough to acknowledge him. Each gives a hug and peck on the cheek. Offer the requisite congratulations.

Our driver pulls up within a minute. Pops out, opens the door. Ladies climb in, I follow suit. Door shuts. Only then do I glance back at Dillon. Can't see me through thick tint. His demeanor unchanged. Straightens his jacket and tie. Spins around, back up the steps, and into the church.

Driver pulls away, "Where to?"

"Just drive. We'll figure something out," I bark.

Sensing my angst, the ladies each place a consoling hand on my knee.

Despite anticipating an early departure, I hadn't planned this far ahead. Turn my head both ways, looking to my dates for advice.

Ambrosia chimes in, "Well, my flight back to LA isn't until later this evening."

"Same here," Chateau adds.

Right now, I need nothing more than to be alone and cry in my room. But needs don't always usurp desire. Because what I want to do is drown my misery in casual sex. Clearly motivated by spite, as humping is rarely enjoyable for me, surely this time will be no different. Doesn't seem to matter. Can't shake the image of Mackenzie in her dress. Simply angelic.

"Sorry, that was so awkward, ladies, but I really had no desire to be there. I'm not even sure why he invited me."

My words are falling on deaf ears. As if my monologue was a tree in the forest. Did anyone hear it? The women now on to other topics. Each commenting on the other's fashion choices.

Shoes. Jewelry and makeup. Dresses.

And the floodgates open. Chateau begins, "Ohmigod, did you see how adorable the bride was?"

Ambrosia continues, "Oh, I know. She was too precious for words. I hope I look that good when I decide to have a kid. Dillon is gonna be such a good dad."

"Oh, I know. That broad is so lucky."

It goes on and on.

This needs to stop. Now.

Never one to be smooth with women, I unzip my pants. Whip my cock out. It's met with reactions not typically affiliated with adult film actors.

Confusion. They're looking at it like it's growing wings or has eyes or something.

"Um, what are you doing?"

Not really sure how to answer that. Thought this a rather straightforward move.

"Look, just because we fuck on camera for a living, doesn't mean we just bang any guy who whips his cock out."

Might take that statement seriously if they hadn't had their hands in my pants moments earlier.

"What we do on film, that's just a job." Her charade of being offended quickly goes by the wayside. Gently rubbing me, she says, "We play hard to get. You've got to treat us like ladies. Take us out for dinner and drinks." Begins rubbing her twat. Ambrosia I think. Forgot who's who long ago.

Ponder what she's saying.

"Ladies, I know that given your line of work, you've done some pretty interesting things in some peculiar places." Seductive winks of assertion. "I've got an idea." Their interest peaked. I have their full attention. Press the intercom, tell the driver to take us to Le Colonial on Woodlawn. He makes the necessary turns, and we're on our way.

"Sounds fancy," the one in yellow says with enthusiasm.

"The food is definitely excellent. Their wine list is second to none. But my favorite thing about it is its location."

Exchange puzzled glances. Not familiar with Chicago and its layout. I elaborate. "It's very close to the University of Chicago." Doesn't mean much to most people, so I continue. "They have one of the best science programs in the country. Some would say the world. It was there that the first man-made nuclear reactor was built." Knowing they're supposed to be impressed, they feign excitement. "Trust me on this one. Nothing gets me harder than the equipment in their labs."

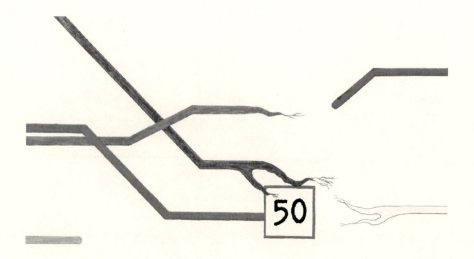

50

Getting dressed, careful not to cut my bare feet. Each step requires precision. Getting from A to B, quite the challenge. Can't move two steps in any direction without the threat of lacerations. Beakers once full of who knows what. Erlenmeyer flasks. Test tubes and broken microscopes. Top of the line, without question. Easily over one million dollars' worth of damage.

I'll leave a check. Payable to "fuck off."

The ladies seemed to enjoy themselves. Take it for what it's worth. They're paid to make sex look far more enjoyable than it is. For a minute, they had me believing I'm good at it. I know better.

"Baby, have you seen my other shoe?" one of them asks. Not sure if she's asking me or the other one. No longer have their dresses to differentiate them. No idea who's who. As if we would have any kind of interaction after today.

Put on my shoes, naked from the ankles up. Leave them to search for what little clothes they have. Start looking in closets for a broom. Not that I mind leaving a mess. Just don't want any blood spilled. No desire to leave a drop of DNA behind.

Well, minus the couple ounces I already left in the ladies' hair, I cleaned up the excess as best as possible.

Begin sweeping up the glass, push it to a far corner. My two companions now fully clothed, if you can call it that. Lean the broom against the wall, find my clothes, get my appearance back together. As much as possible anyway.

"Do you two have everything you need? Purses, IDs, whatever?"

They look at each other to consult. Reaching a consensus, they nod in unison and say yes.

"Excellent. Well, the limo is waiting around the corner. I'll call and tell him we're ready to go, and then we'll get you two off to the airport. Where are you flying out of?"

Their replies coming simultaneously.

A jumble of Midway and O'Hare. All I hear is Mohorway.

Perfect. Let the driver deal with it.

One last check for belongings, and we're out of the lab. Down the hallway toward the elevator. Double doors open, head straight for the side exit. Not deserted, but far from busy. Anyone in the science building at this time, only there for business. Studying, testing, experimenting. No time to waste observing human interactions. You wanna waste time on a pseudoscience, the sociology building is not too far from here.

Left and right, all I see are faces buried in books. Trying to duplicate what I once did. To be atop the mountain of science. Even the world. Will they get there? Maybe. Probably not, but maybe. Odds are stacked against them. Even if they do it. Even if they do the unthinkable, rid the world of an egregious ill, will it be worth it? Are they capable of handling everything that comes with it?

Things such as this, the focus of my ruminations as we near the exit. Spot the limo through a plate of glass ahead. The women already through the doors, steps from their ride. In an ever-increasingly common show of vanity, I check my reflection.

And wish I hadn't.

Run outside, tell the driver to take them wherever they need to go. Apologize profusely, but I have something I forgot to take care of. Exchange the obligatory kiss on the cheek, and they're on their way. I'm headed back inside.

Whether Dillon was right about my mental breakdowns being self-inflicted or not, it's irrelevant now. I passionately hope that's all this is. A delusion. An altered reality.

Up and down the hallway, I pull on every closet door. Same results. Locked. Deep breath. The sound of a squeaky caster grabs my attention. Around the corner comes a cart full of cleaning supplies. Dart over to the custodian, quickly enough to portray urgency. Careful not to scare them off.

Offer him $200 for his uniform, no questions asked.

No problem with him. Takes the money and heads off.

I dress in the bathroom, his coverall fitting snug over my suit. His hat foul with the stench of old sweat. A pair of work gloves to hide my mismatched hands. Finally feeling sufficiently disguised, I head back over. Much to my dismay, the source of my trepidation is still there, chatting away. Grab a mop, pretend to clean. Can't hear a word uttered. Give myself a good enough angle to read facial expressions. There are a few people in white coats, presumably doctors. A few more in suits, likely lawyers. Then we have a few usual suspects.

Cooper Madigan. Silent since the death of his boss and mentor.

Nadira, his lovely wife. Likely there because Nordstrom is closed.

Her father, asserting his power with his posture. Remaining silent otherwise.

That's not what worries me. I never doubted for a second that Cooper would be working nonstop to undo the mess I did to Nicky's will.

No, that I was prepared for.

What I wasn't prepared for was her.

Krystal Madigan.

Apparently not as deceased as once thought.

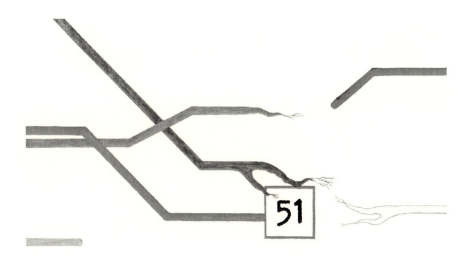

51

Had enough of my redundancy? I've said it a million times. Not sure why it still shocks me, but it does. Dillon just knows *everything*. Simply put, it defies anything rational you've ever believed or been taught.

But as I stand here, looking at a premature tombstone, there's no other explanation for his wisdom. He must be psychic.

There is a strike against this claim, however. A rather big one at that. I have no doubt that I am hallucinating. Whatever is in my blood is corroding my brain. Certainly I'm months, if not weeks, from taking Krystal's place underground.

I hover over the mangled pile of sod.

There is no other explanation for what I'm seeing. I am certain I am going crazy. As a man of science, I rarely eliminate any possibilities. No matter how bizarre or extreme.

Not this time.

How else do I explain the fact that less than an hour ago, I was staring at the owner of the headstone in front of me?

"I know this sounds crazy," he says, sarcasm flowing freely from his pores, "but have you considered the possibility that she was never dead to begin with?"

Fuck you, Dillon.

Obviously, I overlooked that likelihood. Not that I'll ever admit it. Simply bury my head in my chest. My unspoken defeat enough for him.

My humiliation annoys me. Not a big deal when you consider he doesn't seem to mind my little display at his wedding. Thankful Mackenzie isn't allowed to fly for two. Postponed their honeymoon. TBA. Still haven't spoken a word to her since that night in Chicago.

"Or more than likely, she's still dead, but the person you saw just looked a lot like her."

"That doesn't explain the dug-up grave," I say, displaying a false confidence.

Gives me the response I expected. "Anyone could have taken a shovel and moved some dirt around."

Certainly plausible. Even likely. But why?

"Look, man, I'm not exactly sure what to tell you. You got mixed up with some pretty suspicious people. They could have any number of motives to be fucking with you. And who knows? Maybe the girl you lost your virginity to really is a zombie. The living dead. Maybe she was really good at holding her breath. You know, was never dead to begin with." He delivers the last line with a chuckle.

I'm not amused.

Sensing my frustration, his tone shifts to serious. Wraps an arm around my shoulder. Deprives me of oxygen; quite comforting, regardless.

"Dude, right now I think you need to just lay low, clear your head. Maybe take a vacation. Obviously, I don't think you should neglect this. But you're exhausted. You're not all here right now." Points at his head.

Doesn't take a psychic to draw that conclusion.

I nod in agreement. "Yeah, you're right. But I think going anywhere that requires me showing my ID or passport, fabricated or not, is a bad idea. Cooper has probably thrown out red flags to any and all security organization you can name."

Dillon nods, acknowledging the obvious.

"So where are you going to go?"

No need to even think about it. "Easy. I'm going to the last place anyone would think to look for me."

Raises an eyebrow. Seemingly full of genuine intrigue.

"Mom and Dad's house. The place where I grew up."

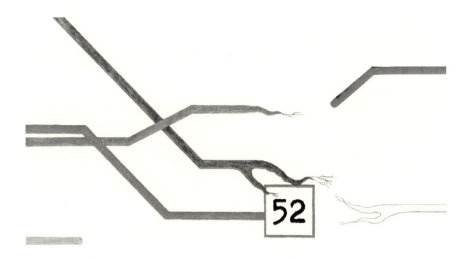

52

My childhood frozen in time. A pristine photograph preserved for decades, remaining untainted. Save for a thin film of dust. I haven't set foot in this house since Dad died. Almost completely paid off at the time he passed. I covered the balance for exactly this purpose. A sanctuary. To be used only in an emergency. If this doesn't qualify, no desire to find out what would.

There's paranoia with every doorknob I turn. Every kitchen drawer I open. Expecting something to be rigged to blow. No destruction so far.

My purpose for retreating here, twofold. Most importantly, safety. Preservation of my life. Cooper and company don't seem particularly interested in me. Must not see me as a threat. Doesn't mean they aren't baiting me. Hoping I'll let my guard down.

Definitely doesn't hurt to play it safe.

If you can call hiding in plain sight safe.

Second function: detective work. Unlikely to find anything helpful in here, still worth a shot. Check photographs, diaries, documents, records, receipts, home videos, old vacation souvenirs, jewelry, closets. Up, down, all around. Need to find some kind of link between Josephine and Paul Watts to Krystal Madigan.

Why was she there at the funeral?

Random happenstance?

Her parents a friend of mine?

It's waited this long. Can wait a few hours more. Need a nap. Desperately in fact. My head hangs in fatigue; I drag my feet toward the room I once called mine. Twin mattress covered with gray-and-blue comforter. Made up as nicely as a hotel. I strip down to my underwear, pry my way under the sheets. Burn fifty calories just getting inside. Sheets and blankets tucked so tight. Nearly pass out just preparing to sleep. Kick my legs furiously. Each movement produces an inch of extra space.

Eventually feeling comfortable, I fall asleep without hesitation.

Dream the sweetest dream. The first in a long time. Literally can't remember the last time I had a pleasant dream. Probably years ago in Nepal.

Would be too easy if all my questions were answered during my slumber. If Mom and Dad showed up and told me all I needed to know. No such luck. They were there, however. One of those visions where you fabricate past events. Things that never happened. But aren't out of the realm of possibility. Not talking about dreams of flying or landing on Saturn.

In my dream, the Bears won the Super Bowl. Mom, Dad, and I glued to the television. Not sure what the year was exactly. I was about eleven though. My sleep peppered with slight alterations of things we used to do. Went camping from time to time. In the dream we were in Yellowstone.

So it went. Half a day apparently. Woke up to notice I'd been out for nearly twelve hours. More fatigued than I was willing to admit. I roll out of bed, straighten the sheets. Remake it just as it was. Obviously unnecessary. I still want to make Mom happy. Maybe Dillon's right. Maybe she can see me right now. No doubt my high spirits are attributed to the last images I saw before I awoke.

She passed years before I cured AIDS. No doubt she would have been so proud. I dreamt I was giving an acceptance speech.

Nobel Prize.

Chemistry. Medicine. Peace. Even economics.

Why not? It's my dream.

The tears in her eyes flowed freely. Gathering in puddles around her feet. Flooding the room. Enough to soak the socks of everyone around her.

A reasonable person would take that as motivation to turn their life around. To do good in the world. Shine like the light of hope the world has needed. Not saying that won't happen. Need to be realistic. One doesn't undo all I've done overnight. Not that simple.

So I start by making the bed.

Moving on to the living room, I begin to dust. Pull the vacuum from the closet. Amazed that it still works after years of stagnation. Four hours later, the house is spotless. No rearranging necessary. Mom and Dad were meticulous. Maybe even OCD. But after Mom passed, Dad stopped cleaning as often. Not sloppy like he wouldn't shave but once a year, bread crumbs in his beard. Nothing that bad. But it took enough out of him that he was never the same.

Content with what I've accomplished thus far, I watch the sun rise. Nothing majestic. Not like watching it rise over the Atlantic. Set on the Pacific. This was better. Took me to a simpler time. A place void of trouble. A place where people like me and Nicky Salcedo only existed in the movies.

Tempted to take a walk around the neighborhood, but I refrain. Best to remain low key. Pace around inside the house, unsure of my next move. Only logical progression being to start my research. I go into Mom's closet, looking for anything that might help. Virtually pillaging her nightstand, taking anything bordering on beneficial into Dad's office. Two hours later, I've gathered a small stack of notebooks, picture albums, and Mom's jewelry box. A long shot for sure. *Anything* helps. Rule nothing out.

I'm physically feeling fine. Ready to get to business.

Emotionally, a different story entirely. So many memories coming back. Haven't even cracked a book. Can only imagine how I'll react actually seeing images of days gone by.

Head back into my room, slip gently under the covers. Nervous I'll violently toss and turn tonight. Leave the sheets tight. It's so snug, confining my movements like a straightjacket. For my own safety really. Takes a little longer to pass out this time. So much to take in. Decades of suppressed emotions and memories manifesting themselves so suddenly. Not exactly intense bawling, my eyes are moist with tears still. Refreshing. Reminded I am in fact human.

Never fear. The thought long passed by the time I woke up. Alert and cocky that my new approach was bulletproof.

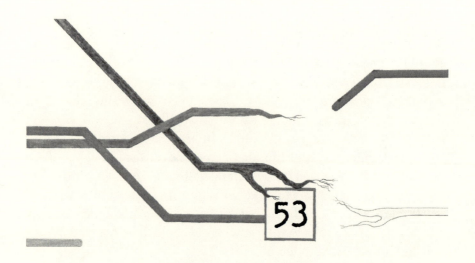

53

My father's former lawyer—biological father, that is—easily the stiffest man I've ever met. Wrinkles cover his face. Not one of them due to excessive smiling. Referring to him as bland would be an insult to the adjective. Nope, personality dry as year-old toast in the Sahara Desert. I squeeze every pressure point on my body I can locate. Anything to stay awake. All the stimulants in the world wouldn't make this guy exciting.

I suck it up. Just a necessary step. At least the guy is a solid dresser. Always skeptical of lawyers who dress poorly.

Suck down my triple espresso. Shocks my senses like a lightning bolt to the taint. Its impact momentary. My gaze focuses on his tie. An Escher-like tessellation. Hypnotic, taunting me. Tempting me back to sleep.

The lack of enthusiasm in his voice doesn't help. "Mr. Watts, thank you for getting in touch with me. I hadn't heard from you since I last spoke with your father. I must admit, I was beginning to wonder if I'd ever hear from you."

Cringe at the word "father." Grin and bear it. Speaking ill of Nicky surely can't help my cause. My face displays a horrendous attempt at despair. Think he buys it. Emotions clearly not his strong suit. "I apologize for any inconveniences my delay may have caused you, Mr. Ball. But I've had a lot on my mind lately. And thank you for meeting with me on such short notice. My gratitude is substantial to say the least."

"Mr. Watts, I represented your father for nearly fifty years. And I don't care what people say about him, he was an excellent man. Very loyal to those who worked for him. I wouldn't be able to look myself in the mirror if I didn't reciprocate the same loyalty."

Words are coming out of his mouth. Not exactly sure what he's saying though. His monotony lulling me to sleep. Everything he says is processed by my brain five seconds later. Every response on a delay.

Looks at me, anticipating a reply. My gaze drifts around, analyzing the art in his office. Most of it absolute garbage. Except for the one by the window. Entirely out of place. Momentarily, debate if I'm sitting in a lawyer's office. Or back at Gumball Alley. A painting of an angel. She's Japanese. Her wings daunting, casting shadows over the people grabbing at her feet. Traditional katana sword in one hand. Baby in the other. I stand from my seat, move closer. Examine the signature.

As expected.

Mackenzie Desjardin.

Never seen this one.

"Where did you get this?" Clearly not expecting the conversation to shift from Nicky Salcedo's estate to a local artist.

"Excuse me?"

"I'll give you ten thousand dollars for it."

An insult to Mackenzie's talent. Should have added a zero. Isn't much, but finally elicits a reaction from him. He's not amused, but at least the muscles in his face depart from their default setting.

"Mr. Watts, if you are interested in discussing my art collection, perhaps you can come back another time. For today, I really think it in our best interest to focus on your father's affairs."

Once again, the word "father" brings me back down. Swiftly move back to my chair. "You're right, Mr. Ball. Pardon me. I haven't slept much lately." False. Slept like a pro in my old bed.

His concrete façade returns. "Very well. As I was saying, your father was very loyal. My best client by far. Needless to say, I did anything he asked me. So I am absolutely committed to making sure everything is settled as he desired."

A tough one to read. Is he suspicious of me? Portrays an image of lackey. Would bend over backwards for Nicky. Follow him into the dark unquestioned. Still, the circumstances surrounding our first discussion must have him slightly unnerved.

"Once again, I would like to express my gratitude." Pressing him, "I'm sure you've had a very full plate with everything going on. I imagine you must have found it quite odd when my father made such an extreme request right before his passing."

Any emotions inside him remain well hidden. My imagination drifts back to Las Vegas. I can easily see this man making a killing at poker. His face gives nothing away.

"Young man, your father was many things to many people. For decades, he wielded a great deal of influence, with which he accomplished quite a bit. Many of those things were highly scrutinized. Were they controversial? Most definitely. Were they unethical? That's not for me to decide. Depending on whom you ask, he either helped a lot of people or ruined many lives. But there is a very definitive common thread over the years." He pauses for dramatic effect. Attempting to bait my curiosity. Prompting me to beg. Not exactly on the edge of my seat. But this is the first sign of him having an actual personality. Sure, throw him a bone.

"Really? And what would that be?"

"He never backed down from his decisions. Whether they were popular decisions or highly criticized by the public, he never wavered. Everything he did, he stood by it. I never once heard the man utter the word sorry. Even when he made decisions that inevitably were bad for business, he just said he'd learn from them and know better for next time." I'm soaking in the description of the man I never knew. Not making me miss him. Nor do I admire him. Still, it's intriguing, learning about a man responsible for much of my personality traits. Mr. Ball goes on, "It was not unusual for him to call me up in the middle of the night with a request. And on the rare occasion that he felt what he asked me to do was not in his best interest. He simply got in touch, told me to change it, and left it at that. Never spoke a word about what he'd said minutes before. It was like it never even happened. I quickly grew accustomed to this. So when he called me and told me to turn over control of his entire company to you, I didn't hesitate. He never did anything without having a reason to do it."

This is true. In this case, Nicky's reason being me threatening to end the life of his "true love." My mother. Or whoever she is.

I'm needing more information. "Well, your cooperation is appreciated. I know it wasn't easy for him to change his mind. He loved my mother very much." I'm making a poor attempt at empathy. "And I know it was tough on him to give control over to me instead of her. But I promised him that I'll take care of her, and that I will."

The phrase "take care of" being open to interpretation.

For once, his face conveys judgment. "Yes, he was quite fond of her." All he says, with a tone portraying so much more. Definitely cynical. Might say he follows my father unquestioned, but this arouses suspicion.

Not asking me for an explanation. I decide to give him one anyway. Open the doors for more answers. "Basically, he was concerned with the state of her mental health. He didn't feel that she was in any shape to run the company."

He's annoyed. Not buying it. And just like that, I sense resentment. He couldn't care less if I got control or any other woman or Cooper. He's pissed because after five decades of service, he got *nothing*. "Mr. Watts, you don't need to explain his decisions to me. As I've stated, he never did anything without being certain it was what he wanted to do."

Not satisfied. I continue my charade. My turn for dramatic pause. Forcing tears to well in my eyes. Show him Nadira's hand. "She shot my hand off! My own mother. She took a gun, pointed it at me, and blew my hand to shreds. I know Dad told me she wasn't completely with it, you know, mentally. But *this!*" Shove my new hand into his face. Unleash the waterworks. No sympathy from Mr. Ball. Not visibly at least. Count to ten in my head. Grab a tissue from his desk, dry my eyes. About to carry on with my sob story, Mr. Ball interrupts.

Sounding impressed. Of what, I've no idea. Yet again, nothing in his face conveys it. "Well, I guess that Parkinson's drug they've been developing works after all."

Random. Please continue.

"I'm sorry, what did you say? As I'm sure my father explained to you, it wasn't until recently that I met my mother for the first time. You're telling me she has Parkinson's disease?" He stares intently into my eyes. Searching for answers. Skepticism encompasses him. Unsure how much to divulge. Attempt to put him at ease. "Please, Mr. Ball, you work for me now. I heard you mention something about a drug. If it's some kind of secret project, rest assured, I'll find out sooner or later." Shoot him puppy dog eyes. Pleading, "Please, this is my mother we're talking about. Tell me." Still appears uncomfortable. One last ace up my sleeve. "Come on, Mr. Ball. My father would want me to know. And it's not like he's around anymore to tell me himself."

Just like that, he shoots me the look I've been waiting for. An entirely accusatory death stare. The one that says he knows I killed Nicky Salcedo but can't do a thing to prove it. Just as quickly, his stare of contempt melts seamlessly into a face of panic, knowing what I'm capable of. Dozens, if not hundreds, have attempted to kill Nicky Salcedo. And I'm the one who actually did it. Mr. Ball knows not to fuck with me.

He relents. "Mr. Watts, your mother's life has been tragic to say the least. I'm not sure what your father told you. I will attempt to make this as concise as possible." Read: he wants to leave my presence sooner rather than later. "Without omitting important details, naturally."

"Naturally."

"From around the time of your birth, your mother's mental health has been unstable. She was attacked shortly after you were born." I nod, letting him know I'm aware of that much. "She's been seeing psychologists and psychiatrists almost constantly for decades." His neutral demeanor bends slightly toward sympathy, sadness. "As is typical of doctors, none of them seem to agree with when or how it happened exactly. But she has been fighting Parkinson's disease for almost thirty years. Most concur that it is linked to her beating in the alley, but of course there is no proof of that."

The plot thickens.

"So my father made it his mission to cure her. He devoted countless resources, money, scientists, tests . . . all to help her?" Saying it that way almost sounds romantic. Until you consider how much money he could make from said drug.

Then again, recall what Dillon said. Nothing Nicky Salcedo's team concocted ever works. More to this story. Want to know what I'm missing here.

"Long story short, Mr. Watts, yes. That's exactly what he did. Years of research and testing. There were glimpses of hope and progress spattered along the way, certainly. But nothing substantial. Not too long ago, however, she began showing drastic improvements. The spasms weren't gone completely, but they seemed to be cut in half overnight."

Takes every ounce of energy to suppress my smirk. Think I'm on to something. Aloof, "How long ago was this?"

"Oh, it's hard to say. They've been working on it for so many years. But this was approximately a year and a half ago."

Falling in line with what I expected to hear. Definitely not what I wanted to hear. My guess? This transformation took place when I got back into Chicago.

I keep my intuition to myself. "Well, I'm no expert in neurological health." False again. I'm pretty fucking amazing at it. "And while it certainly seems strange that it could begin to cure her almost overnight as you said, that would definitely explain how she was able to hold her gun so steady. How she could aim and fire with such precision?" Unconvinced that a miracle drug is actually responsible, I toss out another supposition. "Then again, maybe she was aiming at my face and just happened to miss badly. Fortunate for me of course, but not a good thing if you're hoping to overcome Parkinson's."

No mistake. Her aim was solid. Hand rigid as steel. Easily could have killed me had that been her intent.

I sit silent far too long. Assuming I have no more inquiries, he gets the ball rolling. Throws a stack of papers in front of me.

"Mr. Watts, if there is nothing further, we can get down to the main reason we're both here." I nod, pulling a pen out of my pocket. Give the documents a cursory glance, sign them then read them in their entirety. Read every word, allowing no caveats or fine print to screw me over. Eventually fully satisfied, hand the papers back to my lawyer.

"Thank you Mr. Watts. I'll contact you when everything is final."

"Excellent. Thank you for your help, Mr. Ball." Packs up his briefcase. One of the few who carries paper documents around. No Internet or modern technology here. His hand pulling the door open, I ask, "Oh, Mr. Ball, there is one more thing I could use your help with."

Taking great pleasure in finally being able to say, "Mr. Watts, I'm a very busy man. If there is an issue with which you would like my assistance, you'll have to suggest it to the new CEO." His candid nature takes me by surprise. Oddly refreshing. Nice to see the guy show some character. Some chutzpah even. "Good day, Mr. Watts."

Enjoy a brief laugh to myself. What a weird guy. Oh well. Pull out my phone, call the new CEO.

Ring.

Ring.

Ring.

Finally connecting, "Hello?"

"Dillon, how's it going? I've got some big news for you."

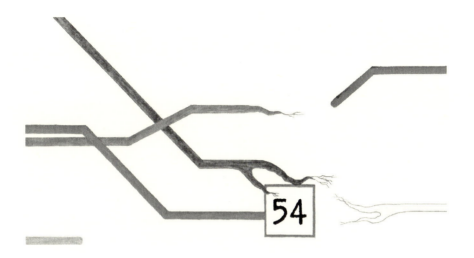

54

Fruitless weeks meticulously absorbing journals and photos. Finally convinced I'm not literally losing my mind. That it was psychosomatic as Dillon said. This undertaking has me rethinking my original assessment.

Words begin dancing on the page. Swirling around like cereal in a bowl of milk. Incessant, no matter how many times I blink. Sleep helps. Only for a while. A walk and fresh air are sufficient. But eventually the mind wanders. My concentration continually weakening. Frustration compounding every time I have a lead. Always a dead end. Never takes me anywhere but back to the beginning.

Who the fuck is Krystal Madigan?

Why was she at my mother's funeral?

Every second that passes without a resolution, the crazier I get. I've read every word my mother ever wrote. Every letter, note, postcard she ever received. Dad wasn't much for sentimentality. Never kept a journal or anything like that.

My agitation coming to a boil, I begin flipping furniture. Tip the fridge over. Roll the couch. Rip drawers off their sliders. House is a mess, like a tornado rampaged through minutes ago. Deep breaths. Calm myself. As much as possible. Another nap is in order. I lie down on the bed I stopped making days ago. The one piece of furniture in the house still in its intended orientation.

Wake up, roll on to the floor, head to the kitchen to begin the tedious process of cleaning up. Rectifying my fit of rage will take days. Crazy how you can undo years of hard work in a matter of minutes. Stand the fridge back up. Nearly throw my back out, but make it work. Glass and plastic bottles rattle around inside. Many of them on the floor. The plug never coming undone, the contents remain cold. The beers on the floor, however, room temperature at best. The disarray makes finding a bottle opener a pointless endeavor. Grab a bottle of a random microbrew from Portland. Wedge the cap in my teeth, pop the top. Chip a tooth and cut my lip. Hardly bothers me when put in perspective.

Carefully opening and drinking two more bottles, I continue with my cleanup. Couch cushions in place, bar stools upright. I move over to the desk. Hands on the lip, begin to lift. Just then I notice a slip of paper. Wedged in the crack, a piece of stationary that must have fallen back there years ago. My heart races. Knowing this will be the keystone. The information to set all my problems right.

I move to the wall, pick the paper from behind the wood.

Milk, Eggs, Cheerios, Salt, Bacon.

A shopping list.

As quickly as it began, my revolutionary find leads to another dead end. Able to keep my frustration in check. Simply crumple the paper, toss it in the corner. Squatted low, prepared to lift the desk back into place, my phone rings. Likely a telemarketer, I gladly accept the distraction.

Don't recognize the number, I answer eagerly.

"Hello?"

"Ted, it's Dillon! You gotta get down here now, man. It's happening, it's finally happening!" He's hysterical. Words flying off his tongue so quickly they barely register. "Her water broke. Mackenzie is going into labor. You gotta get down here, man."

Knowing this day would eventually come. But all the hypotheticals you toss around in your head never prepare you for when it actually goes down. Not anxious or excited. Took months, but I removed myself from this situation. Might be my DNA between her thighs, but that kid belongs to Dillon.

"Dillon. Slow down. Deep breaths, buddy," I say with a laugh. "First of all, where is 'here'? Second, you guys are gonna be fine. You've both been prepping for this for months." In a way, it's been years in the making.

"Northwestern Hospital. Down by Lake Shore Drive."

I cover the phone and laugh. Telling me where one of the most famous hospitals in America is located. In the town where I grew up. Keep the hilarity in this to myself.

"Northwestern? You guys will be fine. They have the best doctors in the country, maybe even the world. Just relax, Dillon. You've got this under control."

My words of encouragement fall on deaf ears. "You've gotta get down here, man. She's gonna have the kid soon, and we need you to be here."

Not sure what his angle is, I shift my tone from playful to austere. "Dillon. I know you're nervous. That's perfectly natural. And I know you're flustered, so you're making spontaneous decisions. But I really don't think it would be a good idea if I went down there."

"Why?"

His one word answer. Incredible that three little letters can so completely trivialize the situation. "Do I really need to answer that?" A long cold pause tells me that apparently I do. "Dillon, that kid doesn't belong to me. Mackenzie wants nothing to do with me. You're going to be an amazing dad. This situation is awkward enough as it is. Please, let's not make it any more uncomfortable. The last thing Mackenzie needs is the stress of seeing my face at a time like this."

Another solid pause. "Ted. Mackenzie is the one who told me to call you."

Remember what I said about removing myself from the situation? Throw it all out the window.

Not sure if he's fucking with me. Playing with the miniscule remains of my emotions. I take the bait. "OK, I'll be there in fifteen minutes."

Pay the cab driver generously to break every traffic law on record. Make it to the hospital in virtually no time. Automatic doors part, running so quickly I nearly crash through the registration desk. About to ask where Mackenzie is located. Don't even get a word out before a pull on my shirt lifts me off the ground.

Dillon drags me into an elevator, hits the button for the third floor. The doors open, and he leads the way, his pace a notch below sprint.

What I see immediately makes me question the logic of women. No idea why they would willingly subject themselves to this. Not to mention the years of diapers and spilt juice to follow. No going back now though. Mackenzie is in this for the long haul. Sweating and moaning, I hope this ordeal is done with sooner rather than later.

Open the dictionary to the word "awkward." A snapshot of this room is all you'll find. What do I say? Where do I stand? Any notion I had that this wouldn't be uncomfortable quickly fades. This was a mistake. How do I slip out unnoticed? Wait for a contraction? Sneak out undetected as everyone debates the pros and cons of an epidural?

Works for me.

But that idea is quickly squashed. Can't leave her in this condition. Not that I can do anything to help. The yelling and sweating continue. Talk of a Caesarean section. She yells to do whatever it takes. Just get the kid out of there already. Any means necessary.

Very foreign territory to me. Even I know things aren't going flawlessly. Increasing commotion makes it hard to decipher the root of the problems. Focus my attention to gain any insight possible.

Then I hear the key phrase.

Nuchal chord.

Dillon's eyes cut into mine like daggers. He has no clue what that means. Motion him over to me. "Dillon, it's very common. The umbilical cord is wrapped around the baby's neck." His eyes now larger than the tip of his dick. Freaking out. I attempt to calm him down. "Dillon, relax. It happens in about one out of four births." No consolation for him. Clearly, he will be no help.

That's when I look at Mackenzie. Our eyes meet for the first time in months. So incredibly brief. But her gaze speaks volumes. I march over to Dillon freaking out in the corner.

A light smack on the face. "Dillon, get over there and help your wife for crying out loud. She needs you. Your baby needs you." And just like that, I feel at ease. Referring to this kid as "your" instead of "mine." Atlas has been relieved of his duties. All those times Dillon's prophetic words have freaked me out. Caused so much anxiety only to come true every single time. Now I get to return the favor.

Sternly, I say, "Get over there and squeeze your wife's hand. Your kid will be fine." Maybe this will help. "Dillon, you think I put you in control of one of the largest corporations in the history of the world just for fun? Of course not. I did it because you're fucking unstoppable. Nothing gets in your way. You're solid under pressure. So get over there and remind me why I put you in charge." Still not convinced. He looks deep into my eyes. Like a child searching for solace in their mother or father's apparent knowledge of everything the universe has to offer. One last time, "Trust me."

Finally manning up to stand by his wife. Heads over, grabs her hand, tells her she's doing fine. The skepticism obvious in his eyes. Doesn't matter. He's doing what he needs to do for Mackenzie.

Her screams and tears point to the contrary, but Mackenzie delivers her daughter without much difficulty. Couldn't let Dillon know, but the nuchal chord worried me more than it did him. Wanted so badly to reach inside Mackenzie and untangle the chord. Somehow, I knew it would be OK. Can't really explain it.

How a woman as tiny as Mackenzie was able to shove something so large through her legs will always astound me. But it's done. Something she's wanted for so long. Her breaths deep and long. Regaining what energy and composure she has left. Dillon consoles her, the doctors and nurses congratulating the lucky couple. Preparing to cut the chord, they hand the scissors to Dillon.

Doesn't even move a muscle for them.

Shares a glance with Mackenzie.

They turn to me. "You should do it."

Speechless. Touched. Give them the socially requisite "Are you crazy? I wouldn't feel right." Despite wanting nothing more at this moment.

They nod in unison, I accept the scissors.

Move my thumb to open the shears, place the blades around the chord. Preparing to make the cut, the last several years play in my head. The unceasing ability of the brain. Truly incredible. Years of images and memories condensed into seconds. Still as vivid as the day they occurred.

I give Mackenzie a smile. So proud of her. Fight back tears as I make the cut. Knowing this moment far more symbolic than just the beginning of a new life.

This chord representing not simply a bond from child to mother. As soon as I sever it, I'm also cutting loose two of the best friends I've ever known. When I walk out the door, it will be the last time I will ever see their beautiful faces. I congratulate them, give them both a kiss on the cheek. Hug Dillon, hand him the manila envelope I brought with most of the information he's going to need. Like a Band-Aid. Just get it over with. Muster the strength and walk away. Literally and metaphorically.

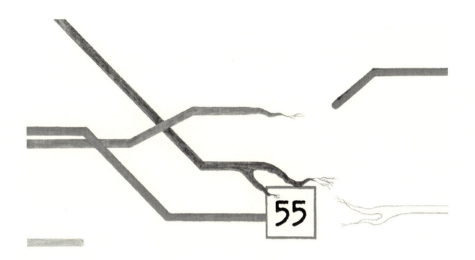

55

Always felt good-byes were blown out of proportion. Not this time. No words to describe how I feel. Sipping coffee at Starbucks a block from the hospital. My latte a poor companion at a time like this.

But as they say, life goes on. I'm not walking out of their lives full of anger or spite. I'm doing it because it's the best thing for their little girl. She needs me in her life like AA meetings need an open bar.

Take my final sips, I'm out the door towards the L. Need to get home, clean up the mess I made. A maid service intrigues me. No company in their right mind would take on that project. I'll make it work.

Walking back, I shiver as I pass the hospital. Look up to the window where I imagine Mackenzie is napping, Dillon passed out in a chair next to her bed. Thoughts that quickly vanish as the sliding doors open. A young man in scrubs rolls a woman in a wheelchair to the curb, hails her a taxi. No broken bones, but apparently weak. Still capable of exiting the chair and entering the car under her own power.

Pulls away from the curb, I get a peek inside.

Krystal Madigan.

Snap out of my shock quickly, no time to waste. Run over to the man pushing the empty wheelchair back inside.

"Excuse me, who was that?"

He's looking at me like I'm crazy. Justifiably so. "Um, I'm sorry sir. I'm not allowed to give that information out." Looks around. Suspects hidden cameras. Maybe his bosses putting his character to the test.

Everyone's integrity has a breaking point. Just need to find his.

Don't have time for negotiations. "My apologies. I don't know what I was thinking." He shrugs, no big deal. Continues on his way. "Oh, but there is something else." He pauses, I walk to meet him. Lean close to whisper a secret, grab the ear, and pinch. Immediately see him tense up, bite his tongue to prevent a scream. "Get me that woman's file, or next time I'm grabbing your balls. Are we clear?"

Nods adamantly. I ease up, follow him to the elevator.

Rolls the empty chair into a corner, tells me to wait by the vending machine. Gone for a few minutes, beginning to think I should run. He's called the cops. Looking for the stairwell, I spot him coming my way.

"Sorry, I took so long. I had to wait for the copy machine."

I pat him on the shoulder. "Good work. And for what it's worth, I'm doing this for a good reason."

Immediately cutting me off, "I don't want to know anything about what you're doing. Please just leave."

Deal. Head over to a different Starbucks this time. Drink a double espresso. As if seeing a dead woman walking wasn't enough to wake me up. Sit at an empty table in the corner, open the folder.

At this point, nothing should shock me. Once again, I'm proven wrong. My turn to look around. Thinking I'm the one under surveillance. This is all some big prank. Decades in the making.

Expecting to see "Krystal Madigan" written somewhere on the page. Instead, plastered all over the documents, staring right back at me ... Penelope Strickland.

Seconds away from redecorating the coffee shop in a fashion similar to Mom and Dad's house. Consider possible courses of action. Conclude my only option is to go to the address on her forms. Take my chances. Death might await me. Better than living with this mental torture. Resolution my primary objective.

The ride is too short. Doesn't provide adequate time to thoroughly read everything in detail. But ascertained she's in for some form of facial reconstructive surgery. A handful of black-and-white photocopies with scribbles on them. The doctor's plan for where to make incisions.

Organize the folder, pay the driver, proceed to the door. Locked. Apartment complex. Need to be buzzed in. Obviously can't call the woman of interest. Go up and down the list, dialing every apartment. Saying the word "delivery" to the first person to pick up. It works. They'll be so disappointed. Need to bring them something later. Maybe a bundt cake or desk lamp.

Find her door on the third floor. No point in knocking. No escaping whatever awaits me on the other side. Step back, collect potential energy. Notice multiple deadbolts. Don't like my chances. Pull out my phone. Find a video on how to pick locks on the Internet.

Oh, the things you can do with paperclips.

I run inside, screaming like a madman. Hoping to distract anyone in waiting. But I'm alone. Walk back, close the door, lock it. Careful to leave everything as I find it, I roam the apartment. No pictures on the walls. Not much of anything really. Sparsely decorated. Very bland. Move into the bedroom. Open drawers at random. Checking the closet. Nothing. Into the bathroom. Nothing. Kitchen is the same. Back in the living room, I sit on the couch. Waiting until whoever she is comes home. Pick up a magazine. One of only three things atop the coffee table.

Make that four things.

Beneath the magazine, a photograph.

You know which one? The one of me as a baby. Two women accompany me. Unsure of who is who anymore.

Nervous, but content I'm finally about to get some answers. Wait for nearly three hours. Growing weak. About to fall asleep, my senses awaken. The sound of a key in the lock. I perk up, hide in the kitchen.

Door opens. The lights come up. Door closes, the locks click back into place. The rustling of bags. She sets them down. The sound of footsteps on the hardwood floor brings her to the kitchen. Jump out, grab her, take her to the ground.

Cover her mouth.

The look of terror in her eyes. Haunting. As if she's never seen me before. Able to tie her wrists behind her back, throw her on the couch. I look her up and down, perplexed. My mind scans the possibilities over and over.

Rule out nothing. No matter how unlikely. Flashback to Maggie lecturing me on Sherlock Holmes. When all other possibilities are eliminated, the one that remains, no matter how improbable, is your solution.

Looking at her, looks just like Krystal Madigan.

But her skin, too weathered to be a woman my age. Time for some process of elimination.

"Krystal, can you hear me?"

Her reaction lays that suspicion to rest. Bewildered. As if she's never heard the name before.

Furious with her predicament, she begins flailing and screaming. Grab a rag from the kitchen, a gag is my first option. Stifles the noise, not the kicking. Wrapping her up, trying to sedate her with magic fingers, her shirt rips in the scuffle.

Suddenly impossible to miss, I see the scar on her abdomen.

If you fear the answer, don't ask the question.

Casting my worries aside, I inquire, "Where did you get that scar?" Remove the gag. Rewarded with spit in my face. Her hair now apparently styled with a machete, I notice several smaller scars on her skull. Not big enough to be surgical scars. Barely noticeable. Likely years old, healed as much as naturally possible.

Feeling confident with this next guess.

"I have a lot of questions for you. It could take a while. So before we get started, would you like a drink, or a snack?"

"Fuck you, Nicky! Why are you doing this to me?"

Brakes inside my head screech to a halt.

Quite an interesting development.

Clearly she's not in peak mental health. Weigh my options. Need to tread carefully. Feeling like I can only gain from what might transpire, "Darling, I'm sorry. I panicked. I thought you were someone else." Approaching with caution, I untie her. "There you go, sweetie. I'm so sorry. Can I get you anything? You want some water or something?"

Finally free, she begins to twitch.

Not nerves or fear of attack. More like spasms induced by seizure.

Numerous possible causes. Instincts tell me Parkinson's.

A minute passes without a response. I head to the kitchen, get her a glass of water and a box of crackers. Takes the water and gulps it down without hesitation. Her hand steady enough that she only gets a few drops on her shirt. Leaves the crackers alone.

"Not hungry? Come on, sweetie, you should eat something."

Looking into my eyes like someone she's known for decades. Lighting up with excitement. The kind you only get when you're in love. Or so I've been told. Try to shake Mackenzie from my head. She interrupts my thoughts, "Nicky! Why don't you take me to that donut shop?"

Playing along, "You mean the one where we first met?"

Smiles wide. The attack of moments earlier erased from her mind. "Of course, Nicky. We haven't been in so long."

Putting pieces together. Wary not to jump to conclusions. Yet apprehensive this is a setup. Alas, curiosity gets the best of me.

"I'd love to take you. I haven't had a cannoli in ages."

"Better than the ones you get in Italy," she says bright eyed.

Reaching out my hand, I help her up. Excited I might get some answers. Quite nervous that I think I'm about to go on a date with my mother.

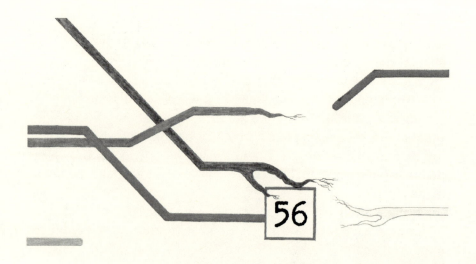

I never liked pistachios. Makes this particular culinary experience difficult to stomach. Pretending to be Nicky Salcedo, I eat two of them for good measure. Gets me questioning if we are in fact related.

The way my guest is looking at me though asserts me that we are. Not that I ever noticed it in pictures or on television. But something about me reminds her of him. For her, it's as if her baby boy was born just the other week. Asking me if I'll take her to the new musical at the Sullivan.

It had major fire damage in 1987. Been a Crate & Barrel since 1990.

Tragic really. Not the theatre fire. This woman. Presumably my mother. Severe psychological trauma. Going on four decades. Which is bad enough. Add to it her Parkinson's, and I'm tempted to put her out of her misery. Not because I'm a monster for once. To end her pain.

Cutting the soft doughy casing of her pastry proves to be a major undertaking. Hand shaking intensely as her fork breaks it apart. Lifting the dessert to her mouth, even more complicated. An occasional drop of mascarpone staining her already filthy attire. Attempting to appear a romantic, I feed her with my fork. Graciously accepts my flirtations. A smitten kitten if ever there was one.

Genuinely hoping she'll say something along the lines of "Remember when we came here all those years ago." Not to be.

Her mind and heart stuck in years past. Hoping to gain some insight, I prompt her, "Pretty tasty, right?"

"Uh-huh. The best, Nicky."

Attempting to be Italian gangster. Find my inner Pacino. "You're tellin' me. The best outside of Italy. And as much as I love the cannolis, that's not even the best thing about this place."

Curious and stuttering, "Oh, really? Well, what's the best part then?"

Acting shocked, I say, "Baby, this is where I met you." She blushes. "Can you believe it's been almost forty years since we met?"

Laughing hysterically, "Oh, Nicky. You're too funny. Forty years! Ha! We only met a little over a year ago."

More or less the response I expected. Not wanting to upset her, play it off. "I know, baby, I was just toyin' with ya. But I guess when you're in love, you lose track of time. Just kinda' flies by, ya know?"

Blushes once again.

The theatre reference tipped me off. This solidifies that her mind is decades in the past. Where to go from here?

She relieves me of that burden.

"So did you get our son back?"

Fuck me.

Noticing the panic in my eyes, she pleads, "Nicky, what's wrong with our son? What happened to him?"

Doing my best to play it cool, "Baby, how much do you remember from forty"—catch myself—"from the other night? Do you remember the dumpster? Anything about that?"

Feeling patronized, "Don't be silly, Nicky. Of course I remember." Sensing I'm withholding something, she pushes, "Nicky, what happened? Tell me!"

"Baby, I tried. But after I took you to the hospital, I went back, and he was gone." Not wanting to get into my entire life story, "Someone found him. They adopted him, and they're taking great care of him."

Tears begin to form in her eyes.

"Baby, don't cry. He got a real good home." Writing checks I can't cash. "They said we'd be able to see him soon though."

You would do the same thing in my shoes.

The waterworks continue. Move around the table to comfort her. "How could I be so stupid? Leaving a baby in a dumpster! What was I thinking!"

Hugging her tightly, doing my best to mitigate the damage. "Baby, you did the right thing. You were in danger. You did it to protect him."

Grab a few napkins from the dispenser. Dry her eyes. Looks at me, pleading for validation. "Do you really think so?"

"Of course I do. That goon was gonna hurt our child. I mean, he hurt you so bad, there's no tellin' what he coulda done to a helpless baby."

"He?"

"Yeah. Your fuckin' husband. But don't worry, baby, I took care of him. He's not gonna bother you no more."

Like she's seen a ghost. "What did you do to Rangi?"

Trying to keep it vague, "Don't you worry about it, babe. He got what he deserved."

Hysterical, "What! Why!"

"Baby, he beat you up in a cold alley. There is no excuse for what he did."

"You keep saying he did something to me. Rangi didn't hurt me."

"Baby, you don't have to defend him. He's not going to hurt you anymore."

Livid, every person in the donut shop staring. Suddenly aware of her ailments. "You think *he* did this to me?"

That's how Nicky told it to me. "Well, yeah. That's what you told me. You were out of it when I took you to the hospital, but you made it clear that he beat you in the alley over there." Pointing in the direction of the dumpster.

Grabbing her head. Looks as if she's trying to rip her hair out. Stumbles out the front door. Her legs not strong enough to carry her at a full pace run. Still, she moves quickly around the corner. I catch up with her, wrap her up. Pull her into the alley. No need to turn this into more of a scene than it already is.

Flailing, I restrain her. Careful not to squeeze too hard. Not sure how much of her spasms are anger related. How much is Parkinson's induced.

Treating my mother like a lover is taking its toll. "Look, what the fuck do you mean he didn't hurt you? That's what you told me. If he didn't do it, then who did?"

Shivering, breaking away. Tucks herself into a ball against the brick wall. I move closer, hoping not to intimidate her. "Baby, talk to me. What really happened?"

Mumbles something into her sleeve. Blows her nose into her shirt. Presumably not the first time, judging by its filthy state.

"I can't hear you. You gotta speak up, baby."

Fighting to speak through an incessant stream of tears. "She didn't mean to do it. It was a mistake!"

She?

This isn't happening.

"What do you mean she? Baby, talk to me. Who attacked you the other night?"

Sniffling, crying, in obvious pain. Can't bring herself to look at me. Eventually the words spill out. Muffled by her arm, but disturbingly clear, "Alison. My sister."

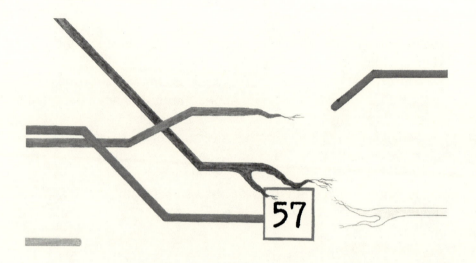

57

Goes without saying, some decisions carry more weight than others. Even the most apparently remedial choices can have profound impact. Turkey or fried chicken? Probably won't alter the course of history. Then again, maybe one was contaminated, the other clean and fresh? Maybe one sends you home early from work, the other back to your routine in a cubicle on the fifty-third floor. More like a prison cell than a place of productivity. Maybe the building catches fire, knocks out power. Maybe you make it out. Then again, maybe you don't. Maybe had you eaten the veggie wrap, you'd be at home, watching it unfold on TV.

Extreme and unlikely?

Of course.

But not impossible.

And now you're thinking that time you threw a recyclable plastic bottle in the trash is what broke the straw on the ozone's back. You're the reason everyone is getting skin cancer.

But seriously . . .

Ever felt the decision you're currently debating could define your life? A permanent label of success or failure hinging on one move? College entrance exams. Job interviews. Shuttle launches. An endless list of events saddled with seemingly unconquerable burden.

So much preparation. Months and months, perhaps years that become decades. How will you be remembered? Will the hard work pay off? Then again, how do you define "pay off"?

Women? Power? Wealth?

We all define it differently. We all define it exactly the same. Happiness. A simple word. A wide variety of interpretations. You want to live a "good life." Try to be more obscure next time.

Success for one is failure for another. Adventure for you is boredom for me. Everyone wants to be happy.

Spoiler alert. It rarely works out the way you want it to. For every dreadlocked hippie protesting animal cruelty, a young boy dreams of being a cowboy. You and I are constantly at odds.

So now the question becomes this: who wants it more?

These thoughts and thousands more stampede through my head as I stand behind Mr. Ball, Nicky Salcedo's former lawyer.

Took some convincing, but he eventually came around. He's at the podium giving a speech I don't really listen to. Have it memorized though. I should. I wrote it. Long story short, we're throwing a charity banquet. At which we will announce that Dillon Pulaski is now in charge.

But we don't say that just yet. Only that we're raising money for a local food bank. That anyone who wants to learn about the company's future needs to be there.

Even Dillon doesn't know about this.

Hoping he's watching.

Guess I can't cut ties with him just yet.

Mr. Ball recites the words I've given him. His tone flatlining, putting everyone in the room to sleep. Irrelevant. He could sing the entire Billy Joel catalogue in Russian for all I care.

Not entirely true. I do need the message out there. As far as I can tell, "Alison" is watching my every move. At least every public move. For once, I'm OK with that. Hoping to draw her to this party.

If she shows, as I suspect she will, I'll need help. That's why to anyone outside my intended audience, I look like I'm having a seizure. Even if Mr. Ball were the most engaging speaker since Martin Luther King Jr., no one would pay him any attention. Everyone wondering what is wrong with my face.

But Dillon, if he's watching, knows exactly what's going on. I'm telling him everything I know. All of the concrete evidence and all of my speculations. Not sure what to do. I find myself saying a prayer that he gets this message.

Because this might be one of those defining moments in my life. The kind that either makes me a hero or a failure. The kind that could literally change the course of history. What happens at this fundraiser could very well determine the future of this country.

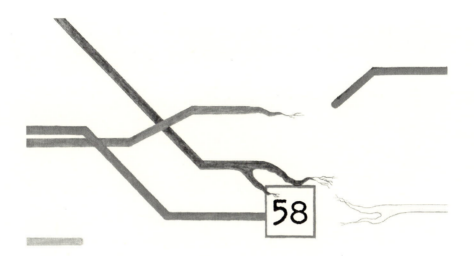

58

The Art Institute of Chicago takes a different role tonight. Most days, a shrine to pedantry and mediocre work. An inferiority complex exacerbated by the perplexing success of the Guggenheim.

Not tonight.

Tonight the Second City takes the spotlight.

The social event of the year. Anyone who is anyone will be walking through the main doors within the next hour. Donors strut around in tuxedos. Designer dresses that will be worn for the night then shoved in the closet to collect dust. Hundreds of people I've never met. Don't have the desire to change that now.

The evening kicked off across the street. Exclusive performance by the Joffrey Ballet: simply breathtaking. Cumulative caloric intake of the entire company: twelve thousand. Men with virtually no body fat tossing around stick figures. I think the piece was called *Dance of the Ninety-pound Fuck-Toys*. But their body image issues make for great art.

The halls of the Art Institute shine bright. Illuminate the current exhibits. Works from artists such as Degas and Munch the main draws.

But *The Scream* isn't one of them, so no one seems to care. Fine by me. The best works in the building are in the banquet hall. A series of paintings done by Mackenzie to be raffled off for charity.

Simply a formality. I'll be taking them home at the end of the night. Price not an issue.

I roam the halls. Determine this place truly is as massive as it appeared on all those field trips years ago. Easy to get lost here. To a casual observer, I'm critiquing the work of some Georgia O'Keefe knockoff. In reality, taking mental notes of everyone. Where is Alison? Who is she with? Will I recognize her, or has she had yet another surgery?

Dinner in less than thirty minutes. The halls increasingly flooded with penguin suits and arm candy. Most of them without a clue who I am. Others gossip quietly but loud enough I don't have to eavesdrop. Wondering who will take over. What about Nicky's other children? Former wives? Cooper the obvious choice, but why not announce it sooner? Why make everyone nervous? Worried about the future of their stocks and financial business that concerns me not.

Move from room to room. Pondering what possessed someone to display this in public. More critical than necessary, but very much on edge. My fragile frame of mind made worse by paranoia. Assuming any second I could be attacked and lose my other hand. Sweating profusely, need to step out for some fresh air.

Heading swiftly toward the foyer, I see Cooper. He notices me too, makes sure that we lock eyes. An evil grin serpentines across his face, tells me tonight will be anything but smooth. Outside, I try to regain my composure. Greet a handful of the hundreds of people I will never see again. My charade of a smile quickly reciprocated with another.

Still haven't seen Dillon. Tempted to give him a call. But all eyes are on me. Nothing I do inconspicuous. Every move subject to scrutiny under a microscope. Check the time, dinner in fifteen. Head back in, greeted by the head of special events at the museum. Says everything is ready to go. They'll open the doors on my word.

Figure why wait. Let's get this show on the road. Give her the nod, and slowly people migrate that way. Deep breath, I make my way into the grand hall. Consumed by anxiety. My only comfort knowing this is helping a great cause. The Good Samaritan Food Bank, Mom's favorite charity. Volunteered there at least once a week as long as I could remember.

Locate my seat. Head table near the stage. Auction items on display. Mainly paintings, a few sculptures. Plus a handful of tickets for the Bears, Bulls, Cubs, and Blackhawks. Sorry, White Sox. You still get the shaft.

I wander around, searching for name cards I'll recognize. The flow of people is slow but constant. Enjoying cocktails, chatting about economics and politics. Standard topics with everyone a self-proclaimed expert.

I head to the bar. Need a cocktail. Just one to ease the nerves. Have to stay composed. Sip it slowly, walking around looking for Dillon. No such luck. By the time I finish, most of the seats are occupied. Head to my table at the other side of the room. Mr. Ball already awaiting my arrival.

Exchange the usual formalities. Casual conversation certainly not his specialty. Suits me fine. I'm not in a talking mood myself. Servers begin shuffling around the room, delivering spinach salads topped with feta, walnuts, and mango.

#Best$250saladever

Next comes the rather ordinary ahi steak or tofu if you prefer. At some point, I notice Cooper surrounded by people I recognize. None of whom I actually know. Alison not in sight. Unless she's been under the knife yet again.

Tiramisu for dessert wraps up the meal portion of the evening nicely.

Dishes are cleared, another round of cocktails is served. The head of the Good Samaritan Food Bank approaches the podium, offers a typical speech of welcome and appreciation. Then introduces Pamela Marcus, head curator of the museum, and auctioneer for the evening.

The first item, a "Campbell's Soup" print signed by Andy Warhol. Next, an abstract sculpture by a local artist. Followed by a rather impressive set of three photographs of "The Northern Lights."

A million here, twenty-five thousand dollars there. It all adds up. Anytime the bidding reaches a lull, Pamela simply reminds the audience it's for charity. The hands fly in the air once again.

Finally, one of Mackenzie's paintings is brought front and center. It's the image I saw hanging in Mr. Ball's office. The angel holding a sword and infant. My eyes find the lawyer, who turns to me and smirks. "It's for a good cause, right?" Laugh a little to myself. Smile for the first time all night. Nice to see signs of a personality emerging from behind his vanilla exterior.

Before Pamela has even finished introducing it, I yell "$50,000."

She recovers from her surprise, and covers it by asking for $55,000. A man at the next table over quickly replies. Then seventy-five. One hundred grand.

"A quarter million," I say with swagger.

A collective gasp. Not exactly a ton of money for a charity auction. But quite a bit for an artist few people have heard of.

Pamela asks if anyone is willing to go higher.

Crickets.

Going once. Twice.

"One million dollars," a lady chimes in from the back of the room. The gasp that ensues completely belittles the one from seconds before. All heads turn toward the back. Curious to put a face with the generous voice. No need for me. I know who it is.

"Wow, that is certainly quite a jump. One million dollars from the newcomer in the back. May I ask your name ma'am?"

Nails on a chalkboard, "Penelope."

#Spurious

Expecting a more elaborate introduction, Pamela continues, "Well then, if anyone can beat Penelope's offer, by all means."

Begin to lift my hand. Open my mouth to double her offer. Quickly interrupted, "Put down your hand, Mr. Watts. Save your money and get yourself a nice manicure. Even from here I can tell your girly fingers are looking dry."

And just like that, the countdown has begun.

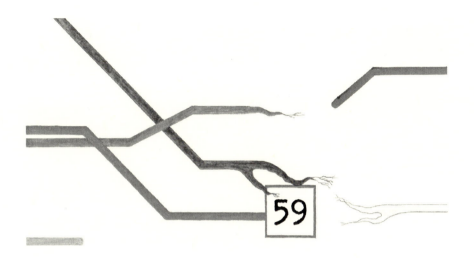

59

All the makings of an epic pissing match. Defiantly bid two million. Strutting confidently towards the front, she ups it to 2.5 million.

Jaws dropping left and right. Takes a lot to shock a room full of millionaires. Pretty sure this is just the tip of the iceberg.

Not backing down, I up it to three million. Without breaking stride, she ups it to four. The room completely silent. Pamela stands mouth agape, unbelieving. Continuing her walk toward me, I rise from my chair, take my place on the stage.

Moments later, Alison begins her ascent. Once on the stage, takes four steps toward me and stops. The audience eagerly anticipating what will happen next. Better than any movie they've seen in decades.

"Are you going to bid again, or is the painting mine?" she asks.

Her tone implies more than the words simply spoken. With apprehension, I begin to bid, "Five mill—"

The last syllable cut off by a gunshot. Aimed not at me, but near me. Gouges a hole in the painting. Shrieks and screams resonate around the room as people make a panicked dash for the exits. "How much is it worth now?" she screams with a haunting timbre.

The room empties out in under a minute. Feels like an eternity. Staring down the barrel of her gun, images of my severed fingers run through my mind. Wonder if it's the same pistol.

Cooper is the only other person remaining. I look to my left, spot a bright red high heel shoe. Likely Pamela's, lost in the shuffle.

Can only look around for distractions so long. Let's get this over with.

"What do you want, Alison?"

Fury in her voice. Impatience burning red across her face. "You know exactly what I want."

Resorting to humor in times of fear, "Look, if you really like the painting, you can have it. I don't really want it so much that I'm willing to get shot over it."

A stupid comment only amplifies her rage. Emphasizing the fact she's holding a gun. "It's probably not in your best interest to be sarcastic right now. You know what I want. Sign the company over to me like Nicky intended. Otherwise, my next shot won't be at your hand."

Interesting she should mention that. "Funny thing about that. You have impeccable aim for someone with Parkinson's." Her eyes betray her. Tries to hide it, but it's too late. Her reaction already tells me I know more than she would like. "That's right. You're not the only one who can dig up information."

"You don't know shit."

"Oh really? Well then, enlighten me. Come on, how about a little aunt and nephew time? Or is it mother-son time?" I hit a nerve, her nostrils flare. Catch Cooper's reaction out of the corner of my eye. Very confused. Moves a little closer out of curiosity. Still maintaining a safe distance from the lady with a gun.

Now standing several paces behind her, Cooper inquires, "Penelope, what is he talking about? Who is Alison?"

Finally getting somewhere. Her reply terse. "He has no idea what he's talking about."

From the back of the room, a booming voice draws our attention. "I highly doubt that." Dillon to the rescue. Looking sharp in a tux two sizes too small. Accentuating his massive stature. Even from across the grand hall, this beast of a man alarms Cooper. My Achilles heel of the moment, I stare too long. Before I know it, Alison has a gun at my head. Kicks the back of my knees. They buckle; I'm forced to a kneeling position. Dillon appears unfazed.

"Who the fuck are you?" she demands. Surely she's seen him before at the restaurant. No recollection whatsoever.

"Well, long story short. I'm your new boss. And I've gotta say, you're not making a very positive first impression."

Can't see her reaction, but I can feel it. Her clutch around my neck tightens severely, straining my breathing. She relents after ten seconds, long enough to give me a headache.

Whispering in my ear, "You gave my company to *him*?"

Confident the final countdown on my life has begun. "Well, yeah. It's what Dad wanted."

Speaking loud enough for the others to hear, "Wrong! He wanted *me* to have it."

Again with her lies. "No, he wanted Penelope Strickland to have it. The woman he apparently loved more than anything else." Which I still find suspect. Not thoroughly convinced he ever loved anyone other than himself. Circumstances being what they are, I'm forced to take him at his word. Watching Cooper for his reaction. Still unclear how much he knows.

"My sister is completely deranged. She doesn't even know what fucking year it is! No, what Nicky wanted was for his company to continue to thrive. And I'm the person who will make that happen."

Taking my chances with a reply, "You have a gun to my head. You've shot my fingers apart. Are you really in any position to be diagnosing your sister's mental health?"

Interjecting, Cooper looks at her, his face blank. "Would someone please tell me what the fuck is happening here?"

"Cooper, just get out of here. I'll explain later. But right now, I've got some loose ends to tie up. It's probably better if you're not around."

Still in awe of what has transpired, relief blankets his face. Thrilled at the free pass to get out now. I'm hoping Dillon will run and grab him. Balance out the hostage situation. Give us some leverage. But he allows him to leave uncontested. Finally approaches the stage where I kneel in front of my aunt. My life hanging in the balance.

"Stay back," she shouts. He stops on her command, roughly ten feet away.

Trying to diffuse the bomb, he calmly replies, "Let's not do anything extreme. I know you're upset, but killing your son isn't going to help."

"I disagree" is all she says.

Her tone unleashes a flood of chills across my entire body. Almost as disturbing, the fact that Dillon doesn't seem to have figured out this woman's relation to me. Fingers crossed he's playing dumb.

"OK," he says. "You want the company. It's yours."

"Dillon, no!" My interjection quickly met with a knee in the back.

His face now breaking into twitches. Sends me a message. Claims he has a plan.

"What is wrong with your face? Are you having a seizure or something?" she asks. Her tone laced with concern. Not for Dillon's well-being. Concerned that his health could delay getting what she wants.

"No, I'm fine. Just a bug on my face or something." He does it again. Tells me he has a gun. Doesn't want to pull it. Can't get a clear shot.

Breathe heavy. Quite certain what I'm about to do is a huge mistake. But one that is necessary. Shoot him back twitches of my own. His eyes light up in horror.

Are you sure?

Mouth the word "absolutely" to him.

Alison begins to question his odd behavior once again. Doesn't get more than a syllable out. Dillon draws his gun from his back waistband. Fires a shot straight at me, passes through my shoulder and into her body, knocks her backwards. She drops her gun, both hands rush to the wound, attempting to stop the bleeding. Dillon runs at us. First kicks her gun out of the way. Takes off his bowtie, secures her hands behind her back. She might be screaming in pain. Doesn't mean she isn't capable of deviance.

Puts the finishing touches on his knot, he calls the paramedics then the police. Both arrive in minutes, working furiously to escort the wounded to my second home. Wonder which doctor will be on call tonight. I'm loaded into the ambulance, watching as Alison is being tended to on the scene. They've cut her dress open, exposing her abdomen. The entry wound bloody as expected. My eyes move down toward her waist. A scar, much like the one I found on the real Penelope. Confirming her story.

From my stretcher, I thank Dillon, remind him that with great power comes great responsibility. Running a company with seemingly infinite resources is no small task, but I know he's up to it. He nods in agreement. And as the doors close and the vehicle pulls away, I cry. Knowing that this time it's real. This really will be the last time I see my best friend.

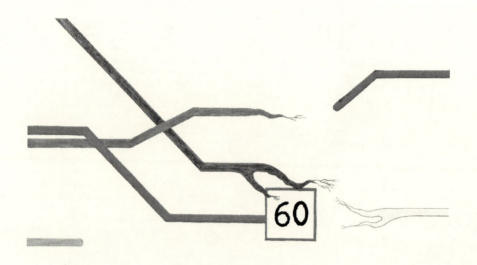

ORD→FML.

O'Hare to anywhere but here.

I've spent my fair share of time in airports. As much as I like to complain, this one is my favorite by far. Anytime spent within these walls conjures up intense feelings. When I land here, it represents a homecoming. A sanctuary from my travels. Relief from a torturous homesickness. When baggage claim was the only thing keeping me from roaming the streets of the Windy City.

But sometimes I can't stand the weather. Or the people. Especially the traffic. This place is my ticket out of here. A gateway to something better.

Today is a don't-look-back kind of day. Time to start over once again. Partly because there is no reason to stay. Mostly because I'll be killed if I do.

I roam the concourse, wandering from terminal A to D then back again. Lugging two large bags. Stuffed so full, making the zippers earn every penny. Not everything I own. Just everything important I could fit into them. Been pacing all over for an hour. Surely must look suspicious. Do I take American Airlines to Ireland? Delta to Beijing? Lufthansa to Berlin is appealing.

Ultimately an irrelevant decision. Still, one I can't afford to fuck up.

Maybe France. Mackenzie and I always talked about going to the Louvre. No sense in reopening that wound. Time to move on.

Australia should be nice. Where is the Qantas ticket counter? I take five steps and remember I hate opera and vegemite.

Always wanted to see Patagonia.

South America does have a certain allure. Then again, so does Cape Town. Decisions, decisions. My train of thought momentarily interrupted. Someone yelling the name Bill across the way.

Moving past United and Southwest, I stop in front of British Airways. Always found it fascinating that their main airport is one letter off from spelling "Deathrow."

I approach the ticket counter. Some lady still yelling "Bill." Not interested in staying in London, but the agent tells me they fly direct to Rome. Leaves in six hours.

Sign me up.

A couple months in Italy are just what I need.

On the verge of finalizing the transaction, I hear a final "Bill." Turn around, find Maggie right behind me.

Before I can ask what she's doing here, she tells the agent, "Make it two tickets. One way." Hands her a credit card.

Very confused, I stop myself from launching into a tirade. Remember, I'm the one who started this. Whatever "this" is.

Ticket agent swipes the card. Softly ask her what she's doing.

"I'm going wherever you're going."

"Is that so?"

"Yeah, Bill. So where *are* we going?"

"Rome." Immediately cut off her elation. "More importantly, why are you calling me Bill?"

"It's a long story. I'll explain after we go through security."

The woman behind the counter is now checking IDs. Giving me an odd look. My license says Samuel. Probably just as confused who Bill is. Quickly dismisses it. The things she must see. Every day, men taking their paramours all around the world. She knows the value of discretion while judging internally. Moving on, I put my bags on the scale, look at Maggie.

"Oh, I only brought a carry-on." Holding up her purse.

My bags are tagged and thrown on the belt.

The agent hands Maggie our tickets and her credit card. Signs her name with nonchalance. Walking away, I ask once again why she's here.

"Would you relax? I said I'd tell you once we're through security. And since our flight doesn't leave anytime soon, I'll have plenty of time to fill you in."

The entire process: security and customs, metal detectors and passports. We're in proximity. To a casual observer, she and I have never met. The forty minutes it takes to finish the formalities drags by in silence. The situation doesn't exactly call for small talk.

"OK, so what are you doing here?" My words bursting forth the moment we're out of earshot.

"Would you just relax? A girl needs her Starbuck's. Do you want anything while I'm there?"

Just perfect. "No, I'm good."

I walk over to the gate. Nearby, a flight to China is boarding. Aside from that, desolation. I take a seat in the corner. Just under five hours until we board. Moments later, Maggie is sitting next to me, sucking down a venti-something. Smart move, getting her coffee fix in now. Rather well documented that the birthplace of espresso has a major shortage of cafes. She places a smaller cup in my hand, "Here you go. I got you a latte, just in case." She smiles softly.

"Thanks," all I say. She's clearly offended. "What? I said I wasn't thirsty."

Rolls her eyes. "What the fuck is up with you? You need to lighten up. We're going to *Rome* for crying out loud! Loosen up."

Grinding my teeth, keeping my voice down. "That's cute. I haven't seen you in months. You just show up out of the blue, buy me a ticket to Rome, and expect us to carry on like nothing happened."

"Hey, you're the one who started it. I was fine turning tricks and stripping until you decided to play surgeon on me." Finally, some indignation coming through in her voice.

I'm rubbing my temples. "Maggie, clearly I haven't forgotten that. Was it wrong? Absolutely. But right now, that's irrelevant. Please explain to me what I'm supposed to think when you show up out of nowhere as I'm trying to leave the country. I know you were working for Nicky, relaying things I told you. How do I know you're not doing the same thing right now?"

"Nicky's dead."

Thanks for bringing me up to speed.

"I'm well aware. But Cooper and that crazy bitch Alison are still up to no good. I've impeded their progress, that's for sure. But they're far from derailed."

Her reaction very peculiar. Not sure how to read it. Fairly certain she doesn't know who Alison is. Knows her as Athena. Maybe Penelope.

"I wouldn't worry about Cooper," she tells me in an omniscient manner. Don't think much of it.

A very long, awkward silence. Tension mounting with every sip she takes. In turn, I slurp down my latte as well. Tasty. Won't let her know that.

Hearing I've finished the last of my beverage, she mocks, "Must have been terrible. So sorry you had to drink that." After an icy stare, a smile emerges.

"Thank you," I tell her. This time with conviction. Dare I say sincerity? "OK, so seriously. What in the world are you doing here?" Her look says she's wondering the same thing about me. "You see, I don't really have a choice. Odds are that if I stay, I'll be dead in no time. So yeah, I'm running away. It's a coward's way out, I get that. But it's a reason nonetheless." Looking at her with genuine concern for once. "Maggie, why are you flying to Rome with me? You don't expect me to believe you just happened to be at O'Hare as I was getting ready to leave, do you?"

Dodging my question yet again, she says, "You're not a coward."

Appreciate her effort. Too little, too late.

"Whether or not that's true, I really do need to leave."

"Why?"

Is she serious? Where to begin? "Things are bad right now." My attempt at brevity fails.

Gives me a look that says, *No shit*. "So is that what you always do? When the going gets tough, you bolt?"

Funny sentiments considering ten seconds ago, she said I wasn't being a coward. What's her angle?

"Who the fuck sent you here?" I ask with a low but stern tone. Appears genuinely insulted at the insinuation. "Look, you want to know why I'm leaving. And I would love to tell you. First off, I feel like you already know the reason why." It's not exactly a secret. "But more importantly, last time I told you what I was up to, you told Nicky Salcedo. You set me up. Nadira's hand? You knew where she was going to be." Doesn't react kindly to that insinuation. "I'm not saying I blame you. I certainly deserved it. But give me a reason to think you won't do it again."

Just stares at me, sipping her drink. Her eyes locked on mine, never straying for a second. Even spills a few drops on her shirt, but isn't deterred. I'm on the verge of walking away when she grabs the back of my neck, pulls me in, and shoves her tongue into my throat.

"You clearly don't know me very well if you think that's going to get me to talk. You know my sexual history. Women don't have the same pull on me that they do on most men." The words I've uttered so many times. Always spoken with conviction. Always true.

Not this time. Something about her is different. And she knows it. Just grins, finishes her drink, stands up, and throws it away. Sits back down. "First of all, I'm sorry. Telling Nicky was a terrible thing to do. But at the time, it seemed like a good move. I had to get him thinking I was on his side. Then when I got him drunk, he would spill the beans." Shifts uncomfortably in her seat. "As for Nadira's hand, I have no clue what you're talking about. Running into her was completely coincidental." Probably a mistake, but I believe her. "How about we just start over? I think it's safe to say we got off on the wrong foot." Understatement of the century. "You fucked up. I fucked up. Let's face it, we're both pretty screwed-up people." No argument here. "So let's just start over." I pause to consider. Debate whether or not she's playing me. "What do you say, Bill?"

There it is again. "OK, what is it with you and that name? Why do you keep calling me Bill? And don't give me the 'I'll tell you when the time is right,' bullshit. If you want me to trust you, start right now."

She nods in agreement. "Sounds fair. So I know that in your dealings you require a certain amount of"—searches for the right word—"*mystery*, let's say." Great euphemism. Point, Maggie. "I know you're fond of pseudonyms instead of using your real name." I concur. "But not just any name. You like using authors' real names. Or maybe musicians." Her perceptiveness quit impressive. "And being the smart guy you are, I'm sure you have a long list of names you could use. But don't forget, I've done quite a bit of reading myself." Reaches into her lone piece of luggage for a trip to Rome. Pulls out a book, places it on her lap. Covers it with her hands. "Safe to say, I'm probably familiar with several authors you've never heard of."

"I'm pretty well-read, but yeah, you're probably right." I smile to myself for once.

"Well, this is one of my favorite authors." Hands me a book.

Scoff at the Mundane by Bill Kalman.

I look it over, read the description on the back.

"So that's why I was calling you Bill. You know, I just thought you could . . . " she trails off. "Sorry, it's not really as exciting a story as you were probably expecting."

I continue to peruse the book, flipping through it. Secretly, I'm touched. Not ready to let her know that. "Well, I guess I could be a 'Bill.' But this guy looks like an idiot. Definitely doesn't look like the kind of guy capable of reading a novel, let alone *writing* one."

But she isn't fooled. Can tell I'm bluffing.

"Well, Bill, you'll just have to read it and let me know if you still feel that way." That's fair. "OK, so now will you please tell me why you're leaving?"

"Not quite yet." Rolls her eyes. "First off, I want to know how you knew I was here."

"Dillon."

Hold on. "You spoke to Dillon?" She nods. "How?" Looking back, I don't even know if she ever met Dillon. Scanning my memory . . . don't think so.

"I've known him for quite a while, actually." My eyes meet hers. Knows what I'm about to ask. Simply nods, looking ashamed. "Yep, we, uh . . . made a couple films together years ago."

"Really?" Not sure how to respond to this.

"Look, it was a long time ago, and I'm totally over that lifestyle—"

Cutting her off. "Maggie, please. I don't care about that. I'm no saint myself. I'm just doing some math in my head. I mean, you're not even old enough to have slept with him the last time he was in the industry."

I'm terrified I'm going to find out the man raising my child is a statutory rapist. Shooting pains in my chest. Feeling nauseous.

My fears quickly put to rest. A laughing Maggie simply says, "I'm actually a lot older than I look. Don't worry about it."

Still breathing heavy.

Dillon knows.

He just always knows. Something I don't even question anymore.

"So now will you please tell me what you're running from?"

Should be insulted at the word "running," but that sums it up aptly.

Look around. Paranoia. Force of habit. "OK, sure." Her reaction almost unnoticeable. But her breathing definitely says *finally*. Rack my brain, try to remember what she knows.

I tell her all about my meeting with Nicky. How I made him sign the company over to me. How I gave it to Dillon so something good could finally be done with all that wealth. How I could finally get Dillon to use his talents. Tell her about killing Nicky's bodyguards. The wreck on the freeway. Surprisingly haven't heard a word about it. Almost concerns me more than the thought of being arrested. Tell her about taking two porn actors to an academic building for a fuck only to spot some kind of meeting with Cooper and a lady I thought was Krystal Madigan.

"I'm confused" is all she says.

Understandable.

"Well, as you now know, Nicky Salcedo was in love with Penelope Strickland, my birth mother. She was never in good health after being beaten in the alley. And she eventually developed Parkinson's." Still haven't mentioned that her sister, my aunt, was the assailant. "But he always had a job for her. Which is odd, since he never really showed anyone any form of charity or kindness whatsoever—"

She interjects. "Yeah, but I've met her. She seemed fine. Rather eloquent actually. And I know Nicky had people working on Parkinson's treatments."

"And that would probably be the end of the story if anything Nicky Salcedo financed ever actually worked. But I don't think it's quite that simple. My aunt, she's a deviant woman. I'm convinced she's not in the best of mental health either. But she was vengeful. I'm almost certain that she was the person you met, the one actually working for Nicky for the last several months. Maybe longer."

"What makes you say that?"

Getting back to the fake Krystal Madigan. Tell her about the lady in the wheelchair. Manipulating the information from the nurse, breaking into her apartment. How she thought I was Nicky. The scar on her abdomen. How we went for cannolis at the donut shop. Eventually leading to a breakdown in the alley.

"You see, my birth mother was actually barren. But she wanted a child so badly, she resorted to desperate measures." Intrigue growing on Maggie's face. She thinks I'm making it up. I wish I were. "How do I put this?" Got it. "OK, so I'm sure you remember the procedure I performed on you."

Dryly, "Um, yeah, it's been a while, but I think I vaguely recall something like that."

"OK, well, as it turns out, it runs in the family."

"Excuse me?"

"Apparently, unsolicited surgeries are in my DNA. You see, Penelope wanted kids so badly that she stole her sister's ovaries." Maggie cringes instantly. "They both have scars right here." I point to a spot above my hip.

In shock, "You're crazy. Didn't you just tell me that a crazy woman with Parkinson's told you this information in the alley behind a donut shop?" I nod. "And you believe her?"

Without pause, "Absolutely."

"So what, your aunt took your mother's job to get even?" she asks sardonically.

"Well, partially. My aunt Alison was able to take over relatively undetected because she had several plastic surgeries. So physically, it was a nonissue. As for the acting part, I can't really comment. Nicky said he thought Penelope was getting better, which leads me to believe Alison wasn't doing a very good job. But I was never there, so who knows?"

"And what did your aunt do with your mother? Obviously, she didn't kill her."

"Well, as far as I can tell, she used her to her advantage. She gave my birth mother multiples surgeries as well, making her look like Krystal Madigan."

Overwhelming look of relief. She's been wondering how she fit in.

"You see, Krystal Madigan is Cooper's mom. She died years ago, I've seen her tombstone. I've done Internet research. But like I said, one day I saw her in a science building across town. Almost flipped my shit. When I went to her grave, it was dug up."

Her eyes the size of saucers. "You don't actually believe that she rose from the dead, do you?"

Can't help but laugh a little. "I hate to admit it, but the thought did cross my mind. But no, I don't believe that. I believe that Alison made Penelope look like that, knowing that sooner or later I would see her. She wanted me to freak out. You know, cause me to slip up, do something stupid because I had control of the company she wanted."

We sit in silence for a while. Digests what I've told her while I stare out the window watching planes take off.

"OK, but it sounds like you've got things pretty much figured out. Dillon's got control. Alison is pretty much powerless. So why are you leaving?"

"Because I don't believe Alison is powerless." I might barely know her, but like it or not, she's kind of my mother. We're related. And I *do* know what I'm capable of. She can't be underestimated. "And I definitely don't think Cooper is powerless. Nicky and he were into some shady stuff. I'm not just talking Chicago politics. I mean on a global scale." She should know. She helped me with the research.

Says nothing, just smirks.

Can't help but ask, "What's so funny?"

Pauses for effect. "Cooper is dead."

Her face doesn't twitch. I'm convinced she's screwing with me nevertheless. "You're funny," all I offer.

"No, seriously, Bill. He's dead."

"OK, now it's your turn to elaborate."

"Not much to say really. I ran into him last night at a bar. He was piss-ass drunk. When he noticed me, he came right over and was all over me instantly. I've never been what I would call 'a fan' of him, but last night was the final straw. I went back to his place, and well, you know."

"No, I don't know." And now I really want to. "What did you do? Poison his drink? Stab him?"

"Ha-ha, no. Nothing that gross. Let's just say I applied one of the methods you taught me." And that's it. She just winks, pulls a piece of gum from her purse, throws it in her mouth.

A dozen or so scenarios play in my mind. What is the woman really capable of? How did she finish Cooper off? Should I be impressed or terrified? Finally, light bulb. "So that's why you showed up?" Give her an irregular smile of my own. "You're running away too."

"Busted," she says. Eyes me sheepishly. "But for what it's worth, and I know this sounds fake given the circumstances, but I was trying to track you down anyway."

I say nothing, wait for her to expand on that.

"It's just—" Searches for the words once again. Seems to be going around. "I mean, can you seriously tell me you felt nothing when you were with me? I know you say you're not very affectionate, that intimacy isn't very important to you. But I really think there's something between us."

I sit there with a blank stare.

"Look at me and tell me you're not interested in me at all. If you do, I won't say a word on the flight. I'll get off the plane in Rome, take a train somewhere else, and you'll never see me again."

As she requests, I look her in the eye.

Open my mouth.

Silence.

I plant a small kiss on her cheek. Shrug my shoulders. She returns my gesture with a smile. A genuine one. Not one of those sarcastic charades we'd been exchanging for the last hour.

A few minutes pass, neither one of us saying anything. Finally breaking the silence, I stand up, "I'm gonna get a coffee. You want anything?"

"No thanks, I'm good."

"Cool, double espresso coming right up." Her only response a cute little giggle. When I return, she takes her drink, I sit with mine. Each holding cups in our outside hand. My free hand interlocks hers.

"Can we switch sides?" Not quite the reaction I expected. I look down, notice Nadira's hand clenching hers. I stand up, move over to the seat on her other side.

"I'm sure Rome has plenty of mafia members who only need one hand. I'll see what I can do."

Shakes her head. Not in disapproval. More like questioning what she's gotten herself into.

If you fear the answer, don't ask the question.

Why am I going to Rome?

Easy. I do my best thinking abroad.

People will forget all about me. What I'm capable of. Five years from now, when we return, Maggie and I are going to seriously fuck shit up.

Go figure. All this time, thinking I was god, turns out I'm just plain evil.

Edwards Brothers Malloy
Thorofare, NJ USA
June 4, 2013